THE STAIN
CRISIS IN CONSCIENCE
A HISTORICAL NOVEL

ED DEVOS

Halo ●●●●
Publishing International

ISBN: 978-1-61244-138-2
Library of Congress Control Number: 2012917878

Published by Halo Publishing International
AP# 726
P.O Box 60326
Houston, Texas 77205
Toll Free 1-877-705-9647
Website: www.halopublishing.com
E-mail: contact@halopublishing.com

Endorsement

Ed DeVos' wisdom – as a leader of soldiers and possessor of genuine faith – has helped set my moral compass these past twenty five years. I wholeheartedly commend <u>The Stain</u> to leaders who want a fresh perspective on the Gospel accounts of our Lord, applied across the centuries to the circumstances of life today. Read this book. A tremendous contribution to Biblical understanding.

U.S. Army Chaplain Ken Sampson

Chapter I

Machaerus
Province of Perea
July 15, A.D. 33

The majesty of another oncoming dawn arrived without
trumpets as I ascended stone steps leading to a spot from which
I could look down upon the main gate of the fortress. No matter
how many times I stood on such ramparts, crouching behind
wooden walls, trembling, locked with my brothers in a wall of
shields awaiting some on-coming enemy, the colors of a new
day—ever-new combinations of pink, yellow, or blood-streaked
purple in an eastern sky—always seized my attention. Yet here in
Machaerus, in this hot, sweaty, festering dunghill of a province
perched on this impregnable fortress, the panoply of colors in the
east coupled with the fading light of stars struggling to remain alive
in the dying western darkness strike me this morning. Were these
verdant, ruddy, turquoise, and flaxen colors mixed in harmony, the
handiwork of Aurora, the Goddess of the Dawn or of some other
Supreme Being instead of simply light shining through clouds?
I smell the air, wondering with a treasonous part of my mind if
perhaps this Supreme Painter might announce his coming on the
wind; yet there is nothing but the smell of the heat, and dust like
powder in the air one breathes. By all the gods, this place truly
reeks of the supernatural. No wonder these Jews see a messiah on
every mountain. I shake my head and move on up the steps.

"Good morning, Centurion," a soldier said, stepping from
the darkness, slamming his fist against the leather armor on his
chest. I returned the man's salute but did not stop. He had been in
the dungeon with me last night and I wanted no memory of those
events in this morning's light. I glanced at my right hand, then
at the leather strips of my lappets, my greaves, and finally my

sandals. There it was: that persistent blotch of darkness I could not remove, spreading across the side of both sandals. I had delayed too long. Unconsciously I turned my foot and scrapped against the stone wall. I felt a strange sense of guilt, but then disgust for feeling guilty. I had done nothing but my duty, a duty performed last night that I didn't want to dwell upon today. The silence of the oncoming dawn was too majestic.

As the light grew, it afforded a commanding view of bare, rocky terrain of peaks and valleys from the walkway that traversed along the inside edge of the fortress' outer walls. To the north were the rough hills of Perea, dominated by Mt. Nebo, which lay several days' journey away. Northwest was the Jordan River basin. Galilee, the second province governed by Herod Antipas, was located far up the Jordan River to our north. West of Machaerus was the Salt Sea and the barren, prophet-scarred hills of Judea beyond. From the fort I could see the trail which led to the Gorge of Callirhoe, a steep, severe cut through the rocky ground leading down to the sea. South lay the territory of the Nabataeans, a nomadic war-like people, against whom this fortress was constructed. These nomads controlled large amounts of land to the south and southwest. To the east were hills and more hills; hills which seemed to stretch on forever.

The dawn's colors blended across every point on the compass of this brutal, barren landscape. Although the early morning air was cool, the hint of wind coming from the west was a harbinger of another sweltering day we would spend sweating on the high rock walls, defending the empire. Today the world seemed to be at peace, but a soldier's duty never rests, and the day's responsibilities began to awake.

From the stables along the northern side of Machaerus' interior walls, I heard the clatter of the horses' hooves and metal couplings smacking against leather bindings as servants hitched horses to their chariots. The horses' owners had been here for a week, reveling in Herod's birthday celebrations, but now the animals sensed the rest they had enjoyed was about to end. The horses pawed the ground, snorting as they strained at their harnesses, seemingly aware of the long distances they would traverse, ready to haul their human cargo across miles of parched desert before their journeys would end as their owners resumed their duties and responsibilities assigned them throughout Herod Antipas' provinces. As their territorial ruler, Antipas wanted these men to remember his birthday and judging by the rivers of wine and groaning tables of food I saw offered during their stay, Antipas' guests would recall his generosity for many days.

As I turned my attention back to the rising sun, my second in command, Valerus, appeared at my side. Although he was seven years older than me, we both understood the difference in rank and our respective responsibilities. I was the Centurion; he was my subordinate. Valerus leaned against the rock wall softened by the blowing dust.

"Centurion, I know Antipas' father, Herod the Great, built this place to secure the frontier, but I wish he'd built it closer to civilization." He laughed. "This is a strong fort, second only to Jerusalem, but I wish it wasn't so close to the armpit of the world."

A stocky man of average height, his short black beard blending well with his dark complexion, Valerus' scars on his right cheek and right ear coupled with his piercing green eyes announced to the world he was not one to be taken lightly. Like most other Roman soldiers, his tin and bronze helmet contained a leather skull cap woven inside to provide extra cushion for his head. A leather strap secured his helmet firmly in place. Although the helmet was irritating and uncomfortable to wear, I insisted my troops do so nonetheless. I'd seen too many men lose their brains because they'd forgotten about tightening that strap in the frantic onset of a surprise attack.

A combination of hard leather and metal made up Valerus' breastplate and other outer garments, all held together by leather bindings. Strips of metal protected his massive shoulders and upper arms. He wore a crimson scarf around his neck to prevent chafing. A large belt encircled his waist, with additional hardened leather strips hanging down from the belt to protect his groin. His sandals, also made of leather, had a thick sole held in place by hollow-headed nails. This particular morning Valerus carried his short sword and dagger, attached by straps to his belt, his javelins and shield remained stored in his room, back in the barracks.

Enlisting as a young man, Valerus had served Rome for more than twenty-five years, and like me, he had seen many blood-spattered dawns. In five years he planned to retire and receive his pension of land owed him for that loyalty. I trusted Valerus with my life. I was fortunate to have him by my side.

"Your eagle reflects the dawn well this morning, Centurion." Valerus referred to the elegant carved eagle adorning the center of my breastplate. I smacked the short staff made of vine wood—my vitis, the symbol of my rank—across the armor.

"It waits to see dawn over the Tiber, my friend. It hates the scenery here."

"How well I know," Valerus said with irony, spitting over the wall in agreement.

Like Valerus, I was armed with sword and dagger, but there was one difference between our uniforms. Around his neck Valerus wore a thin chain of gold with a wreath of golden oak leaves suspended from it. This was the Civic Crown, Rome's highest decoration, an award given to those soldiers who had saved the life of a fellow citizen or soldier. I had no such award.

I looked at him and poked his chest lightly with my vitis. "Valerus, I've known you for many years and you've never spoken about the Civic Crown. What did you do to receive it?"

He stared at the lightening, dusty horizon for a time before answering. "Years ago when I was a young soldier, I pulled a young centurion out of an icy river; he would have drowned otherwise. His father was a Senator, so my superiors wanted me to receive special recognition, though if you ask me, I only did what others would have done." He looked over at me with a steady, sardonic eye. "It was a long time ago. The young man was, and as far as I know still is, a complete idiot." He laughed as he turned to stare back at the horizon, perhaps reliving that day once again.

Changing the subject, Valerus inspected the ground with the eyes of a military professional. "One good thing about this place is that no enemy with any brains would try to test our defenses." He waved his thick arm toward the wall. "Look at these walls. By all the gods, they're thicker than a gravid Ligurian sow. Attackers would have to come uphill, across open ground, giving us plenty of advanced warning. Even with the pudding-headed recruits we have defending this place, it would cost the heathen dearly."

"Who knows…maybe they think their god will simply make the walls fall down."

Valerus laughed, throwing his head back and whacking me on the shoulder with a stone-like fist. "Jericho is that way, Centurion." He pointed northwest. "Don't tell me you believe that old story?"

I said nothing, but smiled grimly. "Too many prophets and priests out here."

"Prophets and priests bleed like other men," Valerus replied, his voice like the stones against which we leaned. I snapped a sharp look at him, but I saw he didn't know what he had said.

With a wry smile, unaware of the hard spot of anxiety he'd awakened, he asked, "Well, now that we've been here a week, what do you think? Can we whip these ham-fisted frontiersmen into a unit fit to stand alongside the Legionnaires in the Army of Rome?"

I smiled again, this time to myself. Good soldiers tended to get straight to the point—no wasted time, no wasted energy and this man before me was every inch a soldier. Through the years in his service to the empire, his moral and physical strength were legendary, a role model to the younger soldiers in every respect. I would have traded a hundred new recruits for ten more like him.

"Valerus, you ask a good question. Machaerus is everything you said: barren, dusty, dry, and isolated. But to you and me, those things really don't matter, do they? Pontius Pilate detailed us to help train Herod Antipas' soldiers—heads of pudding or not— and so we shall." I gripped his upper arm, just under his leather armor. "You and me, Valerus, we are soldiers and we do our duty. Imagine, Rome actually pays us to do something we consider a privilege, something that's in our blood. The gods of fortune smile on us, my friend." We both chuckled quietly as we played out this familiar dialogue as we watched the sun climb slowly into a brewing, cloudy sky.

****

As the first of Antipas' guests drove their snorting horses through the main gate, I saw four ragged men standing just outside the doors. They looked out of place with their worn cloaks and tattered clothes; men of little means, no doubt. Were they beggars here to annoy Antipas' guests, heckling them at the gate before their horses could build speed to race by? I pointed with the vitis.

"What do you make of them, Valerus?"

He looked for a moment. "Beggars, most likely," he replied, with a tinge of wariness in his voice. Old soldiers know it is death to assume anything.

"What else would they be doing here?" I asked, more to myself than of Valerus. He said nothing.

Sitting by a small fire, they appeared to be talking amongst themselves even though their heads were buried in their chests. One man appeared to be crying. "Find out who they are and what they are up to. I don't want them aggravating the guests as they depart. Get rid of them."

After briefly staring down at the clutch of beggars, Valerus nodded and without another word, walked down the steps and out the gate to confront this small group. He sensed my concern and would make certain none of Antipas' guests would have an unpleasant experience as they left the confines of our fort. Having been treated in grand style, it wouldn't be right for them to be harassed as they left for their homes.

I watched him stride toward the knot of men with determination. The wind snatched his words before they reached my ears. Whatever he said caused the four to rise to their feet. I was surprised, however, they did not seem to be cowed by Valerus or the power represented by his uniform. From their gestures, by leaning forward with intensity and looking directly at Valerus, it appeared they had an issue of some importance to discuss; their zealous ardor never in short supply in this passion-ridden land on full display as their arms flayed about, their heads vigorously nodding and shaking, their rags flapping in the growing wind. Then they stopped, and Valerus turned, walking more deliberately through the gate it seemed, climbing the steps to approach me.

"No matter how much time I spend in this Jewish armpit, I'm amazed at what I see and hear," he grumbled as he shook his head. "Those men aren't here to cause any trouble, nor are they here to beg for food." Pointing to one of the men, he continued, "The tall one, the one wearing the dirty gray tunic, tells me he visited our dungeon on several occasions with Antipas' approval to spend time with one of our prisoners before we deployed to this post. Should be easy to learn if his story is true."

"What do they want?" I said, growing impatient.

"They've just one request."

"And what would that be?"

Valerus stared down at the men. "They heard that John, the man who lost his head last night, is dead." Then he turned to look at me and the blood-red streaks in the low clouds stood out behind him. "They want to claim his body. They want to bury him."

****

Last night's events quickly came to mind -- a slave had found me on the wall, staring at the constellation of Leo, the Lion in the heavens above thinking about my wife and children in Rome, wondering if their thoughts were on me as well.

"Centurion, Antipas wants to see you immediately."

"Where is he?" I asked, gathering my cloak, thoughts of my wife now left suspended.

"With his guests in the great ball room, sir."

I nodded, dismissed the man, wiping the dust from the day's activities off my uniform before walking slowly to the ballroom. As I moved through the stone-lined halls, I noticed how quiet it was…strangely quiet; no music, no laughter, no boisterous talking…just silence. Since I had dropped my weapons and bedroll here seven days ago, musicians had constantly been playing their flutes and harps, entertaining a raft of wine-soaked drunks that passed for the ruling class. There wasn't an hour of the day one couldn't hear their racket. Raucous laughter and drunken babble added to the noise from the more than one hundred revelers Antipas hosted; I'd no idea he was wealthy enough to sustain so many mouths. I argued with myself as I went to meet the man: 'disdaining the man before his own guests would not be a good way to start your tour of duty here. Keep to your business.' I grimaced knowing how difficult I found it to take my own advice.

When I walked through the doors of the great room, I saw the musicians holding their instruments, staring. The guests stood in small clusters, a piece of bread clutched in a hand, wine cups frozen in mid-air. No one spoke a word. Around the room light flickered from candles in numerous stands around the hall as a breeze snaked its way through open windows. Aromas of beef, fowl, and fish spread in large platters sat on groaning tables in the four corners of the room, bowls of grapes and figs, pomegranates and raisins remained untouched.

The hair stood up on the back of my neck as I moved across the room. The only sound came from my sandals striking the gray marble floor as I approached Antipas. All eyes seemed to be on him and a lanky young woman reclining near him. Antipas stared at some distant object through one of the larger windows, his gray hair matted from sweat. I wondered what exertion these drunken wastrels could undertake that would cause them to raise even a bead of sweat on their privileged brows.

Laying there on his couch, his body draped in his purple toga, his tall frame, once athletic in his youth now bloated through years of inactivity and pleasure seeking in all its forms. His breath reeked of wine. I wondered what it was about Rome that men like me—hard men, men conditioned to duty and danger and hardship, devoted to loyalty and service and integrity—always seemed to work for men like Antipas—debauched, corpulent beyond belief, devoted to nothing but gluttony, wine, and pleasure. I hid my disgust as I saluted. "Sir, Centurion Aquila reporting as ordered."

As I spoke, he turned to face me, a sneer on the left side of his face, a thin line of saliva leaking from the edge of his mouth. After a long pause he wiped his mouth with his sleeve and spoke in solemn detachment.

"Centurion, I have a task I want carried out right away." He burped, slammed a fat fist into his chest, swallowed, and then he turned his attention to the young girl next to him, her body glistening with sweat, the colorful veils she wore concealing little of the long lines of her young body. Golden bracelets circled her wrists and ankles, long strands of dark hair hanging down about her shoulders. Apparently this young, snapping black-eyed filly had been dancing in a way that brought Antipas panting to the trough.

Shifting his gaze back at me, he held up a finger and declared, "Bring me the head of John the Baptizer to me on a silver platter."

There was no emotion in his order; no signs of either glee or sorrow—only resolve. What was this all about? Why was he giving this order to me? I hadn't been here long enough to know who this John was, what a Baptizer was, or where this man might be, but an order was an order. I looked around at the guests, all staring at Antipas and then at me, mouths open, eyes hard, or frightened, or, in some a strange gleam of surreptitious triumph. There was something going on—something I wasn't privy to, but this was not the time or the place to ask questions.

"As you wish, sir." Without another word, I saluted. I left the ballroom, turning in the direction of the stairs which led down toward the dungeon. I told the first soldier I saw to find Valerus and whoever it was who served as an executioner in this place, and have them report to me in the dungeon.

****

"Centurion . . . CENTURION!"

Valerus' voice jerked me back to the present. Shaking my head, I looked at him. "What do I tell these men at the gate? Can they have the body or not?"

It seemed to be a simple request; the man was dead—someone should bury him. But some instinct checked me. I remembered the shaded, sneaking looks of triumph I'd seen in the eyes of a few who stood around that dance floor, looks that bore Antipas no good will.

"There may be more to this issue than simply putting a man in the ground, Valerus. Let me talk to Antipas first. Where's the body?"

Valerus sneered, "Probably at the dump to be thrown out with the rest of the garbage." Slaves took all refuse well outside the south wall so the prevailing wind would carry the stench from the fort. There would be no reason to delay in keeping a decaying corpse inside the walls, especially in this climate.

As we spoke, I noticed the man in the gray tunic continuing to stare in our direction. I motioned to Valerus but kept my eyes on the man in gray. "Go find the body. I need to discuss this with Antipas. Tell those men we'll get them an answer soon. I've a few other things to speak to Antipas about, so it will be later this morning before we can tell them anything."

Valerus nodded as he muttered, "Well, may the gods bring Antipas' decision quickly; we have better things to do than measure out dead meat—that's why the gods made jackals and buzzards. The gods know we can't miss a minute of training these sorry excuses for soldiers they've given us, or it will be our own sad carcasses they'll be hanging from the wall next."

****

No soldier likes to walk into a situation blindly, yet this was where I found myself. Why would anyone in this part of the world hang around outside the gates of a Roman fort and beg for the body of a man Romans had just killed? It would be like sheep approaching a lion's den and asking for the carcass of one of their lambs the lions had just snatched away. I needed information, and the best source I knew of would be Cuza, the tetrarch's chief servant, and head of the household.

Cuza rose from his desk as I walked into the anteroom. A man in his late fifties or perhaps his early sixties, his hair a mixture of gray sprinkled with a sandy blond color matching the color of his closely cropped gray beard. Short and pudgy, he spoke in a humble yet direct manner. When I first met him a week ago, I immediately liked him. He seemed to posses the qualities of devotion to duty and loyalty essential to a man in his position. He'd served Antipas for many years, I'd been told, and knew everything there was to know about the tetrarch's household affairs, serving as personal aide, advisor, and confidante. It was said that because of his trustworthiness, he also managed all of Antipas' property and wealth. If such were true, it would mean the man was worthy of a significant amount of trust.

"Good morning, Centurion. How can I be of service to you?"

"I need to see Antipas." I tilted my head toward the front gate of the fort. "Some men outside the gate want to bury the man who was executed last night…the one whose head is sitting on some woman's platter, I presume." I leaned forward. "Unless I'm missing something, I sense Antipas has some kind of personal interest here. Before granting them their request, I thought I should speak to Antipas first."

For an instant, a look of sadness appeared across the servant's face. Lowering his eyes he replied quietly, "May I say, Centurion, you are wise to discuss this with him. He had many dealings with John— the name of the man beheaded last night. Yes, he'll want to have something to say about the…about the body. Yes," he said, rubbing his chin absently with a hand, "I believe you should speak to him about this. You will find him at the pool. He goes there every day at this time to relax."

I looked at the slave but said nothing, knowing my instincts had been right. Why was the death of this man so troubling; of such concern, this steward would have to check with his Master about what to do with garbage? I must have let something of my confusion pass across my face for Cuza spoke up.

"Do you have a moment, Sir? Perhaps I can explain the situation to a degree that has not yet been made clear. It might help you understand this . . . this delicate situation."

"As I thought" I said, grunting, sitting down in the one chair in the room.

"Several years ago Antipas fell in love with Herodias, who at that time was the wife of his brother. They were, ah, smitten with each other, but unfortunately also indiscreet. As things unfolded, both Antipas and Herodias divorced their respective spouses and married." I expressed no surprise. It was just another example of what the ruling class did, but as a man faithful to his wife for more than a dozen years, through campaigns in some of the most desolate, parched, women-starved stretches of the world ---well, I had my own opinions regarding Antipas' morality, and it dovetailed with what I'd seen last night in the great hall, watching him stare at some young dancing girl.

"This sad departure from moral virtue occurred," Cuza went on, "while John, the man you killed last night, wielded great influence in this area."

"He looked in no way like a man of influence when I saw him last night," I interrupted recalling the scene in the dungeon.

Cuza nodded. "Ah, yes, yet as I am sure you are aware, Centurion, in this province, there is a great esteem for those who know and are known by God."

"Which god is that?" I asked, interrupting again.

"Yes, well…ah...

"Speak freely. While I'm new here, I need information and you're the best source to provide it. We Romans do not close the mouths of those willing to speak to us."

Cuza tilted his head to one side. "That's not exactly it, Centurion. I simply would not choose to convey offense if it can be avoided."

"Offense? What offense?"

"In Rome, Centurion, you have beliefs in many different gods. In this, well here in Perea, and Judea, Samaria, and throughout Palestine, there is the belief in only one God…what we…the God we refer to as 'the God of Abraham, Isaac, and Jacob'."

I waved a hand brusquely. "Yes, I know of your beliefs. Every Roman knows of this stubborn adherence to your 'one true God'. Believe as you wish; I have no wish to compel you to adopt Roman gods—only Roman law, and I see this is not an issue. So John was some notable prophet or priest of this God of yours?"

"He was more than a prophet, more than a priest, Centurion."

"Do you claim he was this messiah you all harp about?" I leaned forward in the chair. "Are you telling me I killed your messiah?" I hissed.

Cuza held up both hands, a shocked expression in his features. "Oh, no, no, please do not even think such a thing. I meant simply that John knew, and was known, by God Himself, and the people here accepted this as truth. You can understand, then, when John spoke, his words carried great influence. People felt he was speaking the words of God."

Something disturbed me then, something I could not define. I was relieved I had not killed this messiah of theirs, yet I felt uncomfortable thinking any man would presume to speak the words of a god, and more, it bothered me that a great number of people would think it so. Yet if it *was* so, what would it mean to be the man responsible for silencing that voice? I looked again at the dark blotches on my sandals.

"When John learned of this liaison between Antipas and

Herodias, he rebuked them—in public, mind you, Centurion—for their offense against God putting their sin before everyone's eyes."

"Why would this desert prophet call a Rome-appointed Tetrarch to task?" I asked. "Who did he think he was?"

Cuza just looked at me slowly. "But … John's words came from God."

"What interest does your god possibly have in a tetrarch's love life? Doesn't he have more important things to occupy his time, perhaps thinking of ways to lift up this conquered, subjugated Jewish nation of yours?"

The servant ignored my stab at his god. "John called attention to this sin, Centurion, to generate some degree of shame in Antipas and Herodias, hoping they might turn from it. Their public display of disdaining the marriage vows is a great shame in an institution chosen by God, a powerful force in our society. Your Roman culture knows this as well as any."

I nodded, recognizing the truth of his words about shame. "You say, John was speaking, as it were, for your god?"

Cuza paused again, this time looking at me differently. "Yes, one might describe it in just those words…yes."

"And you believe this?"

The man hesitated for only a moment, drawing himself up at that moment looking less like a steward, less like a slave, and more like a free man. "Yes, I do. I believe John spoke for God."

"I see why you've no wish to proclaim such a belief from the housetop." Cuza bent his head somewhat in acknowledgement that as Antipas' steward, he could not speak freely about his opinions. I went on: "So it becomes clear. This desert prophet takes it into his head to bring the Tetrarch and his lover…what was her name?"

"Herodias."

"Herodias to task, admonishing them in public, alleging this god whom you worship was displeased." I suddenly remembered something and jerked around to look at Cuza. "So who was that long, lean, black-eyed vixen laying next to Antipas last night? She had Antipas lathered like a chariot stallion running in the great circus."

"Ah, you noticed ... The girl was Salome, Herodias' daughter."

I stared at the older man as my mind worked through what I'd seen last night. "So this Salome dances…"

Cuza held up a hand. "Let me explain further, Centurion. Herodias, angry about John's criticism, made no secret of her desire to see John dead, and pressed Antipas unmercifully. Yet because Antipas kept his nose in the wind and his ears to the ground sensing the people's reaction to all this, he could not bring himself to put John to the sword. So for the sake of peace and harmony, Antipas shut John up in the dungeon here, thinking perhaps if he could keep John away from the people, it would dampen Herodias' desire to do away with him." He shrugged his shoulders in a helpless gesture. "Foolish, I know. While John was here, Antipas would occasionally wander down and speak to him, going alone, permitting no one to accompany him."

I looked up in surprise.

"No, it is true. We don't what was said. It was strange for Antipas to do such a thing, but he did it, nonetheless. I don't know what passed between them."

Something Cuza had said earlier suddenly rose up in my mind. "You say he was wary of putting John to death?"

Looking uncomfortable, the man replied, "I'll leave this for Antipas to tell you more if he wishes to do so."

I shook myself and resolved to take some time alone, down some straight vinegar. It was not part of my duty to get involved in some Jewish religious haggle.

I stood up and adjusted my armor. "Perhaps, Steward, he may or he may not. But he needs to render a decision about the man's carcass—priest, prophet, or mouthpiece of the gods. It makes no difference to me." I turned away from Cuza, leaving him with a startled, fearful look on his face.

****

The path to the pool took me past Antipas' personal quarters, the open doors revealing the marble floors of smooth, subtle colors and intricate designs, fresco paintings on the walls, and exotic garden plants growing in every corner, fitting a man of considerable wealth. It struck me again how a man who lived in such opulence was worried about the ranting of some Jewish prophet.

The large pool, built to catch as much of the sun as this sun-drenched land afforded, occupied most of the southern side of the fortress's upper level, water flowing into it through several large cisterns. Date palms grew in the corners of the tiled walkway, with beds of lilies and roses intermixed. Swallows, sparrows, and others birds of varying colors dashed from flower to flower, chirping with delight at the sweet aroma from so many flowers, these winged creatures, like these Jews, flitting about as though looking for a messiah under every flower.

Antipas floated in the shallow end of the pool, his eyes closed as water moved serenely over his plump frame. He lifted his head when he heard my footsteps.

"Good morning, Centurion." He lifted up a hand and spread it toward the plains west, toward Judea. "What can I do for you on this beautiful day?"

"I apologize for the interruption, Tetrarch, but I require a moment of your time."

"Yes, yes, of course." He drew himself upright, looking about to ensure we were alone. He looked back at me, squinting in the sun, wiping a few drops of water from a broad, high forehead. "What is it?" He took a deep breath; moving that much bulk, even in the water, must have been strenuous.

"There has been no opportunity since my arrival to present you with an initial assessment of your troops here. We should talk about their condition." While I could have mentioned one major concern, I didn't.

"Yes…I wondered when we would have this conversation, perhaps over today's midday meal? For the time being I just want to enjoy my surroundings." He looked around at the pool, the birds, the palm trees, and laughed. "It was tiring, you know, undertaking such revelry with my guests." He looked at me through narrowed eyes, smiling. "Or perhaps you do not know, stern Roman that you are." Another pause for breath: "And it was quite expensive. Spending my own money always enervates me." He stopped to take a drink from a deep wooden bowl at the edge of the pool and looked at me as though he just remembered I was still there. "Is there anything else?"

"At midday," I said, saluted, turning to retrace my steps across the stone patio. He closed his eyes, a smirk on his face as he slumped back down into the cool water.

"Oh, there is one more thing," I said, stopping near the edge of the pool. "A trivial matter…there are men at the gate wanting to bury the body of the man we executed last night. Before agreeing to this, I wondered if you had any objection?"

Antipas rose up from the water, all sign of indolence disappearing. He rubbed his chin with his right hand for several moments, perhaps uncomfortable with me using the word "*we*".

"Perhaps when we meet for lunch, I'll speak about John and the trouble he caused." Shaking his head, he said quietly, *sotto voce*, "…and still causes." He went on in an irritated but oddly compelled tone of voice, again speaking more to himself. "*Well… by the gods, why not? She's had her wish.*"

He looked up at me. "Give those men the body. I don't know where the head is and don't intend to ask. But, *yes*, give them John's body, and perhaps we can finally see an end to this affair." He sank back into the pool, any trace of pleasure washed from his face.

I retraced my steps recalling the events of last night . . .

Chapter II

Machaerus
Province of Perea
Late evening, July 14, A.D. 33

The dungeon was like every other rock-lined hole in the ground I had seen in my years of service. When Herod the Great rebuilt Machaerus, the dungeon took on new meaning. With horses dragging great iron plows like daggers through the earth, they ripped into rock, shale, and dirt, excavating the stones ripped from the depths, mortaring them together to form walls on the violated ground. It was only after they had made a place for death did they build a place for life, using the walls as a foundation, building the more luxurious parts of the palace above the dungeon, the stones lining its walls down here uncut, sharp, and jagged. With no windows, no cooling breezes blew through these halls, the air damp and heavy with the smell of sewage, sweat, dead men's bones, and rats—both dead and living. Yet upon this foundation of death, there rose up polished marble halls, carved white columns and graceful arches spreading in the sun overhead.

Light came from torches on the wall of the hallway leading to the cells. A tomb-like quiet filled this place, save for the shuffling feet of the guard and the soft dripping of water descending through the ragged stones. Rats scurried everywhere as they aggressively fought each other for crumbs in the dark corners of each cell reminding me of one the size of a small cat I'd kicked across a hallway somewhere in Egypt. In dungeons like this, either these vermin ate what food spilled from the prisoners' rations, or they nibbled on the prisoners. Guards were rotated frequently lest such pestilent duty put them at great risk.

There was a holding area, wide enough for ten men to stand, where the guard was stationed. Swinging my torch around, I ordered him, a man called Xanthus, to take me to the prisoner known as John the Baptizer.

The guard moved down the passage, holding his torch close to the rock ceiling, kicking rats out of the way as he went until they caught the idea and retreated on their own. I could hear a man speaking; I paused, motioning for the guard to stop. We both stood there in the passageway, listening. It was definitely the sound of a man, speaking to someone, but we could not make out the words. As we approached the cell, the words became more distinct. Xanthus stopped at a cell door of thick solid wooden planks, nothing but a small cut at the bottom, where a rusted iron plate could slide underneath to feed a few scraps of dried up bread and two day old scraps of meat to the prisoner. I could hear the voice now clearly. It was a man, speaking to another.

I looked hard at the guard. "Who else is in there with him?" I whispered. "Who's he talking to?"

The man turned to face me, the torch swinging its pattern of eerie light across the jagged wall. "There's no one in there, Centurion. Just talking to himself. Many of them do, you know."

"I've been in dungeons before, and that man in there is talking to someone."

The guard shrugged. There was certainly an easy way to find out. He put his torch in the iron brace hammered into the stone adjacent to the door, put the key into the lock, and then moved back from the door. "Stand back, Centurion." Lifting a knee, he gave the door a massive kick with a booted foot. The door shuddered, dust cascading down around the edges and the voice from inside stopped but the door remained shut, frozen in place.

"Just something to help the lock," he griped, with a tinge of bitterness; he was a young man, probably full of ambition which his time as a guard did not shake. He turned the key in the lock and the bolt slid. He put a foot in the middle of the door and kicked it again before slamming into the door with his shoulder. It opened, grudgingly, turning on its rusty hinges.

The Baptizer stood there in the darkness…alone. I shoved my torch into the cell first, swinging it left and right, to make sure.

"To whom were you speaking?" I asked.

"God" came the simple answer out of the darkness.

I looked at this man. He was thin, understandably so as he must have fought the rats for what food scraps were thrown down to them from the remains of Antipas' table. He stood there, bearded, shivering, with nothing but a loincloth and a thin, manure-encrusted blanket, a piece of trash from the stables unfit for horses.

Yet standing there in a place calculated to strip a man of every shred of dignity, he did not look like a prisoner. The man radiated some strange sense of peace, an aura of calm, a gravitas I'd seen in just one or two men I had known in my life, men suffused with dignity, confidence, and integrity; truly great men. It was as though the filth-crusted blanket around his shoulders symbolized some sort of royal robe of acceptance. I blinked hard, my eyes darted again wondering the reason for the hope I saw in the prisoner's eyes. There was no explanation for his peaceful contentedness, for he must have known the executioner's blade waited for him beyond his rusted cell door.

I stood transfixed, unable to utter a word. It reminded me of when I met Gaius Marius, a descendant of one of Rome's first great general, and an accomplished tactician in his own right, a man of almost god-like bearing. It was the same, standing before John.

"You have something to say, Centurion," he said. It was a statement, not a question, and certainly not from a man with any sense of impending doom.

I found my voice. "You are John? The one they call the Baptizer?"

His scarred thin hands caressed the edges of his ragged blanket. "Yes… I am he." He took a step forward and lifted a hand, pointing it at me. Xanthus stepped forward, but I put out a hand and bade him still. "I baptize with water but there is another coming, Centurion …he who will baptize with fire. You should seek him."

"No…no, John. It is you I seek."

"It was God who speaks, Centurion. I am simply one of his instruments."

"It seems your god has left you to answer for the consequences then."

John bowed his head slowly. "If that be so, I trust good will come from it."

"Your god has strange ideas about what is good," as I gazed around at the barren walls.

John chuckled, a deep, rumbling laugh, his beard shaking. "My God *is* goodness itself. Can your gods say the same?"

Quickly tiring of this bantering, this strange sense of his dignity now seemed to me nothing more than a delusion caused by the workings of the stench in this pit. "My gods have not left me to rot in some hole in the ground, John."

He bowed his head again and shook it back and forth, slowly. "No, you are wrong." He looked up and his eyes flashed with fire, his voice tight leaching passion. "No. Your gods live to keep you in a pit, for they came from the pit to which they will return and they desire to drag you into it with them." His eyes blazed as he continued. "You will die, Centurion, unless…unless you leave the gods of Rome and turn to the God of Abraham, Isaac, and Jacob. Forsake this filth," he said, throwing up his hands to indicate his own surroundings. "Flee from it! Your gods keep you in pits like this so you cannot see it. Do you think they live in sweetness and light and freedom up there?" he rasped, throwing up one hand toward the ceiling, referring I knew to Antipas and those drunken revelers several floors above. John continued to fling words at me like spears. "No, they don't, and you will become like them, despite all your appeals to virtue and hardship and the nobility of a soldier's sacrifice." He spat these last words with disdain.

Then he stepped forward and in one passionate gesture grabbed the leather armor at my chest. "Flee from it!" he sneered, his voice scratchy with passion. "Run. Put it behind you. Leave these false gods in the dust, and live a righteous life!"

Stunned for a moment, I recovered and jerked his hand from my armor, shaking inside. It had been a long while since someone put their hands on my armor and lived to tell about it. "Your piety has bent your mind, John. It is you who lives in this pit, not me."

"No, *you* look around, Centurion. In the days to come, look around you. Watch and listen. You will see the one who baptizes with fire. Follow him. He will lead you out of the pit."

"Is there another baptizer out there in the Judean wilderness, then, with your mantle, baptizing men hungry for any notion of a god?" I struggled to throw words back at him in laughter, but could not; I was trembling too much, the cold frigid air holding me captive.

John looked at me and for the first time, he frightened me with his words. "He *is* God," he said, holding up a bare, thin arm, pointing out through the walls toward the world outside, "and he is walking around out there, his feet in the very dust of this land, God walking among us. And he will baptize with the fire of refinement, of purging, a cleansing, a burning fire, a baptism of death that will lead to life."

Xanthus, an undisciplined youth, strangled a derisive laugh at the prophet's words, and it shook me out of my fear. "Centurion, this place has made him crazy."

John looked at the soldier and then back at me. "I see more clearly than you can imagine, Centurion. It is you who must fear the days to come, not me."

"I think not." I indicated to Xanthus to bring the prisoner, and turned to face John again. "It seems your god has directed Antipas be permitted to remove your head, for the command has been given to do so."

"So this is why you are here," he replied, unshaken, the peace in his tone unsettling.

"Yes. I am here, visiting you in your festering, stinking pit,

John, to see that your head is delivered to the ones upstairs on a platter."

John rearranged the filthy blanket over his shoulders and nodded. Then, with great firmness, he looked up at me and said, "So be it. Blessed be the name of the Lord."

"Bring him," I said to Xanthus, growling angrily. There was no logic behind John's demeanor, but for some reason it angered me beyond reason. I was too young at the time to realize I was angry at John because I envied him the peace he had, a peace that enabled him to face death with such equanimity…but that night I recognized the peace John had was true power, a power capable of disrupting nations and kingdoms should it spread.

We walked back to the holding area, Xanthus pushing John ahead of him, me following, my torch held high. Valerus was there along with the executioner and three other soldiers. Valerus pointed to the soldiers, "I thought we might need a few more men to hold the prisoner steady." I nodded wordlessly, though I doubted it.

The executioner was well muscled with thick arms and neck. Not unexpectedly, he was slightly drunk for executioners tended to dull their own senses with drink before swinging their axes as severing a man's head from his body wasn't something a human soul could withstand with any great deal of frequency. Xanthus pushed John into the center of the room, the handle of the axe tripping John.

I spoke to the assembled soldiers. "By order of Antipas, this man is to be decapitated." They stood there, cold in the dark pit, the torchlight flickering across their stony faces as they received without reaction the news that the man on the ground before them would soon be dead. Valerus bent down, took John under an arm, shoving him roughly into a kneeling position. Xanthus had placed a broad, stained wooden chopping block in the center of the room, and as my strong warrior moved John toward it, John shook himself free of his iron like grasp.

"You can let go, Roman," he said, with unfathomable dignity.

"I will be the first one out of this pit. My prayer is for you to one day follow me."

Valerus looked at me sharply. I shrugged my shoulders. "Prophets."

"There has been no reprieve, Centurion?"

"No." I turned to the executioner, motioning him to come forward. The other soldiers, seeing John bending placidly over the block, his hands holding each side, stepped back. They had smelled the executioner's breathe as well, wanting to be no closer than necessary when he brought the heavy instrument of death down.

John's voice came from the dimness, floating up from the stained block of wood upon which his head rested. His words seemed to echo off the close rock walls and come at me from every direction. "There is only one reprieve, Centurion, for you and your soldiers. Endure the baptism of fire; without it, you will remain in this pit for the rest of your life, and at its end your gods will drag you down with them into the great lake of fire, and there you will burn for eternity."

I said nothing but for some reason these words struck me more than anything else he had said that night.

"Cheery one, isn't he?" Valerus grumbled, his voice like gravel, watching how John was affecting me. Motioning to the executioner, the big man positioned himself, readying his axe. "Are you ready, Centurion?" my trusted second in command asked.

It was customary to give a condemned man a chance to utter final words, but as I stood there debating whether to let this desert prophet have another opportunity to throw some barb-filled words into my soul again, he spoke, looking first at me and then at Valerus.

"I have said what must be said, Centurion. Do your duty. I pray God will have mercy on you and these men."

I stood there, confusion mixing with the bile of anger at this man, his head on a chopping block, asking his god to have mercy on me. I had watched others face the executioner's axe, yet I had never heard one so condemned repay the sentence with a plea for mercy.

Valerus looked at me, waiting for the order.

I lifted my hand, pointed, and nodded. Valerus then turned to the executioner giving his assent. The axe whistled down.

The sharpened steel separated John's head from his body. Drunk as he was, the man's stroke was sure. Blood shot out everywhere in the dim space, splattering against the walls, the wooden block, robes, sandals, and hands. Even as thick silken skeins still pulsed from the now headless body, I directed the executioner to put his prize on a platter and take it to Antipas. Without hesitation, the man bent down, grabbed the head by the hair, and walked off with it. Without any instructions from me, Valerus and two soldiers threw the body in a corner of the holding area, to await slaves who would carry it up tomorrow.

As I looked down, I noticed some of John's blood had splattered on my sandals. I cursed as I grabbed a rag, kicking my sandals in the fine Middle Eastern dust, trying to wipe the leather clean. One of the first things a good legionnaire learns on campaign is that blood not removed immediately from leather leaves a permanent stain. Despite my efforts, the stain remained, the blood leaching into the leather... a permanent reminder of a cursed desert prophet and the words he'd tossed through my breastplate armor like a sharp spear through silk.

Chapter III

Machaerus
Province of Perea
Midday, July 15, A.D. 33

Cuza graciously received me at Antipas' quarters. A satisfying breeze blew through the open windows, fighting the oppressive, increasing heat of the noonday sun. Bright purple drapes provided a rich contrast to the gold cloth covering the couches placed throughout the large, airy room. Rugs made from the finest handpicked wool covered sections of the polished gray marble floor, the furnishings so different from those of my own Spartan accommodations, leaving me with a acid taste in my mouth for all this luxury.

Antipas walked in, wheezing with each step, which made sense in any man who carried such weight in this climate, but I could see in his form where lines of muscle still existed, and his eyes, clearly, those of a younger, harder man. I'd seen this look before; in men who missed nothing of what happened around them, whose entire lives revolved around the sole purpose of ensuring that no situation would ever put them at a disadvantage. I disdained such men for they seemed quicker about most things than me as they assessed dangerous situations, insuring their own skins were well preserved and protected.

"Again, welcome to Machaerus, Centurion. I regret I didn't receive you here earlier this week, but I'm sure you understand," the greeting of a political professional, like a cat balancing on a beam. By all gods, I hated politicians, their placating ways devoid of any real substance.

"I look forward to serving you, Antipas."

He laughed, "Any man who finds this place enjoyable should

be examined by an oracle or gutted, so the priests can draw divinations from his liver." He waved a casual hand at me while he sat down, nodding to Cuza who along with other servants, began to bring in the food.

Lamb, succulently prepared, from where I had no idea, came first, slow roasted on a spit and falling off the bone served with mounds of couscous, golden and feathery, flavored with a fruity olive oil. Cuza placed warm bread, the crust firm, along with the red grapes full and bursting next to the lamb. I picked up a piece of bread, dipped it in the oil, and looked at Antipas.

"Epicurus leaves his mark here, I see."

Antipas waved his hand around in the air, encompassing the entire fortress. "Yes, yes, I make it a point to take my enjoyments wherever I can find them."

I looked at him while I chewed the bread, made of finely-ground grain unavailable in the villages and certainly not the normal fare in a Roman soldier's barracks.

"When my father decided to secure this eastern border and rebuild this . . . this 'edifice', he paid scant attention to the finer aspects of life in what is, sadly, the armpit of the world, so I changed it. If one doesn't like one's environment, one simply changes it, wouldn't you agree?"

"If one has the authority, the means, and the wisdom, yes, I suppose so . . . why not?"

Antipas nodded, lifting his immense goblet of wine to his lips as I concentrated on the lamb, wolfing down a tender cut of shoulder before there was any more conversation. He was faster than me, eating an entire leg of lamb before feasting on the bread, and then the couscous. We said nothing as we ate, and I avoided his gaze, staring instead out through the tall columns out into the Judean wilderness. There was fruit, cool and sweet. Cuza surprised me when he set custard made from goat's milk before me to finish the repast.

Antipas belched before setting down his goblet, wiping his hands on a towel held out to him by one of the younger slaves. "So Pilate assigned you to train my guards. They're raw and inexperienced, more of a danger to themselves than anyone else. You will be stern with them as you instruct them in the Roman ways?"

"Of course. I will be what they need, Tetrarch."

"Ah, the stoicism of Rome meets the passion of the Galilee!" He laughed quietly, no doubt at some private joke. He quaffed his wine, wiped his mouth again, and looked at Cuza, holding out his cup to the man. "So what news do you bring from Pilate? Is he well? Does he enjoy Caesarea?"

"Pilate sends his compliments. He is well aware of how you have kept Galilee and Perea safe and prosperous and he looks forward to visiting you soon."

Antipas smiled, speaking with a hint of mockery, "As am I." Fixing me with a more serious look, he said rather brusquely, "So tell me more about your mission here."

I wanted no part of any squirming political relationships, nor did I want to get between Pilate and Antipas as there was no future in anything like that for a soldier. I met his eye directly. "My task here is simple. My second-in-command, Valerus, and I will train your people to a standard approximating that of the Legions."

"And why would Rome dispense its knowledge of warfare so freely?"

"So its trusted friends like you can have well trained soldiers at your disposal, and if needed, these soldiers can be employed by the Emperor to help keep his lands secure as well."

Antipas regarded me for a moment with a stare aimed at penetrating my soul but he said nothing waiting for me to continue. "Rome trains auxiliary units from almost every land…"—I almost said, 'from every land we've conquered,' but felt that would be inconsiderate—"where the Legions are. Your men, when properly trained, increase the force at his disposal and he is most appreciative."

The man leaned forward from his seat, "What? Are you saying he intends to take my men and use them for his purposes without any consideration for my needs? A contemptuous idea." As he spoke his voice grew louder with each word, his face reddening.

He stood up and began to pace the floor, spitting out, "I've given that man so much." Mumbling under his breath, "*The nerve of him . . . after all I've done for him!*" Turning toward me, his face now crimson, he exclaimed, "You say Rome would use my men . . . . my men for its territorial conquests! How dare you!"

"Tetrarch, I did not say that."

The man looked sharply at me. It was obvious few men ever told him he was wrong or his thoughts misplaced, but I needed to be set him straight immediately. "Antipas, I never said the Emperor intended to take your men and conquer new lands."

"But you said …"

"What I said was he appreciates having your men trained. Could he request some assistance from you in the future if the situation warranted? Yes, but right now I know of nothing to suggest anything like that is on the horizon. Valerus and I are here to increase the battle readiness of your men for your use. I repeat, I know of nothing to suggest the Emperor wishes to deploy your forces as part of some conquest."

Antipas' eyes glared at me. "Don't coddle me. I know about this mission you're talking about. I'm not the simpleton some take me for so don't insult me with your condescending drivel. Even if you're right about the Emperor, we both know Pilate has an additional task for you. You are here to judge my administration and report your findings to Pilate. You're nothing more than a spy! Isn't that right?!" his voice laced with sarcasm and contempt.

Before I could respond, Antipas continued his attack with the speed of a hundred arrows shot all at once. "Yes, you're here to train my soldiers, but you're also here to look over my shoulder to insure I don't stray too far from Rome's vision for these lands. Does Pilate take me for a fool, that I would harbor a mole in my midst?"

I hesitated, taking a few grapes from the tray before us, stalling to consider my response. No doubt Antipas' source in Pilate's headquarters was well placed. With my purposes here now fully exposed, what could I say to rein in the man's rancor? Meeting his attack with another would lead nowhere. I rose to my feet looking south out the window at the Nabataean hills, composing my thoughts before returning to my seat, choosing my words carefully. "Antipas, you're right. I am here for two purposes. First and foremost, I'm to assist your soldiers in reaching a higher level of proficiency. That is my primary task. Let me ask, if the Empire is not secure, does anything else matter?"

Antipas said nothing at first, skepticism written on every wrinkle of his face; his answer bland, without emotion, "That's true, the highest priority is to have our lands secure."

"Good, we can agree about that. . . And as you suggest, Pilate wants me to provide you assistance in your lands so they continue to prosper. I apologize if this was not made clear to you before my arrival."

Antipas made a sudden grab for his wine goblet but missed it, scattering its contents all over the marble floor. Ignoring Cuza and another servant who instantly appeared to clean up the results of his unconstrained rage, he stormed at me. "You Romans! Why is it you believe you can fix everything, control everything just by the power of your words and your Army! You truly believe everything under the sun is yours to manipulate. Oh, your words are meant to placate me, to soothe me, Centurion, but right now, I see you only as . . . as a spy."

From his perspective, he was right. I was a mole, a threat, a constant reminder of how Rome restrained him, holding him captive with bureaucratic ropes and chains. How could I allay his fears, his solicitude? Was there any way for each of us to find dignity and common ground in this discussion?

We looked at each other for a time, each evaluating the other. Finally I offered, "Can we agree you and Pilate have the same goals?"

"What do you mean?" Antipas replied, his eyes sullen and foreboding.

I wanted to shout, '*You oaf, can't you see the advantages to you in this arrangement,*' but I held my words in check. "You and Pilate both want peaceful and prosperous lands. Neither of you benefits if there is unrest or anarchy in these lands, nor is there any benefit to either of you if these lands become economically unstable."

He rubbed his chin, nodding his head slightly in agreement.

"And since the Emperor appointed you to oversee Galilee and Perea, can we also agree he did so because he trusted you?"

"Yes, I believe that."

"Has the Emperor given you any indication he has lost confidence in you?"

Antipas' eyes questioned me before answering, "No, I've given him no cause for that."

"Are your provinces still important to Pilate?"

"Yes, of course, you . . ."

"Antipas, I'm here simply to make sure if a situation arises that might hinder you or Pilate in the accomplishment of your mutual goals, I may be a resource, one not beholden to you for some political favor, to help resolve any issues before they become major stumbling blocks to either of you. Could such an arrangement be helpful to you?"

The tetrarch's eyes flickered for a moment, assessing my words before accepting another fresh cup of wine from Cuza, twirling it around in his hand, seemingly gaining confidence from its contents. Rising from his seat, he began to pace around the room, his royal robes swishing around his frame before he stopped abruptly. "I want to trust you, I really do. I can see where a man like you may be useful to me. You appear reliable and I sense you can provide a calm voice in a storm. I will consider your words carefully."

He turned away from me looking south again at the brown hills. He remained still for several minutes before commenting soberly, "It was my father who desired I be the Tetrarch of these provinces. After his death and after a laborious process, Caesar Augustus affirmed this appointment, for which I'll be forever grateful. I believed then, as I do now, the Emperor knows he can depend upon me to do his bidding. What you say about both Pilate and me desiring peace and prosperity is true. Nothing is gained by either of us if unrest or discord raises its ugly head." Turning back to face me, he asked, "So how do we work together to achieve these mutually desired results?"

I now appreciated Antipas' position to a far greater degree than before. Here was a man who would always live under the shadow of the memory of his famous father. He desired fame and fortune to come his way through his own ability, his own drive; not because of his father's legacy. Yet he was practical enough to know that, regardless of what he accomplished, he would always be under the watchful eye of Rome. Living under this structure for many years, he understood this far better than me.

Rising to my feet, our eyes now level, I said, "Antipas, I believe the answer is a simple one -- honesty. While you may not always agree with my observations, I pledge my thoughts, ideas, and recommendations will always be given without bias or prejudice, without hidden agendas or double meanings. The words I speak will always be what I believe is best for both you and Pilate."

Antipas nodded a trace of a smile on his face. "Well said, Centurion. It will be good to hear opinions unencumbered by desires of personal gain. A man in my position is exposed to far too many sycophants."

He sat back on his couch, his hand cradling his cup of wine as he brushed some hair from his face. "You should be a politician. You may have the gift."

I laughed, "Oh, no. I'm just a simple soldier, nothing more, nothing less."

Snickering, he appraised me once again. "You are an unpretentious man, an intelligent man but one with few Augean ambitions. I don't see many like you." After a brief silence, Antipas indicated our meeting was over. "We have accomplished much today. Rather than consider the military matters you wanted to discuss, join me at dawn for a day's enjoyment of the Salt Sea. We can talk about my soldiers as we bask in the refreshing spring waters there."

Hesitating for a moment, I nodded "Of course". It was not what I wanted to do but . . . "Before I leave, I have one question about last night. Since you have many under your command to do your bidding, why did you require me to take charge of killing that man last night?"

The ruler chuckled as he sat forward on his cushions. "A few moments ago, I indicated I found you reliable. Rather than challenge me in public last evening, you saluted and carried out the task without hesitation." A sly smile filled his fat face as a freshening breeze came through the windows spreading his garments out like a great cape. "John's death was not something I had planned but once I trapped myself, I had no recourse." He turned to face me. "Once I realized my error, I decided to take advantage of the situation to test you." He stopped, his chin rising slightly, seemingly assessing me once again before declaring, "And you passed. You did your duty even though I sensed it was not one you necessarily agreed with."

It was now clear everything I heard about this man was true. Despite reassuring words delivered in an engaging tone, the man was like a fox, crafty and devious, willing to use anyone to achieve his purposes. His aim would always be directed solely at improving his position in whatever game was being played, always putting his position, his welfare ahead of all others. I had just told him of my determination to be honest with him and now he was telling me his values and his beliefs were contradictory to mine. Instantly I wondered when he would try to take advantage of my truthful, duty first mannerisms again. What a bastard!

"I'm glad I passed your test," my comment terse and succinct, trying, perhaps unsuccessfully, to hide my contempt for the man.

With nothing else to add, I excused myself and returned to my headquarters still shaking my head over being used by Antipas. How could I be so naïve? Part of me wanted to beat the man to a bloody pulp, but my orders required me to serve him well. This would be a greater challenge then I first envisioned.

****

"A magnificent scene, isn't it?" Antipas asked as he sat upon his white charger and me on a brown stable mount hurriedly procured for me before beginning our descent to the Salt Sea.

Although weary and on alert from yesterday's discussion, the man was right. Any artist, even one with modest capabilities, would be pleased to adorn his canvas with the beautiful landscape spread before us. High craggy mountains stood upright in all directions, the sun's early morning rays reflecting off rocky cliffs above us spreading warmth on the turquoise water lapping at our feet. Bright white, salt stained rocks and sand graced the shore of the sea, and across the glassy water to our west sat sandy brown cliffs and tall peaks, positioned like sentries guarding the western shoreline. The tranquility of the place stilled my soul after a restless night recalling yesterday's discussion with Antipas.

Our journey to the Salt Sea began under a few wisps of pinkish clouds in the eastern skies, heralding the start of another day, a light breeze coming from the west. Our party consisted of ten men: Antipas, Cuza, two other servants, and five soldiers with me. We carefully descended down the Gorge of Callirhoe on the steep winding trail no wider than one horse-width, numerous loose stones and rocks laying in wait to trip the unwary traveler, plunging him down the abyss on either side of the trail. With danger lurking at each step, each of us, after glancing at the unforgiving depths, concentrated on staying in the center of the path knowing any misstep would prove fatal. Once we reached the shoreline we gave out a collective sigh of relief as we appreciated the beauty around us even more.

The simple pleasures at my feet captured my attention as small waves splashed ashore effortlessly, moving small white pebbles on the shoreline back and forth nudging them gently first in one direction and then in another in a timeless ritual. Dismounting, I reached down to feel the smoothness of the small stones before Antipas interrupted me, pointing toward the distant mountains to the west. "Over there is the southern part of Judea. Many who live there eke out a meager existence by farming the rocky ground and raising a few animals. A few enterprising souls mine the salt deposits, shipping their bounty by caravan to lands in all directions including Rome."

I took in the mountains he indicated. Looking about I answered, "It's amazing how the gods have brought all this landscape into such harmony."

"Humph, well I am glad this place meets with your approval," annoyed that he was not the center of my attention. I reminded myself once again; *Stay alert – remember he is only motivated by his own self interests.*

Gesturing to the hills around us, Antipas went on. "As you look north, that green, lush gathering of small trees and brush in the distance is where the Jordan River completes its journey from Galilee, its waters providing the primary inflow from which there is no outlet. The resulting stagnation, coupled with bordering lands rich in mineral salt, produces water with a salt content that is four times greater than the Great Sea." Dismounting from his horse, he sauntered south along the shoreline. "Let me show you the spot where we'll spend our time this morning."

Once we reached some large gray boulders strewn along the shoreline, he stopped. "Past these big rocks, those waterfalls you see above us bring down clear, salt free water from underground springs in the mountains back to our east. The water then collects into pools before it enters the sea. It is these spring fed waters we'll enjoy today." After looking around to admire the scenery once again, he continued. "The people who lived here long ago called this place, the 'Springs of Callirhoe.' Today it is better known as 'The Baths of Herod' because my father loved this spot."

He gazed at me, making sure I focused on him. "After my father died, my brothers and I began our reigns simultaneously. Archelaus, two years my senior, governed the provinces in the hills of Judea, Idumea, and Samaria while Philip, one year my junior, rules the two provinces north of Galilee, Traconitus, and Iturea."

"Obviously, you have met the expectations of the Emperor. What about your brothers?"

Antipas huffed, "An interesting question. While Philip and I successfully continue on the path our father envisioned, Archelaus ruled ruthlessly, killing more than three thousand people, and more importantly, he was not a good manager of money. As such, Rome removed him from office ten years ago, exiling him to Gaul along with his reprehensible wife. That's why Pilate rules Judea today. From Rome's perspective, despite our loyalty to the Emperor, there will always be concern that Philip and I do not fall into the same trap as our brother."

He rubbed his chin. "When I hear myself make these statements, I have empathy for Pilate. Perhaps if I were in his position, I too would have assigned an individual like you to watch over a man like me. An interesting thought, isn't it?"

Rather than reopen yesterday's banter, I shrugged, "Something to consider, I suppose."

Neither of us spoke for a time as we watched the water fall from the heights above, the steady beat of the water playing its rhythmic melody on the rocks. Then Antipas pointed southwest. "In those hills hides another fortress built by my father, an immaculate place called Masada. Constructed on a high bluff, it commands a highly defensible location. Perhaps one day, we'll visit it."

With his explanation of the surrounding terrain complete, Antipas led the way over the last few rocks to gaze at the pools of spring waters. Handing the reins of our horses to a servant, we stepped close to the nearest pool, its water transparent. "My father first brought me here when I was a young boy. I've often thought that despite the military and territorial imperatives of Machaerus, one of the reasons he reestablished the fort was so he could enjoy these springs on a regular basis, although his first priority were the Nabataeans to the south. He never wanted to be surprised by them coming out of the dark so he concentrated on strengthening the walls and the parapets." He smiled brightly, "I, however, being more of a polymath, wanted to bring the finer things to the region, a product of my spending my youthful years in Rome."

Surprised, I looked up. "I didn't know you were educated in Rome."

"Ah, yes, for many years. I love that city. While I've used some money to bring the comforts I enjoy to our secluded hovel here, the majority of my funds and effort for the last twenty years has been on building the city of Tiberias, specifically to honor the emperor and my love for Rome. It has been a labor of love for me."

He seemed to drift off for several moments before signaling Cuza over, giving him instructions about our midday meal. Once the servant bowed his understanding and hurried off to see to his tasks, Antipas disrobed. Unlike the other days I had seen him, today he dressed as a plebian, a gray simple piece of cloth held in place by a leather belt rather than the delicate purple and crimson clothing he seemed to favor. Once undressed and throwing his clothes off to the side, he lowered himself into the nearest pool of water, his flabby body now fully exposed. Too embarrassed by the sight of his bulging frame, I watched the waters run down from the craggy rocks above as they splashed into the deep blue pools. When Antipas called for me to join him, I deferred, telling him I wanted to first inspect the security positions of the soldiers guarding us from the rocks above.

****

Each step up the rough rocks to top of the cliff invigorated me, stretching my legs, reminding me of my roots as a soldier, the feeling of being in tune with the beauty and harmony of nature, away from the intrigue and self importance of Antipas. Once on top of the rock and after filling my lungs with the clean air, miles and miles of open, desolate country lay before me testifying to wonderment of the gods, the majesty of sky, hills and mountains, every color of the rainbow blending together in magnificent synchronization. To be here, now, in this place, this was my calling, my destiny, serving Rome as one of its warriors.

Before my mind could be lulled further into a state of unbridled reminiscences, a soldier surprised me as he made his presence known from a rocky boulder above and off to my left. "Centurion, can I do anything for you?" the man asked,

I turned to look up at the man. "Soldier, why are you here?"

The soldier thought before responding, "To guard the Tetrarch from marauding bandits, Centurion," the young soldier stammered a bit. He was typical of Antipas' auxiliary formation: tall and rangy, unseasoned in the basics of soldiering, yet willing to learn and be molded under the grip of skillful leadership to become a mature, robust soldier.

"Correct. Would you agree for any bandits to be successful, they will be looking for us just as we search for them?"

The soldier thought for a moment, his words tumbling out, "Yes . . . I guess that's right."

I now stood directly in front of the young man, his eyes straining, trying to avoid my stony stare. "So if we agree the bandits are looking for us, why would you want to silhouette yourself on the top of this cliff where anyone with half a brain can see you from a great distance?" Pointing to some rocks a few steps to the left, I said, "Why don't you stand guard behind those rocks there so the metal on your uniform does not shine out like a beacon? From that position, you can still maintain vigilance over the same ground to our front without exposing yourself to the wandering eyes of those who might wish to harm us. Does that make sense?"

"Yes, Centurion. I see what you mean. That would be a much

better location."

"Good. Now I want you to go around to the other four soldiers up here and pass this knowledge on to them."

"Yes, Centurion," the young man said with conviction as he saluted.

"Your name is . . ."

"Avram."

"Avram, I'm now placing you in charge of the other four men. I'm depending on you to instruct them on what we've just discussed. If you need me, I'll be down there in that pool of water below. Do you have any questions?"

****

Unlike Antipas, it took me more time to enjoy the water because of all the fastenings holding my uniform together, but the effort was worth it when the exhilarating liquid flowed around the loins and muscles of my body. As I delighted in the cool pool, Antipas gave me a quizzical look. "You're a cautious man; part of your character or from lessons in your past?"

Ducking my head into the water before responding, I said, "My instincts come from my father who was also a soldier. And over the years my experiences as a soldier have taught me the value of common sense."

"Is the placement of guards a result of instincts or common sense?"

"Both. Your men must learn I expect them to do the right thing every time, without taking shortcuts or making unwise assumptions."

Antipas brushed some hair from his forehead. "I assume one of the benefits from you and Valerus, that's his name isn't it, is security at Machaerus will be increased."

"Yes, and there'll be other improvements, some obvious, others less so."

Antipas sloshed some water over his body, the trickles of water needing time to reach the pool because of his size. "Your name means eagle, doesn't it? That's most fitting for a soldier to be named for a creature known for its cunning and its hunting skills."

As Antipas was speaking, my thoughts flashed to my father who died on a battlefield in Gaul while serving under Varus. When some of his past comrades came to our home to pay their respects to my mother, they testified to his strength and courage as he fought to his last breath. "I'm proud to follow in my father's footsteps. My decision caused my mother some distress, but in time, she grew to understand. My wife, Claudia, is the one who endures many days without my presence as she raises our two children." How I longed for my wife and to be with our daughter Flavia, and son, Felix. When could I join them? Soon, I hoped. What a great day that would be . . . then I realized Antipas was talking, thoughts of my family of no interest to him.

". . . tell me about my soldiers and Shallium, the man who leads them. I have known his father, Uthai, the overseer of Nain, one of my small towns in the southern Galilee, for many years." He stopped. "Are my men good enough to meet the expectations desired by Pilate, by the Emperor?"

I sat up slowly, letting the water run over my legs, glancing up to make sure the soldiers above us were not privy to this discussion. "Right now, no. There is much to be done. In the next few weeks, I will have more definitive thoughts for you. However, based on your relationship with Uthai, what I'm about say will not please you."

The ruler's face snapped up, his eyes opened wide, his hands shaking as though he needed a large cup of wine. "What do you mean? What will not please me?"

Taking my cue from his startled look, I plunged ahead. "Right now, Shallium's leadership concerns me. Your situation here is similar to many other auxiliary units on the frontier. The genesis of the problem stems from recruiting both the soldiers and their leaders from the same general location."

"What are you telling me? That he is not a good leader; that he must be replaced?"

"Shallium is a good man who cares a great deal for his soldiers, but therein lays the problem. He may almost care too much."

"Your words make no sense. How can a leader care too much for his men?"

Ignoring Antipas' tirade, I went on. "As I'm sure you are aware, he has known many of his soldiers before they joined the army and this new relationship is difficult for everyone. Simply put, Shallium cannot be friends with his subordinates. He is their commander and your soldiers, despite their familiarity with him, must see him in that role."

Antipas rubbed his eyes for a moment, but said nothing, a pained expression on his face.

With his attention now in my grasp, now was not the time to be tentative. "Your men must learn to respect his authority. They must understand his decisions are not open for debate. There may come a day when he must order them into battle and they must have complete trust in him so if that day comes, they fight knowing he is right and the sacrifice of their lives may be necessary. Right now, I don't believe this type of relationship exists."

Antipas' angry look slowly abated, his eyes taking in the hills to the west. He let the water play over his body for several minutes before admitting, "There is wisdom in your words. Shallium and his men grew up in the same region of southern Galilee and northern Perea. No doubt, many of them have known each other all their lives, and I must confess, I've seen them enjoying time together, telling jokes, and eating together. It never occurred to me any harm might come from their close relationship."

The placating, self preserving side of Antipas' personality then came to the fore, his words and look mirroring his plea. "Can you resolve this issue, Centurion, or must we send Shallium to another location? What will his father say? What will he think about me?"

What kind of a ruler was this man who was more concerned

about hurting his association with a subordinate than concentrating on the problem at hand? Why did soldiers, men of war like me, have to be under the thumb of those who lacked moral courage, spineless frauds who reveled in their titles but not in their requisite duty? I thanked the gods once again I was a soldier, not a politician.

"Centurion, what can you do? How can you get us out of this dilemma?"

I almost laughed as I thought about how this same man who boasted earlier of testing me was now reduced to a feeble, whining excuse of a leader, wanting me to solve a predicament of his doing. What an incompetent fool!

Holding back a smirk, I answered, "If this cannot be corrected soon, Shallium should be reassigned, but for now, I intend to challenge him. Since you've known the man's family for some time, I wanted you to be aware of the situation before I took action."

Beginning to get control of his emotions, Antipas' eyes blazed as he tried to appear to be a steadfast leader. "Yes, challenge him, test him." His words came out as commands but his voice begged for a positive response. "I wouldn't be pleased if my relationship with Uthai was crippled. It is my utmost desire you teach and motivate his son. Handle this quickly and quietly. Do I make myself clear?"

As I nodded my agreement, my anger began to boil up again about the weakness of such men as Antipas, who wished to exculpate himself by delegating the issue to me thereby closing the door on this subject. "As we discussed yesterday, my goal is to maintain peace and build prosperity in my territories and having one of my town leaders upset with me could prove nettlesome. I've one issue I'm dealing with now and I don't wish to have another."

What was he talking about? "I was not aware of any unusual issues or concerns. From all I've been told, things are going well here."

Antipas chuckled. "Actually, you're part of both the issue I refer to and the solution."

"I don't understand."

The man looked at me for a moment, judging me once again. "John's death delighted Herodias, but because the common people respected John so much, I may be answering to them for some time. It is my hope this entire affair is forgotten soon so we can return to a state of normalcy."

Maybe now I would find out something about John, but did I really care? While part of me wanted to brush all this aside, something deep in me pushed for a response. "I heard this man rebuked you, so I understand how this must have angered you, but why execute him in front of all your guests? Why take such a step then?"

"Ah, a good question." After the ruler took a deep breath, his words came out slowly. "As you may have heard, several years ago Herodias and I were drawn irresistibly to one another. Against all good common sense, we divorced our spouses and married. If we had been common people, we risked death by stoning, but as the tetrarch, I thought we could weather any criticism. But I hadn't counted on John."

I saw John again in my mind, his eyes, his strident tone, his unflinching determination. "I can understand why you say that. He and I spoke briefly before his death . . . a strong forthright man, a man with deep conviction."

"Yes, exactly. He railed against our union, calling it sinful and against god's will and he did so in a very public way, forcing me to silence him." The man stopped to swat a small bug off his arm. "So I arrested him and imprisoned him to isolate him from his followers. Herodias badgered me relentlessly to have him killed."

I gave a knowing nod. "From my brief time with him, he didn't appear to be one who would change his position on matters he felt strongly about."

"A fair statement. Anyway on the last night of my birthday gathering, Salome, that vixen, danced in such a way, I found myself wanting to please her in any way I could. I was so drunk I promised to give her anything she wanted, even half my kingdom. I was a fool thinking as though I was young again. Anyway, for some reason which I didn't comprehend at the time, after I told the girl she could have anything she wanted, she left."

As some more cool water played across his soft hairless chest, the man went on. "When she returned, she asked for only one thing. Not for a palace or for gold, not for jewels or anything I would have gladly paid. This innocent looking young girl asked for John's head on a platter!" For a moment, his eyes filled with sadness, and then it disappeared. "Then I called for you. I didn't really want to kill John, but I had to save face in front of all my guests. Since they all heard my exchange with the girl, I had little choice."

I sat still, wanting to blurt out, *'If you're the ruler, you can do whatever the gods guide you to do,'* but instead, I asked, "So why did Salome want John dead? What did he ever do to her?"

"Later that night I asked myself those same questions. After some investigation, it became obvious. When Salome left me, she went to see her mother asking for guidance as to what she should request of me. It was then Herodias saw her chance. She is the one who instructed Salome to ask for John's head. While you and I may share some guilt for John's final outcome, it was really Herodias who killed John. Not me. Not you." His voice trailed off.

Here was another side of Antipas to be leery of, his constant effort to escape responsibility. I was glad my life was simpler, more straightforward, devoid of intrigue and double meanings or quandaries too complex to grasp.

Dunking underwater, my thoughts turned back to John's death. I killed others before, but those men thirsted for my blood and that of my soldiers. John's death was different. As a man who revered his god, did his thoughts and views warrant his death? As I wrestled more on the subject, I rationalized others bore the blame for his death, not me, and while his death was unfortunate, John was just a man. Like every man, his destiny was to die one day, his death occurring earlier and more savagely than most anticipate. While tragic in its execution, the matter didn't seem to warrant any more of my time. My focus had to be upon my mission knowing the sooner it was accomplished, a return to my family could be my reward.

Antipas got out of the water and began to sponge off. Perhaps his mind had also been on John. I don't know. I didn't ask. "Enough of this. Let's see what Cuza brought for us to eat."

After enjoying our meal of bread, cheese, and grapes coupled with some casual conversation, we retraced our steps up the trail to Machaerus. In the letter I wrote to Claudia that night, I told her of my first week in this strange land. I told her about the beauty of the sky and the brown-green hilltops. I told her about the surprising luxuries found in our fort transported here by Antipas. I told her about the Salt Sea, about the white rocks and the quiet shoreline, and about the cool waters plunging down from the waterfall. I told her about how the people of this land dressed in long flowing garments to protect themselves from the heat of the sun. I told her about the wind which seemed to come without warning and how it blew sand in every direction.

Before sealing my letter, I glanced down and stared once again at the blood on my sandals. Concluding that John's death, while brutal in the manner it occurred, was of no significance. I made no mention of it.

Chapter IV

Machaerus
Province of Perea
Evening of July 17, A.D. 33

The soldier's canteen next to the barracks was divided, the larger section for soldiers and a smaller section consisting of one wooden table and two benches tucked away in a dark corner reserved for myself and others I invited to join me. As Valerus and I shared our meal of salty fish and crusty bread, a large jug of wine leftover from Antipas' birthday celebration sat in the middle of the old, scarred table, the recipient of numerous attempts to carve figures and names in to it with knives too dull for the task. After studying the words and numbers gouged in the wood, I determined this table occupied its current space since the days of the Herod the Great. What great stories it could tell.

From our dark, out of the way observation post, we silently watched the young soldiers drink themselves into oblivion while playing games of chance. Their shouts of glee and despair intermixed as they gambled away their meager funds, their noise level proportional to the volume of wine consumed, the revelry growing louder as the evening wore on.

"Look at them," said Valerus. "We were like them once, exhausting all our time and energy trying to look like men. Amazing how much time and money we spent trying to find maturity when it was closer than we thought."

I smiled at my friend and confidant. "I've only been gone for a day and suddenly you've become a philosopher, or has your wine now found its voice?"

"Ah, you know me better than that. I only mean maturity comes on like a slowly ripening fruit. While many things can help it grow – physical and moral challenges, death, love, among them – it takes time coupled with experience to reach the maturity they long for."

Watching Valerus grab another piece of dry bread which crumbled in his hand, I recalled my recent lunch with Antipas, the lamb falling off the bone, the food prepared in expert fashion, wondering if Antipas ever ate the rot gut we had in front of us. I vowed to bring this subject up to the man at the next opportunity. ". . . we can help 'em. We can season their skills and their will but ultimately it will take experience for it all to come together." He stopped to fill his cup from the almost empty jug. "Alright, back to what you were saying . . . You were telling me about Antipas' reaction to your concern about Shallium. What's your plan? Are you going to invest all your efforts on this lad or look for another to lead this mob?"

Throwing the last bit of my fish down my gullet I looked at Valerus. "I've already taken the first step. The lad, as you call him, is to meet me on the hilltop northeast of the fort tomorrow at dawn where I intend to challenge him to become a leader. Either he will want to grow into that role or he'll back away." I chuckled, "Care to wager?"

"Ah, Aquila, I've known you for a long time. If anyone can motivate the man to excel, it's you. Now if I were talking with Roscius, that scoundrel we served with in Egypt, I'd say Shallium should quit right away and I wouldn't blame him, but with your abilities, I'd say the odds are better than even our young man will want to follow in your footsteps."

I nodded at my friend. "Always hedging your bets, ah, well, we'll know soon enough. In the meantime, where will I find you tomorrow?"

"Out the east gate teaching these neophytes the finer points of hand to hand fighting. That should toughen 'em up and give 'em some confidence," assessing the young soldiers near us as he spoke.

I followed his glance wondering who among them was the toughest, the best fighter, the best javelin thrower. "Good. Keep an eye out for any who may have some leadership potential in case my persuasive powers are not equal to your lofty claims." I swallowed the last of my wine, wiping away the last of the savory liquid with my sleeve. "Since dawn will show its face soon and we have two months to wipe this addle pated bunch into shape, I suggest we get some rest."

Valerus looked up as several fists flew among the men in the far corner of the room. We watched as cooler heads quickly separated the two would-be combatants both of whom too drunk to land any debilitating blows. "Two months you say? I'd like three with this rabble but it can be done in two. No distractions to concern ourselves with in this hell hole."

He sat still for a moment, thinking more seriously on the subject. His words came out slurred, "Yes, two months will be enough . . . Have to make Pilate happy." Without another word, the man threw his head back and gulped down the rest of his wine before heading off to his room, stumbling as he walked away, pushing aside the drunks who stepped into his path.

****

As I dressed early the next morning, my thoughts turned to those who had mentored me, men like Tadius and Albius, their memories and lessons giving me comfort and confidence in my chosen approach toward Shallium. Although normally impatient, the lessons from my mentors suggested a slower style today to give this man the benefit of the doubt, their counsel proposing I put little weight on the few short pithy sentences given to me upon my arrival. Remembering their teachings, I walked up the steep hill overlooking Machaerus' front gate.

Watching the first hint of the dawn bouncing off the small swiftly moving clouds above, the cooler air announced a change in the weather. I wondered if the gods were telling me something, but then I rejected that notion; after years of silence to my appeals, why would they choose to speak to me now?

Sitting down on the largest rock on this hilltop, I had a commanding view of the main gate of the fortress, the walls of which now took on a darker tone, almost black, giving rise to why some called this place, 'The Black Fortress'. Captured by the solemnity and the quietness around me, I almost missed seeing Shallium pass through the gates heading in my direction. Nearing the crest of the hill, he spotted me as he marched effortlessly up the last grade, stopping before me to salute. "Good morning, Centurion."

While returning his salute, I assessed the man before me. A large man, Shallium was at least ten years my junior. With his sandy colored hair and tall, well proportioned physique, it was understandable why he would be considered for a leadership position. A friendly smile came easily to him, and he appeared comfortable as we began to talk. As I looked closer, my instincts alerted me to the softness of his hands and the features on his face. Did he have the inner drive, the mental toughness, the passion to lead soldiers?

"Shallium," I said, "we've had little time to speak last week and so I wanted to learn more about you and why you joined the army."

The young man seemed a bit surprised at my subtlety, but after a moment he grinned, his eyes gazing toward the northwest. "My family comes from Nain, a small town in the southern part of Galilee. Ever been there, Centurion?"

When I shook my head no, his eyes brightened. "It's a small town. Most of the townspeople make their living growing olives and figs below the slopes of Mt. Tabor. The sky always seems so blue there, the grass is a lush green, crops grow tall ..."

As his words tumbled out, I could see him embracing his hometown. While I too wished I could focus on home, this was not a luxury afforded me; my duty required my concentration on the task before me. As a professional soldier, our credo was *Duty first, everything else second.*

" . . and straight, quite different from the brown rocks and this hard crusty ground under our feet."

Wishing to turn the conversation, I said, "I understand Antipas trusts your father a great deal."

"My father will be pleased to hear that. He has been the town's leader there for many years."

My eyes now fixed the man. "Tell me why you decided to join the army, to be part of auxiliary unit here? Certainly with your father's authority, you could have remained in Nain, eventually attaining some position of influence."

Shallium looked to the east, the sun almost ready to make its full presence known above the hills. "That's true, Centurion, but I wanted to make my father proud of me and I thought my service as a soldier for Antipas would please him."

"Is that the only reason?"

The man rocked back slightly on his feet hesitating some before answering. "No. In all honesty, I believe if I become an exemplar soldier, this will boost my qualifications to follow in my father's footsteps in cities larger than Nain."

He stopped, a sheepish grin coming across his face. "And I like being in charge, and others seem comfortable with me in that role. After taking my soldier's oath, others found it natural for me to be chosen as the leader of the men with whom I took my oath." Then he paused. "But I must confess I struggle with always being seen as the one in front, the man others look to for guidance and decisions. There are times when I just want to be part of the crowd, times when I don't want to be always looked at as the leader."

Shallium stopped, staring at me. "I need someone to train me. Are you that man, Centurion? Are you the one to show me how to be a leader?"

Ignoring his questions, I asked, "Shallium, your soldier's oath requires you to be brave, obedient, honest, and loyal. But to be a leader, much more is required. Our leaders must be courageous, willing to lead others to their death. Is this a responsibility you desire . . . The courage to lead others into battle?"

His eyes dropped down, studying the small rocks at our feet, saying nothing.

"The leadership I'm talking about doesn't have its roots in wanting to please a father or gaining experience for political appointment. Leading men of this army requires a willingness to die for the Emperor and for Rome." Thrusting out my vitis, I shoved it into his face. "This piece of wood is a symbol of authority, a symbol of what it means to lead men for the glory of Rome. Is this what you want to hold in your hand some day? Are you willing to do all it takes to earn the right to carry this?"

Shallium glanced at some far off object on the northern horizon. After a long silence his words came out slowly and thoughtfully. "A week ago my candid response to you would have been my primary motivation to please my father, and by doing so, curry favor from Herod Antipas. But since you've come here, Centurion, I've watched you as you talk to the soldiers, and perhaps more importantly, as you listen to them. I see the bond you share with Valerus. Although you're his superior, there is an unspeakable trust and respect that unites the two of you in a single purpose. I want to experience that same trust with my men, many of whom I've known since childhood."

Turning to look at me, his words came out ringing with passion, "And so, Centurion, my answer today is I want to be the leader of these men because it is the right thing for me to do. I feel it in my bones, in my very being. I want to be a leader like you. Will you help me? Will you teach me to be a leader?" As he completed his thought, he straightened his back, his eyes boring into mine.

Now it was my turn to look away wondering if this man was he playing me for a fool. Did he understand the sacrifices required, the time and effort necessary to reach such a goal? Was he ready to turn away from his youthful friendships, ready to lay down his life for others?

I examined the man once more. "I can teach you everything I know about being a leader, Shallium, but in the final analysis, the true judges of your success will be your soldiers because it is their respect you must earn. Can you live with their judgment knowing failure may mean a lifetime of disgrace and disappointment? Is that a risk you are willing to take?"

Holding my gaze on the man, I continued, intending every word to be as sharp as my dagger. "I'll leave you now. Consider everything we've said here today. Look into your heart. Pray to your gods for their divine assistance. Pretty sounding words and good intentions mean nothing. Either it is in your heart to become a leader or it is not. If you totally commit yourself to that end, I will help you succeed. If, however, you're not fully committed to this calling, don't waste my time or yours."

Thinking about Valerus and those soldiers with him, I faced Shallium again. "Whatever decision you make, it will follow you the rest of your life. Make sure it is the right one for you, not the right one for your father, or for your friends, or anyone else. Just for you. Give me your decision here tomorrow morning. Then we will either begin or end your training."

****

I found my stalwart second-in-command covered with sweat and dirt, his arms and legs flying about as he demonstrated another technique to the group of fifteen soldiers under the shadow of the fort's eastern gate. Judging by the heavy panting of the younger men, it was no surprise that none of fledglings had been able to get the better of this experienced warrior in the finer points of unarmed hand to hand combat. While no extremities appeared permanently damaged, many of the soldiers bore deep bruises from well placed blows inflicted by my friend upon their young frames. Despite the welts and swelling of various body parts, spirits were high.

When he saw me approach, Valerus called the group to attention. With a smile on his face, he announced, "Centurion, these young soldiers keep trying to get the better of this old man, but they're learning to appreciate how experience coupled with proper technique will always win out over misplaced exuberance." Smiling at the soldiers, he won their hearts and their allegiance as he gave them unfeigned praise. "But from what I have seen, these men are far better then you and I were at their age. I am proud of them. They have the fighting spirit we seek." No wonder other soldiers followed this man willingly into mortal combat. What a motivator!

I winked at him, laughter in my voice. "Given that, it's best I take you away from here before these men spring a few surprises on you. From the bruises I see on your body, you may have unknowingly revealed some of your most closely guarded secrets."

This grizzled veteran guffawed. "Perhaps you're right. I don't want to give them the benefit of all my knowledge in just one day." With that, he turned back to the soldiers. "Good job today, men. Hoist a jug of Antipas' finest on me tonight. Meet me here early tomorrow morning with your new best friend, the *gladius*, the short sword. Rest well."

After receiving the salutes of the soldiers, we walked back toward the main gate, but once out of their sight, Valerus began to limp badly on his right leg, the same one he injured several years ago during a violent struggle with a massive big-boned heathen on the frontier of Gaul. As he took one gingerly step after another, he grimaced, "I'm glad you came when you did . . . I'm not sure how much longer I could have lasted. Did you notice the big one with the red hair? Name is Reuel. Keep our eye on him. He has potential. Strong. Almost broke one of my best holds."

I nodded my understanding as I saw some blood come from the area of his old wound. "Make sure you treat your leg properly, old friend. These men need you and so do I."

He soiled the ground at our feet with some fresh spit as he attempted to walk in a more upright manner, but after a few slow tentative steps, his efforts to hide his discomfort failed, the limp returning just as before. To help him, I slowed my pace down as we neared the barracks telling him of my conversation with Shallium. While we still made no wager, Valerus hinted he felt the man might not be mentally tough enough to lead the soldiers he trained this day. For arguments sake, I took the contrarian view praying to the gods I was right, but as always, they saw fit to ignore my request.

****

The next morning, a pinkish-pale blue tint in the dark eastern skies gave evidence of another brilliant day in store for Perea as I made my way up the hill to meet Shallium. To my surprise when I reached the peak, the man stood in attention, his uniform immaculate, its polished metal reflecting the first of the sun's rays, his footwear clean. Since we knew the purpose of this meeting, neither of us wasted time on insignificant chatter. After inspecting his uniform once again, I cut to the heart of matter. "Shallium, what have you decided? To be a leader, or let another take your place?"

His eyes locked on to me with an intense look not present the previous day. "Centurion, you gave me much to think about last night: about my father and the impact my decision would have on him and about the friends I have known for years. I focused on my life and how, as an old man, I wanted to look back and see how I used the gifts god gave me." He stared down at Machaerus. "I believe I was sent to this place to become a leader of the soldiers here. Today I rededicate myself to that end. I am ready for my training to begin."

I slowly nodded evaluating his words. "Very well. Move your belongings into the spare room next to mine. It will be crowded but this will allow us to train at every opportunity. This will also separate you from those you've known for so long. Second, you will no longer eat with or socialize with them. Valerus is responsible for their training while I will devote my energies to your training. Later, you'll be placed in charge of the soldiers once again. Any questions?"

"No, Centurion."

"Good. Meet me outside the southeastern corner of the fort."

****

The next two months passed in a flash as Shallium proved to be a man of his word, doing everything asked of him, working from dawn until late into the evenings, taking little time to rest, pouring his whole being into becoming a leader of men. During these fast-paced days, the young man became an expert in all our weapons while driving himself to be the most physically fit man at Machearus, no small feat since both Valerus and I were accomplished in all areas of fitness: running, swimming, jumping, marching long distances, all while carrying heavy loads.

Shallium invested his evening hours in reading and studying information I provided him concerning the details of military tactics, as well as the history of our army and its leaders, from Publius Cornelius Scipio Africanus, the man who defeated Hannibal's armies, to Caius Julius Caesar. He learned quickly, his progress challenging me to find more innovative ways to transfer all my skills to him. As I reflected upon this experience later, my involvement with this man brought me great joy as it gave me an opportunity to pass on my legacy to another.

Meanwhile, Valerus focused on the soldiers, sharpening their skills in the use of the javelin, the sword, and the dagger. He led the way in improving their physical fitness, their use of engineering equipment, and the fundamentals of preparing defensive positions when they halted for the night, drilling into them the understanding that good fortifications were the price one paid for a peaceful night's rest. When we compared our thoughts each evening, we shared with growing pride the accomplishments of these men.

While Antipas expressed satisfaction in my periodic reports to him on Shallium's progress, I knew he was most relieved because this growth insured his relationship with Uthai would not be scarred. Because I was responsible for the young man's training, I knew if Shallium did not meet expectations, the tetrarch would be quick to lay blame on my shoulders, sharing none of this responsibility.

****

As the two month goal of training Antipas' soldiers approached, Valerus and I employed members of Antipas' work force to construct a series of obstacles and targets in the rugged rocky ground south of the fort to display the capabilities of Shallium and his men. When the day arrived to demonstrate the soldiers' prowess to Antipas, he asked me of my expectations.

"If Shallium and his men execute as I expect, you'll be able to provide a sterling report to Pilate and to his father." Antipas gave me a hard stare, before turning his attention to watch this young man lead his men up the hill, rendering his salute to his tetrarch. Once Antipas returned the salute, the unit began its first challenge, one which required them to maneuver in a checkerboard formation called a *quinux* up a treacherous rocky hill, testing their ability to maintain good order in the rapid march expected of them.

Although several soldiers suffered some minor injuries as they scurried up the steep incline, the unit pressed on through the obstacles satisfactorily, exhibiting their proficiency with their individual weapons as they crossed several more embankments and charging up another steep incline. Antipas gave me a quick smile as he watched his men, nodding his approval. "Well done, Centurion. You and Valerus have performed a miracle."

"It is Shallium and his men who have done the work. Before we praise them too much, let's see this last maneuver. It is the most difficult."

"And what would that be?"

"Rather than me explaining it, assume you are an enemy in a protected fortification being attacked by your men. Tell me how you would defeat them as they approach you in the formation now moving in our direction." Without another word between us, Shallium's men came over a rise toward us in the tortoise formation or *testudo*, the soldiers' long shields overlapping one another's to protect each other from projectiles coming from overhead, front and the sides as they advanced in a half crouching, half walking manner toward us. Very little of the men's bodies showed as the overlapping shields of the advancing soldiers enclosed the entire formation. While the movement was slow, it was steady. Finally, Shallium brought his men to a halt an arm's length from Antipas before he moved to the front of the formation and reported to the tetrarch with a crisp salute.

"Well done, Shallium. Well done," Antipas clapped his hands shouting loudly for all to hear, a big smile on his face. "You men make me proud! Even though I knew you would not run me through with your javelins, I could sense the power of your steps. Well done. . . Well done indeed!"

"Thank you, sir. Your soldiers worked hard for this moment."

Antipas smiled back, "You can be assured your friends and relatives throughout the land will hear of your deeds."

Turning to Valerus and me, Antipas nodded his pleasure once again. Waving his hand to Cuza, the servant appeared instantly at Antipas side, and upon hearing words whispered in his ears, he walked in haste toward the fort as Antipas faced his soldiers again. "Tonight there will be a banquet in the soldiers' canteen in your honor. All the best foods from my stores will be available. It is my way of showing my appreciation to you all."

It was a proud day for me, and then with little warning, it became one of saddest.

****

The grand celebration filled the night air as all soldiers not on guard duty gathered in the canteen, laughter and raucous gaiety coming from everyone's lips, wine flowing down the throats of these deserving soldiers splashing on the floors and on the tables, but no one cared. Antipas, true to his word, provided the best foods available, all deliciously prepared by his personal cook, choice cuts of lamb, beef, goat, and fish set on the tables in great abundance, the men showing their gratitude by quickly devouring every morsel leaving few scrapes. These men knew they accomplished a great feat and were ready to stand side by side with the Legions of Rome.

When Valerus arrived the second hour of the celebration was in full swing. As he made his way slowly through the crowd, the soldiers greeted him as they passed on their admiration and thanks for his leadership and teaching. It was an exhilarating moment for me as I watched my friend receive the accolades and praise he so richly deserved. When he saw me, he came directly toward my table. As he got closer, I noticed him moving with a considerable limp on his right leg, his face ashen, pain showing on his face with each step. He sat down on the bench with a thump.

"What have you done?"

"Remember some weeks ago when I aggravated my old injury?"

"Yes. You hid the bleeding quite well and I told you to take care of it. You said you would, but from what I see, the injury now needs some serious tending."

Through clenched teeth, Valerus grunted, "I thought I had it under control, until several days ago I reinjured the leg in same area as before. Instead of it healing, it continued to get worse, and from the looks of it, I may have done significant damage, certainly more than I first thought." I watched him as he slowly un-wrapped the crimson stained cloth which he had tied around his leg, a foul miasma filling the air even before he completely removed the bandage. In the dim candle light of my dark corner, I saw the yellowish, green pus squirting from the injury. I examined his bandage, a mixture of blood and squalid pus covered it, deep dark redness surrounded the wound, dead tissue around the center. A low moan, much like that of a wounded animal, came from Valerus' lips. No doubt my stalwart companion of many years needed prompt medical attention.

"Why didn't you tell me?" I stammered, trying to keep the ire out of my voice, knowing his answer even before he gave it.

With his voice quavering, his gruff response did not surprise me. "Aquila, we've known each other for a long time. These men needed us; both of us."

Looking at the soldiers before us as they told their raunchy jokes and slapped each other's backs, Valerus smiled through clenched teeth. "Look at them! They needed us to show them how to be soldiers, how to be men, how to battle through obstacles, how to overcome discomfort and hardship. This wound's a small price to pay to see them celebrating their triumph." With pride in his voice he continued. "And because they needed us, I would allow nothing, nothing to get in my way. Nothing could make me quit. But now it's time to fix this leg." He looked around the room once again casting his eyes upon the soldiers whom he loved. Then he grabbed my large cup of wine. Hoisting it to his lips, he took a huge gulp of Antipas' finest before passing out.

****

Quickly summoning a few of the nearby soldiers not so drunk they couldn't follow simple orders, we laid Valerus on the table and carried him from the canteen to his room at the far end of the barracks. As we made our way through the drunken throng, the foul smelling air became heavy and still, fear and concern replacing the laughter and joy which filled the rooms only moments before. I ordered one of the soldiers to find Antipas' physician and to have him report to me without delay.

In Valerus' room, we made him as comfortable as we knew how, elevating his leg and putting cold compresses on his face. When the physician arrived in a few moments, he directed me and the soldiers to move away from my friend so he could conduct his examination. At my urging, the soldiers returned to the celebration but their mood had sobered considerably. I stood near as Lael, the physician, began to assess the injury, each touch of his delicate, probing fingers bringing a grimace to the warrior's face as he tensed up, anticipating the pushing and probing of the tender skin and of the muscles and bones so close to the skin's surface. I only had to look at Valerus' eyes to know this strong courageous man was dealing with a pain unlike any he had ever experienced. After the physician gently touched the infected area, a new stream of the pus erupted from deep inside the injury. Lael looked up, motioning me to follow him.

Once outside the barracks it took several deep breaths of the cool, clean night air for me to realize the horrible smell which filled Valerus' room came from inside my friend's body. Lael looked at me. "Centurion, I know this man is your friend, and you've been together for many years, so I will leave this decision up to you. Do you wish me to tell him, or do you want to?"

My face broke into a cold sweat, tears clouding my eyes. Not Valerus! He is too strong! Men like him don't die from a leg injury. I tried to remain calm, but the words came in a rush. "Are you saying he is going to die from his leg wound? Are you saying I'm to prepare my friend for death?"

"I certainly hope not. But for him to have any chance of survival, I must amputate his leg above the knee. The infection he suffers from is called gangrene. Removing part of his leg is the only chance of stopping the disease from spreading to the rest of his body. The infection may have already gone too far, but I can't be sure. So I ask you again, do you want to tell him or should I? Either way, his leg must come off tonight. We can't wait. Any delay only increases the chances the infection will spread." Lael looked at me. I had seen him only a few times before but now it was time to trust him. Amputate! The word never sounded so cruel.

I looked at the distant stars shinning in the black sky, a shooting star, brilliant with its swift tail, flashed across the sky. Then another made its way behind the first, and like its predecessor, it faded away into the darkness. Barely recognizing my own voice, I said, "I'll tell him. He should hear this from me. Give me a few moments before you come back to . . . to do your duty."

The physician gave me a sincere look. "It will take me a little time to gather the necessary instruments and my assistants." He fixed his eyes upon mine. "Thank you, Centurion. You're a good man. You know, of course, if there was any other way . . ." He walked away into the night leaving me alone to search the heavens for answers from my gods but nothing came from them. Only silence. What would I say to Valerus?

After delaying as long as I dared, I slowly walked back into Valerus' small room. He looked up, his eyes filled with agony and distress. "I guess I've overdone it this time, Aquila. I have been knifed and speared, fallen down cliffs and rocky ledges, but each time I recovered without any permanent injuries. This is different. The throbbing seems to be coming from inside my leg. Does our doctor friend have any magic potion, something to deaden the pain?"

Even as the sweat dripped from his forehead, he tried to smile. "And to think, we're missing a great celebration." Without warning, another wave of torment came from deep inside his body causing him to moan once again. He moved around on his bed seeking a more comfortable position as he closed his eyes, the sweat now pouring from his face and into his beard. He had to be told; the sooner, the better.

Putting my hand on his shoulder, I said, "As I suspect you know, my friend, your injury is severe and it must be dealt without delay. The physician believes your life is in danger. From what I can see, I think he's right. The infection in your leg is called gangrene, and it appears to be growing rapidly. If left unchecked, it could spread into the rest of your body and kill you." Valerus' eyes now wide open, his gaze fixed on the ceiling above.

"The only way to save your life is to amputate your leg above the knee." I spoke softly, but there was no way to diminish the impact of the words.

Neither of us spoke for what seemed a long time. This hero of Rome groped for words as he stared upward. "My whole life has been given to Rome. I have fought for her. I have killed for her. I never married because of my sense of duty to her. And now I must give her one more thing: my leg."

His eyes moved from the ceiling to me. "When you and Lael went outside, I guess I knew it would come to this. I suppose I'll go by ship back to Rome. The army will give me some land due me, and I'll draw out the money I've saved in our legion's savings bank unless some scoundrel has stolen it. Then I'll settle down to find myself a good wife." He stopped for a moment still gathering his thoughts, a quick smile came. "Aquila, maybe I'll find a woman as good as yours but we'll just have to see about that, won't we?"

I laughed. "When the women of Rome find out what a hero they have in their midst, they'll be beating down your door for a chance to be chosen by you."

The man tried to laugh, but coughed instead. "Well, let's hope you're right." Looking at me, he pressed his lips together to gain strength for the trial ahead. "You know, Aquila, I believe I've given Rome something else of great value. In the past few months, I've given her a new set of trained soldiers who meet my standards. These men will fight like me. They have the heart of lions. My legacy is safe with them and I'm pleased about that." The effort to get these words out was almost too much for him as he lay back closing his eyes.

Behind me I heard the physician come into the room leading three other men. Without turning I hollered, "A few more minutes!" When I heard them back away from the door, I looked back at my friend. "I will make sure you are cared for my friend. The gods will travel with you."

Valerus opened his eyes once more, a fear showing in them not present before, tears gushing forth. "Aquila, I know you'll do your best, but I'm scared. Scared because I wish I had more trust in our gods." Shaking his head from side to side, he exclaimed, "I wish I knew the God of John the Baptizer. I envy that man. He seemed to know his God so well . . . trusting in him in a way I've never seen in anyone before. He had no fear in his heart. I wish I had that same confidence." Then he suddenly gripped my arm with the strength I didn't anticipate, shouting out, "Aquila, how can I know John's God? How can I know his God?"

Now it was my turn to be frightened. How I could answer Valerus? He saw something in John which I too had seen, but didn't have the courage to express. Did my fear come from lack of confidence in my gods; that they weren't as powerful as we wanted them to be? All I could do was to shake my head, my words coming with little conviction. "The gods will take care of you, Valerus. They will watch over you." I pulled my arms slowly away from his bed, signaling Lael to come do his work.

Stepping back outside, the fresh night air cleansed my lungs again as I searched the stars for answers. While my pleas to my gods had been infrequent at best, I now cast fervent prayers skyward toward Aesculapius, the god of medicine and then to Mars, our god of war, the god who protects soldiers. When no response came from either of them, I petitioned our greatest god, Hercules to intervene, but nothing came from him either. Surely if these gods of mine were trustworthy and all knowing, surely they would intervene on behalf of one of Rome's great warriors. They must! They had to! And later they would care for me as well. They would, wouldn't they?

My thoughts came to an abrupt end, my friend's cries of pain breaking my train of thought. Was Valerus' pain just in his leg or was it in his heart as well? Where was John's god now when my friend needed him? Would this god respond to Valerus' cry?

Chapter V

Machaerus
Province of Perea
September 23, A.D. 33

When Cuza ushered Lael and me into Antipas' chambers early the next morning, the ruler sat in his lofty wooden chair, his mood sullen, his eyes bloodshot, staring at us as we stood before, growling, "What is it? And before you say anything, I know about Valerus' leg."

Lael dropped his eyes before speaking first. "Sir, I had no choice. Left untreated, the gangrene could have cost the man his life. He needs to be transported to Caesarea with all speed. I can make him comfortable and stabilize him for a short time, but he requires more treatment then I have can provide. Once he reaches Caesarea, he should be placed on the next ship bound for Rome."

Antipas gave his physician a stern look before stifling a deep yawn with his fist. "After what I saw yesterday, I owe this man a great deal and I want him properly cared for." Turning to me, he asked, "Centurion, your thoughts?"

While part of me yearned to shout '*I'll accompany him to Rome*,' knowing I would see my family again with an opportunity to finagle an assignment there, ridding myself of having to coddle this untrustworthy, deceitful ruler, I knew in my heart that wouldn't be right. My duty was to complete my mission. To do anything else would dishonor me and my rank. "I recommend Shallium lead the detail to take Valerus to the coast while I continue to train your men."

His eyes lit up in surprise as he gave me an amused look. "I agree. We'll do as you suggest. Upon reaching Caesarea, Shallium will see to it Valerus is given passage on a ship bound for Rome."

The man then looked down at me, rubbing his stubby beard for a time. "Since Shallium will be in the city of Pilate's headquarters, let's use this opportunity to inform the governor about the training status of my soldiers. I want you to prepare a dispatch for him to go along with mine." He then pointed at Lael. "Prepare Valerus for this departure seven days from now. In the meantime care for this man like he was my own son. I hold you responsible for his well being. Do I make myself clear, physician?"

A frightened look came suddenly on the face of the man next to me whose only response was an energetic bob of his head. Without any other comments, Lael and I left Antipas, the doctor clearly shaken as we emerged into the light of the day. "Centurion, do you think he meant what he said, about holding me responsible?"

"You've been with the man for years, what do you think?"

Pale, Lael blurted, "He seldom makes idle threats." After a few more steps, he turned to me, "Excuse me, Centurion. I have a patient to check on."

****

Knowing Valerus' final destination was Rome, I spent my next few evenings composing a letter to Claudia, focusing on a variety of family matters. Even though it would be many months before a response would come from her, I felt closer to my beloved as expressions of affection flowed from my heart.

With this first letter now complete, my assessment of Antipas' soldiers took longer as I detailed the improvements made by the soldiers, paying particular attention to the accomplishments of Valerus. In my missive I recommended that similar comments accompany our valiant soldier on his journey to our homeland.

Writing these letters gave me an excuse to spend little of my time with my trustworthy friend. No matter we said at his departure, chances of seeing him again were slim. While I parted company with many other revered soldiers at various postings, saying farewell to Valerus would be different. Our bond transcended rank, my trust in him unmatched in any other soldier. I would miss him greatly.

****

A few wispy thin clouds in the west were the only spots in the sky to spoil the crystal clear blue dawn as Shallium's detail stood ready to depart, the men talking among themselves, the horses snorting as they pawed the ground impatiently. Antipas watched the proceedings off to one side. When four soldiers carried Valerus out from the barracks on a stretcher, some apprehension arose from all those assembled as the men tied the stretcher securely to a travois, an 'A'- shaped wooden frame whose rear legs trailed in the dirt, behind one of the horses. After securing Valerus' head and shoulders high on the triangle to the horse, the men then tied his feet and legs to the wooden legs with more cloth wraps. Despite the abundance of soft clothes around and under his body, we all knew his journey would be uncomfortable at best, excruciatingly painful at worst. With Antipas' not so veiled threat still in the forefront of his thoughts, Lael assigned his most trusted assistant to care for Valerus throughout the journey in hopes of averting any catastrophe.

With the preparations complete, I looked down at my friend, my well rehearsed words sticking in my mouth. Finally a few thoughts tumbled out as I hardened my face knowing the unavoidable good-bye was now upon us. "Valerus, you've always been there when I needed you. I owe you a great debt." I gestured to the soldiers around us. "You set a high standard for these men and I'm sure they will live up to it." Nothing else needed to be said. I handed him the letter addressed to my wife which he carefully tucked into the folds of his garments.

Now it was Valerus' turn, struggling mightily to sit up on his elbows, the exertion causing beads of sweat to pop out on his face. "Aquila, it has been my honor to serve with you through the years." His eyes then moved from one soldier to another, before returning to me. "It is I who owe you . . . You brought me to this place and I leave content knowing part of me lives in these men." He smiled up at them once more, expending every ounce of energy in him as he saluted them before falling back on his cushions.

We then gripped each other's arm one last time before I
tore my eyes away, nodding in Shallium's direction. With our
dispatches now secure in a pouch fixed to the saddle of his big
brown stead, he saluted both Antipas and me. The young leader
looked at Valerus and me again, sensing our pride, our loyalty, and
our love of one soldier for another, a love understood as only those
in the brotherhood of arms could fathom, a love birthed from the
willingness to give one's life for another, a love uncommon in any
other profession.

After a final check of his men, Shallium led the way out
the gate, small clouds of dust rising behind him from the dry,
windswept soil. Quickly making my way up to the highest tower
at the fort, I watched the procession until the winds erased any
evidence of their existence.

****

I spent every waking hour of the days following Valerus'
departure with small groups of soldiers, knowing the more I
immersed myself in their training, the less time I would have
to think about my friend. To my delight, several of the younger
soldiers who immersed themselves in Valerus' teachings began to
emerge as potential leaders. These men brought me great joy in
knowing their growth came directly from the foundation laid by
my friend whose steady hand, instructive tongue, and his desire for
others to succeed, motivated and encouraged this creation of new
exemplary soldiers who, without his nurturing, would have died in
the womb of lethargy and slothfulness.

****

Shallium's return a few weeks later brought satisfactory reports
on several fronts. Antipas reveled in the knowledge Pilate studied
our reports in detail while Shallium pleased me with his report
about how the governor took a personal interest in arranging for
Valerus' departure for Rome on the first grain ship available. As
we shared a meal of goat, fruit, and strong drink at my corner of
the canteen the night of his return, Shallium's eyes lit up as he

retold his story for the third time, slurring his words, "I wish you could've seen how the crew of the *Octavius* treated Valerus. It was as though he was a conquering Tribune, the ship's captain giving me his word he would see to our man's every need."

"What caused this captain to be so accommodating?" I asked refilling our cups for the fourth time.

"Ah, a good question, perhaps because of Pilate's interest or perhaps because I gave this seaman sufficient funds to insure Valerus had all the wine he could handle." He smiled, "That may have had something to do with his level of cooperation as well," adding coyly, "I know it didn't hurt."

After downing his cup in one gulp, he sputtered, "Oh and before I forget, Valerus wanted me to tell you your letter to your wife will be delivered as soon as possible. From what the captain indicating it could be a month or two depending on the weather before they reach Rome."

"A long trip for sure. I appreciate all you did. You and Pilate both went out of your way to help Valerus and I'm grateful."

Despite the enormous amount of wine that had passed through the man's gullet, he suddenly gave me a serious glance. "After all you and Valerus did for me, it was the least I could do for you. After all, where would I be without your interest in me?" Then a befuddled expression came across his face. "There is one more thing, something Valerus asked me to tell you."

"And what was that?'

"Seemed strange to me but he said you'd understand. He said to tell you to keep searching for John's god. I'm not sure why he was so insistent I tell you that, but that's what he said."

I sat still for a moment, thanking Shallium once more for caring for my friend before managing to stumble out of the canteen into the cool night air. Above me the night sky greeted me once again reminding me of the night Valerus lost his leg, the stars sparkling in all quadrants, a half moon slowly marching across the darkness spreading enough light I could not escape seeing the stains on my sandals. John's god! What was Valerus' message to me in those simple words – keep searching for John's god?

****

A few days later word came for me to report to Antipas early the next morning. Entering his private chambers at the appointed hour, the ostentations of his rooms no longer surprised me although I wondered if Antipas ever considered the Spartan conditions existing in the bulk of the fort. Before I could devote any time to that subject, the man greeted me warmly, thrusting a cup of wine into my hand. Was there every a time when this sot did not have a cup of the grapes' nectar in his hand?

The tetrarch said little as we sat on the soft cushions in his seating area both of us chewing on the delicious grapes and pomegranates from a tray a servant set before us, Antipas washing them down with a large gulp of his wine as he examined me, a satisfied smile on his face. "Aquila, I've studied the letter Pilate sent me in response to those we sent him. It seems our leader is quite pleased with the progress of my auxiliary unit. Your words must have given him comfort when he penned his words."

He stopped to taste his wine once again, smacking his lips together as he swallowed the succulent juice, settling back further into his cushioned seat. "It seems my trust in you is well founded. You're indeed an honest man, a pleasure to have here, an asset to someone in my, shall we say, delicate situation."

I set my cup down knowing it was too early in the day to seek pleasure from its contents. "As I said, I intend to provide you and Pilate the truth as I see it."

"Yes, yes I know that but still, it's valuable for me to know you're a man of your word."

"Tetrarch, my letter to Pilate told him about the improvement of your soldiers emphasizing the roles Valerus and Shallim played in the soldiers' accomplishments. I'm sure you agree with those sentiments."

"Well yes, of course. Both of those men deserve special recognition." He then gave me a half-hearted grin, his words dripping with sarcasm. "I feel much safer knowing those who guard my walls are now well trained."

No sooner had his comments filled the air when anger consumed me. This man knew nothing of a soldier's sacrifice, the blood, the sweat, the blistered hands and feet, the countless hours of repetition required to perfect the skill and cunning necessary to face down an enemy. Now he mocked those who allowed him to sleep comfortably in his palatial surroundings while they stood guard on the cold, windy nights throughout palace. I could not leave this man with such vile scruples soon enough.

"Antipas, be thankful you have such men around you . . . men ready to sacrifice their lives for you."

"Yes, of course. I meant no disrespect to my men . . . "

"Does Pilate have additional orders for me; a new assignment perhaps?"

Antipas chuckled softly. "Ah, Aquila, why is it I sense you wish to leave me? Have you forgotten? Your mission is only partially complete. While you've trained these men here to an acceptable level, we have Galilee to consider; more men there than here in Perea, that territory more expansive, more diverse. No, my friend, I can't have you leave yet. There is more to do."

Chomping on a few more of the almonds and pistachios from the tray, he sat back for a moment. "Sallu, the leader of my soldiers there, seems competent enough, but I'm not about to return you to Pilate until you assess his leadership." Spitting a few shells out of his mouth, he now grabbed a few grapes, swallowing them before grinning at me. "I value your counsel, Aquila; your calm, quiet manner. As I said, after you assure me Sallu and his men are equal of the men here, we'll discuss your return to Pilate, although the final decision is his of course."

I tried to mask my disappointment, but what he said made sense. I needed to see my mission through to the end regardless of my feelings toward this man. Grabbing my cup, I swallowed its contents in one gulp reaffirming the logic of his statement in my mind. "Antipas, you're right . . . I've given little thought to Galilee. Based on Shallium's progress, I suggest he be given full control of these soldiers so I can travel to Tiberias to begin this assessment."

Antipas gave me a quick smile. "Precisely what Pilate and I were thinking. Leaving Shallium here alone will require monitoring, but yes, we're in agreement." Antipas put his cup down, gesturing with both his hands. "Now regarding Galilee, Pilate informed me he appointed another to assist you there, a fellow named Maurus, who Pilate is sending directly to Tiberias. You are to meet him there in a few weeks."

Maurus. We had served together years ago in Gaul. While most in his position exercised strict discipline, the man tended to exceed the norm. He was certainly no Valerus, but who was? "Sir, I'm sure we'll work well together. We served together some years ago. Does this two to three week timeframe fit into your plans?"

The tetrarch slumped deeper in his seat, the cushions swallowing him in luxury. "Yes, very well. I'm ready to return to Tiberias, a place much more fitting to a man of my tastes." Hugging one of his cushions he went on, his eyes sparkling, "You haven't been to Tiberias yet, but as opposed to this dung hole, it's exciting diverse population, tradesmen of every description, its colorful surroundings along the Sea of Galilee will captivate you. Seeing it now makes it worth every gold coin I spent."

Getting to his feet, he walked slowly over to the nearest window, smiling at some unknown pleasure before turning back to me. "Yes, I would like for you to leave for Tiberias in a few days to begin your evaluation of my men there." He paused for a moment. "And perhaps you can avail yourself of some time to enjoy everything the city has to offer." With a playful smile, he went on. "The city can provide whatever companionship you desire."

I put my cup down. To his depraved mind, his thought that I required or desired physical companionship was wrong. To me, the desire and satisfaction he alluded to could only be met with my wife by my side. No other woman could fill that void. It was her arms I longed for and no one else would satisfy me. Ignoring his inferences was my best course of action. "Antipas, since I'll be leaving soon, if you've nothing else for me, I have much to do."

With the wave of the hand and a shaking of the head, Antipas dismissed me. We were two different men, driven by different desires, different goals, and different values. I thanked the gods for the differences.

****

The dawn for our departure was unusually cool, the result of heavy rains during the night which tamped down the dust, a brisk wind from the west pushing a series of small clouds rapidly to the east. Shallium stood at the front gate of the fort, watching the final preparations before handing me a letter. "This is for my father if you pass by Nain." Then he reached out to grasp my arm tightly. "Your counsel will guide me in the days ahead."

Nodding, I muttered the best guidance I could muster, "Make me proud, Shallium. Make me proud." Mounting a gray stag, I glanced around to take a final look at the fort, my eyes gazing at the now familiar dark walls of this edifice before settling on that part of the wall where men huddled early one morning to ask for John's body. When would the memories of that man end? That night still haunted Valerus. When would that memory stop for me?

Behind me was a force of twelve soldiers and three servants, the soldiers all selected because of their leadership potential, each armed with a heavy javelin or *pilum*, a short sword, and sharp knife. While recent reports told of aggressive bands of thieves roaming through the desolate country-side between Machaerus and the Jordan River, logic suggested these marauding bandits would not choose to tangle with our detachment. Because these groups had well-earned reputations for ruthlessness and brutality, particularly if prisoners fell into their grasp, I briefed my detachment on the consequences if confronted by such men, the soldiers understanding the need for absolute unwavering vigilance in the days ahead.

Cuza selected the three servants to care for my horse and the donkeys upon which we loaded pickaxes, shovels, and other equipment for constructing our night entrenchments along with our cooking necessities of kettles, foodstuffs, and water. One of these three was Kish, Cuza's son, a powerfully built young man, short in stature like his father, a smile never far from his face. With beaming pride, Cuza told me, "Centurion, my son will take my place one day. He has been to Tiberias many times. These three will care for you and your men as necessary and upon reaching the city, Kish will be in charge of making preparations for Antipas' arrival."

As to the soldiers, I appointed Reuel, the soldier singled out by Valerus several months ago, to be my second in command. Showing considerable promise over the last few weeks, I wanted to test his reaction to this greater responsibility.

My plan called for us to travel on a little used trail through bare, wild hills and valleys of northern Perea until we neared the southwestern slope of Mt. Nebo, the highest mountain in this region. A westerly turn would then take us downhill to intersect with the crossing sites over the Jordan River, where after fording the river we would parallel it north to Scythopolis before heading northwest to Nain. Our travel would conclude the following day as we intersected the main road which led straight to Tiberias, a trek estimated to take five to six days. We drew supplies for four days, anticipating we would be able to obtain food from the merchants near the crossing sites along the Jordan or at the Roman garrison at Scythopolis.

While the hills were more rigorous in the first several hours than I anticipated, we made good time despite severe changes in elevation. Moving along at a brisk pace for the better part of the morning hours, I called a halt well below the crest of a large hill, signaling Reuel to join me. "One of the procedures you learned from Valerus was that during the heat of the day, halt your unit, establish security and rest for several hours before marching for a few more hours before establishing your camp for the evening."

"Yes, Centurion, we practiced this several times."

"Good. Instead of me seeing to the details, I want you take charge of this rest halt. Organize your men so they know to occupy these same positions on our perimeter for the rest of our journey. Brief me on your actions in an hour. Do you have any questions?"

"No, Centurion." Almost without hesitation, he propounded, "Avram and Maor will assist me."

These two appeared to be good choices. Both men were smart and quick learners. Avram was the soldier who had received my personal attention overlooking the "Baths of Herod" while Maor was a short stocky fellow built like a rock. I asked, "These two appear to be credible choices, but did you choose them for their military expertise or because of friendship?"

Reuel's eyes narrowed, considering my question. Without any dilatory thought, his answer came back clear and direct. "Centurion, I chose them, not because they are friends of mine, but because they're good soldiers and the others respect them."

With that settled, I watched from a distance as Reuel gathered the others around him. Rather than fall for a simple trap I had laid, he moved the detachment to the crest of the hill above, some distance from where I had stopped only part way up the slope.

It was then I knew then Valerus was correct; with additional seasoning and experience, Reuel had a good eye for the terrain as he correctly deduced the best location for our halt was on the high ground with good observation in all directions rather than on the slope where I stopped which offered no opportunity to view the landscape around us. After confirming the high ground was the better location, the young soldier selected locations for the men by twos around the perimeter, assigning them this same relative placement for the rest of our journey thereby reducing the time required to establish any hasty position.

The soldiers than began preparing their fighting positions, dirt and rocks mounded in front of each man to provide protection from enemy arrows and spears as well as affording us protection as we hurled our javelins toward the enemy. With this activity was underway, Reuel sought me out, escorting me around to the locations he selected. With only a few minor corrections necessary, I encouraged him. "You've done well. When we make camp this evening, follow me around as we establish our night security. Then for both halts tomorrow, you will be in charge once again. Rest now. We move in an hour."

****

Our move north along the dusty trail continued, reaching another tall hill two hours before dusk. With our soldiers now knowing their places in the perimeter, they wasted little time in preparing their defensive positions. As Reuel and I walked about, we noted the stubborn crusty ground did not yield quickly to the men's efforts. "Centurion, I don't think we'll finish before nightfall," one of the soldiers exclaimed as we inspected his position.

"You're right, but if you knew bandits would attack tonight, what orders would you issue?"

The man wiped the sweat from his brow before swinging his pickaxe again with greater energy, taking another small bite out of the ground. "Keep digging."

I nodded my agreement, blessed to be in the company of men willing to do the right thing without complaint, men who could be depended upon in this tough, unforgiving environment.

As the digging and moving of rocks continued, I gave Avram responsibility for posting guards on each point of the compass. With twelve soldiers available, four men would always be on guard, the rest rotating through this duty throughout the night. To increase our ability to respond to any threat, everyone slept fully clothed, weapons at our side.

Once I was satisfied with our preparations, the soldiers not on guard began to eat their evening meal of porridge of wheat cereal eaten supplemented with lard and vegetables heated with small fires built low to the ground, washing down their meal with vinegar or diluted water. Soon darkness wrapped its arms around us, the constellations in the heavens above keeping their vigil watch over us. It was a pleasant evening, a cool refreshing breeze blew across the hills, our animals quiet as they settled down under the care of the servants, the crackling of our small fires soothing us, the whispers of the soldiers about us. The glory of the moon cast its light down upon us as it slowly rose over the hills to our east. Looking at all this beauty around us, I mumbled something about my gods, Luna, the Goddess of the moon and Nox, the Goddess of night, thanking them for sharing their splendor with us.

It was Avram who asked, "Centurion, you Romans have many gods. Why so many?"

I looked up at the dots above pondering a suitable response. Did I really want to become embroiled in a discussion about my beliefs? Yet, this man deserved an answer. "An interesting question, not one I've thought about often. Yes, we have many gods; one for war, for medicine, for wisdom, for earth, grain, and harvests. I could go on and on but I'm sure I'd forget one or two. Why do you ask?"

"It just seems so complicated. How do you know which god is answering you?"

I sat still, my eyes fixed on the red hot embers of the fire. "The honest answer is sometimes I'm not sure they do."

Avram poked at the fire with a long slender stick, the wood freshened on the fringes of the fire. "I guess that's true of our God as well. We approach him through the priests who teach us and help interpret things for us. A few times I've sensed his presence, yet most of the time, I don't. I struggle with keeping all the laws. When our Messiah comes, I fear, like many others, I'll pay a heavy price for my waywardness." The young man gave a great sigh before concluding, "Like your gods, sometimes ours is a mystery to us as well." After a long silence, he stood up. "It's time I check on the guards."

The man faded into the darkness, his steps quiet. I was glad he left. Debates about religions seem to go nowhere. Like a spinning top there seemed to be a great deal of motion, but when the top came to rest, nothing much was resolved. Rather than focus on the nebulous, I closed my eyes concentrating on my family. They were my motivation. Did anything else really matter?

****

The second day's travel began at dawn, following the same pattern as the first, resting in the heat of the day, halting well before nightfall to construct our position, Reuel and the others applying lessons learned from the previous day as we moved along. Because of the hard, difficult terrain we experienced the first night, I called a halt sooner this day to give us ample time to establish our defensive positions. From my maps and from the commanding view we had from our campsite on a large knoll, the Salt Sea sat in its magnificence to our southwest while the short, sharp curves of the Jordan River along its thickly wooded banks could be seen to our west. Our plan remained intact. Tomorrow we would work our way down the hills to refresh ourselves at the Jordan.

With our perimeter established and inspected by Reuel, guards posted by Avram, food cooked and eaten, the darkness closed in around us, the cool air combined with a stiff westerly breeze suggested this night would be cooler than the last. Once again the bright stars showered us with their luminescence, the moon seemed close enough to touch. Sleep came soon as the familiar night sounds comforted me.

****

In my dreams I saw my children running through the grape fields around our home, Claudia's smile telling me of her love . . . a time of joy and laughter . . . then there were terrified shouts and cluttered noise. Blood curdling screams now became inter-mixed with the vision of my children running toward me in fear. As I learned later, more than two dozen ghostly figures emerged from behind large boulders below the north side of our camp, rising as one as they dashed from the shadows, their attack preceded by their sharpened arrows and spears filling the night sky, their loud screams piercing the quiet as their assault began.

Reuel, on guard on that side of our camp, was the first to catch their movement. After shouting a warning, he hurled his javelin at the closet man just before an enemy spear caromed off his shield. Without knowing the accuracy of his throw, he took on two more bandits as our other three guards rushed to reinforce him, giving those of us who had been resting, time to join the fight.

As I moved in behind the first four men, I saw Avram heave his javelin through the star-lit night air with deadly accuracy, slamming one man to the ground, the point of the javelin protruding from the back of the intruder's shoulder. With several attackers now out of the contest and their element of surprise spent, the battle became a swirling maelstrom, hand-to-hand fighting raging in all quarters, each of us engaged in mortal combat, sometimes fighting one man, for brief periods, two. The fight was intense and savage, pitting muscle against muscle, skill against skill, shrieks and howls coming from all directions, blood flowing, bones cracking, all moving about in a choreograph of horror and deadly strife. Within a few minutes our superior proficiency with the javelin, sword, and dagger began to swing the momentum in our favor, our soldiers employing all the tricks and techniques drummed into them by Valerus, his spirit alive all around me, each soldier a mirror image of how he moved as they wielded their instruments of death.

While we concentrated our efforts on the threat to north of the camp, I heard Kish's frantic scream behind us, coming from the center of our perimeter. "Centurion, they're more over here!" In the dim light I saw Kish and the other two servants challenging this new threat, their daggers in one hand, while trying to hold the reins of our frightened animals in the other as they fought with several bandits whose focus seemed to be on stealing our animals and supplies. Before any order came from my lips, Reuel and Maor sprinted toward this new danger. Fighting like lions protecting their cubs, these two made short work of the thieves, attacking with their swords with deadly efficiency, the shrieks of the bandits blending in with the cries of their comrades now lying at our feet.

With their attack doomed, the thieves still able to run away did so, melting into the gloomy underbrush below our position. After sending Maor and one other man to make sure their retreat continued, I surveyed the battlefield. While the outcome of the clash appeared to be one-sided, Reuel suffered a substantial gash to his left arm as he saved our animals and supplies from being confiscated. With no way to permanently stop the bleeding, it was evident he needed more treatment which I could provide. Another six of us had minor injuries.

Eight bandits lay dead before us with five others on the ground thrashing about in varying stages of dying, their loud cries pleading for mercy. With no way to care for these wretched vermin, nor having any desire to do so, I ordered their execution, sending these five to meet whatever god they worshipped, my soldiers carrying out my orders without hesitation. With the night now quieter, we reflected on the past few heart pounding minutes, the clamor and confusion of the battle giving way to exhilaration and hushed, excited talk among the soldiers, a natural reaction after surviving a surprise attack from an enemy bent on cutting our lives short.

Through this quiet prattle, Reuel, his teeth clenched in pain, asked, "Centurion, "do you think Valerus would have been pleased with us? Did we fight like him?"

Amazing! This young soldier was not asking about the seriousness of his injury. He only wanted to know if his revered teacher would have been proud of his efforts. What a question! I stammered, "Yes, Valerus would be proud of you and all these men. You gave an account of yourselves for Legionnaires everywhere to emulate." I looked around at the other men, blood and sweat, dirt and grime on every face and uniform. "Tell me, Reuel, why did you react so quickly? Did you hear something, see something before the attack?"

The soldier thought for a moment. "No, not really, but I felt something, sensed something wasn't right. It was too quiet, too still. The sounds of the night were absent. Something just wasn't right."

I considered his thoughtful comments. "This means you have become a true soldier, a combat tested soldier. You sensed something awry and it alerted you." Turning to the others I proclaimed, "Did all of you hear that? When your senses speak to you, don't be afraid to act. If you feel something's wrong, if your intuition is speaking to you, pay attention. Act on it! Those two or three seconds can spell the difference between life and death. It did tonight. Reuel's reactions and instincts saved us. If he had ignored his gut, it would be us now on the ground with our heads cut off and our hearts open to the stars above."

I looked into each man's eyes in turn. "I will write Valerus and tell him of your actions. Kish, you and your men are to be complimented as well. Your cry about the men coming behind us made a difference in this outcome. Cuza and Antipas will hear of your deeds."

Smiles and nods of approval came from these new battle-tested soldiers now confident knowing their training and equipment was the difference between life and death. Looking down hill, I issued my next orders. "While I don't expect those bastards to return, be ready. Assume your places on the perimeter. Avram, retrieve our two men from down the hill and resume your guard rotation. We have two, three more hours until sunrise. Reuel will remain with me and Kish so we can treat his wounds. We'll head toward the river at first light."

****

The aromas of fresh baked bread and lamb cooking on a spit filled our nostrils as we drew closer to the river. Emerging from the trail near the crossing site, we saw the sources of those comforting smells as four large groups of Jews camped near the crossing spot we intended to use, their large congregations gathered around huge tents as they refreshed themselves and enjoyed the late afternoon breeze. The loud chatter so prevalent before we made our appearance gave way to an uneasy stillness which spread throughout the entire area when the Jews spotted our small party. While there no demonstrations of hostility directed toward us, it was clear our presence made many uncomfortable as they fixed us with silent stares.

In recognition of this lack of acceptance, I chose to establish our camp some distance away from the other assemblages, near the river next to a small grove of large tamarisk trees. After a nod from me, the soldiers began to clear the area around us of brush so we could see anyone approach, the soldiers now acutely aware of the significance of securing our site from any surprise. While we did not expect any hostilities, the soldiers impressed me with their vigor and work ethic, the experience of coming close to death motivating them, helping them to understand there were only two kinds of soldiers on any battlefield, those who were skilled and observant and quick, and those who were dead.

With preparations for our stay now well under way, I concerned myself with caring for Reuel, changing his dressing again after cleaning the wound with the cool, clean river water flowing near us. Once satisfied with my efforts toward his healing, I took special interest in the nearest Jewish camp, the one closet to us. Made up of young and old, male and female, it was by far the largest of the camps. A man wearing a gray, well worn tunic seemed to be watching us with intense interest. After taking several furtive glances at him, I remembered - he was the man who asked for the body of John.

Chapter VI

At the Jordan River
Border of the Provinces of Judea and Perea
November 14, A.D. 33

The man in the gray tunic; by the way some in his camp stared at us, I could only guess what he had told them. They must now be wondering why we chose to stop here. Was their concern because we were Roman soldiers or was it something else?

With our camp established and a modest guard posted, the soldiers began to eat their evening meal as a bright orange red sun sank lower, partially hidden by the sharp mountain peaks to our west. The evening rituals in campsites around us commenced, the noise of children at play slowly abating, pleasant sounds of flutes and lyres and gleeful singing coming from around their campfires, contented satisfied sounds from well fed animals blending softly into the background. While disquieting glances still came in our direction, we observed no signs of animosity.

Although no redness or swelling appeared around Reuel's wound, now was not the time to take any chances. While only a trickle of the blood came from the slash, the requirement remained to completely stop the bleeding and to reduce chances of infection. Until I found someone who could do that, our efforts centered around keeping pressure on the wound, redressing it often after rinsing the injury with clean water.

Avram was the first to draw my attention with a slight move of his head to several older men from the largest of the Jewish camps approaching our perimeter. Although they did not appear armed, our soldiers nevertheless became alert, our interest increasing the closer these men came. When they halted a comfortable distance outside our perimeter, I went forward to meet them accompanied by Avram, who positioned himself several paces behind me. One of our visitors, the eldest, closed the distance between us. A frail man, his steps were slow and labored, his back bent forward severely hunched in an awkward angle. While discomfort showed on his face with each step, he maintained his balance through the long sturdy wooden poles he held in each hand. What little hair he had was almost clear. After approaching to within a few feet of me, he surprised me with his vibrant, strong voice.

"Welcome, Centurion. My name is Tobias. My friends and I don't mean to be presumptuous, but it is unusual for Roman soldiers to make camp here. May we inquire as to the purpose of your stay?"

Gesturing to the mountains to the east, I said, "We mean no harm. Bandits attacked us last night in those mountains. While we sent them back into the hills with the memory of our skill as soldiers, one of my men suffered a worrisome wound to his arm. We came here to treat him and our other minor injuries." I pointed again toward the mountains, "Based on the thrashing we gave those would-be thieves, I don't believe they'll be bothering you or anyone else anytime soon, but if you travel east, I suggest you increase your vigilance."

As soon as these words came out of my mouth, the Jews began to talk excitedly among themselves, their hands and arms flailing about in all directions, this information about bandits was obviously new to them. When they quieted down, older man addressed me again, his voice conveying genuine sincerity. "Centurion, we are grateful you and your men taught those thugs a lesson. Your presence here will certainly give them pause before they decide to attack anyone in this area." He studied me for a moment longer before asking, "How can we repay you for this great deed?"

Amazing, here was a Jew offering to help a Roman, willing to give soldiers assistance rather than quarrel with us over the slightest inconvenience. Under the normal day by day occurrences in this land, a subdued adversarial relationship existed between the two cultures, so despite the circumstances that brought us in close proximity this offering was clearly outside the norm.

I smiled at the man's unanticipated show of kindness. "I'm most grateful for your offer. While we've done our best to care for our wounded, if you have anyone with medical expertise, I'd like him to examine our most seriously injured soldier."

The old man looked at me, studying me again, before turning to rejoin his colleagues. After taking a few painful steps, the others of his party huddled around him for support. Soon after the old man spoke, a heated argument ensued, some men scowled at him, their arms upraised in protest, their voices hushed yet vehement in their opposition to whatever he proposed, The majority, however, seemed to stand firmly behind the one called Tobias. Finally, the old man reached a decision, one which did not appear to have universal agreement.

Facing me once again, he explained, "Excuse me, Centurion, for I needed to discuss your medical issues with the others. As you perhaps know, we Jews have certain legalities we contend with from time to time, one being since you're a Gentile and you are considered unclean, we cannot touch your wounds or we'll be committing a sin."

The old man paused to look back at his cohorts. "However, we have a young man in our midst with some medical training. Since you and your men have done us a great service, I see no reason why he can't advise you on a treatment requiem. I will see to it he comes promptly to you, bringing with him some medications that should prove satisfactory. Later if you have any other requirements, we'll assist you as we can. Right now, I think it best we give your medical concerns priority." With that, he turned and waved his hand to one of his men who hurried toward their camp.

With that action taken the old man looked back at me, his eyes penetrating deep into my soul. With the slightest of nods, he closed his eyes momentarily, his lips tight. "Our man will be coming to assist you soon. Although he is quite young, you'll find him knowledgeable and compassionate as well." The old man stood like a rock leaning heavily on his wooden poles. "May I ask you a question on another matter?"

"Of course . . . How can I refuse?"

Sadness came across the man's face. "One in our party says he saw you some months ago at Machaerus. Says he saw you the morning after Antipas beheaded John the Baptist. Is that true, Centurion? Were you there when John was killed?"

He held his eyes on me unflinching, his questions and boldness stunned me. What could I tell this man? That I gave the order to the executioner, that John's blood was on my sandals? I had to say something, but I was under no obligation to say anything. Finally I replied, "Yes. I was there when John died. He spoke of his faith in his god with his last breath and that he looked forward to meeting his god. From what I observed, I believe he met death without fear." I nodded in the direction of the Jews' camp. "The man in your camp was one who came the next day to claim John's body for burial."

The old man continued to examine my face closely. Thankfully, he did not ask my part in John's death. He simply nodded his understanding. "John was a prophet to many of us, teaching us a great deal about our God." The old man turned to face the river, examining the waters in the fading light as they jumped over and around some rocks, the babbling of the cool, clear liquid the only noise interrupting the silence between us. The white haired man seemed to stand a little taller, a little straighter. "Centurion, for now, let's care for your wounded."

After taking several painful, hard earned steps toward his camp he paused to look back at me. In a quiet, almost reverent voice, he said, "Thank you for your honesty." Then he resumed his slow, torturous movement, the others of his group providing him support as they slowly walked away.

****

A tall, thin fellow, roughly the same age as my soldiers, the physician, if I could call him that, had strong, dark, handsome features, and sparkling dark green eyes. Despite the tough deportment of my men, some still wearing bandits' blood as badges of honor on their uniforms, this man did not seem awed by our demeanor, carrying himself in our midst in a quiet confident manner. After walking about our men asking a few questions, he assessed our injuries beginning with Reuel, but because of his religious laws, he was careful not to touch any of us, rather giving me specific instructions as he eyed the wounds from a distance.

After looking at Reuel's injury, the physician told me to liberally spread oil and wine over and around the five-six inch gap after I once again cleaned the wound with clear water. Throughout this process, Reuel stoically endured the sharp pain that registered in his eyes while several of the other soldiers held his arm still, the oil and wine designed to kill any infection that had crept into the gap in the skin. After a second dousing of the area, the physician advised me to bind the area with the heavy clothing wrappings he provided, impressing upon me the requirement to follow this same procedure three times a day until the wound completely closed. While not able to suture up the gash as I desired, this man impressed me with his ability to transfer his knowledge to me. Despite the minimal light now available, he advised me to treat our other injuries with the oil and wine combination which we did. As he left, the young man left sufficient quantities of both liquids and an abundance of clean clothes for our use in the days ahead.

With my attention focused on the care of my men and with the darkness enveloping us, I failed to notice Tobias' reappearance outside our camp. When I acknowledged him, he slowly staggered to the center of our camp, painfully lowering himself down upon a large rock close to the burning embers of our small fire. With the flames dancing before us, I studied the man out of the corner of my eye, his countenance displaying superior intellect as he enjoyed the warmth of the fire, his snowy white hair giving testimony to many years of experience. We both stared in silence at the blue-yellow flames of the burning wood for a long time.

The old Jew spoke first. "Centurion, if these trees looking

down upon us and the rocks at our feet could talk, they would give testimony of some wonderful stories about the history of my people. Abraham, the father of our nation, erected an altar to our God not far from here. And then many years later, another of our great prophet, Moses, brought our people from Egypt through the lands south of here through the area you traveled through yesterday."

"Was he the one who lead your people into the land you now occupy?"

The man poked at the fire with a short stick before answering. "No, he disobeyed God and died somewhere in the area around Mt. Nebo, his burial location known only to God."

"Disobeyed your god you say? He must have done something horrendous."

The man ignored my comment. "To God, sin is sin. The size of the sin is of no consequence, and despite Moses' stalwart leadership of his people, God punished him. Joshua, Moses' principal subordinate, then led our people upon Moses' death crossing this river near this spot we now sit into the land decreed to us by a promise made to Abraham long ago."

Wondering what this old man was going to tell me which would be of interest to me, I chose not to challenge him. After the medical assistance provided to us, I thought listening to his idle banter about old prophets and myths was a fitting price to pay. After a brief lull, the old man's purpose for coming to my fire became clear.

"These men are significant to the history of my people, but our present times are being shaped by others, men like John who baptized so many of us."

I held up my hand in protest but before my words came out, the old man stopped me. "I know your question, Centurion. Baptism, why is it so important to us? It is a sign of our intent to turn away from a lifestyle that displeases God to one focused on him. That may not mean much to you Romans, but to us, it's significant."

He looked at the river, the faint starlight reflecting off the moving waters as they continued their steady flow south. "I've been praying to God, thanking Him for the life of our beloved John. Even though Antipas isolated him in prison for many days, we've not forgotten him." He paused before concluding, "I don't know why but God has told me to tell you more about John."

I sat up in an attempt to halt all this talk. After a great sigh, I said, "Forgive me, but you have your god and I have my deities. I've no need to learn anything more about John."

The old man stared patiently at some far off star in the eastern sky, ignoring my comment. "While I'm sometimes confused by God's instruction, I've learned over the years that while I may question him, his instructions aren't to be taken lightly; they're to be obeyed. Hence, I'm here to tell you about John."

I looked at the man searching for some chink in his manner but it seemed nothing would take him off his appointed course. Leaning back on my rock trying to appear totally disinterested, I hoped for a brief oration. I quietly laughed more to myself then to my uninvited visitor, "Since you give me little choice, I'll sit here with you but only for a short time. We've a great distance to travel in the morning."

After poking the fire with his stick, he launched into his tale. "When Antipas' father, Herod the Great, ruled Judea, a priest named Zachariah and his wife, Elizabeth, lived in the hill country south of Jerusalem, diligently following all of God's commands. Despite their fervent prayers for a child, God never granted them this request. Although disappointed, they remained steadfast, their desire to follow God unwavering."

A small flame sprang up from the fire as he continued to stoke its dry outskirts. "One day as Zechariah performed his priestly duties in the temple at Jerusalem, an angel appeared before him. The man trembled in fear, but the angel told him not to be afraid; God was going to answer his prayers, Elizabeth would bear a son, and they were to name him John. The angel also said this child would be great in the sight of God, filled with his spirit, and the

91

child would prepare others to serve God."

When Tobias stopped to take a breath, I couldn't contain myself, guffawing as held my hand over my mouth. "Do I have this right? Some vision tells an old priest his barren wife is going to have a child? And not only that, this child will grow up to be some kind of leader. Quite a story, old man. Forgive me but how can you be so certain this is true?" mordantly ridiculing him with each word. "Sounds like just another old Jewish tale filled with mystery and intrigue, another of your riddles with no end in sight."

Ignoring my derision, he plowed ahead. "As a Roman, I'm sure it is difficult for you to understand our belief in God, but as one of Zachariah's relatives, I can assure you, every word I'm telling you is true." He pointed a bony, scarred finger at me. "Please let me go on. There is more to tell."

"Humph," I sighed. "If you must."

The old man looked sharply at me as though he was ready to walk away, but then his face relaxed and he resumed his yarn. "The angel also told Zechariah that John would lead our people back to God with the spirit and power like Elijah, another of our great prophets. When our beloved priest began to ask questions much like yours, the angel responded, telling him because of his unbelief, he would not be able to speak again until after the child was born."

With this I threw my hands up, smiling, "You've got me now. Are you're telling me because this fellow questioned this angel, he wouldn't be able to speak again until after the child was born? You certainly have a strange god or maybe just a strange angel. But I've got to give it to you, it's a good story."

Without defending his previous words, Tobias stared straight into the fire. Finally he slowly shook his head. "While I'd like to tell you more tonight, I've given you enough to consider. I'll return in the morning. . . But before I go, let me leave you with one question . . . When you talked with John, was your heart stirred by his unwavering belief in his God?"

Stunned, my thoughts went back to that night in the dungeon, recalling the steel I saw in the man who was about to die. My eyes narrowed as I looked at Tobias. "No." I tried to keep my voice steady. "No, there was no reason it should have been."

Ignoring my response, the old man rose gingerly, using his wooden supports to steady his body as he rose to his feet. "God knows and sees all, Aquila. You can try to hide from Him but you can't." As I watched him melt into the darkness, I heard those words reverberate through my brain ---You can't hide from God. Is this part of what Valerus was communicating to me? Then another thought struck me. The old man called me "Aquila." How did he know my name? I had never mentioned it to him.

****

After several hours of tossing about the details of my encounter with John, I arose well before dawn, rekindling the fire with some dried wood collected by my men throughout the night. A string of foaming dark clouds overhead blotted out the stars accompanied by a strong westerly wind giving way to a rumble of thunder farther to the west foretelling of an intense storm heading in our direction. As my eyes watched the passage of the ominous sky above, I wondered again what Tobias knew of my encounter with John. So engrossed in these thoughts, I almost missed the guard's signal, alerting me the old man was once again entering our camp.

"Centurion, I wanted to come and finish my story before the storm swallows us." The old man wrapped his cloak around him tighter as a big gust of wind swept through the tree tops near us as he sat down, not waiting for an invitation.

While I would have preferred to forgo any more talk about John, I reminded myself once again of the kindness this man showed my soldiers. Moving over to give the man some room by the coals, he resumed his tale without preamble. "As I mentioned last night, because of Zechariah's disbelief, when he came out of the temple, he couldn't speak, using signs to answer what questions he could. Once he returned to home, we assume he shared with Elisabeth through signs what the angel said." With a twinkle in his eye, this Nestor smiled, "Imagine her surprise, her heart filled with great joy and happiness after all the disgrace and ridicule she endured for so many years,"

I wanted him to stop him, but some enigmatic thought inside me caused me to want to hear more. If only a part of Tobias' tale was true, it was an interesting account as he continued to draw me along.

"As the months went by, our family's anticipation grew as we watched God bless this wonderful couple. Then the great day arrived and the baby was born. Eight days later, as is our custom, we gathered to witness the circumcision and the naming of the boy, but Elizabeth stunned us when she spoke up boldly saying his name would be John."

"Why the concern?"

"In our culture children are normally given the name of some relative and there was no John in our family linage. Exasperated we all turned to Zechariah expecting him to correct this wrong."

"So what did he do?"

"After giving all of us a wry smile, he grabbed the nearest writing tablet upon which he wrote, 'His name shall be John!' As soon as his fingers stopped writing, his mouth opened as he sang praises to God. After things quieted down a bit, he told us everything the angel said, the sum of which I've related to you. It was a great day for my family."

Tobias paused to look up as the thickness of the clouds steadily increasing, the winds above us swirling about with growing intensity, thunder booming out its message, much closer now. "I know you want to be on your way. Only a few more points; this story has been told over and over again in our land for many years. It was not surprising to us John grew up to fulfill all the words given to his father."

I sat back thinking about the words of this white haired man. "How is it you know so much about all this? That you tell this with such certainty and passion?"

A smile came across Tobias' face. "As I told you last night, I was there, Zechariah is a relative. What I didn't tell you was that he was my brother, John was my nephew."

I could only stare at the man across from me. Even though I helped kill this man's nephew and although it seemed Tobias had some insight concerning that, he appeared to bear no ill will toward me. Despite the rapidly approaching weather, I changed the subject. "What was his boyhood like?"

"Oh, there is much to tell about that . . . I'll give you just a few details. As he matured, he spent much of his time alone in the wilderness, his hair grew long and disheveled, his clothes came from camel's hair, a large leather belt encircled his waist, his primary sustenance coming from locusts and wild honey. His focus was on communing with God, absorbing his message."

Even as I looked at the clouds above me, the scent of moisture heavy in the air, I muttered, "And so with all this knowledge he began to preach to you and the others?"

"Yes, that's right. His speech was loud like the thunder approaching us, his words shook the foundation of those who heard him – words marked with conviction, spirit and grit, all this from a humble and sincere man, his messages spoken as though they came straight from God. John kept saying he was forerunner, a herald of another who would come after him, a man we call Messiah."

I looked up at the word Messiah. "So despite all the things spoken about John and his relationship with your god, he was not your long overdue Messiah?"

Tobias sat back deep in thought. Looking up at the boiling sky above, now showing more colors, red and yellow mixing with gray and black as the dawn came, he said, "No, John was not our Messiah. It seems his role in God's plan was to help us prepare for the His coming. At least that's how we interpreted what we heard." Struggling to his feet, his body rebelling against the movement, the man finished his thoughts. "You'll learn much more about all this when you reach Galilee. I hope the remainder of your journey is successful."

The old man bowed once again before trudging back toward his camp, peals of lightening now streaking through the nearby hills across the river, the thunder shaking the ground around us, booming out in almost a constant refrain, leaving us no place to hide.

As I watched Tobias walk away, I wondered about his words – it seemed as though something, someone was pulling me or maybe pushing me in some undefined, unknown direction. Clearly it had something to do with John, and maybe his god, yet, what business was it of mine? Why should any more of my time become intertwined with the life of this Jew? I had a task to accomplish, a mission to see through to the end.

Trying to put all this behind me, I saw my men were packed, ready to move before the brunt of the storm hit us. Because this idle talk with Tobias had wasted an hour of good travel time, the men stood ready to leave this place, even Reuel who gave me an encouraging smile and a nod which told me he was able to travel.

We filled our water jugs with fresh water as we crossed the Jordan, turning north on the next leg of our journey, the heavy rain now pelting us with each step, enveloping us in a wet gray shroud.

Chapter VII

West of the Jordan River
Province of Galilee
November 16, A.D. 33

As the rain hammered us, the muddied waters flowed down from the hills to our west making our travel troublesome as each stream bed we crossed was a rushing torrent, the normal dry rocky ground now a slippery mess, each step a struggle causing us to take two days to reach Scythopolis, a town dating back twenty five hundred years. The unpretentious town of several thousand souls sat on the southeastern edge of Galilee, three miles west of the Jordan River, fifteen miles south of the Sea of Galilee, an area over the centuries which changed hands many times, from the Egyptians to the Canaanites, and now finally to the Jews under Antipas' leadership with Roman supervision.

After climbing the three hundred feet up the steep trail from the river bed, we entered the city, passing both an amphitheater and a large auditorium on our way to the Roman garrison located near the town's center. Once inside garrison's walls, it pleased me to find that an old acquaintance, Savius, served as commander of this outpost.

****

"Another good story, Savius. I remember it well. But I must confess, with all those camel riders who lived there, I don't miss that dry, unforgiving Egyptian desert. May I never see that country again," I said as I emptied my wine goblet for the fourth time.

"Ah, you and me both, Aquila, you and me both," my old friend laughed heartily as he refilled our goblets. He hadn't changed in all the years I'd known him, thick hairy forearms, a curly dark head of hair, and a quick vulgar tongue, still able to drink me and any two other Centurions under the table.

"So back to your bandits . . . You said about twenty to twenty five of them?"

"Yes, but now the number is closer to twelve still breathing air," amusing both of us at my comment as the red nectar continued to loosen our tongues. "Oh, and before I forget, thanks again for sending your man to examine Reuel's arm. I thought the oil and wine combination given to me by the Jews would work, but it's good to have confirmation. I wanted to trust that Jew but sometimes they make you wonder."

Savius looked at me through red eyes as the red liquid we guzzled began taking an even greater toll, belching his thanks before returning to an earlier topic. "I know what you mean, strange people, these Jews . . . You said you were on your way to Tiberias but you're going to Nain first. Why? Not much there but some grapes and figs growing on the hills around there; certainly no entertainment there for you or your men. When you reach Tiberias, I can give you names of some fine young damsels there if you like," as he flashed a quick smile my way.

I quietly laughed at my friend. "Ah, Savius, you're drunk. Have you forgotten? We've had this discussion before. I don't need that kind of entertainment although I can't speak for my soldiers. I told you, the leader of Antipas' soldiers at Machaerus hails from Nain. I'm going there to pay my respects to him."

"Ah yes, I remember now," as he took another swallow from his cup. "Reminds me of a story I heard a few months ago about Nain. Shows you how crazy those people must be," a giddy drunken laugh came from my friend. "A preposterous story if you ask me."

He looked around the dingy canteen, our table in a drab corner away from the soldiers, the setting much like I enjoyed with Valerus at Machaerus. "The way I hear it seems a young fellow, not more than a pup, name of Amittai or Amitti, something like that, died there one day some months back. As the townspeople went through their wailing process like they always do, some rabbi or priest or whatever appears out of nowhere, goes and talks to the grieving mother, and then tells this dead boy to get up out of his coffin, and guess what?" He took another gulp of the rose colored liquid. "This is the best part . . . Supposedly this boy gets up, throws off his burial garments and starts walking around! Can you believe it? What a confused lot, these Jews. First they say the lad is dead and then he's alive. People have got to be crazy to believe that," slurring his words the longer he spoke.

I laughed again. "Now I know you're drunk."

"No, Aquila, I swear, one of my soldiers heard it from a farmer from that area. I don't believe a word of it, mind you, but it should make for good table talk when you see the man there. Yes sir, good table talk. More wine?" he asked as he filled up my goblet one more time.

****

Early the next morning we set off in a northwesterly direction through the Valley of Jezreel, Mt. Gilboa to our left, Mt. Tabor to our right front. The cloudless sky gave no indication of the great storm from several days ago, the only evidence remaining were some deep ruts along the path still holding shallow pools of water. As we marched along, I reminded the soldiers of the battles fought on this ground through the years by men with the names of Gideon and Saul, Jewish leaders who fought the Midianites, the Amalekites, and then the Philistines. Because of their Jewish heritage, my men knew the history of these conflicts and searched for signs of these clashes, but the relics of old remained hidden below our feet.

As we approached Nain in the late afternoon with our last steps up the steep, rough trail leading to the town, I called a halt near a stone well outside the town, the few townspeople gathering their water yielding space for us to refresh ourselves and to wash some of the dust off our faces. Dominating the surrounding countryside was Mt. Tabor, standing east of the town. Shaped like a cone, Tabor rose to a great height above the valley floor, the verdant trees on its slopes in sharp contrast to the grassy plains around its base. Coupled with many fig trees and olive groves we could see in all directions, it was a majestic blending of greens, flaxen, and russet. It was easy to see why in the Jewish tongue, Nain meant pleasant or delightful.

With most of the dirt now off my face, I was ready to meet Uthai, Shallium's father. After issuing instructions to Reuel regarding a suitable position for the night, I hailed a young man working in the nearby field. With a questioning look on his face, the lad put down his hand-held plow along the edge of the field as he walked slowly toward me. Stopping in front of me, he asked cautiously, "Centurion, is there something I can do for you?"

This youth was shorter than me, of medium size, his frame sturdy and vigorous, everything about him suggesting he was a picture of good health. Like so many others in this land of brilliant sunshine, he was tan, his hair a sandy color, his clothing simple but functional for working long hours in the fields. I took him to be younger than most of the men with me.

I looked down at the boy. "I'm looking for Uthai, one of your town's leaders. Where can I find him?"

"His home is on the main street as you enter through the gate, fourth house on the right. Is there anything else I can do for you? a puzzled look on his face.

"No. It's certainly no business of yours why I ask for him." Who was this boy to question me! "What's you name boy?"

"Amittai."

Amittai – could this be the one Savius had mentioned - a boy thought dead but now alive? I looked harder at the lad, harkening back to Savius' story. My face must have indicated something because the young man asked, "Are you alright, Centurion? Is anything the matter?"

"Your name . . . I heard it recently. Is there something I should know about you, something special?"

The youngster gave me a muddled glance. "Well . . . when most people come to our town, they want to talk with me, not with any of the town's leaders." His words carried no hint of boastfulness or arrogance although it was a peculiar statement.

Seeing my discussion with this boy, my soldiers drifted over. As they began to gather around us, the young fellow shot me a pensive glance as he held his ground while my men shuffled in closer, the two of us now in the center of a loose circle.

"See here, young fellow, I've no idea what you're talking about. Why should anyone come to this town to talk to you? What makes you a celebrity in this backward part of Galilee?" chortling as I spoke, my soldiers taking up this theme, mumbling similar questions.

The lad's eyes signaled his concern as these rough, battle tested warriors made verbal sport of him. He moved closer to me seeking protection as sarcastic comments came at him from every direction before he stated, "Centurion, I apologize. I didn't mean to offend you. I forget not everyone knows my story."

As the taunts began anew, I held up my hand for silence. When my men quieted down, I asked, "Lad, we've had some long days on some difficult trails. We're tired and hungry and my patience is short, but you've awakened my curiosity. You say people come here to talk to you. Now why would they do that? What makes what you have to say so important?"

The frightened look on the young man's face slowly subsided. "Centurion, if you really want to know, my story will only take a moment. Then when you meet Uthai, he can verify what I tell you."

I rubbed my mouth to get some of the dust away, scratching some bug off the back of my neck, giving the lad a quick smile. "If your tale is a good one, you can be sure I'll tell him about meeting you." The men around us mocked the boy, "Yes, let's hear this great story. We're ready for a good laugh," my hand quieting them down again, their verbal folly giving way to amused smirks.

Perhaps awed by our uniforms or our lack of respect, the lad's first words came out in a halting, stumbling manner, but when he realized he held our attention, he became more garrulous the longer he spoke. "Some time back, I was very ill. So much so, people here say I died." Broad smiles came on the faces of my soldiers at the mention of the word, but they decided to play along, at least temporarily. Sensing this, the young fellow talked with greater speed.

"The people here told me they wrapped me in burial clothes and placed me in a coffin. As I understand it, my funeral procession was making its way out of the city," pointing to the avenue leading out from the town a hundred steps away, "when a stranger and his followers approached the procession asking who died. The townspeople pointed to my mother, telling the man that I, her only son, was dead and my mother was in great despair because since my father dying years ago, if I died, she'd be alone."

My men couldn't bear this any longer. They jeered the story teller, making him the butt of their ridicule. "Let's get this straight. You say you're dead and some stranger comes along to find out what's going on? What kind of imbeciles do you take us for? We're not idiots," the cries multiplying as their anger and disbelief grew.

The young man looked at my soldiers before shifting his gaze back to me. In a quiet, reverent tone he claimed, "I know all this sounds strange, Centurion, but it's true. And there's more."

"Go on," I said, motioning my men to be still.

Without waiting for any further interruptions, the lad's words tumbled out. "After being told about my mother, I'm told this stranger approached her and told her not to cry. Then he touched my coffin, saying, 'Young man, I say to you, get up!'" The boy now pointed to a spot on the narrow road not far from us. "It all happened right there. I don't remember hearing his words, but when I woke up, I was wrapped in burial clothes, so scared I pulled them off as quickly as I could and started talking to anyone, everyone! Those around me cried and shouted, raising their arms in celebration and joy, my mother by my side, tears running down her cheeks as she kept hugging me and hugging me. Later when things settled down, the townspeople could talk about little else except about this man who called me from the dead, saying he was a great prophet who spoke about God coming to help our people."

When the story teller took a breath, several of the soldiers cried out, "Centurion, he's drunk. No one can do that that; when you're dead, you're dead. Just like those cutthroats we killed a few days ago." Another soldier chimed in, "You don't look dead to us. How is it you've come back to life? No one can do that!" Another followed with, "He's under some spell. I've heard this story before from an old drunken fool. Didn't believe it then, don't believe it now." Another shouted, "The heat has gotten to him." Several other soldiers, Reuel and Avram to name a few, remained quiet and contemplative, staring directly into the young man's eyes searching them for the truth.

After calling for quiet once again, I smiled at the young man. "What an entertaining tale! You can be certain I'll ask Uthai about this. But before we go, let me ask, does this man who brought you back from the dead have a name, this so-called prophet, or sage, who, according to you, has the power over life and death?" mocking the boy as a few of my men carried through with similar queries.

Despite all caustic jabs aimed in his direction, the boy assumed a bolder, more spirited demeanor, one which replaced the fear and trepidation present moments before. With his back now straight as a javelin, the lad announced, "I apologize again, Centurion. I didn't mean to rile you or your soldiers." He gestured with his hands to those townspeople who were working in the fields around us. "To those who live in this area, this story is well known. Ask anyone, they'll tell you. As far as this man who you ask about, some think he is more than a great prophet."

The young man bowed his head slightly in obeisance before finishing his thoughts. "Some think he may be a great healer. A few even hint they believe him to be our Messiah. I don't know about that, but I do know this man brought me back to life." The boy stopped for a time before proclaiming, "I long for his return. I want to thank him because he gave me life!" Fixing me with a steady gaze, he continued, "You asked the man's name. Perhaps you have heard of him. His name is Jesus. He comes from a town to our northwest. Jesus of Nazareth is the one who raised me from the dead."

With that, the young man nodded to me and after being allowed passage from the circle of soldiers, he walked back toward the field, picking up his plow before resuming his duties with the others in the fields.

****

Knocking on the well-worn wooden door of Uthai's home, I tried to ignore the story or tale or lie or whatever it was as I concentrated on watching Nain's people move at an unhurried pace on the streets, some involved in social conversations, others conducting business with merchants peddling their merchandise. The town was laid out in a rough square and with no walls encircling their houses within it, holding pens for the animals extended out from the homes away from the center of town forming the periphery of the village. While I anticipated my uniform would bring some reaction from the inhabitants, most paid scant attention to me, their focus on their daily activities. Stones and mortar bricks cemented together formed the majority of Nain's homes, the predominant color a dusty brown, mats of reeds and in some cases thorn bushes tied in bundles constituted the roofs of many homes while the more affluent, like Uthai's, had substantial roofs made of bricks and wooden beams, strong enough to be used as additional living space.

An older man with a short gray beard answered my knock. Shorter in height than I expected, he bore a striking resemblance to his son. After staring momentarily at the bronze and polish of my uniform, he asked, "Centurion, can I help you?" but before I could respond, recognition spread across his face as he looked at me with greater interest. "Forgive me, you look familiar. Yes, yes, I remember now. I saw you at Machaerus some months ago."

While I expected to be asked to remain outside the home, the man surprised me with a most unusual invitation, directing me into his home. "This is a pleasure. What brings you here? A word from Antipas perhaps; something about my son?"

"Sir, I bring greetings from Antipas. My soldiers and I are traveling to Tiberias, and because we were passing your town, Shallium asked me to deliver this letter to you," saying all this as I reached into my tunic, handing the precious cargo to him.

With trembling hands, the man held the letter as one would hold a treasure of gold coins. Looking up at me, Uthai exclaimed, "If you will forgive me, it has been many months since we've heard from our son. Please let me usher you out to our courtyard where you can refresh yourself while I take this to my wife so we can read this letter together. I don't wish to be impolite but. . ."

"Of course, I understand."

"Please follow me," he said as he led me through the center of the home to the garden area which was open to the deep late day azure sky. As we passed through a wide, airy interior hallway of his home, we passed several rooms on both the right and left, rooms which appeared to be sleeping areas and for preparing and eating their meals.

Before I could even sit down on one of the two benches in the courtyard, Uthai returned carrying a bowl of water and several pieces of clean cloth in one hand and large jug of wine and a goblet in the other. I understood immediately I should take off my sandals to wash my feet. While not so much a Roman custom, it was expected of me as a guest in this man's home. The purpose of the wine was obvious. With a smile on his face, the excited father exclaimed, "Please excuse me . . . Thank you again for understanding." With anticipation in his voice he began to retreat into the main living quarters but then he paused, looking back at me.

"Centurion, it is not the accepted practice for us Jews to host Gentiles in our home, but as head of this town, I find it necessary from time to time to associate with many people for economic and governmental purposes, and besides, you've given my wife and I a great gift. How can I possibly refuse hospitality to you? Make yourself comfortable. I'll return shortly."

After cleaning my feet and sampling the first cup of the delicious red wine, I examined my surroundings. In large clay pots in each corner of the garden grew multi-colored flowers which drew an occasional small bird and not just a few bees dancing around the exposed petals. The surprisingly even floor was dark gray, made from flat clay stones. Everything was simple and neat. A stairway led up to a well constructed solid roof which doubled as an open air room above the main part of the home. With the lateness of the day, my senses captured the smell of freshly baked bread coupled with the aroma of a delicious meat, lamb perhaps, on a spit not far away.

While I wanted to stay in this moment, my mind kept returning to the young man's story. He spoke with such conviction, yet it still seemed so farfetched to be true.

Uthai returned to the garden carrying a small tray of grapes and pomegranates, and after grabbing the jug and filling both his cup and mine, he smiled, "Please follow me to the roof. The view up there is spectacular." After climbing up the steep, stony steps, we both stopped and looked over the rooftops of his town, the beauty extending in all directions, the dark shadows of mountain and lighter colored hills blending together, a few small puffy clouds well to the west, all under the sun's rays, which began to soften as the day began to close. The westerly breeze added to our comfort as we both enjoyed the wine along with the delicious fruit.

"Centurion, you have given my wife and me a great gift today, words from my son written in his own hand. What a memorable day." He smiled in reflection of some past memory before turning to me. "Do you have children?"

"Yes, a son and a daughter, both still quite young. They live in Rome with my wife. Once I finish my duties here, I pray to the gods I'll join them soon."

The older man nodded, "Well with that possibility, I too will pray your desires are met." He paused to again study the scenery around us before his voice became more business-like. "So how is Antipas? Since I assume he intends to travel to Tiberias soon, does he intend to come by here on his way north?"

"Well, first, let me say Antipas sends his warmest regards. He will be traveling to Tiberias soon, but he gave me no indication of his route. As for any business matters impacting you or Nain, I've heard of no issues to cause you concern."

"Well that's good to know. Antipas' responsibility of ruling two provinces is enormous, but if he comes this way, I'll be delighted to host him." Uthai stopped to look at me. "So why are you here, sir, just to deliver a letter?"

"Actually, yes. With several routes to choose from to reach Tiberias, I thought it fitting to pay my respects to you and let you know of Shallium's accomplishments." After savoring another taste of the gods' nectar, I went on. "It has been my pleasure to spend many hours with him in the past few months as he accepted the challenge to lead soldiers; a challenge which he is meeting better than expected. His men have confidence in his leadership and Antipas views him as a reliable, trustworthy leader."

Uthai stared at Mt Tabor, its tall stately trees visible in the distance. "When my son left here to join the army, he was much like a raw stallion, ready to charge, yet unsure as to the proper direction. I believe you when you say he is doing well in his leadership role, although I suspect much of the credit must go those who nurtured and trained him. His letter indicates you played a major role in his development. Is that true? Were you one of those who molded and shaped him?"

Looking out over the landscape, I nodded, "Yes, I was, but Shallium is intelligent enough and motivated enough to take our thoughts and ideas, and blend them into his personality. Like most good soldiers, we're a combination of our upbringing, coupled with the personalities of our mentors who teach and challenge us." Turning back to Uthai, I said, "So yes, I'll take some credit for his maturation, but not all of it. I propose we drink to his continued success."

We both hoisted our cups of wine, drinking heartily as we allowed nature's beauty to enfold us in her arms. I drank in the calm sunset, the air becoming noticeably cooler as the wind died down, the blinking candle lights from the homes below. Low muted voices mixed with the baying of animals as the people of Nain started their nightly ritual of settling down for the evening. Tranquil and peaceful, everything seemed to be in its proper place. As my eyes finished their wandering over this pastoral scene, I said, "You live in a wonderful place, Uthai. Calm and quiet." Did I really want to spoil this setting? Couldn't the story of the young man be left unsaid?

The older man nodded, "Yes, it is." Studying me he went on. "I sense there's something else, something troubling you."

Despite my misgivings, not knowing where this would lead, I blundered ahead, wanting, needing to know if the boy had played me for a fool. "A question did arise as we approached your town this afternoon. Something a young man told me and my men. It was a most entertaining story."

Uthai stared at me. "What was it about?"

"The lad told us that some time ago he died and a prophet appeared and raised him from his burial coffin. My soldiers and I had a good laugh over this, although the young fellow seemed quite sincere. He went so far as to say you could vouch for him. Is there any truth to what he told us: he was dead, a man saw the funeral procession, telling him to arise, and now the lad shows no ill effects? Any truth to any of that?"

Shallium's father said nothing for a long time as he stared at the western skies, the last pink and reddish rays of the sun still favoring us with some light. Finally he looked at me, his eyes sparkling. "So this young fellow told you we were carrying him out of the town in his coffin, the boy's mother crying uncontrollably. Then a stranger stopped us, telling the boy to get up, and the young man arose in a daze. Was that his story?"

"Yes, that's it exactly."

Uthai took another swallow of his wine before speaking. "Centurion, I can vouch for this story. You see I was one of those carrying the coffin that day." He stopped to pour more wine into our cups."I saw it all. The man who called the boy from his coffin that day was as close to me as I am to you right now, his arm almost touching my sleeve.

I watched the first twinkle of the stars in the eastern sky, before taking another large gulp of wine. How could this be true? Astonishing! Why would such a thing happen in this small, out of the way village?

"When this prophet, as you called him, told us to lower the coffin, we followed his direction. I watched as he ordered the boy to get up. And when the boy, draped in the clothes of death, obeyed, I pulled my hand away in fright as he gripped mine to get his balance. We thought he was a ghost! We were terrified!" Uthai stopped, perhaps reliving that the day once again, before his words now came out in a flood. "Then when the boy flailed away throwing the death clothes off his body, he stood right in front of me. If I had not seen it with my own eyes, I wouldn't believe it, but I tell you it's true."

His gaze now went from house to house below us. "Amittai is the name of the young man who spoke to you." Pointing to the north side of the village, "He lives with his mother there, the last house on the edge of the town. Almost the whole town witnessed the events that day. A day of sorrow became a day of unspeakable joy. We continue to look for the man who healed Amittai but he's not returned."

Uthai now turned toward me. "As you can imagine, we have many questions. That day came and went so fast, I know we didn't think properly thank him. If you see Amittai before you leave, be assured he told you the truth. His name means 'truthful' and he is very serious about living up to his name."

Shaking my head, I asked, "If this is all true, why haven't I heard about this before? Surely such news should have traveled fast?"

"Within our Jewish community it has, but as you've indicated, unless you were here that day and witnessed it all with your own eyes, it is difficult to believe such a story." Then he shrugged his shoulders, "And besides, why should we share it with you Romans? What would you do with a man capable of performing such miracles?"

"Why should we care? If you keep the peace, pay your homage to Caesar, what difference would it make? This is your land, not ours?"

Uthai stared at me for a time. "You are an unusual Roman. Naïve perhaps yet you seem to have a certain sensitivity not found in others who wear your uniform. For some unknown reason you've been privileged to understand what happened here at Nain." He looked at the brightening stars to the east. "I also fear for what some of our Jewish leaders might do? Would they arrest this man? After what Antipas did to John, many have concerns. I suppose we'll have to wait and see, won't we?"

Neither of us spoke as we watched more stars fill the night sky, stars so numerous they were like the grains of sand on the shore so close to together, they seemed to touch one another as they slowly rotated across the dark sky. With my business complete, I thanked Uthai for his hospitality, telling him we would be leaving the area early in the morning as our goal tomorrow was Tiberias.

****

I found my campsite on a small hill overlooking the town. After making a cursory inspection of Reuel's perimeter, my mind wandered back to the day's events. While I enjoyed meeting Uthai, I needed to escape from another story about a higher power I could not comprehend. Could there be such a man who could circumvent the natural flow that life led to death? I faced death stoically, knowing it would come to all of us in some way at some time, maybe through the sword or disease, through sickness or through the aging process. Nothing could reverse the inevitable.

To be free from the bonds of death was impossible . . . Utter folly . . . It had to be. To think otherwise was lunacy. Yet John seemed to look forward to his death in some strange way, and somehow the old man at the river seemed to have a similar trust. This optimism about the afterlife was foreign to me and now here was a story about a prophet raising a young man from his death shroud.

The young man from the fields believed everything he had been told and experienced; Uthai believed it; no doubt many of the people living in Nain believed it, but I couldn't. It just didn't make sense. Nothing could defy the wisdom of the ages. No god was that powerful!

Chapter VIII

Nain
Province of Galilee
November 20, A.D. 33

As my feet hit the ground early the next morning ready to put all this prophet talk behind me, I pushed my soldiers along our route from Nain taking us on a well traveled path through the fertile fields past the lower slopes of Mt. Tabor. A clean dulcet aroma of grapes and olive trees coupled with golden grain growing in the fields accompanied us as we passed through the lush meadows, the people we encountered polite, but not overly friendly. To these peasants, the Roman uniform represented occupation, men bent on pillaging hard earned assets, men to whom a degree of obeisance was required. To them we were a necessary evil thrust upon them, uninvited guests at best, thieves of their culture and land at worst. Despite our differences, it was most pleasurable hike as each side kept its distance from the other.

Closer to Tiberias, the road swelled with travelers and merchants going to and from the profit centers of this city of fifteen thousand. Cresting the last significant hill, we stopped to gaze at the panorama stretching out before us, the sprawling urban area and the deep blue of the Sea of Galilee dominating our view east of the city, a view so spectacular it could only have been made by the gods. Avram was the first to comment. "Centurion, what are the names of all these towns around the sea; there are so many of them?

"If my studies are correct, as you look left of Tiberias, the first small town to the north is Gennesaret, a town known for its fertile lands and many gardens. I understand they grow walnuts, palms, figs and olives there."

"What about the large town north of there?"

"That would be Capernaum, large enough to be called a city." Turning to the back of our formation, I motioned to Kish to come forward. "Kish, tell us about Capernaum."

The young man smiled, "I've had occasion to enjoy its pleasures several times as I worshipped in the synagogue. Many of the boats you see on this side of the sea call it home, and because it is on the main road between Damascus and Jerusalem, a great deal of commerce flows through the area requiring a customs house and a substantial Roman detachment."

Maor now jumped into the discussion. "Kish, what about that smaller village further to the east, the one right along the coast?"

"A fishing town with a number of spring-fed pools flowing into the town's center from the hills above. Some people believe those waters contain some special healing powers to them, but I've never known of anyone who was cured there. That doesn't stop some from spreading false hope about all that. Name of the place is Bethsaida."

"Looks like some rough, high country directly east of us across the sea. Is that Hippos?"

"That's right, Centurion. The land on that side of the sea is much rougher then this side, the ground there similar to Perea, much rockier compared to the fertile land here."

I pointed to the southern end of sea. "I assume that's the outlet for where the Jordan begins its journey south, through that conversion of swampy ground and trees down there?"

Kish followed my glance. "Yes, exactly. That's the birthplace of the Jordan, all the water that flows through it ends up in the Salt Sea." The young man gave a great sigh. "I'm always pleased to be here, so much different than Machaerus, the blues of the water, the verdant, emerald greens, the softer features of the land blending together by God's creative hand."

"Humpf, yes, *god's hand*," I mumbled under my breath. "That's all you Jews think about, god." Shaking my head hoping that was the last time today I would hear about 'god,' I announced, "If we are to enjoy the city and shake the dust off our uniforms, we need to finish this march."

****

With our pace quickening, it wasn't long before our eyes beheld some of the details of Antipas' city, the two large stone pillars marking the main gate. Before we could take another step, one soldier burst forth with a question on the minds of most of the men. With a gleam in his eye, the young man, no doubt spurred on by others, asked, "Centurion, can we assume in a city this large, there'll be adequate recreational opportunities to keep us occupied when off duty?"

The others laughed at the subtleness of the query, but they anxiously awaited my answer, nudging each other, sheepish grins on several faces. To these men, whose life experiences revolved around the small towns and villages in the bleak and unforgiving areas of the wilderness, they envisioned Tiberias to be a place of endless enticements, filled with intoxicating allurements, all leading to evenings of boundless pleasure that here-to-for they only dreamed about. To them this sprawl of humanity was an opportunity where all their dreams and fantasies could be fulfilled.

I laughed at the question. Soldiers never change. Even on the dustiest of trails, or during days of scorching heat, days of torrential downpours or cold, dark nights, soldiers' thoughts could shift with little encouragement to the pleasures of wine, women, and good food, not always in that order. Having been a young soldier once, I understood their youthful interest in this subject. "While this is my first time here, I suspect a city this size will have all the entertainment possibilities you can imagine. But hear this. I expect all of us to behave in a manner which is befitting of the Army of Rome. Some of the activities you are contemplating are acceptable, but there are limits. By now, you should be man enough to understand where these lines are drawn. While this place is certainly far different from Machaerus, I don't want to see or hear about any of you stepping over that line."

The soldiers nodded their heads trying to hide their smiles as we continued our descent. While my warning would not dampen their enthusiasm or willingness to seek debauchery in all its forms, at least the issue had been addressed. Sooner or later some, if not most of these men behind me, would be tempted to test the limits of my word.

****

As we marched through the main gate, excitement filled the air as Roman, Greek, and Jewish cultures mingled, blending together in a cornucopia of languages, clothing, and customs these cultures represented. Fortunately for us, my mastery of languages and the power represented in our uniforms allowed us to navigate through the streets without undo interference, nor did it hurt, that our sweaty, miasma odors, the result of our hard travel, kept many away who ventured within an arms' distance of us.

The soldiers gazed in awe of our surroundings. Tradesmen on every street peddled every conceivable type of merchandise as they bought, sold, and bartered their wares, shouting and gesturing in every possible way to make a profitable exchange. The qualities of their goods ranged from the very best to the very worst, leaving the responsibility to judge a fair price a matter of discernment left to the customer and buyer alike in this fast paced business environment. I also noticed, as did the soldiers, that despite our dirty faces and our well worn looks, enticing smiles came our way from several of the sharp eyed beauties we passed.

With so many sights and sounds enveloping us, we slowly made our way to Antipas' palace, soaking up the atmosphere in hopes of remembering what we saw and heard for later examination. What did Antipas say? Tiberias was his crown jewel. Based on my initial observation, no one could fault his assessment. This city was full of life and vitality; a madhouse of activity.

****

Once inside Antipas' palace, I busied myself first with making sure my soldiers were taken care of, a task accomplished efficiently with the assistance of the palace staff and Kish's knowledge of its surroundings. Then I sought out Sallu, the leader of Antipas' soldiers to learn if Maurus had arrived.

Within a few minutes of my asking, Sallu greeted me in a most gracious manner. Short and stocky, he was a descendant of the tribe of Benjamin, one of the twelve Jewish tribes described in their history, his dark eyes matching his dark curly hair, his mannerisms and speech confirming his reputation as a focused, demanding task master. If his competency equaled his reputation, unlike the challenge of leadership at Machaerus, service here would be relatively easy. During our short discussion, he mentioned Maurus' arrival several days before and that the man was out observing training. With a few hours of daylight remaining and wanting to stretch out my body after the monotonous marching of the past few days, Sallu escorted me to the appropriate training area.

In a dusty corner of the garrison, we found Maurus intently watching some soldiers display their prowess in hand to hand fighting. Unlike the day I watched Valerus train soldiers on similar skills, my new second in command stood apart from these men rather than getting personally involved in the demonstration of techniques. It struck me how different his voice and comportment were from that of my departed friend, his tone and mannerisms gruff and brusque, heavy on criticism, less so on encouragement. The soldiers listened, but I sensed their attention came from duty, not so much out of respect. When he became aware of our presence, Maurus called the group to attention. "Centurion, welcome to Tiberias. It has been a long time since we served together. I look forward to assisting you here."

After a few pleasantries, we agreed to meet at the canteen later that night to discuss our mission. As I walked away from the training, I cautioned myself once again to give this man a chance, and not be too quick to compare him with my departed comrade.

****

The next week passed quickly as I spent the majority of

my time observing Sallu and his soldiers, learning through my observations, these soldiers were physically fit and experts with their weapons. Like all military organizations, there was room for improvement, but from my inspection of these men, there appeared no glaring errors that would necessitate copious amounts of energy to correct.

One night at the soldiers' canteen, I asked Sallu his view of the military issues confronting him. As I expected, he gave me a candid response. "While my force is large and trained to a razor's edge, the truth of the matter is there is no significant military problem here, no real threat. While the people could stage a revolt at anytime, we have no information suggesting the likelihood of that is imminent."

After taking a large swig of his wine, he continued. "The people here don't have the will or the desire to confront either my auxiliary units or elements of the Legion. Nothing could be gained by any attempt on their part to challenge us."

I nodded, "I agree and so therein lays our challenge. How do we create training events to keep you, your subordinate leaders, and your soldiers interested enough to continue to train? In my experience, when a unit believes it can accomplish every task assigned, the unit's expertise and morale slowly begins to erode." I stopped to look at the man. "Training must be challenging to an ever increasing degree, or otherwise boredom will be our enemy. What we must do, my friend, is to develop new and interesting challenges to test both the will and skill of your unit."

With that settled, the two of us spent the rest of the night thinking as we drank, turning loose our creative juices, discussing long into the night ways to challenge his men. It was a worthwhile exercise.

****

With our training plans now developing on the appropriate path, I invested my free time in acquainting myself with Antipas' handiwork in building this monument to Emperor Tiberius, knowing the tetrarch had drained his coffers of considerable funds dry. Everywhere I looked, Rome's culture was in full display, the lines of the buildings clean, bright tall colonnades on many edifices rising to the sky, the evidence of the power and dominance of Rome in abundance, every turn of the head the eyes catching another glimpse of Roman tradition or a bust of one of our heroes. Symbols were ubiquitous; in the theater where trained actors performed Roman comedies, in the stadium which hosted athletic and social events, and at the forum where citizens debated the issues of the day. Within the palace, the tetrarch's desire to show his opulence and affluence knew no limits; a roof made of gold similar to the emperor's home in Rome, life size statues of famous Romans in every room along with furnishings decorated with the most extravagant materials.

Despite the man made marvels of Tiberias, one of the highlights of this city to me were the warm springs the gods created by warming the waters in the sun drenched hills above the city and then allowing them to collect in refreshing pools around the outskirts of the city as they descended toward the sea. I was there at one of my favorite springs when word reached me of Antipas' arrival.

Expecting the difficult journey to have taken its toll on the tetrarch's portly frame, upon reaching the palace I anticipated it would be several days before he recovered enough to see me. However, after informing Cuza of my availability, he surprised me when he ushered me almost immediately into the tetrarch's presence, my thoughts turning to '*What now?*' Such urgency portended trouble, but what kind?

Upon entering his large living area adorned in a similar ornate fashion to that which the man enjoyed at Machaerus, the ruler seemed pleased to see me. "I trust you've found some pleasures here in Tiberias. Once I wash off the dirt of the past few weeks, like you, I'll set my course on enjoying all the splendors afforded me in this wonderful place. Have you enjoyed yourself thus far?"

"The city is beautiful. I must say you have honored the

emperor in every corner."

"Well that's my intent," Antipas said as he spread his arms about, luxuriating on the soft cushions which held up the many folds of his body. Looking out the window staring at the blue brilliance of the Sea of Galilee, he asked, "Aquila, do you like to fish? As long as I've been here, I've never tried my luck on those waters. I'm sure the view from out there would give me a different perspective of Galilee."

"While I've never been much of a fisherman, but perhaps a day on the water might be good." I was not overly excited about the possibility, but one did not turn aside an invitation from the man holding the key to one's future. "Perhaps if we did that, we could use that occasion for me to give you my assessment of your soldiers here. Unlike when we discussed this topic at Machaerus, my report should be more to your liking."

Antipas laughed loudly, the fleshy part of his body rolling about with each guffaw. "You're an amazing man. I can always count on you to redirect my attention to business first, pleasure second. Of course, I want to hear your report. From what you just said, we'll talk about my soldiers on our fishing trip, mixing business with pleasure. I'll tell Cuza to find a boat for us to go out the day after tomorrow. Is there anything I should be made aware of before then?"

"No, nothing that can't wait until my fishing lesson."

After Antipas dismissed me with a wave of his hand, I turned my attention to inspect javelin training, finding the soldiers' skill acceptable, well above standard. While watching these men, my mind drifted to my position at Tiberias. Because of Sallu's leadership, it seemed to me there remained little I could offer in the way of major improvements aside from inventing some new training challenges. Unfortunately, based on my meeting with Antipas, he felt comfortable having me around, yet why waste my time and expertise? Perhaps from Antipas' perspective, he wanted me close to render favorable reports to Pilate. Whatever the reason, until he made a decision to the contrary, my duty remained here.

But like all soldiers, when a degree of boredom sets in, thoughts turn quickly to home and loved ones. I was no exception.

****

Word reached me the next evening to meet Antipas at the stone wharf nearest the palace at dawn for our fishing expedition. Arriving with the first hint of a new day streaking across the eastern sky, Antipas, Cuza, and another servant surprised me by already being at the wharf. Cuza led the way to a boat, introducing Antipas and me to Serung, the captain. Dark skinned with a muscular, strapping frame developed through years of performing all the labor necessary to keep his vessel sea worthy, his watchful look reminded me of what I'd seen many times on the faces of experienced soldiers. Deep calluses covered his enormous hands and his puffy tired eyes told me he spent much of the previous night preparing to host the tetrarch's fishing venture.

Shaped like many of the other boats moored around us, Serung's boat was larger than most, capable of holding the five of us comfortably. Before he untied his vessel from the stony barnacle filled dock, he familiarized us with the features of his craft. Attached to the long sturdy wooden pole fixed to the center of the boat was a single dirty white cloth sail, the primary means of propelling us across the water. Underneath the two seats that crossed the width of the vessel in the front and rear sat two heavy wooden oars for our use in case the wind did not cooperate in a satisfactory manner.

"This is what will bring us fish," the captain said in his deep baritone voice as he held up several hand lines made from heavy fabric wound tightly. "We'll drop our lines over the side at some prime locations, our bait some smelly pieces of fish I caught yesterday, and if all goes well, you'll have fish for dinner." Then Serung smiled, "If that method doesn't meet with their approval, we'll be forced to catch our scaly friends the hard way, by throwing out nets." Looking at our startling faces, he grinned, "Let's hope God smiles on us, and we don't have to do that. Even though I brought several small nets one man can throw, they're heavy even without any fish in them." To help us understand the difference between professional fishermen and those not skilled in this art, he added with a quick smile, "I left the heavier nets on shore since they take several experienced fishermen to handle them."

After releasing the heavy ropes holding us firm to the wharf, the westerly breeze generated the power necessary to propel us easily into deeper water where the dazzling landscape on all points of the compass captured my attention. The towns and cities I had seen when we approached Tiberias from the west, now seemed close enough we could touch them with our outstretched fingers. We shared the water with many other boats, all trying to catch the elusive quarry before the heat of the day. It was an ideal setting, the early morning sky a deep blue, russet greenish hills on all sides, and the calm, sparkling water at our fingertips. Serung explained, "We've only a few hours to catch our prey before they either stopped biting or we face the possibility of an afternoon storm brewing up."

With such beauty so close I gazed intently at the northern shoreline. "Is that Capernaum to our north?"

"Yes, Centurion. It's a large city, although not as ornate as Tiberias. The smaller village to its right at a distance is Bethsaida where I grew up. Most of the boats you see around you come from those two towns." For some unknown reason the man gazed at me as he spoke, "Perhaps you should visit there someday."

Sensing we were in a location where he felt the fish lurked, our captain deployed two large lead anchors, one attached to the front of the boat and the other to the rear. As the anchors splashed into the water, he announced, "These anchors are significant to our success today. They will keep us from moving off this one spot regardless of how hard the winds blows. These anchors were my father's. He taught me many things, first to be a fisherman like him and then, like these anchors, to have some solid immoveable truth to be the bedrock of our lives. Every time I lower these anchors into the depths, I thank him for his teachings and how I fortunate I am to tie my life to something permanent – my God."

Watching the line attached to one of these heavy weights play out into the depths, his statement meant little sense to me at first until it struck me. Was my life anchored on something permanent, something solid? Thoughts of John came flooding back to me. His anchor was his god, a solid, permanent fixture. My anchor was my army and the eagle which symbolized it. Was my anchor as strong as John's?

Serung handed fishing lines to Antipas and me, but the tetrarch declined for us both, passing the lines to Cuza and the other servant, telling them to fish for us as he led the way to the bench at the back of the boat. We barely sat down before the two servants successfully wrestled two black fish a little larger than their hands into the boat, closely following with three larger tilapias which gave them a better fight. With their senses now piqued to enjoy the experience, Antipas felt free to talk. "So, Aquila, tell me about my soldiers. Do they meet your standards?"

"Yes they do. Sallu is a good leader, stern yet approachable, knowledgeable but not so stubborn as to be closed to new ideas. There will always be things to learn and to train on, but from what I've seen, his unit now is better than Shallium's, the soldiers here knowing if they make too many mistakes, there are many other places they could be reassigned not as comfortable as Tiberias. This understanding helps motivate them."

"Good to hear. What about Maurus?"

I hesitated. I treasured loyalty, a key element in our code as soldiers. I expected loyalty from my men just as they expected my loyalty in return. "While he is different from Valerus, he is a good soldier. Although sometimes gruff and overbearing, he is fair and he can be counted on to get the job done." Then I ventured into a recondite, touchier subject, shifting around on the bench before doing so. "With his relationship with Sallu now established, I'm not sure I can contribute much more to your unit's success here. Maurus can do everything here I'm responsible for."

Antipas looked at me before shifting his eyes to watch his head servant haul in another large tilapia. "Save that one for dinner tonight, Cuza."

Rubbing his chin, he leaned back against the wooden frame of the boat for more comfort, the half sneer, half smile across on his face. "Aquila, surely you haven't forgotten your two functions: first, to train of my men and second, to help Pilate and me watch out for what is in Rome's best interest. From what you just said, your first mission is well on the road to success, but I'm concerned about anything which might disrupt the delicate balance of power here in Galilee. Sometimes these peasants have a mind of their own. At times their religious fervor can blow in several directions at the same time and since Galilee is much larger than Perea, its diverse cultures can blend together forming an amalgam which can prove to be uncomfortable from time to time.

He stopped, applauding Cuza once again as the servant hauled in an even larger fish. "Since we have been here only a few days, I'm going to enjoy your company a little longer and assess the situation more completely before I consider recommending your return to Pilate. That sounds reasonable, doesn't it?" his words spoken in a soothing tone like fine oil being spread on the skin of a beautiful woman.

After contemplating his position, I nodded, "I understand." What else could I say? Unless Pilate needed me for something more important, Antipas held me in his grasp. I hoped my disappointment was not too apparent.

To his credit, Antipas then showed remarkable perception. "Aquila, you're a good officer and a good teacher. The day will come when you will be rewarded for your service, but right now, I need to make sure all is quiet here before I consider having you replaced by someone who may not have your abilities and insight. I hope you understand my position."

I nodded my agreement. His words made sense. Through some quirk of nature, if our roles had been reversed, I would have been inclined to make a similar decision. At least the subject had been broached again and the door remained ajar.

Still thinking about Antipas' words, I saw Serung cast an experienced look into the western sky, darker ebullient clouds now blocking out the sun. Catching Antipas' eye, he said, "Sir, the darker clouds in the western sky are showing signs of life. Since we've plenty of fish in the boat that need cleaning, it is time to head for shore before the winds and waves make things unpleasant."

Even before Antipas nodded his approval, the fisherman began to retrieve his anchors. With the threatening sky becoming more ominous by the minute, he made good time returning us to shore ahead of the approaching storm. As Cuza told me later, our captain was cleaning the last of the fish when the rains and the lightening came in earnest, the evening meal of the fresh catch a delight even though I made no contribution to the feast.

****

The days turned into weeks and the weeks into months. With Maurus' assistance, the training events Sallu and I developed were bizarre yet the soldiers reacted well to them, thriving on several of the new tests, standing a little taller each day. After observing one of our training exercises, one involving a house search for some thief, Antipas made it a point to tell Sallu and me his recent dispatches to Pilate included testimony of our efforts to train his soldiers. His comment caused me to wonder, *"Is it time to ask to be reassigned again?"* I prayed to the gods for an answer, but as was their custom, they made no response. I continued to believe reassignment would come, but when?

Late on the last day of January at the conclusion of another arduous day of physical training, I found Cuza waiting for me at the entrance to my quarters. "Centurion, Herod Antipas wishes to see you right away. It is a matter of some urgency. Please come with me."

Without taking time to wash the grime and dirt off my face and hands, I followed the servant as he proceeded briskly toward Antipas' inner living area. We found the ruler there pacing back and forth muttering, sweat coming in large streams down his face staining his gold and purple tunic, his arms flaying about in all directions. I saluted but he didn't acknowledge the courtesy.

Finally looking at me his words came out in quick short bursts, his voice barely under control. "Centurion, I've received several reports of a man here in Galilee making speeches and saying things to my people much like John did months ago, talking about sin, saying the people should turn to God. Could it be that John is back from the dead?" Without waiting for my response, his rampage now in full stride, he spat out, "Some of my advisors think this man is John! Others think he might be another prophet . . . You and I both know John is dead. We saw his eyes turned up in death, his head separated from his body, his blood on the platter, but if this man is not John, who can he be?"

The speed of his pacing increased as he shouted, "Can't be John! Just can't be!" He stopped and stepped right up in front of me, his foul breath reeking of wine, his face only a few inches from my nose, staring at me, his voice trembling, the look in his eyes telling me the man was terrified, panic stricken. "What do you know about this?"

Caught off guard, I took a step back before answering calmly. "Sir, this is the first I've heard of it. I'll dispatch some men to investigate this at once. If the man you speak about is popular with the people, our informants will know something. He shouldn't be too difficult to find."

Flinging his arms about, Antipas set off on another round of circling the room. Then he slowed down, coming to a halt to stare out one of the windows, gazing for a moment at the rays of the retreating sun. Rubbing his hands together, he seemed to gather himself, trying to gain control of his emotions. "Yes, of course. You're right. We will send someone to find him, to find out the truth. We must send out someone I trust, someone who I can rely upon." As he rubbed his chin, his walk back and forth became slower, more controlled. Then he stopped and looked at me, his eyes blazing. "I know exactly who to send." His gaze continued to fall on me. "You, I want you, Centurion, to find this man and find him quickly. Take whatever you need; whoever you need!" Antipas' face was red with rage. He began to pace again before spitting out his directive in a loud venomous hiss, "FIND THIS MAN!"

Chapter IX

Tiberias
Province of Galilee
January 31, A.D. 34

Even though Antipas was badly shaken, his orders were clear: find this man. I knew it wasn't John: his head lopped off, his body long ago buried, clear evidence of his demise on my sandals. So who was this man who was bringing Antipas almost to a state of paralysis? It struck me once again what a spineless, shallow man Antipas was, a man desiring to publically demonstrate courage and grit while inside beat the heart of a pathetic excuse for a leader.

With no time to dwell on that subject, some basic questions required answering. Who was I looking for? What had he done to attract such attention? Where was he last seen and when? Obviously Antipas knew the answers to some of these questions but he shared none of them with me. He was too disturbed, too agitated. To approach him for any of this information would only incur his wrath. Where could I turn regarding the details of this matter? The answer was Cuza. He was always at Antipas' side listening, watching, following the directions of his master, the silent yet efficacious man behind the scenes. Later that evening, I stopped the servant as he left Antipas' living area. Bowing deeply, he asked, "Can I be of assistance to you, Centurion?"

"As you know, someone is causing your master great distress. From what he indicated, this man must be somewhere in Galilee, but I need some information to begin my search. Since you're always at his side, you hear everything he hears. Can you give me a name, a place, some clue to help point me in the right direction? Based on Antipas' state of mind, my last resort is to ask him these questions."

Cuza nodded as he led me into the garden where we stood underneath the spreading limbs of two olive trees, the stars sparkling through the branches overhead, a full moon with its round luster silently making its appearance over the eastern sky, its light poking through the limbs of the trees, a light breeze adding to the peaceful setting, the sweet smell of flowers remaining in the cool early evening air.

The servant studied me but said nothing. Was he measuring me? He closed his eyes and gave a great sigh before breaking this long period of silence. "Your questions appear simple, however they're difficult; difficult because the answers may lead to consequences beyond anyone's control." He stopped to take in the stars above us. "I've been with the tetrarch for many years. I've seen him perform admirably and with great understanding. And at other times, I watched him blatantly sin against Almighty God, like when he married Herodias which led, as we both know, to John's death."

He rubbed his cheek for a long time before he asked, "If I help you, what do you think will be the outcome? What assurances can you give me your pursuit will not lead to the death of another good man?"

This servant, this slave was questioning me? What nerve! With my temper rising quickly, I spoke out my fury through clenched teeth. "Your speech borders on treason, Cuza. You're asking if you can trust me? . . . Me, a Roman Centurion! My loyalty, my willingness to abide by the truth is not in question here!"

The man gazed back at me – as one man looks at another man – not as servant answering a superior. Courage and conviction came through his next words. "Centurion, you're loyal to your Emperor and to the eagle of your Army. You answer to them. My loyalty is to my God and I answer to Him."

We both stood silently, each evaluating the other. Cuza's eyes went skyward again as he studied the night sky in all its glory. I looked in the same direction, seeing the sparkling lights but nothing more. What was he looking for? Were the answers he sought found in those faraway shining orbs? Finally he turned back to face me. "You're right. I know much of what concerns Antipas. I asked God for his blessing to tell you what I know. In my prayers he told me to trust you and so I shall."

God. Prayers. When would this ever stop? I let the cool air slow my thoughts and my fervor to accomplish the task given me. If this man felt led to trust me, then he deserved an honest answer in return, servant or not, this conversation fast approaching a point of mutual understanding that crossed the bounds of Roman and Jew, of superior and subordinate. We now faced each other, man to man.

"Cuza, regarding your questions, I've no way of knowing how this will all end. Because of what you've heard and because you know Antipas so well, I suspect you have a far better idea than me about the ultimate outcome of my search. What I do know is Antipas is greatly troubled and he's given me a task. I don't seek to place anyone in peril. My task is to find this man and report back to Antipas. What he decides to do at that point is his decision, not mine."

The man searched my face, his eyes steady, holding me in their grasp. "Centurion, one honest response deserves another. My task in this world is to serve Antipas, my earthly master. While I take this mission, this life's assignment seriously, the highest priority in my life is pleasing and obeying my God."

I held up my hand still frustrated by all this religious nonsense. "Why must everything in this country revolve around your god? Why is that important?"

"Because I follow my God's leading and direction in all matters." He paused. "Your soldiers hold you in high esteem because of your character, because you are a man who knows right from wrong. Perhaps that is why God wants you to hear what I know."

After looking around to insure we were alone, he said, "When John taught the multitudes at the Jordan, my wife, Joanna, and I found time to go one day and be baptized. We became followers of John, true believers of God through his message. After Antipas imprisoned him at Machaerus, God called upon me to bring the two of them together in hopes Antipas would see the errors of his transgressions. While I prayed many times for a change of heart in Antipas, I will carry the memory of John's bloody head on that platter to my grave. It was a sad day."

I shook my head slowly. "You carry a heavy weight on your shoulders, Cuza. Loyal to such opposite men: John and Antipas. It must be difficult every time you see Herodias considering her part in this tragedy, yet how is this related to the man Antipas talked about? Who is the one I'm looking for? Is there really a man who is stirring up the people? Or is just a hoax?"

Cuza gave me a wry smile before speaking in hushed reverence. "The man you seek is real. I've not heard him speak, but Joanna has. She tells me how he heals the crippled and the sick, how his eyes shine when he talks about the majesty of God and how crowds travel great distances to hear his voice and feel his touch." The excitement in the man's voice grew. "She tells me while John's message was strong and powerful, this second man speaks as though he has authority over all matters regarding our God. As John told us months ago, one day another would come whose message was more powerful and of such stature John could not even untie his sandals. From everything Joanna and others have told me, I believe the man you seek could be the one written about in our scriptures, our Messiah, the Savior of our people."

I stood still, waiting. Here was more Messiah talk. Rather than divert my attention to these comments, I focused on my goal. "From what you've just told me, Cuza, I'd like to meet this man regardless of Antipas' charge to me, but there is clearly some urgency for me to report back to Antipas. What is this man's name?"

The servant gave me a knowing smile. "I believe you heard his name at Nain." He gave me an encouraging pat on the back. "I wish you well in your search, and when you find this man, perhaps he will satisfy the stirring in your heart. Goodnight."

Jesus of Nazareth. That was name the young man told me. How did Cuza know that? Did one of my soldiers or Kish share that with him? What was I in the midst of, and why me? I turned to my gods beseeching them for a response, for some guidance. Their silence remained defining, the only resemblance of an answer from any god came when the moon cast its bright light down upon the blood stains on my sandals. While I fought against it, my mind replayed the events of that night once again.

****

The thought jerked me out my sleep in the middle of the night – Nazareth – Start the search there. After telling Sallu and Maurus I'd be gone for several days, I hastily detailed Reuel and another soldier to accompany me as messengers. From a quick study of the maps, I estimated we could reach this small town in a day. While there was a small Roman garrison there, I chose not to depend upon them for anything, the fewer who know of my journey, the better.

Our route to Nazareth early the next morning took us westward across the major trade route which ran from Damascus to our northeast, south to Jerusalem. We continued west through the valley floor filled with wild flowers and a variety of trees - olive and fig, mulberry and lemon - all blending together in a redolent aroma. While it would have been easy to get caught up in the peacefulness of this place, our goal lay in the higher hills which dominated this beautiful countryside.

Nazareth sat at the top of the hills we saw in the distance. With sharp cliffs on the eastern slopes facing us confirmed my understanding the town lay close to this drop off, the best approach was up a trail on the northern side of the hills. While small fields of corn and wheat grew near the trail, the ground tended to be rocky and barren. Near dusk we passed the first few modest homes signaling the end of our journey to this town a thousand people called home. Since the sight of a Roman was not uncommon here, we met no interruptions as we walked our horses through the narrow streets finding a modest inn near the center of town.

After washing most of the dirt off my feet and hands, I met my two soldiers in the dingy, dark dining area of the inn, our only light coming from several candles placed strategically around the small room. When we sat down at the empty corner table, two other men who occupied the table in the opposite corner quickly finished their food without a word and left, leaving us alone. The meal of fowl, quail I guessed, and lentils we ordered from the innkeeper came soon enough, some crusty old bread and goat cheese alongside. A large jug of red wine was also brought to our table, the strong scent drawing our attention. The food was warm, the quality reasonable, reminding the three of us why we sought comfort in an inn rather than spending the evening at the nearby Roman garrison.

As I was finishing my meal, the innkeeper, a portly elderly man, his clothes giving off the aroma of the food we just ate, approached our table, a concerned expression on his face. He was no doubt, the owner, the cook, and the caretaker of this one-man business. After a short bow he asked permission to sit down.

With my approving nod and after pulling another bench close to our table, the man asked, "Centurion, with your garrison just west of town, it's most unusual to have Roman soldiers staying in my inn." He muttered, "I'm pleased to have your business, but if I may, what brings you to our quiet town? Are you staying for just one night?" Going through his battery of questions without pausing for a breath, it was obvious he was uncomfortable with us in his establishment. I was also sure, as the town's innkeeper, it was his responsibility to funnel all visitor information to the rest of the townspeople.

I glanced at Reuel who understood the discussion between me and the innkeeper might require confidentiality. Raising his eyebrows, he motioned to his comrade, the two of them excusing themselves, moving to the vacated table at the other corner but not before securing another jug of wine for their trouble.

Before beginning a dialogue with this man, I reminded myself of the talk I had given myself during the day's travels. After these last six months with Jews all around me, I had begun to understand some of their mannerisms and their views toward me as a Roman. While I knew the vast majority would always see me as an enemy, a conqueror, if I approached any Jew with the typical stern officious tone of a Roman Centurion, an insurmountable barrier would undoubtedly appear between me and those from whom I was seeking information. My demeanor, my manner had to more open, disarming to a point, treating others as I would wished to be treated, knowing I would not get any details about Jesus unless I sincerely wished for others to share what they knew. Could I do this? Could I be a better listener? Here was the first test: *keep my stern, serious, commanding voice out of the conversation.*

"Innkeeper, we've come with peaceful intentions seeking information about a man who hails from your town, a man called Jesus of Nazareth. What can you tell me about him, and perhaps, can you direct me to his home where I may speak to him or to his relatives in the morning? Again, my intentions are peaceful. I mean no harm."

The man hesitated a bit, his eyes shifting back and forth from me to my soldiers who laughed in the corner over some joke as he wrestled with my request. Finally he said, "Yes, Jesus grew up here. Spent most of his life walking these streets. Hasn't been around here lately. Why do you ask?"

"I've heard his name recently. Could you tell me about his family?"

The man poured himself a large goblet of wine. After filling my cup, he wiped the sweat off his brow with the filthy cloth tucked in his woven belt. "Father was Joseph, a man whose linage can be traced back to King David, perhaps our greatest king. He was the town's carpenter." The innkeeper bobbed his head up and down. "His work was of such quality, many of his pieces are still in use today." The man looked down at our table. "In fact, he made this table maybe twenty five, thirty years ago, that table over there as well," he said pointing to where my soldiers sat. "They've got a few scars on them and you can see the wear, but the workmanship is superb."

I nodded my agreement as the man continued. "Besides being a good carpenter, he was a good man, a man of integrity." The innkeeper stared at the door for a moment as though he expected

Joseph to suddenly make an appearance. "Even though he died some years ago, I remember his face, his laugh. Mary, his wife, some years younger, still lives here. A most gracious woman. Jesus was their first. Four other sons followed: James, Joseph, Judas, and Simon as well as several daughters." The man stopped, keeping his focus on his wine goblet.

"Anything unusual or different about Jesus as he grew up?"

The man laughed softly. "Centurion, almost everything about that boy was unusual. Joseph and Mary were good parents to all their children, but as the first born, Jesus received special attention. Very polite boy. Don't recall him ever getting into the mischievousness most children seem to find. Like the others, he spent his early years close to his mother until at age five, as is normal for our children, he attended the synagogue school studying Moses' writings and those of our other great prophets. Even now, Jesus' teachers still talk about how his inquisitive nature challenged them. He was a remarkable young man, serious, mature well beyond his years. After he completed his synagogue education, he sat under Joseph's tutelage, learning to be a skilled carpenter and craftsman."

I took a large swallow of wine before asking, "Anything else stand out about him?"

The man thought for a moment, some faraway look on his face. "Here is something you may find interesting. When Jesus was twelve, Joseph and Mary went to Jerusalem to celebrate the Feast of the Passover. On their way back here they discovered the boy was missing from the traveling party; couldn't be found anywhere. After an exhaustive search, they decided to return to Jerusalem, searching frantically for him throughout the city for three days. Finally, they discovered him at the temple courts asking questions of many learned scholars and weighing their responses. Imagine a young lad trading comments with some of the best minds in the land."

I nodded, thinking about my children lost in a large city. I could picture my frantic search for them and then my relief when at last, I held them safe in my arms.

The man in front of me stared at the unadorned wall of his establishment for several minutes before speaking. "There is another story I'll share with you, even though it's not one I'm proud of." Remaining quiet, I knew something troubled him, something in the depths of his being.

Gathering himself, he gave a great sigh before his words tumbled out, his eyes now staring at some small spot on our table. "Several years ago Jesus traveled south to the Jordan River where he was baptized by John, his cousin; the same man killed by Herod Antipas some months back. Anyway, after this baptism, Jesus came back here and left his carpentry business to his brothers, focusing his energies on studying the scriptures."

The portly man shifted slightly in his seat, his head still down, his voice barely a whisper. "One Sabbath morning as was his custom, he joined the rest of us in the synagogue. On this particular day he stood, unrolled the scroll of our prophet Isaiah to a specific passage and read, 'The Spirit of the Lord is upon me because he has anointed me to preach good news to the poor.' All of us in the congregation sat still not knowing what to say. Then Jesus said very distinctly, 'Today this scripture is fulfilled in your hearing.'

"Well I'll tell you, the crowd couldn't stand it. The whole place erupted, people turning to each other asking, 'Is he saying he is the Messiah? It can't be! He is Joseph's son!' Most of us were very angry at the audacity of this man. Then everyone turned against him when he said, 'No prophet was accepted in his hometown.' We all became incensed, shouting 'Blasphemer! Blasphemer!' as we drove him out of the synagogue, shoving and pushing him toward the bluffs east of town, right to the brow of the cliffs, intent on watching him being dashed on the rocks below. But somehow, almost like a miracle, he seemed to walk right through us and left untouched." The man stopped, looking at me with sad eyes as he slumped back in his seat, his shoulders dropping.

Neither of us spoke until I rose from my seat. "I'll get directions to Mary's house tomorrow."

He glanced up at me. "Sir, I normally don't seek to spend my time with Roman soldiers and certainly not with a Centurion . . . yet something told me to share these stories with you. You're different from the others who wear your country's uniform." He downed the remains of his goblet as he smiled up at me. "We'd make a strange picture wouldn't we, Centurion; you, a symbol of Roman power, talking with a simple innkeeper from a small remote village about a carpenter's son. Yes sir, a very strange picture."

I nodded my agreement but said nothing. Later on my straw bed, the innkeeper's words kept me tossing: Jesus was raised in Nazareth . . . related to John . . . sent by his god to be this long awaited Jewish Messiah. It didn't make any sense. Jesus was an interesting man, but Messiah? He had no credentials for such a title, no training, no wealth, no pedigree. Yet, could the accounts at Nain be so easily dismissed? My last thought before my fatigue gripped me was the innkeeper's observation: was I really that much different from my fellow officers?

****

Early the next morning, I made the short walk up the dusty street to Mary's home, my two soldiers remaining at the inn awaiting my instructions. Mary's home, like so many others I observed at Nazareth and in the other small villages, was a one story brown and sand colored structure made of bricks covered by mortar, the roof made of thatch grass. The front of the home was neat and orderly, fine workmanship in evidence on all the woodwork around all the windows and doors. Attached to the left side of the home was a smaller open-air structure, saws, chisels, and other tools hanging from the beams supporting the grass roof, several benches and tables scattered about with hammers and planes near them. A thigh high rock wall separated the home and the attached work space from the dusty street where I now stood. Before I could approach the front door of the home, a man a few years younger than me came out from the work area.

So focused was he on his work, he took no notice of me as he sat on one of his benches under the lone sycamore tree in the yard working on a door frame propped up against the tree. Small strips of wood began to fall to the ground as he expertly drew his small plane back and forth along the edge of the wood, taking time every few strokes to run his hand across the wood inspecting its smoothness, his rhythm unhurried yet effective. Like professionals in many trades, each of his movements was instructional to a novice like me as he applied his skill to the project with choreographed efficiency. After watching him for a few moments marveling at his application of his craft, I called out to him asking if I could speak to Mary.

The man stopped his work, blowing away some more dust from his last swipe of the plane as he examined his work. Satisfied, he got to his feet, walking over toward me. He was of medium stature, his long dark hair matching the color of his beard, the color of his eyes, a deep blue like the sky, his frame strong. "Why are you asking for my mother, Centurion? I'm sure she's done nothing to warrant any concern."

Another test. Could I first be a man before thinking of myself as a Roman officer? "I'm sure you're right. I have a few questions I'd like to ask her about her son, Jesus, if she is available."

The man took time to mop the sweat from his brow with a dark stained rag that magically appeared in his hand. It was then I noticed his large forearms, undoubtedly the result of many hours plying the tools of his trade. "Jesus is my brother, although I haven't seen him in some time. My mother's not here either, away for a time visiting some distant family members south of Jerusalem. Don't expect her back for several months." The man paused, "Word reached me you might be looking for her. What can I do to help you?"

I smiled, both at myself and at the man in front of me, marveling at how quickly word came to him of my interest. "Since your mother isn't here, could you spare me a few moments to tell me about your brother. I mean no harm."

The man hesitated and then pointed to the bench under the tree where he had been working. "Guess that couldn't hurt. Have a seat."

A few steps took me through the opening in the rock wall and after brushing the accumulation of wood chips off the bench I sat down and asked, "Your name, sir?"

"I'm James, the second son of Joseph and Mary. Jesus is my older brother by several years." Looking at the man closer, I noticed his hands showed numerous scars and bruises. While I had seen him practicing his trade with great aplomb a few moments earlier, these marks told me of the many hours of trial and error required to master his craft. "What concerns you about my brother?"

I looked at the carpenter for a moment. "I've heard his name mentioned in various places and wanted to learn more about him. As I told your innkeeper last night, your brother is a most interesting man." Now was not the time to bring up Antipas' interest, certain any mention of his name would result in the sundering of my efforts.

James gave me a hard penetrating stare, perhaps judging me as one worthy of hearing anything about his brother. "My brother is a man of great integrity and high morals, but there have been some times when I, like some others, have difficulty understanding him, times when it almost seems like I never knew him." Then he stopped. "I'm not sure, why I'm telling you any of this. Maybe it's because our innkeeper spoke highly of you. Is his judgment correct?"

"James, your thoughts will be held in confidence. As I said before, I'm here to learn more about your brother." I caught myself – *Antipas sent me on this mission* - yet the more I found out about Jesus, the more I wanted to learn about him for my sake, not just because of Antipas' order. "What can you tell me about him?"

The man's hand went to his mouth, rubbing it thoughtfully. "While we enjoyed a normal childhood, it was apparent to all of us siblings my brother's interest in the scriptures was much deeper than ours. Whereas most of us labored through our studies, his thirst for knowledge about the prophets and their writings was unquenchable."

"Sounds as though he undertook his schooling with more vigor than the rest of you."

The man laughed, "That's a good way to put it. And because of that, we envied the attention he received, perhaps jealous may be a better word," as the man's head dropped. "Like the rest of us boys, when he finished his formal education at the synagogue, he worked with our father learning this trade. In time he became skilled in this profession, pouring all his energies into it, trying to match our father's skill. His workmanship was always of high quality and he never charged more for any work than was appropriate." James stopped, looking down at his hands. "Then one day everything changed."

"What do you mean?"

He picked up a nearby plane, caressing it as only a man skilled in its use could. "After he received some type of special anointing from John, our cousin, Jesus came back here with several other men who hung on his every word. One of the first things he did was to turn his entire carpentry business over to me. When I asked my mother about this, she gave me the strangest look, telling me not to be concerned, telling me later Jesus had more important things to do. From my point of view, I found it quite distressing."

James stopped speaking, appearing to be deep in thought as he stared at one of the distant hills to the east. "When was the last time you saw him?" I asked.

"Ah it's been a while . . . your question brings back some strange memories."

I looked up, "Why do you say that?"

After kicking the dirt with his sandals, James' words came out slowly at first. "Some good friends of ours from Cana, a small town a few hours north of here, invited our family to attend a wedding there. It was the typical week-long celebration with many banquets for the invited guests."

"Must have been quite a crowd."

"It was, almost the whole town turned out for the celebration. On the third day of the gathering, because of poor planning on someone's part, my mother noticed the wedding party was running out of wine. I was sitting near her when, for some bizarre reason, she told Jesus to do something about this. I wondered what could he do, but the two of them spoke in hushed tones for a few minutes. The next thing I knew, my mother told the servants standing nearby to go with Jesus and follow his instructions. Without another word Jesus and the servants left the banquet and when the servants returned a short time later, they each carried a large jug into the banquet area setting them in front of the master of the banquet. After the man sampled the liquid from the jugs, he announced to the entire wedding party with an addled look on his face these jars held the choicest wines."

I looked at James. "I don't understand. What happened?"

"Those were my questions. Later I quizzed one of the servants who told me when Jesus left with them he found six large stone water jars each capable of holding twenty to thirty gallons of water for ceremonial washing in a storage area. As you can imagine, these were not the cleanest of jars."

James played with the plane for another moment before putting it down. "This servant told me Jesus instructed him and the others to fill these unclean jars up with water and then draw some out and take it immediately to the master of the banquet. Although quite baffled by his words, the servants complied. Somehow, Jesus mysteriously changed the water into choice wine. I have no idea how he did it, I just know he did."

James stared at me, adding, "From that day on, my brothers and I have been more confused than ever about Jesus. We've even heard rumors that he's healed men who had been lame and blind, but I've never talked to anyone personally who claims to have witnessed this. As far as I know, these words may all just be rumors."

I glanced at the man, appraising his tale of the water being changed into wine. "Some of what you've heard may have some foundation." I thought of the young man at Nain but said nothing about him. "I must admit I too am puzzled by things I hear about your brother. Any idea where I might find him?"

"No. Whenever I hear things about him, it's always after the fact although I understand he spends much of his time near Capernaum."

I nodded my head. Capernaum. "Before I take my leave, is there anything else I should know about him?"

James looked at the carpentry tools surrounding him before answering, his head down as though deep in thought. "Maybe just one thing. For some time I harbored some resentment toward him. He was an excellent carpenter. Our business was thriving when he left it all behind. Your questions this morning have helped me recall some of our early years, some of the good times our family experienced. My brother is a remarkable man. Perhaps in my dealings with him my tongue has gotten the better of me from time to time."

I sat quietly before saying, "I'm not sure what you mean."

"Centurion, for many months my brothers and I have had great difficulty when we hear stories about our brother. We . . . we have trouble believing them. But the more I hear about him, or least what's attributed to him, the more I want to believe that what we hear about him is true. And like all men, from time to time, we allow our tongues to spout out words filled with venom and guile before we think of the harm they might do. I know I have."

As I took my first few strides back toward the inn, James' words reminded me of how my quick tongue, my quick judgment of the strengths and weaknesses of others, caused alienation of some from me. Yet the more steps I took, I knew as a Centurion it was my role to assess, adjudicate, and yes, judge those around me. James' words made sense for a common man, but not for me. My role required much more. If I offended others by my brisk nature and quick tongue that was their issue, not mine.

Chapter X

Tiberias
Province of Galilee
Early evening February 5, A. D. 34

A waft flowed through Antipas' throne room causing the candle light to produce haughty dancing figures along the walls as the setting sun threw its fading rays around the room as I walked in, Antipas leaning forward in his royal chair, anticipating my arrival. Three of his closest advisors hovered about, their faces alternating between grinning and glaring at me. Wiping some wine from the corner of his mouth, the ruler slurred, his voice impatient and shrill, "Well, Aquila, what do you have for me? Have you found this rogue who is causing me distress and sleepless nights?" Antipas leaned back, the creases on his brow deeper than normal, an anxious look on his face.

While retracing my steps back to Tiberias, I dreaded this meeting. His questions were neither unexpected nor was the uncertainty of his mood. Despite my preparation for this hour, my thoughts remained unsettled. What should I tell Antipas; everything I had learned about Jesus or none of it or maybe something in between? The latter course of action seemed best. If I blabbered out everything I'd heard thus far about Jesus, raising the young man back to life at Nain, his comments in the synagogue, changing water into wine, these few comments could generate a hornet's nest of activity much like a week's long torrential rain descending into a dry sun baked wadi, flooding a barren creek bed with an unstoppable flood sweeping away anything in its path.

My experience in the army taught me a simple truth: the first report of any action always contained threads of incorrect information, elements requiring revision and further clarification as additional details surfaced. With this in mind, I judged it best my comments paint a broad picture so as more details emerged, a more complete portrayal of the evidence could be revealed in its proper context. Something about Antipas' mood and those of his advisors, all of whom desired to curry favor from him, told me whatever was said tonight could be the first steps down a precarious path from which there might be no recovery.

"Sir, let me first say what I tell you should give you relief from your sleepless nights."

Antipas' hand went to his chin, rubbing it, a sign he was listening with great interest.

"After you gave me orders to find the man who is stirring up your people, I began my search in the town of Nazareth."

One of his advisors, the one with the pot belly and bald head, laughed as he interrupted. "Why Nazareth? That dump, that no nothing, do nothing spot on the map."

I looked at the surly drunken fool, fixing him with a gaze intended to convey a message of disgust. If he had been one of my soldiers, he would have received far worse than a repulsive glare. After staring at the fool for a long uninterrupted moment, my attention shifted back to Antipas. "I started my search there because we received a report earlier of a religious leader from that town who might fit the description you gave me. Through several interviews I conducted in there, I'm convinced this man is not John nor is he holding himself up as such. As you stated several days ago, John is dead and I've found no evidence suggesting he has risen from the dead. The man from Nazareth is a Jewish preacher, well versed in the scriptures, who has performed what some refer to as miracles. It will take more investigation before I can provide you detailed information about him. My comments today are based on only a few days of inquiry and are intended to alleviate your concerns about John."

Waving over one of the nearby servants to refill his wine goblet, Antipas immediately relaxed as he settled back into the soft cushions of his chair, a huge sigh coming from deep inside his chest, relief spreading across his countenance, the wrinkles on his brow now receding. With the nod of his head he sneered, "So, if I understand you correctly, I can rest knowing we are not dealing with John once again. Is that right?""

"That's correct."

"A great relief to me, Aquila . . . a great relief," sighing once again as he emptied his wine goblet in one gulp, calling for the servant to fill the cup once again before closing his eyes, a smirk coming slowly to lips. After a few moments of reflection, Antipas stared at me. "Now regarding this man from Nazareth, continue your search for him. We must learn more about him and these so-called miracles." He looked at the men surrounding him and laughed. "It's certainly not beneficial to have his kind giving hope to the population in something other than what my magnanimous government can provide, can we? If this man you're talking about is hindering me, well . . . we'll handle him at the appropriate time and in the appropriate manner later." He gave me a villainous smile. "We know how to deal with his kind don't we, Centurion."

A shiver ran through me. Antipas was talking about killing Jesus or, at the very least, imprisoning him away from those he might influence. But killing him? Here this cowardly ruler was suggesting I could be the instrument of his violence once again, a judgment he didn't have the courage to do himself. Why kill a man who helped others, who healed the sick, and who may have brought someone back to life? This cruel thinking needed to be redirected.

Ignoring his minions who were as gutless as their ruler, I said quietly, "Antipas, I don't believe we're at the point where we need to consider eliminating such a man. As you told me before, it wouldn't be in your best interests to incite the people's ire. If the man we're speaking about is healing the sick, it sounds to me your people would take umbrage to any action against him. Our proceedings   need to be carefully thought through first, not undertaken on a few bits of information that, when more thoroughly investigated, may have little validity."

The tetrarch leaned forward in his seat considering my words as he took another large gulp from his goblet. "I understand, Aquila, your counsel is as always sound." With a shrug, he finished his thought, "If later we find something more sinister about him, we can always bring some penal justice to bear if and when it is required."

Smirking at the men at his elbows, he pointed his finger in my direction. "Continue your investigation and keep me informed." With the order given, he focused on his wine and his other advisors, their laughter following me as I exited the room.

****

Upon leaving Antipas' chambers, I sought out Cuza. Having been present in the back corner of the room throughout my discussion with Antipas, he witnessed our exchange, his somber look telling of his concerns. "Thank you for trying to help Antipas understand Jesus is not a threat to him personally, but I fear if Jesus ever comes before either Antipas or others like him, he'll be in grave danger." The servant looked down, stealing a glance at the stain on my sandals. "It was good of you not to mention Jesus by name."

"It was neither the time nor place." I pressed my lips. This man in front of me knew so much but shared so little. While he trusted me in part, would his confidence appreciate? "Jesus' brother, James, mentioned Capernaum. Does this agree with knowledge you have about Jesus' whereabouts?"

Cuza gave me an intriguing glance as he slowly nodding, "Yes, Capernaum would be a wise choice. If you go there talk with Lucius, the Centurion of the Roman garrison. He's been stationed in the city for a number of years and he is revered by the Jewish leaders having contributed substantial funds to them to help build their new synagogue. He's a good man."

Cuza paused for a moment before continuing with greater conviction. "Yes, if I were you I would search for Jesus at Capernaum." Without another word, he bowed and walked away.

Was I a leader in this drama or just a puppet on a string being pulled here and there by some great power in a maze that seemed to have no exit?

Searching for some answers, I spent the next few hours walking through the streets of Tiberias seeking a quiet place of refuge. With the sun now well below the horizon, the stars and moon dominated the sky, my wanderings led me to the wharf where Serung moored his boat. Seeing the anchors on the vessel, they reminded me again how my life seemed to be adrift, being tossed about by the unruly tides and winds of life, confusing me, weakening my confidence in my inner core, unlike Serung's anchors which his vessel secure on solid rock on a stormy sea.

Greeks philosophers, men such as Aristotle, Anaxagorsa, and Socrates whom we Romans studied and admired, wrote about the complex meanings of life, of knowledge versus ignorance, and how lives should be examined. Their words sounded grand and meaningful, yet what good would their teachings and reflections be to me now? So much rambled through my mind – the Jews' God, their fixation on a Messiah, miracles now attributed to Jesus – what was true, what was false? I was not a deep thinker, one who dwelled on complex knotty issues, one who spent countless attempts to solve the mysteries of life. Confusing me even more was Valerus' unexpected plea to seek John's God. Like me, my friend was not one easily entangled in the complexities of this world. He and I were alike: simple soldiers wishing to leave the deep thoughts of the universe to someone else, yet . . . As I stood on the wharf watching the tethered boats bob up and down on the dark waters of the night, my eyes focused on the outline of Capernaum in the distance. Where the answers to my quest there? Part of me screamed '*Yes*' while another part of my mind responded with a quieter more hushed response, denying that my questions could be so easily answered.

****

Capernaum. Even though it was only a few hours away by horseback, I elected to have Reuel accompany me. I was growing to enjoy his company, not only because of his intelligence, but because he exhibited the traits of being a superb leader one day. A man of few words, when he offered his opinion his comments were well thought out, containing choice morsels of information rather than meaningless drivel. Fast becoming my personal bodyguard, I trusted him completely.

It was an easy ride early the next morning along the coastal road, the Sea of Galilee on our right, the low hills of Galilee on our left. Far to the north we caught glimpses of Mt. Hermon, the dominating mountain in the region. Known as the mountain of snow, Hermon's three snow covered peaks graced the area with white sparkling luster shining down from its slopes, snow and ice packed in its lofty elevation ready to release cold water south in the spring and summer months to feed the Sea of Galilee.

With this glorious nature alive in all directions around us, the rhythmic gait of our horses allowed my mind to wander. Surely some Supreme Being or Beings orchestrated all of what my eyes saw today. How else could this synchronization of land and matter be thrown together without someone, something knitting it into such harmony? Something had to account for the multiple shades of blue on the Sea of Galilee changing each moment as gentle tide lapped on to the pebbled shore coupling with the browns and greens of the gentle land. Likewise, what being built the massive mountain to the north that supervised the landscape like a shepherd caring for his flock with the cloudless sky above it all with no end to its depth, the dazzling sun preeminent overseeing this spectacle with its magnificent rays of light. Yes, there had to be gods like Jupiter and Mars, Venus and Vulcan, cooperating with each other, otherwise how could this amalgamation of matter come into being? The earth was far too large for only one god to have brought all this into being; all this orderliness was far too complex for just one god.

****

Once inside Capernaum's gates, the strength and the grandeur of the city's numerous buildings confirmed its prosperity, the homes equaling those found in Tiberias, the streets wide, the merchants trading their goods at a frenetic pace in the commercial area near the front gates. Before reaching the Roman garrison, we passed the Jewish synagogue, its tall colonnades giving this structure a regal appearance, white limestone dominate instead of the local black basalt, the main building two stories tall, a variety of figures adorning the walls. In the adjacent garden was a large fountain, its elaborate decorations paying tribute to the city's long and colorful history.

After passing through the main gate of the Roman garrison and leaving Reuel to care for our horses, a guard directed me to the Centurion's secretary who ushered me down a long, wide hallway into a large room, one side facing an open air portico. Before I could begin to enjoy my surroundings, a tall, athletic officer entered the room, introducing himself as Lucius, the Centurion of Capernaum's garrison. He was a model soldier with impeccable military bearing, his uniform immaculate, metal shined to the highest standard, his eyes a steady blue. I judged him to be ten years my senior, a conclusion reached because of his receding hairline and his stature as my superior by several ranks in the Centurion ranks. A short, thin servant, certainly older than his master, stood motionless at his side. After receiving a friendly nod from his master, the servant bowed, scurrying off to perform some task.

Lucius guided me out into the portico where several large date palms cast their shadows over the tile floor, a cool refreshing breeze providing respite from the increasing heat of the day. After sitting down on two of the wooden chairs near a large table, my host began our conversation. "Aquila, it's a pleasure to meet you. I've heard good things about you, your reputation as a first class trainer has found its way to my ears."After some small talk about several mutual acquaintances, he asked, "So what brings you here? Has Antipas dispatched you to give me some training advice or are you here to inspect my Legionnaires at Pilate's behest?"

I laughed, "Ah, Lucius, you know better. You require no help from me to keep your men in a ready state. My role in this frontier is to bring the auxiliary units under Antipas up to a standard to give creditable assistance to your Legionnaires if and when they are needed." I leaned forward in my seat. "I'm here on a mission assigned specifically to me by Antipas, a task requiring sensitivity and confidentiality. As I think about it, I don't believe Pilate knows anything about what I involved in."

The older man eyed me closely. "Well, now you have my curiosity with this mysterious introduction. Fortunately, it's quiet right now in our city and in the surrounding area so you're not interrupting anything of great importance." He paused for a moment. "Your choice of words - sensitivity and confidentiality - piques my interest. Do I detect a sense of urgency connected with your visit as well?" It was obvious a man of his stature had dealt with strange tasks over the years training him to be unflappable in such cases, a trait common to most senior officers. "So what is this challenge our Galilean ruler requires of you?"

As I was about to speak, Lucius' servant appeared at his side, placing a jug of cool water on the table before us along with a platter of assorted cheeses, grapes, and other small pieces of fruit for our enjoyment. With a smile from his master, the man left as silently as he had appeared, Lucius watching him depart. "Jorim has served me for many years, so long, in fact, we consider him part of our family. Because of this relationship, he anticipates what I want without a word from me." Setting his eyes upon me, he gave me his full attention. "So please, tell me how I can be of service to you?"

After a quick sigh to clear my thoughts, the words began to tumble out. "Lucius, to put everything in context, let me start at the beginning. As I suspect you know, some months ago, Antipas killed John, an influential Jewish prophet. In the last week, Antipas received word of a man traveling throughout Galilee teaching and preaching to the people in a manner reminiscent of John." I stopped to sip some of the water from the cup in front of me. "Some of Antipas' advisors suggest the man here in Galilee may be John come back to life. Others believe him to be one of the Jewish prophets of old. These reports troubled Antipas even though he saw

John's bloody head adorning a shiny platter months ago."

The senior officer sat still before commenting without emotion. "I've heard stories about John so it's understandable why Antipas would be concerned. If he really believes a man from his past haunts him, his fear is natural." He stopped for a moment to sample several grapes, laughing as he ate them. "I wonder how Mors, our god of death, would react to someone escaping his grasp, but please continue."

"Since I've been training his soldiers for some time and he trusts me, he gave me the task of finding this second man and solving this mystery. Based on my initial findings, I informed Antipas several days ago this man in question is not John returning from the dead. While this calmed him down, he still wants me to find this second man. From what I've determined thus far, I believe the man I'm looking for is Jesus of Nazareth. It seems he may have some connection with Capernaum as I've been told he frequents this area." I stopped to catch my breath glad to be sharing this burden with such a distinguished soldier. "I've come to see if you've heard of him and since you've been stationed here for a number of years, it seems if anyone knows anything about Jesus or his travels near Capernaum, you'd be the one. Any assistance you can give me would be greatly appreciated."

Rather than answer my questions, Lucius leaned over to grab a few more grapes off the platter. "So what have you learned about Jesus thus far? Why do you think he is the one you're interested in?"

"An interesting question. The first place I went after receiving Antipas' directive was Nazareth. Although I haven't shared this with Antipas, on my way to Tiberias, my route took me through Nain where I met a young man there who claimed Jesus raised him from the dead. As fantastic as that sounds, one of the town's officials verified the lad's story. My thinking was if this was the same man that concerned Antipas, a logical place to start my search would be at his hometown. Several days ago, I traveled there and spoke to two men, one of whom was Jesus' brother. Both men talked about some strange powers Jesus seems to possess. Their words coupled with those I heard in Nain make me suspect Jesus of Nazareth is the man I'm seeking. Until I can confirm my suspicions, I'm withholding Jesus' name from Antipas."

I sat back, relieved to be rid of my burden. After a short pause, my inner thoughts spewed out. "Incredible as it seems, some believe Jesus may be the Messiah the Jews are always searching for but they're so scatterbrained, it's hard to tell if their comments have merit. It all sounds too fantastic to me. Our gods are logical, although remote and silent most of the time, they seem logical nevertheless." I stared into the bright sky above. "I apologize for rambling on so." I sat up straight fixing my superior with my gaze. "Have any of your informants, your confidants, told you about anything like this, anything at all?"

Jorim appeared as unobtrusively as before, filling our tray with more refreshments and replacing our water with wine. After thanking the servant, Lucius nestled back on the heavy cushion of his chair remaining still for a long time. "As I mentioned before, Jorim, has been a trusted and faithful servant for many years. Not too long ago, he became quite ill, suffering from some type of paralysis. I prayed to every god I could think of, to Aesculapius for medical help, to Minerva for wisdom, even to Jupiter, but nothing happened. In fact, if anything, his condition worsened to such a degree, we didn't expect him to live."

"What did you do?"

"In my desperation because I've been posted here for a number of years and have excellent relations with the Jewish leaders throughout the area, I asked some of the elders in their synagogue for help. They spoke about a man who exhibited great faith in their god who traveled frequently near here and who had a reputation for healing the sick. At my urging, they sought out this man on my behalf telling him of Jorim's condition."

Fully engaged now, I stammered, leaning forward in my seat, "Were they able to find this man, this healer?"

"Yes, and after some discussion with them, he agreed to come here. Imagine a Jewish preacher coming at the request of a Roman officer. When I heard he was on his way, I was so humbled by his willingness to help I sent him a message telling him if he would just say the word, I believed Jorim would be healed."

"How did the man respond? Did he still come?"

"According to those who took him my message, when he read it, he turned to those with him, telling them he'd not seen faith like this in all of Israel. My friends hurried back to give me comfort but before they arrived, Jorim rose from his death bed miraculously cured! No sign of paralysis, no after effects, his suffering gone in the twinkling of an eye. As we talked later to piece together exactly what happened, it seems his restoration to good health occurred at the same time this healer received my message. We still marvel at the experience and as you can see for yourself, my servant appears quite healthy."

I sat back in my chair, reflecting on this story. Before I could ask the obvious question, Lucius stared at me. "The man you seek is the one who healed Jorim . . . His name is Jesus of Nazareth."

****

We sat still for what seemed a long time, saying nothing, watching the birds dart from tree to tree singing their gleefully melodies, the gentle breeze flowing about us refreshing us it passed through the open spaces, Lucius' story running through my mind again and again. Why did Jesus care for those he didn't even know? There was no hint of him seeking publicity or fame and fortune through his actions. Rather he seemed to exhibit a quality of humbleness in all he did; but why? What was his motivation? My mind in a muddled mess, I excused myself to wash my hands and face in hopes of regaining some balance and equilibrium. As I walked back to the portico, Jorim crossed my path and bowed. I wanted to ask him about what I had just learned, but I didn't know where to begin.

Before I could even open my mouth, the servant took the

lead. "Centurion, I believe I know why you've come here. If I am correct, my master told you of my illness and of the inexplicable outcome. There I was dying, laying there in intense pain, suffering from a disease no one could cure, but then in an instant, the affliction, the pain disappeared. It was though at the snap of a finger my body became clean of all its impurities. I can't tell you how it happened, I just know it did. As Lucius and I talked about this afterward, the only explanation that makes any sense is it came as a result of my master's faith in Jesus." The servant smiled, bowed again, and walked away.

Returning to the portico, I told my host of Jorim's thoughts. The older man asked, "So what is your next step? Where will you go from here, back to Tiberias or somewhere else?"

I thought for a time. "Based on what you've told me, I'm even more anxious to find Jesus but where should I concentrate my search for him? Any idea where I might find him, where he spends his time? Maybe the better question is if you were me, knowing what you know, where would you focus your attention?"

Chuckling, Lucius smiled as he threw his hands up, "I wish I knew. Whenever I hear about his supposed whereabouts, I send men out, but by the time they get there, he's disappeared. Sometimes I hear he's at our synagogue, but before I can react, he vanishes. He may live here in Capernaum although I've never been able to confirm that. I know he's talked to large gatherings of thousands on the hills west of here. His day by day whereabouts is another mystery to be solved." He added, "From my perspective, I still want to thank him for healing my friend."

"Given all that, if you were in my place, where would you look next?"

Lucius quietly watched the birds flit from one branch to the next, their attention focused momentarily on some flower or bug. "Trying to find Jesus is much like watching these birds. They are quick, pausing to stop for an instant to make their presence known and then they fly off again. Jesus knows the territory. He seems to have an instinct that takes him to places where he can deliver his message where it will have the most impact. He's been seen on the eastern side of the Sea of Galilee, in Tyre, in Nain, in Caesarea Philippi, almost everywhere in Galilee except Tiberias. I've heard he's even visited Jerusalem a time or two."

Lucius stopped to consume another grape, carefully choosing his words. "Almost without exception wherever he has gone, he's healed men and women of varying illnesses including blindness, but I've haven't answered your question, have I?" He tossed down a taste of his wine. "If I were you, instead of trying to find this most elusive man, I'd concentrate on finding one or two of his dedicated disciples, those men closest to him who are always near his side. Some of these men are residents of Capernaum. Three or four others come from Bethsaida, the fishing village east of here."

More men, more names? This puzzle kept getting more convoluted yet if I had to trust someone's judgment in all this, Lucius was a good choice. "So you recommend I go to Bethsaida?"

"Yes. That would be my first choice. And I'd start by looking for a fisherman there named Philip. If you find him, expect some reluctance, after all, you're a Roman Centurion. Expect him to be suspicious of your uniform and what you stand for. Remember you work for the man who killed John. Mention my name to him. That may help. I wish you well on your journey. If I can be of more assistance, speak to Jorim."

****

After a few other parting comments, I found Reuel, directing him to see Jorim to pack some food items for us. With our bags now full with several days of supplies, we set off for Bethsaida.

After an hour's ride east along the shoreline, we stopped beside the tranquil waters of the sea on the western outskirts of the village. Laid out before us was the fishing fleet of Bethsaida, small fishing boats capable of holding up to three men, most of them tied up to their mooring rocks waiting for the sun to set in the western sky before launching to seek their elusive prey.

Rather than drawing too much attention to ourselves, it seemed best for us to wait on the fringe of the fleet and make inquires about Philip from there. With several hours until dusk, I found the shade of several large date palms most inviting. From our location, we had a good view of the vessels arrayed before us. After we took the load from our horses' backs and secured the animals, Reuel stood guard some distance away, giving me an opportunity to prop my head on my saddle where I could enjoy the warmth of the sun as it mixed with the breeze coming across the water. Despite the serene and unhurried pace of this place, thoughts whirled about as I reviewed once again Lucius' testimony.

Chapter XI

Bethsaida
Province of Gaulanitis
February 14, A.D.34

Sharp words taking place behind me pulled me awake. Standing near our horses and Reuel was a tall thin man whose appearance suggested he was one of little means, his cloak ragged, his long graying beard matching the color of his hair needed tending, his speech animated, yet his hands and arms flew about as he spoke with great enthusiasm. Reuel motioned him to remain in place so he could wake me as he placed himself between me and our visitor. "Centurion, I can't understand much of what this man's telling me. I think he wants to know if we're looking for Philip. You want to talk to him?"

"Yes. Bring him over."

With the wave of his hand, Reuel motioned for the man to approach. Was this going to be another test for me to listen and not judge? The man gazed at all the glitter on my uniform and my knife in its sheath before he stammered, "Centurion, I hear you're looking for Philip. Perhaps I can help."

How could this be, did the wind have voices? Were my thoughts carried in the air so others knew what I wanted before words even came from my lips? The man pointed a bony finger at a small boat tied up to its mooring rock a short distance away. "That's his boat right there. I came here to find him myself. Looking for a friend of his, a man named Jesus. Ever hear of him, Centurion?"

I glanced at Reuel, but he only returned my gaze, making no comments. This thin, unkempt man now held my complete attention as I studied him with greater interest. "Are you speaking about Jesus of Nazareth? What is your interest in him?" my words sharper, more pointed than I intended.

Hesitating, the man gazed past me, studying the sea, and then at the clouds which began to billow in the western sky over the Galilean hills. Drawing himself to his full height, his words came out with unexpected boldness. "Centurion, I'm almost forty years old, may not look it but I am. For over half my life, I was blind as a result of some incurable disease I got as a child, never knew what it was called." He stopped to gather himself as tears began to well up around his eyes.

"Not long ago, Jesus and some of his followers passed through Bethsaida, Philip and most of the others who normally travel with him were part of that group. Because my relatives had heard Jesus would be passing this way, two of my brothers led me to a place where they thought Jesus would walk by. Just as they anticipated, when Jesus approached us, my brothers shouted out to get his attention. When he stopped to see what the commotion was about my brothers begged him to heal me."

I shook my head. "So you say you were blind. Doesn't look that way to me."

"That's because of what happened next." Pointing to a cluster of date palms further up the shoreline, he continued. "Jesus took my hand and led me over to that grove of trees right there. When we got there, he spat into my eyes and then he put his hands on me and asked if I could see. I told him I saw what I thought were people walking around but I wasn't sure. Then he put his hands on my eyes a second time," the man stopping, tears now streaming down his cheeks.

Reuel and I glanced at each other. The man was talking so fast I asked him to slow down.

The man wiped the tears from his face, nodding, "Alright I will . . . Now where was I? Ah yes, when he took his hands away from me this second time, I could see my brothers, the hairs on their chests and arms, their skin, their fingernails for the first time in a very long time! I could see the blue green water of the sea! I could see the deep limitless sky and the white and gray clouds overhead, the green blades of grass! And I could see Jesus, this wonderful man who healed me as he looked at me with those penetrating eyes that seemed to pierce deep into my soul. Do you have any idea what that is like, Centurion? To lose your sight and have it restored again, to live in total darkness day after day and then suddenly be able to see again?"

Speechless, I shuffled my feet on the sand seeing the stain again on my sandals as the sun cast its rays down upon us.

The man out of breath with excitement exclaimed, "I've so many questions. Why did Jesus choose to heal me? I'd never done anything for him . . . After he healed me, he asked me to keep this secret, but how can I? All those years of darkness gone in a flash." He smiled to himself, perhaps recalling that day once again. "And you know, Centurion, Philip was there that day. I saw him. He was standing right there next to Jesus."

I searched the man's face for some sign his story was all some mirage, some fabric of falsehood in his tale but my eyes saw only truth in his words and on his face. There was nothing I could add, nothing to say. Another miracle. Part of me wanted to discount his words because of his obvious economic impoverishment, but I couldn't. This man had no reason to lead me astray. Why were the gods showering me with such knowledge?

Still lost in my thoughts, the man's words brought me back to the present. "Centurion, I'll come back later. There is one thing; could you please tell Philip I was here?" Without another word, he bowed and walked toward the village.

All these stories with no end to them, only new beginnings, each story leading to more questions, not answers. No one who experienced a healing touch from Jesus was a king or a man of wealth. No payment was asked for. Each tale led to a changed life. Each story centered on one figure: Jesus of Nazareth.

I sat back down to look at the calm and tranquil waters before me, small waves hitting the shoreline with a soft hush, first pushing the grains of sand further inland before drawing them back ever so slowly toward the sea. The scene was peaceful and predictable, a gentle westerly breeze adding to the solemnity of this place. To Reuel's credit, he left me alone as he moved further up the beach as he maintained his vigil.

So much had happened in these past months that called my ordered life, my service to Rome into question. Was my life being changed by these stories? Why were the gods exposing me to all these things? As I gazed into the deep sky praying for enlightenment, all I received in response were sounds of the breeze touching the nearby trees and the water striking the shore. Nothing of substance came my way.

With my mind wrapped around all these questions, I almost missed Reuel's purposeful move to place himself between me and another man who approached the shoreline behind me. I turned, finding myself looking at rather unremarkable fellow. He was of medium height with a moderate black beard, his long hair almost the same color with a few sprinkles of gray thrown in. He looked to be about my age, his simple fisherman clothes covering a body which appeared quite muscular, his forearms enormous. Although he had a ruddy, weather beaten complexion from his days on the sea, his bright blue eyes twinkled with life. He and Serung seemed cut from the same mold.

Despite Lucius' counsel, there was no evidence of any fear or trepidation in the man as he nodded at Reuel, walking deliberately in my direction. Stopping in front of me, the man's deep bass voice boomed out, "Word reached me you're looking for me, Centurion. Name's Philip."

****

I tried to keep my voice calm despite the excitement welling up in me. "Yes, I am. My name is Aquila. Lucius, the Centurion in Capernaum, suggested I speak to you about Jesus of Nazareth. I'm told you've been in his company for some time and you may be able to answer some questions about him."

Philip did not appear to be awed by being in the presence of Roman uniforms or by my mention of Lucius. He stared at me for a few moments before responding, his voice sharp with no indication of cooperation in it. "Pardon me for asking, but why does a Roman officer need to know anything about Jesus? What concern is he to you?"

For a brief moment I considered lying to this man, or at the very least, dodging his question but those alternatives seemed to be folly as Philip's sources had already provided him information about me. Speaking the truth seemed to be the only course of action. "Jesus' travels have come to the attention of Herod Antipas and he dispatched me to learn more about him. I assure you I mean no harm. I'm simply trying to gather some facts about the man."

Philip turned his attention toward the western horizon as the sun made its daily pilgrimage lower toward the hills before returning to set his eyes upon me. Speaking without any signs of fear, he proclaimed, "You present me with a dilemma, Centurion. Even though I've many heard good things about Lucius, I have grave concerns about giving you any information that will get back to that spineless Antipas. We both know he killed John."

Philip stopped there for a moment. "I'll pray about this tonight as I play my game with the fish. When I return early tomorrow morning, if God directs, I'll respond to your questions. But if God tells to me not answer you, I'll follow that instruction as well. Right now the fish are calling me and I must attend to them." Then with a short bitter laugh, he pointed out to the water, "My success in these waters determines my ability to pay the taxes levied upon me by men like Antipas and Tiberius. Pray for my success this evening. I'll be back at first light." Without waiting for a reply, Philip turned about, hefting a large net over his shoulders, nets that appeared to be quite heavy as lead sinkers hung around the entire skirt of the braided rope, reminding me of what little I knew about his profession.

Following his movements, I watched Philip stow his nets into his boat which was like many others dotting the shoreline, his boat designed similar to Serung's. While his craft could accommodate up to three men, it appeared this evening this fisherman would seek his catch alone. After making a final check of his equipment, the man untied the rope which held his craft to its mooring stone and pushed his vessel out into the shallows. At no time did he glimpse back.

In times past, the man's lack of difference to my uniform would have earned him quick justice from my sword but not today. Was it his boldness, his demeanor, or his trust in his god or was I the one who was changing? While Philip's curt exit disturbed me, there was something about the man which caused me to let him go without interference. He said he would talk to me in the morning if his god directed so all I could do was wait: trying to force words from his mouth by coercion seemed futile. While patience was not high on my list of virtues, if this man needed time alone with his god, and if he rewarded me with valuable information, how could I complain? Philip's god was so much different than my deities.

****

As the eastern skies signaled the dawn of another beautiful day, Reuel spotted Philip's boat among many others moving in our direction. When he reached the shallows, the fisherman stepped into thigh deep water pulling his vessel ashore with a rope. As the bow touched dry ground, he pulled the craft up onto the shore before securing it to its mooring stone. Then he gathered some wood from along the beach and began to build a fire not far from where I sat.

After a few minutes of effort and when his fire showed signs of life, Philip walked back to his boat and secured two large fish which he brought to his fire which he then proceeded to clean, seeing to his task with a long sharp knife. When he judged the fish suitable for cooking, he brought them to his now burgeoning fire, placing them on some stones near the center of the flames and looked at me, giving me a brief nod. Reuel remained with our mounts as I joined one of Jesus' closest friends by the fire.

No words passed between us as we sat down on two of the large rocks near the warmth of the burning wood, my companion smelling of fish, sweat and smoke, his tired eyes telling me of his long productive night. As the fish cooked over the open fire, their sweet aroma holding my attention, we both knew a carpenter's son from a small village in an obscure land would be the focus of our conversation.

Philip spoke first. "It was a pleasant night on the water. The breeze was down so the waves did not cause me any concern. Since many of my fellow anglers chose other places to fish, I had one of my favorite spots to myself. As you can see, we can share in the bounty God blessed me with last night for my boat is filled with many like these two." He smiled as only a fortunate fisherman can, reaping the fruits of his labor after a successful voyage.

Turning the fish over to cook on the other side, the delicious fragrance of the catch drew us to eye the prospects of the meal to come. "Joy filled my night for another reason, Centurion. Joy because I spent time close to my God in prayer." He stopped and looked at me for what seemed a long time before returning his tired eyes to evaluate the cooking process in front of us. "In my prayers God told me to trust you, and to answer your questions about Jesus. I must admit he surprised me with those instructions because everything about your uniform suggests you and I have little in common. You carry weapons of war, my master talks about peace. You and your kind oppress, my master speaks of liberty and justice. Many who wear your uniform wish to dominate and control, my master speaks of love and living in peace with one another."

He stopped once more to appraise me. His words came out almost in a hush yet with profound conviction. "While I have reservations about God's instructions, I will follow them nevertheless. Before we begin, let me first say Jesus is not here. He and several others are in the mountains north of here. I have no idea when they'll return, although I expect them to be gone for at least three or four days. So, Centurion, how can I help you?"

I realized my time had not been spent wisely: I was ill prepared having not thought through which specific questions to ask this man. In halting fashion, I stumbled, "The more I hear about Jesus, the more he intrigues me. Where did you meet him? How long have you been with him?"

Philip poked at the fish as he glanced down. Was it my imagination or was he focused on the stains on my sandals? "As John's ministry spread throughout the area around the Jordan, he attracted several disciples, men drawn to his words, his teachings. When Jesus went to the river, John told those around him Jesus was the 'Lamb of God', a reverent phrase indicating Jesus' closeness to our God. Two of John's disciples, with his blessing, followed Jesus, hanging on every word he spoke. These two were Andrew and another man named John, good friends of mine, fishermen by trade raised in this area. They found themselves so inspired by Jesus' teachings Andrew immediately sought out his brother, Simon, telling him he believed they had found the Messiah. The second man, John, likewise went to find his brother James, telling him the same thing." Philip took a piece of fish into his mouth, and after sampling it, he handed me a piece.

After digesting his words about Andrew and John, I asked, "Are you saying these two simple fishermen, who are not scholars of your religion, determined Jesus might be your Messiah?" I chuckled softly, "How could they know that? Without having a thorough background in religious studies, how could they possibly know this?"

"A valid question. If you ever speak to Andrew or John, ask them. I believe their response would be tied to what they learned from John, coupled with what Jesus taught them and how he related to them. Perhaps I can answer your question this way: you have a great deal of experience in leadership. From your experience, as you meet men in authority over you for the first time, how do you determine who is a good leader, one you would follow even if it meant death? And conversely, how do you determine a leader who is suspect?"

I searched back in my reservoir of leaders I had known through the years, quickly recalling examples on both sides of the coin. The lessons learned from those many years came forth. "Two men can say the same words, but through the differences in their speech and their tone, the way they look you in the eye, their mannerisms, their posture, I've learned whom to trust and who not to. Call it experience, call it a sixth sense, or as one old soldier once told me, 'You just know in your gut who to trust and who not to.'"

"There's your answer. Andrew and John knew in their hearts Jesus was teaching them the truth about our God. Using your words, they just felt it in their gut." Philip stopped to eat more fish, not waiting for me. "But back to how I met Jesus. When James and Simon joined Jesus and their brothers, they too became convinced of the truth Andrew had proclaimed." Before eating another mouthful, he gestured to Reuel to come share in our bounty.

Philip continued his story as my companion ambled over to grab a large piece of the tasty tilapia as he sat down by the fire. "I was fishing near here many months ago when I saw the five of them watching me from the shore. When I brought my boat in, the six of us gathered around a fire to share a meal much like we're doing now. I could tell as we ate my four friends held Jesus in high regard as they listened to everything he said." He stopped, his eyes staring out over the calm waters. "When Jesus began to speak to me, like the others, I knew, I just knew this man, this tall, strapping man, with large powerful hands, long hair, and piercing eyes was a man of God. He spoke about God and heaven as though he had been there. While he is a man of flesh and blood like you and me, when he speaks, it as though he knows God personally."

Philip turned his attention back to the fire, neither of us saying a word. We each nibbled on some small pieces of the catch, watching the waves make their subtle, soft sounds on the beach not far from our fire. What could I tell Antipas about Jesus and his followers? These were peaceful men, whose leader healed the sick and the blind. Could these men constitute a threat to Rome or to Antipas? While I kept searching for some sinister plot underlying all I'd heard, there seemed to be nothing to suggest a rebellion or a revolt was about to occur.

"As I said, God has given me a peace to tell you these things but I don't know why. I've never told this much in so short a time to anyone else, except to those in our close neat group. I just know you're to hear what I have to say. There is much more I could add, but I don't know how much time you have or how much you really want to know about Jesus. There are times when I feel as though I know him quite well, but then he'll say something which makes little sense to those of us closest to him."

"I don't understand . . . What do you mean?"

The fisherman chuckled to himself. "One day he talked about Moses, who wrote about a man named Jacob who thought he was climbing a ladder toward heaven. It is a wonderful story. Jesus told us that day mortal men like my friends and I would see heaven open, and we would see angels ascending and descending to earth. We couldn't tell if he meant this literally or figuratively so we just sat there, dumbfounded." With a faraway look at the hills to our west, he declared, "When I'm on the water fishing by myself, I use those moments to reflect on what I've heard Jesus teach us over these many months we've followed him."

Rather than interrupt, I sat still, trying to absorb the words, the gestures, the feelings that flowed out of this man, so much to soak up, to grasp, to understand. "Since the early days of his teaching, more men have joined our intimate group. There are twelve of us now, some are quiet and reserved, others are more vocal and intense, some boisterous and zealous, some skeptical, and some passionate. Our professions range from fisherman to a tax collector. When we travel from place to place, we take little with us for subsistence, believing, as Jesus taught us, God will provide. And you know what is amazing, Centurion? He always does."

"You mean you take no food, no money to care for your needs?"

"Just the bare essentials . . . and we've never gone wanting, not even once."

As a man who prided himself on preparation with an eye toward any eventuality, I found this apparent lack of organization astonishing, shaking my head in wonderment.

Philip's mouth turned up in a smile as he continued, shifting his body around. "One day Jesus led us in a discussion about bread. He told us to not work for food which spoils but for food that endures for eternal life. Then he said only God can give us the true bread from heaven and he, Jesus, was that bread which came down from heaven."

I tried to understand what Philip said, but found his comments enigmatic, my Roman mind having little perspective to appreciate the meaning of Philip's words. "Such befuddling words . . . What did he mean?"

"Centurion, believe me, we too were puzzled. Talking amongst ourselves, we tried to make sense of his comments but couldn't. Seeing our confusion, Jesus began to teach us some remarkable truths, saying first, he was the bread of life and anyone who came to him would not go hungry or be thirsty."

Philip's eyes turned to look at the water. "He then said he came from heaven to do God's will, finishing this teaching by telling us whoever believes in him would have eternal life. After he said those words, there was quiet around our camp for a long time. Later as my friends and I discussed this, we began to embrace the idea Jesus really might be the Messiah." Philip sat back with tears in his eyes. "While I know I want to believe everything he teaches us, I still have moments of disbelief, of questions, of doubts. There are even times when I feel filled to overflowing with the goodness of God, and yet there are other times my heart is overcome by evil thoughts and evil desires. It's almost like I'm part good, part evil. I wish it were not so. I suppose it is just my human nature."

Caught off guard by Philip's comment, I had no response. He was one who spent many hours with Jesus, sharing meals with him, hearing him teach, watching him interact with the people of the land. I had no perspective to add any worthwhile thoughts. After an uncomfortable silence, I said, "I'm not qualified to speak about your thoughts in that regard. Do you think it is possible I can meet this remarkable man? Could that be arranged?"

Philip did not answer but gave me an indifferent shrug.

To dig more at what this man had experienced, I asked, "Do you know in my search for Jesus, I've talked to two people who believe Jesus has power over life itself?"

The man's eyes snapped up, staring at me, his words coming out with wonder. "If you're talking about Nain, I was there. I saw everything. It was incredible to watch, to be a part of that scene. And my friends and I have seen many other miracles, so many they would fill a large book. Even though we see what happens with our own eyes, the raising of the dead, the healing of the blind and infirmed, we can't account for any of it using earthly logic. The only justification we have is Jesus is who he says he is ---The Son of God!"

I looked at Philip first and then at Reuel, who had continued to nibble on some fish but kept his head down. Could there really be such a person, a god living on earth as a man? Was Jesus this man? Part of me wanted to shout yes, YES! But another side of me shouted with equal vigor, impossible, IMPOSSIBLE! My gods don't live on this earth. Why should another god live here? Where was truth in all this?

As my mind threw the question back and forth, one side won out. I smiled. "Friend, are you sure you're just a fisherman? Your stories come out with great passion and with great enthusiasm. Maybe you should be a merchant selling expensive wares rather than spending your nights searching for elusive fish." I sat up straight, remembering my background, my training, my goal. I looked at Philip. "While part of me is captivated by your words and the testimony I've heard from others, I'm a loyal soldier of Rome. I believe in things I can see and touch. You and others have given me much to consider but now I must render my report to the tetrarch. I don't know what he will do with this information, but duty compels me to report all that I've learned." As I stood, Reuel rose as well to untie our horses.

Philip came slowly to his feet, his voice clear and unwavering as he took hold of the reins of my horse. "Think long and hard about what you've heard from me and the others. Despite your tone and your rhetoric, I see confusion and doubt in your face. Are you trying to convince me of your disbelief or yourself? The man paused for a moment. "Consider this, Aquila. Jesus is either who he claims to be or he is the greatest liar the world has ever known. We believe him to be who he says he is. Right now, it appears you've made a decision to reject him. I pray you will revisit your decision, and that you reach a different conclusion the next time." He released the reins. "I pray you will have an uneventful journey back to Antipas."

I looked at Philip a final time before turning my back to him spurring my horse in the opposite direction. Was my horse taking me toward Antipas, toward Tiberias, or was he taking me away from Philip's words and his trust in this carpenter from Nazareth?

Chapter XII

The quick gait our horses equaled my state of mind as we rode next to the shoreline retracing our steps in the direction of Capernaum, neither Reuel nor I uttering a word, my heart pounding. Why were some people mesmerized by Jesus yet I remained entangled in doubt and uncertainty? Was the problem with me or with them? I had never been a religious man, turning on every whim at the mention of a god. I knew my belief in our Roman deities was fundamental to my culture but to place too much dependency upon them to rule over every aspect of my life didn't seem practical. Yet, was even my modest faith and belief in my Roman gods for naught? Could it be that Jesus was everything Philip thought him to be? My mind wondered back to what I knew or didn't know.

The clutter and confusion in my soul ran rampant with all these names and thoughts mingling together like a ball of clay forming nothing of substance. John, Valerus, Tobias, Uthai, Amittai, Serung, Cuza, James and the innkeeper, Lucius and Joram, the blind man and now Philip pulled me, tugged me, and twisted me every direction. Why was I being led on this path, this journey that seemed to lead nowhere? Why me?

Finally realizing our pace might to be too quick for our horses, we began a slow canter, the horses panting their appreciation as they sensed I might be pushing them beyond their limits. Killing these animals through my neglect would serve no purpose. It was not their fault I wanted to escape from my fears and my doubts as rapidly as possible. Even as we dismounted and began an easy walk, my mind continued to race, still trying to make sense of it all. Could Jesus really be able to do all these miracles attributed to him? Did anyone really have that kind of power? I kept asking myself, what *man* can do these things? And if he could, where did his power come from? And what about the compassion he seemed to have for all those he ministered to? All of what I learned became just more pieces of a very large puzzle, each piece more mystifying, more mind-numbing than the previous one, much like a maze inside a maze. Was I the one to solve this enigma or was I just to gather the facts leaving the solution of this mystery to someone else?

****

I stopped our march on the shores of the sea not far from the outskirts of Capernaum. Leaving Reuel to care for our animals, I decided to walk along the edge of the shoreline in hopes the peacefulness around me would help clear my mind. I had to tell Antipas something but what? Perhaps I should seek the counsel of Lucius. While he was close by, I dismissed that notion. It was my responsibility to render a report to Antipas, not his. While the senior centurion might shed some light on my time with Philip, he was obviously taken with Jesus because of the healing of Jorim, his views colored by his closeness to his servant.

Setting on the shore watching some fishermen casting their nets from the boats not far from shore, my mind recalled the man who approached me on the beach at Bethsaida. Was it just yesterday? He claimed Jesus brought his sight back to him. He didn't sound or act like he was under any spell or trance. He sounded excited and grateful. Then there was Philip. His candid and open comments sounded uncontrived and earnest. His honesty in expressing his doubts and fears didn't seem invented to fool me. But to think this Jesus was the Jewish Messiah, the son of God? That was just too much! He affected many lives in positive ways, but why? Was he planting seeds for a revolt beyond my comprehension or could it be all his actions stemmed from simple compassion and love for these people?

My mind kept saying it would be easy to surrender to all I

heard, but was it right to do so? Was there more investigation to be done, more people to talk with, more stories to examine? With my mind still spinning, there was one answer: To do my duty, return to Tiberias, report my findings to Antipas about what I knew or thought I knew and let him decide the proper action. With this settled and rather than cause our horses any potential distress, I told Reuel we would walk at a leisurely pace for a time. I was in no hurry to reach Galilee's capital city.

****

As the scenes along the shoreline refreshed my spirit, I rationalized all this nonsense about Jesus was Antipas' problem, not mine. He was the ruler, not me. This was his territory, not mine. He was the tetrarch. This was his problem to solve, not mine.

With no words passing between Reuel and me, we caught glimpses of our destination. Maybe after briefing Antipas, I could wash my hands of this whole affair and get back to my mission of training soldiers. I was good at that. I was not adept at analyzing this religious babble, these twisting, turning religious games. It was time to let Antipas handle the devout spiritual men of his area. I was tired of it.

Without any preamble Reuel broke our silence. "Centurion, thank you for allowing me to accompany you these past few days. It helped clarify some things in my mind."

Turning to the soldier, I asked, "I'm not sure I understand."

"May I speak candidly, Centurion?"

"Yes, of course."

The soldier stopped his horse, giving the animal a gentle caress on his head as his steed showed its appreciation by quietly pawing the ground, a satisfying whinny coming from deep inside the animal's chest. This tall sturdy man stared out to the sparkling blue waters of the sea before focusing on me. "Prior to your arrival at Machaerus, several soldiers told me they'd been at the river one day when John the Baptizer spoke. According to them, he was a mesmerizing speaker, his words powerful, full of confidence about a world to come. They said John looked straight into their faces telling them should be content with their pay. As you can imagine, this statement caused quite a stir among my comrades but by this bold statement, John gained their respect."

Reuel kicked a small rock at his feet before he continued. "Although some distance away from many of your discussions these past few days, I overheard many of the things said to you about this man Jesus, and like you, I want to learn more about him. After everything you've heard, do you believe he is the Messiah many of these people are talking about? He must be a most remarkable man and I find the stories about him most compelling. You, as a Roman with your Roman gods, must have many questions and doubts. I, on the other hand, as a Jew but one who has not always been forthright in my religious practices, find all this almost overpowering."

Was Reuel seeing all this clearer than me, seeing the truth for what it was? Was I trying to make everything too complicated, too rational, searching for some earthly logic where none existed? Was Reuel seeing the simple truth that was eluding me, challenging me?

"I don't know Reuel. I just don't know." Neither of us spoke for the remainder of our ride back to Antipas' crown jewel.

****

Even after a day of being away, Tiberias felt like home. Since we arrived late in the day, my first thoughts turned to enjoying a good meal before laying my head on a familiar cushion. I wanted a comfortable atmosphere where casual conversation would surround me without raising new challenges, new demands. I found Sallu and we shared some wonderful stories that night. Like most soldiers' stories, some of our tales were true, some were embellished, yet all were entertaining even if we'd both heard the same yarns many times before.

****

Early the next day I entered Antipas' outer chambers in anticipation of seeing the tetrarch. As I waited, I strolled down one of the elaborately decorated hallways, a bust of Julius Caesar, our most famous general who led the way on the battlefields of Gaul seventy to eighty years ago, catching my eye. As I studied the man's face, it reminded me of Rome's power and prestige and that it was my duty to serve her, requiring the confusion within me to be put aside. Before I could spend more time on these thoughts, I felt Cuza's presence behind me, a heavy cough coming from him, filling the air.

"Cuza, are you alright?"

"Yes, Centurion, just a spell. It'll pass. Are you looking for Antipas?"

"Yes. I was hoping to meet with him this morning. When will he be available?"

The man smiled, "Not for a while. Antipas and Herodias left yesterday to visit some friends in Tyre. He neglected to mention to you of his annual pilgrimage to that wonderful resort by the great sea. He instructed me to tell you to send him a brief summary of what you've found out on your recent travels. If, however, you learned something of great significance, you're to go there immediately."

A puzzled, yet relieved look came across my face. "How long will he be gone?"

Cuza smiled, "If he holds to his pattern of the last few years, he will stay there for almost a month until traveling to Jerusalem to celebrate the Passover. Unless he gives instructions to the contrary, we're to meet him in Jerusalem the first week in April."

I mumbled, "Well, I think what I have to communicate to him can be done in a message." Giving Cuza a quizzical glance, I asked, "Another month you say . . . Why didn't you go with him?"

Coughing once again this time from deep in his chest, he spat out a mixture of yellowish-reddish phlegm into a large dirty towel he produced from under his tunic, taking time to clear his nose and mouth before answering my question. "I've found when he goes there, this is a good time for me to insure all the documentation to administer the two provinces is in order. While he relaxes at the beach, I have time to plan his affairs without the day-to-day concerns of seeing to his whims." The servant gave me a questioning look. "So if I may ask, was your visit to Capernaum helpful? And Lucius, did he add to your reservoir of information?"

I stepped away from Cuza, focusing on the activities outside the nearest window. A zephyr blew the petals of the flowers outside ever so slightly causing them to move from side to side, the bees dashing from one flower to the next, collecting the object of their desire as they sampled the various colorful nectars. How could these simple products of nature have such peace, such rhythm in their short lives while I experienced such turmoil and confusion in mine? Yet as I watched this scene play out again and again, maybe the gods were giving me an answer, a reprieve. With Antipas' absence, here was an opportunity to think, time to wrap my thoughts around all I had heard and seen, time for some sagacity to be applied to this puzzle with no end. Still looking out the window, I responded. "Lucius intrigued me with the story about Jorim's healing and at Lucuis' urging, I spent a night at Bethsaida meeting a blind man who told me Jesus healed him and then I spent time with Philip, one of Jesus' disciples. It was a most interesting several days."

I stopped. "You said, I could send Antipas a brief summary of my findings? When will you be sending something to him?"

"I intend to send a dispatch three or four days from now. Will that give you sufficient time to compose your thoughts: a short report, simple, direct to the point, perhaps?"

" Yes, three days is more than enough time." Returning to my room to consider how best to structure my epistle, it occurred to me once again, how some invisible hand seemed to be leading me to go deeper and deeper into finding out about this man Jesus. I couldn't help but wonder if this would lead me toward my family or away from them.

****

I invested the next three days drafting my letter to the Tetrarch:

Antipas, since my last report I have continued to gather information about the man traveling through Galilee whose actions remind you of John. The man in question is named Jesus of Nazareth. He is a carpenter by trade, a humble man who has a sharp mind for religious matters which attracts some followers to his side because of his considerable knowledge of the scriptures. In his travels throughout Galilee he gives comfort to many who were sick or diseased and while he draws the attention of the people, it is significant to note that no signs of political unrest directed toward either you or Rome follow in his wake. Once again let me emphasize Jesus is not John the Baptizer, although John was a distant cousin. My recommendation is we continue to monitor the man's movements but take no overt action against him as there is no reason to stir the people up by calling any more attention to him or his actions than is necessary.

When I handed my report to Cuza, he asked for permission to read it which I granted. As he considered my words, his hand went to his chin in thought. "This should satisfy Antipas for the time being, but if he hears much more about Jesus, I fear he may want to take some action against him. I'm just not sure about what form that will take." He paused for a moment, looking up at me. "For some reason, your report is bland, almost dull. It contains no details, no emotion. What are you leaving out?"

While Cuza saw through my insipid account, I wondered if Antipas would be as astute and demand specifics about Jesus or would my comment again confirming John was not the man in question satisfy him for the present? "You're right, while I could write much about Jesus and the miracles attributed to him, if I did the reactions of our leader might quickly cause the entire situation to spiral out of control. For now, I just wanted to give him a simple brief message. If he wants more details, he'll ask for them."

While Cuza nodded his head in agreement, his concern required additional clarification.

"Let me ask you, what do you think Antipas' reaction would be if I wrote him about the man who would testify Jesus brought him back from death or about another who would tell how Jesus healed him from blindness or the words of Jesus' brother telling me about Jesus turning water into wine? How would Antipas react if I told him Jesus speaks about a heavenly kingdom as though he has been there? I stopped for a moment to catch my breath. Gazing at servant I said, "Right now, I don't want to take the chance!" There I said it.

"If I told Antipas any of this, I think you would agree, he would consider Jesus a grave threat, a dangerous man because many trust him. If Antipas knew any of this, I fear he would arrest Jesus immediately."

"You raise a weighty issue, Centurion. I understand your concerns. Once Antipas' wrath is unfurled, it is almost unstoppable. Like a hungry lioness in search for food, once she gets scent of a prey, nothing gets in her way."

I fixed my eyes on the man in front of me. "So we agree: the less said for now, the better." After a long pause, my words spilled out. "I confess, Cuza, I'm not sure what to think. Is Jesus a magician who twists the minds of everyone he meets or is it possible he is a god, certainly not like any of my Roman gods, but a god that interacts with the people in some personal way? Is that possible?"

No response came from the servant for a long time. He coughed long and hard, recovering from this spell only after he downed a large cup of water. When he spoke, compassion and understanding filled his voice. "Aquila, I too have been filled with wonder when others talk about Jesus. How could a man accomplish all the things attributed to him? I can only respond to your questions by saying that when I've talked to witnesses of his deeds, I trust their words. I hear belief in their voices and see it in their eyes and if I could look into their hearts, I suspect I would see their faith in this man as well."

He stopped for a moment, another heavy cough forcing him to catch his breath. "I think you are wise to not tell Antipas everything. Without the framework of knowledge you have about Jesus, he wouldn't understand your communication. Perhaps later when you're face to face with him, you may have an opportunity to share some of this with him." He gave me a reassuring smile which for some inexplicable reason warmed my heart, giving me great comfort. "You have traveled quite a journey."

I stammered, "Yes . . . yes, I have. And I have no idea where it will lead. Regarding your thoughts about Antipas, I agree. At some point I suspect he will view Jesus as a threat. The two have nothing in common. From everything I have been told Jesus seems to pay no attention to the wealth of any man. His focus is on the plight of individuals, caring about providing for their needs, and perhaps even for their needs in the after-life or heaven, as he calls it. Antipas, on the other hand, is consumed with self; his wealth, his power, his prestige, his personal comforts. Look at this city and at Machaerus: temples of grandeur of self-centered desires, little thought or concern given to the people he governs." My frustrations getting the better of me, I stopped. Had I gone too far with my thinking or not far enough?

"Cuza, I apologize. My comments are unprofessional. As a Roman officer, I should not express such opinions in such a public manner. They are disloyal to your master. I would appreciate it if you would dismiss them from your mind. I've spoken too boldly."

Without another word, I handed my message to Cuza after sealing it with my mark. The servant took the letter, his voice and manner neutral. "I will see this goes out with my dispatches in the morning. Unless he gives other instructions, we must plan to leave in three weeks. Like you, I have a duty, and mine is to prepare the palace at Jerusalem for his arrival." As the man walked away, he turned, "Aquila, rest assured your deep feelings about this matter are safe with me."

With my message now in route to Antipas I turned my attention back to the training of Sallu's soldiers, those men whose lives I felt responsible for even though I was not their commander. I continued to push and push for excellence, not knowing if I would return to Tiberias after my journey to Jerusalem. I poured every ounce of my being into maturing these men, glad for the opportunity to put a portion of me into their military skills. It was my duty.

Chapter XIII

Antipas' Palace at Tiberias
Province of Galilee
Morning, March 22, A.D. 34

Jerusalem. With the date for our departure established, my sense of anticipation grew as time grew shorter to begin the journey to the Jewish capital. When passing through there nine months ago, I spent only one night in this city as my orders required me to reach Machaerus without delay. Now with this opportunity close at hand, it seemed as though I would now be able to take advantage to explore the history I'd heard so much about.

The more I considered this trip my mind began to conjure up a scenario that a return to Tiberias might not be necessary. While Antipas had said nothing to indicate the veracity of this hope, I held on to this belief nevertheless. Call it intuition, a sixth sense, something in my bones told me I would not be returning to Tiberias anytime soon. With this in mind, I devoted all my time helping Sallu prepare to lead his soldiers in whatever endeavors he was called upon to do. The more time I spent with him, the more my confident I became in his ability.

As final plans were made for our four day journey, I decided Maurus should accompany me, directing him to prepare a detail of ten men who had shown leadership potential, similar to my journey from Machaerus to Tiberias. The concept was to use this movement as a training ground to test and train those soldiers to help determine who should be considered for advancement. Not surprising, Reuel was among those chosen. I also directed Maurus to act as commander of this movement and perform all duties as if I were not present. As I learned from personal experience and from Caesar's writings on the Gallic wars, leaders can become causalities at any time and therefore their subordinates must be ready to assume a higher level of responsibility at a moment's notice. By passing the overall responsibility to Maurus for the actions of our soldiers during this movement, he too would be receiving vital training.

After consulting our maps, Maurus chose a route that would take us south past Mt. Tabor and close to Nain. From there we would then enter the province of Samaria, traveling along mountainous roads leading past the towns of Shechem and Shiloh before reaching Jerusalem from the north. Our party consisted of twenty men: Maurus and me, our ten men plus Cuza and those servants he needed to prepare for Antipas' arrival in Jerusalem.

In the midst of our preparations, our company increased by two: Joanna, Cuza's wife and their son, Kish. Because of my experience with Kish on our earlier trip, I was delighted to have him along. Joanna was another matter. While I knew her to be a pleasant looking woman in her mid forties, comely with brown hair, slender in build, I questioned Cuza about her ability to keep up with my soldiers. With a smile on his face, he laughed. "Centurion, sometimes you can be quite narrow-minded in your view of the world. I've lost count the number of times Joanna has made this trek with me. My concern about having her along is I hope she doesn't embarrass your soldiers as they try can keep up with her." His comment left little doubt about the matter.

****

We made good time on our first day, establishing our campsite south of Nain, the soldiers under Maurus' leadership constructing their fortifications according to doctrine in near record time. Because some of these men accompanied me when the bandits attacked us months ago, they had no reservations as to the necessity of nightly security preparations. My chest swelled with pride as Maurus and his men worked in harmony during this evening ritual, no wasted time or energy, just focused effort. Although I could have visited Uthai to renew my acquaintance with him, I gave myself the excuse I needed a restful sleep. Deep in my soul, I knew the real reason; I wasn't ready for another retelling of the day Jesus came to this town. I hoped all that was behind me.

Around the crackle of an open fire watching the sliver of a quarter moon making its steady climb above our heads, Cuza broke the stillness of the evening by telling me about the land of Samaria which we would enter next day, describing how the trails made sharp turns which could be used by any aggressor to ambush parties along the road. Maurus, listening with a careful ear, spat into the fire. "Cuza, my men will make short work of any bandits dim-witted enough to attack us." He laughed, "If it weren't for your wife traveling with us, I'd almost invite some thugs to try us on for size. They'd be no match for us."

I looked at Cuza, "Maurus has a point. If we take our normal precautions, there should be little concern. Anything else we should know about?"

"Just understand the Samaritans are different, blood relatives of the rest of the Jewish nation, but they're considered outcasts by many."

"And why's that?"

"This all goes back almost six hundred years when the Assyrians swept through our country, ravaging it. A number of mixed marriages came about between the Samaritans and the conquerors, these half-breed marriages angering many Jews, so much so that when my people returned to these lands roughly one hundred years later, they avoided the Samaritan territory at all costs, wanting no part of them.

"And so that still affects relationships today?"

Cuza gave a wry smile, "Yes, we bear grudges for a long, long time. For their part, the Samaritans choose to separate themselves and live without interruption in this dusty, hilly countryside. I suspect if you asked some about the details of the rift, some people couldn't give many specifics. It's a family feud where family pride won't allow those now living to forgive the past transgressions of their long dead relatives." Pausing for a long time as he watched the moon's rise, he added, "It almost as though it's easier for us to harbor resentment and bitterness than it is to seek reconciliation and forgiveness before we consider how people and situations change. Many times we can see the fault in others but can't see it in our own lives. Don't you find that to be true, Centurion?"

"Yes, I suppose. I've known some who are so prideful they can't see their own mistakes." I stopped to stare into the fire giving the matter considerable thought. "It's always easier to identify a problem in someone than it is to see one in our own lives."

Cuza looked at me before applying a stir to our fire with a large stick stoking the embers into a new round of crackles amidst a brighter flame. "You're right, of course. Reminds me of a conversation Joanna and I had once. She told me about hearing a man speak on that very subject, saying something like, 'Why do you look at the speck of sawdust in your brother's eye and pay no attention to the plank in your own eye? How can you say to your brother, let me take the speck out of your eye, when all the time there is a plank in your own eye?' The man then went on to say, 'You hypocrites, take the plank out of your eye, and then you'll see clearly to remove the speck from your brother's eye.' "

"Ah, there are the words of an intelligent man. He understood the basic problem . . . Obviously a most learned man."

The servant smiled and nodded his head slightly, his next words holding me tight. "Yes, a most learned man: a simple carpenter from a town west of here, Nazareth."

My mouth dropped open. No words came forth. There was nothing I could add.

After a long pause the servant changed the subject. "We should reach the area around Shechem and the small town of Sychar tomorrow. Shechem is significant to our people because one of our first patriarchs, Abraham, built an altar there over a thousand years ago after God told him this land would always be in the possession of his offspring. Then years later, Joshua gave his farewell address near there before he died, foretelling of the many struggles the

Jewish people would undergo, also stating that God would always be faithful to us."

"What about Sychar, anything of importance there?"

Cuza glanced at me and gave me a slight nod of the head. "Sychar's claim to fame is that Jacob, another one of our ancients, built a well there which still exists."

As Cuza described these places and these famous men, I couldn't help but admire a people whose history passed seamlessly from generation to generation wondering how our Roman civilization would be remembered by historians thousands of years from now? Would we be remembered for our strength and military power or would we pass into history, forgotten like a leaf falling from a tree?

When he finished, we sat back staring into the fire. "This is an amazing land filled with many interesting people. Has your god watched over his people for all these years as he promised? Has he ever removed his protective cover over the Jews?"

Chuckling softly, the servant thoughtfully commented, "You've come straight to the heart of the matter. Yes there have been numerous times over the years when God disciplined us as we wandered away from his instructions, yet despite our disobedience, we believe in His unconditional covenant to Abraham. We know God has always loved us in spite of our transgressions. Our problem historically is we have not always obeyed him as he commanded."

I scratched a knot on the back of my neck thinking about my gods. Would we Romans ever love our gods, to hold them in such high esteem? Before I could pull myself into that thought anymore Cuza's words brought me back to his.

" . . . I can't help but think if Jesus is the Messiah promised by God, it will be the greatest gift He can give us, but I wonder what will happen? As you learn more about Jesus, I pray it may be clear whether or not he is the One." Cuza stopped for a moment reacting once again to a disruptive, thick cough that went on for several minutes. "While Antipas searches for the truth about Jesus to satisfy his curiosity, we also want to know the truth about this carpenter as well. From that perspective, your quest to find the truth about Jesus is important to many."

I sat examining the colors coming from the hot embers of our fire, the flames of blue and yellow and red mingling together. "Cuza, right now it seems I've learned all I need to about him. Unless by chance he shows up in Jerusalem, I may have heard the last of him. As for me, it's time for sleep. Dawn will come sooner than we wish."

****

We reached Shechem late in the day, the wind swirling around us creating great plumes of dust from each step we took, an uncomfortable day at best, a miserable day at its worst. Maurus selected a position for the evening on a spur of the hill overlooking the smaller of the towns, Sychar, its living quarters arrayed before us surrounded by a low rocky wall. Like Nain, each family had an area set aside to care for their animals. Judging by its constant use, the town's well was only water source for the town.

With the last rays of the sun now dipping below the horizon, Cuza joined me at my observation post as I watched the town below settle down for the night, the animals giving off contented sounds as they sought shelter, candlelight flickering throughout the houses, the sounds of someone softly playing a lute being answered by another filled the night air. During the day my eyes saw how the old servant seemed to have some difficulty, his steps slower and halting. "Are feeling alright? I noticed you weren't your normal spry self today."

"A long term problem, I'm afraid. Sometimes my legs don't cooperate with my intentions, but there's nothing to be concerned about. Been dealing with this issue for years." He then started another story.

"Jesus and his followers passed by here a while back despite the rift between the Jews and Samaritans I told you about last night. I suspect if you were to go into that town below and ask anyone there about Jesus they would be glad to add some details to what I'm about to tell you."

I didn't want to hear another story or consider another puzzle piece in this never ending saga. I was tired of this game. Wishing I could escape yet knowing there was no exit available, I sighed in exasperation, "So what happened down there?"

The old servant smiled. After wiping away some sweat that suddenly poured down his face, he began, "After spending time south of here, Jesus and his men chose this route because it was the shortest way to Galilee." Pointing with his finger, he said, "That well we see down there is Jacob's well, the one I mentioned to you last night."

"Yes, I remember."

Nodding the old man went on. "When they arrived here, Jesus sat down by the well alone. When a woman from the town came to draw water from the well, he asked her for a drink, a most unusual request since as a Jew he was going against all conventional protocol, associating with a Samaritan. As the story goes, Jesus went even further in their conversation by engaging her in the discussion in which he said he could give her living water. When Jesus told her things about her past life only a prophet could know, she was greatly troubled."

I stopped him. "Cuza, slow down, you're confusing me. What did Jesus say to her? What do you mean 'living water'? What does that mean?"

He paused to wipe more sweat off his brow. "Your confusion was like the woman's. She asked him about the water and about his words which seemed to indicate he was greater than Jacob. I'm told Jesus stopped her in her tracks when he uttered words suggesting he was the Messiah."

"Not again . . . So what happened?"

"After their conversation went back and forth for a few minutes, she tore off back into the town. I can just see her racing into the village telling the others to come see this man at the well and hear what he had to say. Whatever she told them, it motivated many in the town to descend upon the area. When they approached Jesus, he began to speak to them. I don't know what he said exactly, but whatever it was caused them to invite him and his men to stay, and so they did, for two days. That must have been quite a scene, everyone hanging on his words."

Staring down at the well and the small town, I too pictured Jesus amongst the people, talking to them. Whatever he told them must have been significant for this story to be told over and over.

"Cuza, do your stories ever stop?" Before I could look in his direction, I heard a thump. The old man lay still on the ground, his eyes rolled back into his head, his chest heaving up and down, gasping for air, sweat coming from every pore of his body, his mouth slightly open, his skin a pasty white.

I put my hand under his head to raise it off the hard ground while calling to the others who were nearby. Reuel was first on the scene. After telling him to get Joanna and to get me some water and dry clothes, I tried to comfort this good man wondering all the while if I was holding death in my hands?

Joanna and Kish arrived quickly. Taking her husband from me and gently cradling his head in her lap, she made soft sounds as she whispered into his ear. In the meantime Kish placed some rocks under Cuza's feet, raising them above the level of his father's head, explaining this would increase the blood flow to the head. After a few moments, some color returned to the man's face, his breathing easier, the perfuse sweating subsiding.

As the night air grew cooler and the winds became quiet, I wondered if this night would be Cuza's last. Joanna looked at me, "Centurion, thank you for responding to my husband's needs. He's experienced spells like this before and has always recovered after a short rest. He should be able to travel tomorrow although our pace may have to be slower. Kish and the other servants will help me see to his needs now. Again, thank you."

I nodded and backed away to give Kish and the others room to care for this beloved man, a man I considered to be a friend if the gods would permit a Jewish servant and a Roman Centurion to have such a relationship. Searching the sparkling lights above, I prayed to my gods for Cuza's well being, but I felt no warmth of any answers in return. I wondered if it was it time to turn to Cuza's god. Would he answer? Since I didn't know this god and he certainly didn't know me, I made no attempt. With nowhere else to turn, I focused on getting Cuza to Jerusalem as quickly as possible without jeopardizing his health any further.

****

Our march the next day was slow and ponderous, carefully executed as Joanna saw to Cuza's every need. The road became crowded as we shared the rutted trail with other small groups headed in the direction of Jerusalem, almost without exception these travelers making their pilgrimage to celebrate their Passover at the Holy City. With the increased numbers sharing the road, I cautioned Maurus to give special attention to our security when we halted for the night. While it didn't seem likely anyone would challenge us, maintaining security continued to be one principle of war I didn't intend to violate. At a moderate pace, Jerusalem was a day's journey to our south.

From our night encampment perched on the crest of a large hill above the town of Shiloh, we could smell the turquoise blue water of the Great Sea far to our west brought to us by the strong westerly breeze. Cuza and I sat near our fire, admiring the introduction of another night, the brightening stars sparkling in all their glory above us.

"Were you comfortable today?" I asked.

"Yes, reasonably so. I feel much better. . . better than I have in the last weeks. Yesterday was just one of those spells I experience every now and then, although as each one passes, they seem to grow in intensity. When you get to be my age, Aquila, you'll begin to feel your aches and pains. While we ignored them in our youth, they are not so easily dismissed as we get older and grayer." He nodded his head as though speaking to himself, his words coming out with a renewed vitality. "But enough of such talk. Let me tell you about this place."

With that, the servant started my nightly education explaining Shiloh's importance to me, pointing to a spot across the valley, telling me this area had once been the site of a large sanctuary, a gathering place for his nation over a thousand years ago. "At one time, Aquila, this ground was the center of the Jewish nation. The Ark of the Covenant, a symbol of God's presence and instruction was housed in the sanctuary here. Although it was destroyed many years ago by the Philistines, because of its historical significance, we still hold this ground around Shiloh near to our hearts."

When he finished his dissertation, I asked, "Cuza, these history lessons you've given me over the days have been most interesting. How is it you Jews are able to maintain such a tight grip on the past? You know the ancient heroes, speaking about them as though they walked this ground today. You know their stories, the details of the land. Nothing seems forgotten. It's remarkable how your present times are linked so tightly to events that occurred many years ago. Am I wrong about this?"

The old man's furrowed brow signaled his deep contemplation. He stirred some embers in the fire, watching them take on new life. "We Jews believe in our souls God gave us this land forever; that this dry rocky, sometimes barren, yet fertile land, this land of milk and honey, will always be the land of God's chosen people, our land."

He paused for a moment to wipe the tears from his eyes. "Our history, indeed our entire way of life, is tied to this land. My ancestors are buried in this ground all around us. The blood of past generations who fought and died to keep this land in our possession stains the rocks we traverse today. It is important for us to remember the sacrifices made by our forefathers so we, the living, can see and feel the land under our feet deeded to us by God. It is important for us to have kinship with our long departed patriarchs and prophets who set the course of our beliefs. It would be wrong for us to ever, ever forget their sacrifices."

Looking at me with fire in his eye, the man's voice remained steady and firm, "Unlike you Romans who make your way to Gaul and Egypt and other foreign lands to conquer and expand your Empire, we've no desire to do such a thing. We've no desire to ever leave this land. We have no need to conquer new territories because this land is our home, bequeathed to us by Almighty God. Our history tells of the agony of being conquered by other armies, other kings. We know the pain of being threatened and then exiled from this land by the likes of men like Nebuchadnezzar. And we know the joy of the returning to this land a hundred years later."

The man stopped before spreading his arms as he looked about the darkened terrain spread before us. "While some of our people leave this land from time to time for various reasons, all of them know they can always return and they will be embraced. Because of our ties to this sacred ground, we simply want to be left alone to enjoy this gift from God."

The old man was right. We Romans sought conquest, lands to feed our burgeoning population, lands to buffer us from those who wished to defeat Rome. Our national pride was built on subjugating others, like Gaul, and Britain, and the Jews. Out of respect for Cuza I remained silent.

"Aquila, you're a good man. Thank you for giving me the opportunity to speak my mind to you without fear of wrath or judgment. You're a noble warrior not given to abuse or unsavory actions like so many who don your uniform, but to my fellow Jews no matter how good you are, how noble you are, no matter how kind you are as an individual, the uniform you wear will always be a symbol of a nation set on conquering and ruling over God's chosen people. While you and I can respect each other individually, from the larger perspective, there will always be strife and conflict between your Roman eagle and my people until someday your army tires and leaves this land."

Cuza's boldness penetrated deep into my soul. I had always

viewed my surroundings through the prism of a Roman soldier. Rome was always right, its motives always pure, expansion of territory necessary for the well being of our people. But now with Cuza's words ringing in my ears, I could see how we could be viewed: not as saviors or as kind benevolent dictators to the people in whose lands we occupied. To them we were conquerors.

After a long period of silence on both our parts, I tried to fill the void. "You've shed light on the discomfort I've felt from some I've spoken to at various times since I've been in your country. You've given me much to consider." I remained quiet as I stared into the fire. Seeking refuge from further discussion, I said, "It's time to check on our guards." Then I made my way to bed down for the night. After what Cuza said, sleep avoided me once again. With Jerusalem not far away, I wondered what would await me there.

****

Sharp ear-piercing shrieks came from out of the darkness. Drawing my sword, I leaped up from the ground expecting to confront some enemy, the other soldiers around me mirroring my posture. Then the shrieks intensified, this time mournful, filling the air with sounds communicating grief and despair, this noise coming from inside our camp, not outside. It was a woman's cry followed by a man's and then other softer, tear-filled plaintive wails began, all this commotion originating from the area where the servants bedded down.

Moving toward the sounds, Kish met me a few feet from the shelter where the wailing, the crying, the weeping came from. With tears streaking down his face, he gestured toward the tent. "Centurion, my mother just found her husband of many years dead."

I took a step back. "Dead? I just spoke with him a few hours ago. He seemed alert and refreshed. Said he was feeling better."

The young man nodded, shielding his grief as he wiped some tears away on the sleeves of his garments. "He's not been well for some time. That is one of the reasons he didn't go to Tyre with Antipas. He needed to rest to regain his strength. He was saving himself to return to Jerusalem, the city he loved so much. He wanted to see it one more time to embrace it during the upcoming Passover. That was his fondest wish but . . ."

Cuza, my guide and my confidant in so many ways on my journey was now gone. His counsel would be missed, the second of those who gave me strength: first Valerus and now Cuza. I sheathed my sword and stared at the moon as it cast its silver and gray light over the land. I turned back to Kish voicing my simple heartfelt words. "I'm sorry for your loss. What can I do to help you and your mother?"

Before he could reply, cries from his mother and other servants drew his attention, additional wails now came from the other servants as they added their lamentations and their exclamations of sorrow. As I came to understand later, these expressions of grief would go on at various levels unabated until the conclusion of the burial process.

Kish searched my face. "Centurion, my mother and I will talk soon. As is our custom, the burial will take place before the sun sets, sometime later this day. I will keep you informed of her desires and I'll pass on your concern to her. For now this is something we must deal with in our traditions. Again, thank you for your offer. Your kindness is greatly appreciated." As the young man turned to be with his mother, he paused to look at me once again. "Centurion, you should know my father thought a great deal of you. He trusted you . . . with matters few others can ever understand." The young man gave me a slight smile before turning to help his mother.

****

The burial of Cuza took place late in the afternoon one hour before sunset. Kish and Joanna, surrounded by the other servants, buried the man in a deep grave near the peak of the mountain not far from our campsite overlooking Shiloh. Although I only observed the preparations made throughout the day, there was much activity connected to the burial; servants cleaning the body before they wrapped it in linen clothes, the hastily constructed bier upon which the body was transported up the mountain to the burial site. Throughout this process, the wailings continued individually and then collectively when they lowered the body into the grave. It was a solemn ceremony as Kish led those present in several traditional chants as the tears and wailings continued before dirt and rocks of his beloved land covered my friend for eternity. Somehow that seemed fitting to me. He was now part of the land he loved so much. During Kish's recitation of some old Jewish sayings, I prayed to my gods that Cuza's god would greet him warmly.

Later that evening Kish came to my fire letting me they would be ready to travel at first light. Joanna wanted to arrive in Jerusalem by tomorrow evening.

Chapter XIV

Northeast of Jerusalem
Province of Judea
Early morning, March 27, A.D. 34

Our march began slowly at first, Joanna and Kish, their steps
methodical but without enthusiasm, walked together arm in arm,
their heads were up, looking ahead perhaps for the first signs of
Jerusalem. As the day wore on, our pace imperceptibly increased,
mirroring that of others traveling in the same direction, everyone
sensing the nearness of our goal. As I experienced many times
before when formations of soldiers neared the end of a long
journey, their pace increased in anticipation of what laid ahead.
When we caught our first glimpse of the city, I halted our party to
treat everyone to the sight of the beautiful city to our front with its
towering walls and peak of the great temple.

Kish came alongside me taking a great gulp of water from his
water-proof bag. "Quite a sight, isn't it, Centurion?"

After wiping some sweat from my brow, I replied, "Yes, it
is. I didn't have much time to get a sense if the city when I came
through here before."

"It will be a busy place with the upcoming celebration,
pilgrims of our faith coming from faraway lands. There'll be many
merchants after your Roman coins, trying to attract you to every
kind of goods and services you can imagine." He waved his hand
over the area. "As for the city itself, it sits on a series of closely
knit hills on a rocky plateau. When we get there, you'll be able to
appreciate it even more because its elevation allows cool breezes
to spill over the city from the west giving us cooler temperatures.
As you can see from here, the thick walls and watch towers, some
thirty five of them, help protect the city."

I looked at Cuza's son, thinking now how naturally he assumed the role as my teacher. "As I recall Antipas' father made a substantial contribution to what we're observing."

"Yes, he did. The last major assault on Jerusalem occurred around fifty years ago when Herod the Great, recaptured the city with the aid of your army. It was his vision that restored much of the city to its former grandeur, expending enormous amounts to reconstruct the temple, improving the walls and other defensive structures in addition to building his own palace inside the western wall of the city we'll enjoy tonight."

He then pointed to where the foot traffic appeared to congregate. "See how entrance into the city is controlled by a series of eight gates which have names like the 'Sheep Gate' or the 'Valley Gate' and so on. These gates are simply openings in the walls which can be closed quickly if the city is threatened. Those watch towers you see are strategically placed near each of the openings in the walls for additional protection. For example, the palace where Antipas calls home when he's in Jerusalem is near the Corner Gate, which has three large watch towers, Hippicus, Phasael, and Mariamne, protecting it. Those towers are the ones you see on the right side of the city as we look at it."

I looked at the soldiers around us, their impatience showing. Who could blame them? After spending these last few days on the hot, dusty trails, they looked forward to the attractions of this city. As I ordered the resumption of our march, I wondered how Joanna and Kish felt as they saw the city their beloved Cuza longed to see once more. Putting aside the events of yesterday, I too felt a sense of anticipation, my thoughts wondering if a private discussion with Pontius Pilate would be possible, a discussion of the training accomplishments of Antipas' soldiers and perhaps, if the subject came up, a dialogue about a reassignment to Rome at some later date. Maybe . . . .

Pointing toward the eastern side of the city, Kish seemed a bit puzzled. "Centurion, looks like something is going on near the eastern gates, some kind of commotion there. I've never seen anything like that before. The size of the crowd is staggering."

I followed his glance. Was there a revolt in progress? Kish was right; a great number of people seemed to be flooding in that direction, increasing in size by the minute. "Kish, do you need my assistance to take the servants and your mother to Antipas' palace?"

The gloomy countenance on the young man's changed momentarily to a smile. "Not hardly, Centurion."

"I apologize. Of course you don't." Flustered a bit by my thoughtless remark, I went on. "I'm going to take our soldiers in the direction of that crowd. At the next crossroad, you head for the palace and the soldiers and I will take the left fork, the one heading toward the crowd."

As I turned to outline my thoughts to Maurus, the rumble of the gathering became more pronounced. It wasn't my place to interfere with anything Pilate's soldiers were assigned to do with regards to these goings-on, but perhaps my ten men could be of some assistance. The only way I could find out was to be near the crowd.

****

As we approached the rear of the mass, it was much thicker than I realized, growing more packed and louder with each step. Some in the throng sang out joyfully, many held palm branches gesturing at what appeared to be a rider near the front of the procession. Because we were near the tail end of this crush of humanity, we had no idea who or what caused the ruckus. While I assumed it all had to do with the man in the van of the demonstration, based on the size of the crowd, chances of my ten soldiers halting or slowing down this mob appeared nil. All we could do was follow in hopes of learning what this was all about.

With the back of the mob now all around us my soldiers, at my behest, grabbed one middle aged man who was running past us waving a small thin palm branch. Even though the man was out of breath from his efforts to stay up with the rabble around us, I demanded, "What's this all about? What's going on here?"

The man stared at me as he studied my uniform, fear crossing his face first before his anxiety began to melt away, his eyes now showing a new confidence coming over him. He straightened his back, his voice strong, unwavering. "Centurion, don't you know? That man up ahead could be the one to save us, the one our prophets wrote about years ago. What a day this is! I'll be able to tell my grandchildren I was here the day he came." Before I could ask him anymore, he bolted past my soldiers, disappearing into the crowd as he raced to catch his friends.

As the first man got away, Maurus grabbed another man and brought him to me, this one much older than the first man, unable to keep pace with those streaming past us because of his feeble, tired frame. "How do you know this man is the one your prophets wrote about? Did he give some sign or say something?" my voice insistent and probing. "What makes you think he is . . . " I stumbled over the next words, "your Messiah?"

This older man kept a steady gaze on me, his eyes and manner became stronger, a resiliency coming to the fore as he pointed to the front of the crowd, "Centurion, our prophet Zechariah told us our Messiah would appear to us riding on a donkey. That man up there is fulfilling that prophecy. He could be the our liberator, the one who will lift us from your oppression!" The man paused, laughing, "You Romans better get ready to pack up. Your days here are numbered. " He looked at us standing around him, defiance written all over his countenance.

"You insolent dog," spat Maurus, drawing out his sword to beat the man on his head but before the blow fell, I grabbed his arm. My warrior looked at me, his brow turned up in disbelief before he slowly brought the sword back to his side, confusion on his face.

I shook my head. "Not now, Maurus. Not now. Let this man go. There are too many of them for us to hold them all back."

"But these miserable swine need to be taught a lesson," his anger increasing.

The old man began to tremble as he stooped between us, his

earlier confidence now shaken. Staring down at him, I asked, "What's the man's name ahead, the one who you believe is your Messiah?"

The man glanced first at me and then at Maurus whose sword was still not sheathed. Sensing no harm would come his way, the man revealed to me more than I wanted. "Centurion, you Romans are always behind the times, aren't you? Your spies haven't told you?" Drawing himself up to his full height, he exclaimed, "Well, I'll tell you. You'll hear it soon enough anyway. His name is Jesus . . . Jesus of Nazareth. I'll wager you haven't heard of him before, but you'll be hearing plenty about him in the days ahead. Yes sir, plenty about him."

Jesus! Jesus, now close enough I could see the back of his head as it bobbed up and down as he rode the donkey. What could I do?

"Maurus, turn this man loose and follow the crowd from the rear. If you see any harm about to occur to any Roman citizen, step in. I'm going to go on ahead to get in front of this mob to get a better look at this fellow drawing such attention."

Before Maurus could salute, I melted into the outside of the crowd, pushing and shoving my way forward as rapidly as I could, the crowd yielding to my bulk, my uniform, and my insistence, my goal to reach the city gates before Jesus passed through them. After much effort I established a position just in front of the narrow gate where Jesus would have to pass right by me. Many in the crowd who stood near me were apprehensive about my presence, but their attention shifted away from me as the object of their jubilation came closer and closer. Their shouts of "Hosanna" and "Blessed is he who comes in the name of the Lord" drowned out their concerns about me as their anticipation grew and grew the closer the man came.

Suddenly the crowd in front of him parted and there he was, his head erect as he rode on a simple docile donkey, gazing at the people as they threw their palm branches and cloaks along the road to show honor and respect. Philip the fisherman from Bethsaida and some other men who I assumed to be other close followers of

Jesus walked at his side helping to clear a path through the crowd.

Jesus' features at first appeared unremarkable, a man a little taller than the average, his clothes made in the simple style like many of those praising him, his long hair and beard a dark shade of brown groomed in a manner similar to the custom of the day, yet as I watched him closer, those along the edges of the crowd received a touch of his hands as they stretched out theirs. As the procession came slowly closer and closer toward me, I felt I was only one man in the midst of so many who sought his attention, the noise, increasing in volume as the crowd shouted the words, "King" and "Hosanna" as he drew nearer.

When he was within a few feet of me, I looked at his eyes which gave evidence of his intelligence, his sense of purpose, his love, and his humility. His gaze seemed to rest on each individual in the massive crowd, if only for a brief moment, but when his eyes met mine, they did not move. I felt as though he could see into the deepest parts of my heart and my soul and I wondered what he saw. Did he see my confusion, my questioning attitude of who he was or might be but before I could say a word he was gone, swallowed up by the crowd as he made his way into the city.

How unusual for a man to receive such accolades, his entrance almost like a triumphal king, yet it was made on a most humble manner on a donkey instead of riding a large powerful white charger with an army of warriors behind him. He carried no sword or helmet, his only weapon was a message that resonated with these people. Looking about, I realized I was the only one in the crowd who was dressed as a soldier of war. While others had weapons for their personal protection, everyone else in this swirling maelstrom had only their voices as their weapon of choice. Strange how a leader armed with only words and a humble spirit could inspire so much hope in others they believed they could conquer an army equipped with steel and soldiers trained to weld their destructiveness in a most efficient manner?

As the multitude streamed by into the city and the crowd thinned out, Maurus and the other soldiers reached me. "Centurion, what is this all about? Why all this exaltation for one man?"

"Seems this fellow has captured the people's attention because he has given them hope and that hope has touched their lives. Maybe once their Passover Week begins in earnest, what we've witnessed here today will be just a memory, quickly forgotten amongst all the pandemonium of the days." Did I really believe what I'd just said? The words sounded practical, but were they reality?

As the last of the crowd swept by us, I made up my mind to put this behind me. "Maurus, the path is clear for us to go to Antipas' palace and get some of this dirt off us. Do you know the way?"

Maurus smiled. "Yes." Without another word, he took the lead allowing us to reach Antipas' home away from home without disruption. After greeting us and welcoming us inside the palatial residence, the servants, their mood still somber from the death of their respected leader, told me they would inform Kish of our arrival.

****

The front of Antipas' royal palace faced east toward the center of Jerusalem while the back side of the structure was part of the western wall of the city, taking up several city blocks. As I came to appreciate, Antipas' father must have been a man of considerable skill, blending a variety of construction materials together with the most elaborate furnishings, combinations of rich silk cloth colored in the most luxuriant blends of gold, crimson, and turquoise imaginable expertly arranged to make sure visitors knew they were in the presence of wealth and power.

After settling into the quarters assigned me in one of the upper suites in the Hippicus watchtower, I put my head down on the cushiony bed for a moment recalling Jesus' eyes and how they seemed to have entry into my most inner thoughts, wondering what he learned about me. Was I just another man among many he encountered or would our paths be destined to cross again?

****

A loud knock on the door startled me. Was that the morning sun coming through the room's small window? Shaking myself awake, the knock became more insistent. Upon opening the door, an excited servant asked me to join Kish downstairs in one of the large meeting rooms. Did this mean Antipas had arrived or was it something else? Surprised at the request and even more flabbergasted sleep came so easily to me that night, I found Kish pacing the floor, his manner exhibiting nervousness and excitement, apprehension and dread all rolled in one. "Centurion, thank you for coming. Before Antipas arrives here in a day or two, I wanted to meet with you in private."

I gazed at the man. Before I could respond, the servant walked out on to the adjoining open air portico next to a beautiful garden brimming with tall date palms, several stone benches on the outer edges and by the chatter, home to many varieties of birds and bees all seeking sustenance and refuge among the many flowering bushes spread throughout the garden, the space reminding me of the garden at Lucius' headquarters in Capernaum.

In the midst of such beauty, Kish turned to face me. "First, Centurion, thank you again for the kindnesses you showed my father these past months. I don't know if he expressed it to you in that manner, but in all his dealings with other Roman officers, you stood out as one who tried to understand my people, our culture, and our religion. No doubt you were his favorite."

I nodded my head, my senses alerted me to the soft whisper of silk and quiet footsteps behind us, turning to find Joanna meeting my gaze, the redness around her eyes communicating the sadness in her heart, yet she wore a quiet smile. "Thank you for meeting with us, Centurion. My son is right. Your honesty and integrity made a great impression on my husband. You should also know he shared with me some of the challenges you've faced recently as you've discovered more and more about Jesus." I chose to remain silent knowing this woman still in grief needed time to reflect on the events of past and of the uncertainties before her.

"Centurion, from your look, I can see your uneasiness about what will happen to Kish and me. Let me assure you, your concerns are unwarranted. Although my husband suffered from poor health for some time, his many years of faithful service to Antipas did not go unnoticed. In fact Antipas agreed several years ago to honor my husband's wish that Kish would take his father's role in the household when this event of the past days occurred. And as part of this arrangement, Antipas also agreed I would be able to live under his roof for as long as I desire. It is a most unusual arrangement, but it shows the value and depth of my husband's service to the tetrarch."

I look at her astounded. "Thank you for sharing that with me. You have answered one question I had. Nevertheless, is there anything else I can do to assist you at this time?" thinking to myself, perhaps Antipas had more principles than I had given him credit.

Before responding to my query, Joanna moved gracefully to one of the stone benches, making room for the two of us to sit, Kish standing close by. After both of us took a seat, she stared at me for a moment before glancing away to watch some of the birds flit about, going from one beautiful flower to another. Smiling as she watched some of the scarlet and russet colored creatures vie for the prime places to feed, she exhibited a reassurance in her circumstances I found calming, knowing now her well being was assured.

Turning toward me, she said, "As Cuza shared with you once, I've had the privilege of sitting under the teachings of both John and Jesus. Unbeknownst to anyone else except my husband and my son, I have supported Jesus and his followers monetarily for some time. It is something I felt God called me to do and I was glad for the opportunity. I tell you this to help you understand the depth of my belief in this man, but now without my husband to keep me informed of his movements and the reactions of men like Antipas and those he associates with, I must rely upon others." She fixed me with a hard stare. "Will you assist me, Centurion? Will you let me know how I can help Jesus as he faces men like Antipas and those who are in league with him? I am most fearful of what may happen to this man and I need someone dependable to . . . to help me."

I stared at the woman. I wanted to be a comfort to her, but this? Was she asking me to be an informant, a spy? Was I being used for some nefarious plot, some intrigue I had no business in agreeing to? "I'm not really sure I can help you." Part of me wanted to shout out, "*I'm not a traitor, woman, not a traitor to Rome.*" Yet another part of my being counseled me to listen to her, to learn more about what she was asking before rendering judgment.

Joanna showed no signs of acknowledging my quandary as she peppered me with questions. "Was Jesus in the crowd you saw entering the city yesterday?" Without waiting for my answer, she continued. "From what I'm hearing, Jesus may have left the city late yesterday. If he did, I wonder if he'll return today, and if he does, what will that mean to those of us who believe in him? Aquila, what will Antipas do, or the priests, or Pilate? Do you believe they will allow him to be here in their midst stirring up the people or will they leave him alone? I just don't know what to think or where to turn. Will you help me, Aquila?"

Not knowing exactly where she was leading, I left the bench to walk about having no desire to commit to a course of action from which there might be no recovery. While I trusted Cuza enough to answer questions such as this, he was dead, no longer able to help me or his wife in matters she was alluding to. Could I put my trust in his spouse with my innermost thoughts, in her zeal to take some path unknown to me, which might lead to putting me in jeopardy? Perhaps a morsel of information would satisfy her for the time being.

Turning back to the two of them, I responded, "Let me answer your first question. Yes, Jesus was the one the people honored yesterday as he came through the gates. I saw him face to face. That commotion we saw yesterday from the road was his entry into the city. He was the object of all the noise, all the adulation. Energized, the people waved palm branches as they shouted his name, filling the streets as they cried out his name, saying things like "Hosanna" and "Blessed is the coming kingdom of our father David."

"You saw him? So he was in the procession!" Talking now to herself, she stammered as she began to walk around the garden. "Of course, that makes sense. What a scene that must have been with all the people praising him. Oh how I wish I could have been there! Tell me all about it, Aquila. Did he say anything to you? Did you speak to him?" her words tumbling out like a raft moving downstream caught in a fast flowing river.

I looked at Kish for a moment. His eyes told me he too was as interested in my reply as much as his mother. "Centurion, just so you know, like both my mother and father, I too am a believer in what Jesus speaks about. I was the one who accompanied my mother from time to time as she followed Jesus. Please tell us what happened when you saw Jesus." With a voice filled with calm confidence, he went on, "Centurion, my father left out very little of the discussions you two had these past few months so I hope you believe we can be trusted with anything you would have shared with him."

Something in his voice, his demeanor caused me to believe him. With Cuza gone, I needed to trust someone with my muddled thoughts. I looked at the two of them, my eyes darting from one to the other before going on. "Jesus didn't say anything to me, but his eyes communicated understanding. It's hard to explain his look. It was so penetrating. It was as if he could see right into my soul even though it was only for a moment." I was about to add more when an older servant I had not seen before quietly approached.

The man stared at my Roman uniform before pulling Kish off to the side, whispering into his ear. Before allowing him to speak anymore, the young man stopped him with a raised hand and looked at the older man as he pointed toward me. "We can trust this man. Give me your report again."

The man hesitated, gaping first at Kish, then at Joanna and then at me, a glint of fear in his eyes as he appraised my uniform once again, his eyes settling on my weapon. Despite his pensive manner he began. "Early this morning Jesus went to the temple area. Because of the large crowd expected there, many merchants had set up their booths in the temple to sell their goods, including sacrificial animals needed to celebrate Passover. The money changers also set up their booths to exchange currency for those here from far-off lands. As they so often do in situations like this, these businessmen hoped to take advantage of the crowd to charge higher rates than normal." He glanced at me before concluding with bitterness in his voice. "We've come to expect such activity from their kind."

I held up my hand, stopping the man. "So with Jesus seeing all, what did he do?"

The old man became quite animated, his hands and arms flying about as he described the scene. "After looking around at this cacophony fixated on money, he flew into a rage going from one merchant's booth to the next, overturning their tables, dumping their goods on the ground, gold coins flying everywhere. Then he untied some of the animals to be sold and smashed the cages holding the doves to be used for sacrifice, feathers flying about in all directions like a white cloud. He threw benches around as though they were match sticks. The man may not appear so, but underneath his garments he is strong. No one tried to stop him as he shouted, 'My house shall be called a house of prayer' and with fire in his eyes he told the merchants they were turning the temple into a den of robbers and thieves."

Kish asked, "So what happened then? Did any soldiers come? What did the priests do?"

The servant took a breath to collect his thoughts. "When things quieted down a bit," he laughed, "and as the feathers settled back to earth, Jesus went to one of the corners of the temple. Some of the blind and lame I saw in the procession yesterday went to where he sat hoping he would heal them of their infirmities. Many came up to him there. The merchants and the money changers ran to seek help from the priests and teachers of the law who witnessed all this, chattered away like magpies in the opposite corner of the temple. For the longest time none of them had the courage to challenge Jesus. Finally, after much discussion, several of the priests approached him, noting his healing of the infirmed. I heard from those who were nearby say the priests said something to Jesus about the children who were also there praising him. I don't know what his response was but the priests didn't appear too pleased with his words."

Kish reached out his hand and placed it on the man's shoulder. "Thank you for telling us this. You can be sure the three of us will hold your words close. Is there anything else you heard you think we should know about, anything at all?

The man lowered his head, tears welling up in his eyes as he nodded ever so slightly before his words came out like a hammer shattering glass. "Just before I came here, one of my friends overheard several of the chief priests talking about how they intended to deal with Jesus. One of them even mentioned they should consider killing him. I've no way to confirm this and I'm not even sure which priests were having this discussion, but ... I . . . I thought you should know." Tears now came flowing on to the man's face.

Kish wrapped his arms around the man's shoulders, the man's tears flowing unashamedly as Cuza's son comforted him. He then thanked the man once again for his report and walked him out of the garden. When he returned, he asked, "What do you think, Aquila? Could this be the excuse the priests would use to dispose of Jesus?"

I turned to gaze at the beautiful surroundings sheltering us from the all whirlwind surrounding Jesus. Without any intention of doing so, I was fast becoming trapped between the Roman and Jewish worlds, a place I did not seek nor did I wish to be a part of. I needed an escape, a refuge from this cage. "Kish, you've been around Antipas and his associates with far longer than I. What do you think? Where do you see all this going?"

Kish's face took on the mannerisms like his father. Smiling, he said, "I have no doubt what this man told us is the truth. I wish I'd been there; watching those tables flying about, feathers floating up into air, the priests watching their money, their prestige, their pride being tossed about, all the while afraid of what the people would think about them, afraid of the adulation being given to Jesus. It must have been quite a sight."

The man stopped, rubbing his cheek much like I had seen his father do. "My father would know what to do" pausing, speaking in a quiet voice, "I wish he were here." He stood quietly as his mother helped wipe the tears away. Then he took a deep breath to gather himself. Standing a little taller, a little straighter, he offered, "I think the priests are boiling mad. Jesus confronted them in the places these men cherish most; their money and their pride. Because the priests have reputations to uphold and money which they grasp with an iron fist, I don't see how they'll willingly part with either one. I wonder now if Jesus will leave to go back to Galilee or stay around Jerusalem for the Passover. Remaining here seems to me almost a guarantee he will be arrested on some charge."

Before Joanna or I could comment on this, Maurus came into the portico, announcing his presence with a salute as he looked about at the others. "It's all right Maurus. What is it? Do you have something for me?"

"Centurion, word has reached me that Pontius Pilate wishes to see you first thing tomorrow morning. You are to report to him at his headquarters in the Fortress Antonio. No other information was given to me regarding the purpose of this meeting except you are to go alone."

Pilate. His headquarters at the fortress. Could this portend a question of my loyalty? A concern about my seeing Jesus as he entered the city? Before fear gripped my tongue I muttered "Thank you." Alone. I was to go through alone. What did that mean? After dismissing Maurus, I bade a hasty farewell to Kish and Joanna and beat a retreat to my quarters wondering what awaited me tomorrow.

Chapter XV

Pontius Pilate's primary headquarters for Judea was in Caesarea, the beautiful town located hours west of Jerusalem on the Great Sea. However, when there were major celebrations in Jerusalem bringing multitudes into the city, the Governor moved his headquarters to the Holy City into the Fortress Antonio just north of the Temple.

After a fretful night, playing numerous scenarios in my head concerning Pilate's summons, I arrived early to acquaint myself with this place of power. Once past the entrance to the fortress with its customary guard force, I sought out the small legion chapel located just off the main entrance of the building, a sanctuary which housed the symbol of our legion, the golden eagle. As I expected, the soldiers guarding the entrance to the chapel were the epitome of the Legion, tall and well proportioned men with rock solid jaws, immaculate uniforms, each a battle-tested warrior.

After receiving their salute and entering the chapel, the centerpiece of the room was the eagle made of bronze and gold fixed upon a highly polished oak pole, its spreading wings, sharp talons, and its steady unflinching gaze symbolizing all that was good about the Roman Army. This symbol reminded me of my roots: my father and his service, the men who knew him, and the men with whom I had served. My life, my very being revolved around this symbol and all it stood for: the courage, honor, and the glory of Rome. As young soldiers, we learned about the history of the eagle and about the soldiers who revered it, our Legions following it from victory to victory.

One of stories taught me involved Julius Caesar's invasion of Britannia almost eighty years ago. At a critical moment as our soldiers floundered in the surf, unable or unwilling to continue their assault on this foreign soil, the standard bearer, the Legionnaire charged with carrying the eagle into battle, leaped from his boat, jumping into the foaming, uncertain waters. As he ran headlong toward the enemy horde, the rest of the Legion saw the courage of this one man. They cheered his daring and jumped into the swirling waters behind him, overcoming the enemy forces as they followed their eagle to victory. The Jews could have their Messiah and their miracles but our army had its eagle. Did I really need more than that?

As my mind kept replaying other events of heroism and courage from our glorious past, I began to pray once again to my gods asking Minerva, the Goddess of wisdom to go with me as I met with Pilate, wondering again what lay ahead. If Pilate knew of my search for Jesus, was my loyalty, my allegiance about to be challenged? While these negative thoughts continued to hold me tightly, one of Pilate's secretaries signaled me. "Pilate will see you now, Centurion."

Following the man down a long hallway, he ushered me into Pilate's private office, a workplace I found to be smaller than anticipated, furnishings neat and functional, unlike Antipas' flair for the elaborate and gaudy. After receiving my salute, the governor came from behind his small writing table to greet me, pointing toward the two simple chairs in the room. Because my prior dealings with the man over a period of several years had always been at a distance, he surprised me by the warmth of his smile. Pilate was a man of medium stature although he stood tall and had a commanding air about him. His reputation as a shrewd administrator was well documented having been in his current position for over five years after replacing Valerius Gratus by Tiberius' order. I searched for a hidden meaning behind his affable greeting as I prepared myself for the unknown.

"Centurion, my time is short today, but it is good to see you again. What has it been, eight, nine months since we last hoisted a cup together?"

"Yes sir." Amazing. Before leaving the headquarters at Caesarea and assuming my posting at Machaerus, the last time I saw Pilate was at a drunken dinner with many other officers in attendance. Because of his highly inebriated state, his memory of anything about that night astounded me.

"Well it is good to see you again." With that perfunctory comment, Pilate began praising the training improvements achieved at both Machaerus and at Tiberias. "You must have made quite an impression on Antipas. Every letter he sends me includes some comment about how pleased he is in your abilities. As the one with overall responsibility for this region, I appreciate of your efforts in this regard because I know how difficult training auxiliary formations can be. I also want you to know that before he sailed for Rome, I took the opportunity to spend time with your second in command at Machaerus, Valerus. Despite his grievous injury, he showed himself to be a most impressive soldier." Pausing for a moment, he continued, "And he spoke quite highly of you."

The man stopped to sip something from his cup on the table between us although he didn't see fit to share its contents with me. "When I heard you were here in Jerusalem, I wanted to take a moment to learn about your career aspirations, your goals. You've served Rome well in this disgusting, flea bitten land and soon time will come for your exemplary duty to be rewarded." He sat back on his chair, waiting. "So what will it be, Aquila? Some plush headquarters where you can enjoy the finer aspects of life? Or more time with another legion? What's your preference?"

My head whirled about. Among all the scenarios I anticipated, this was not one of them. What could I say? I started off stumbling and babbling my words, not knowing how to properly express my longings. "Sir, as you know, my father's service inspired me to be a soldier. My initial assignment as a Legionnaire ..."

Pilate held up his hand stopping me, smiling as though he

enjoyed my discomfort. "Aquila, don't waste my time with things I already know: your service in Gaul, your promotions, your service in the Legio VI Ferrate and now the Legio X Frestensis, about your decorations for courage and so forth. You haven't answered my question. When your mission is finished to Antipas' satisfaction and mine, where would you like to be reassigned? Surely you have thoughts in this regard."

Embarrassed by my ramblings, I tried to recover. "I apologize, sir. Your question caught me off guard. Let me say without reservation, it is my greatest desire is to return to Rome, perhaps as a leader in the Praetorian Guard. Since my family resides on the outskirts of that city, to serve the Emperor there would be ideal."

"Yes, I can understand that." He grinned at me. "That corresponds with what Antipas indicated in his writings to me." Leaning back in his chair, he fixed me with his stare. "I understand from Antipas you've become a valuable asset to him. From my knowledge of you, I would have been surprised if he said otherwise. Yet I'm curious, why do you suppose he feels comfortable in having you so close? That has not always been the case with other officers I've sent him. While Antipas and I disagree about many things, it seems we both appreciate your talents and gifts."

Leaning back in my chair, I blurted out, "Perhaps I give him comfort because of my honesty. There are few in his extended circle of advisors who give him that kind of advice. Most others in his inner circle appear to be sycophants at best, cowards at the worst. While Antipas can be self absorbed, he requires someone around him who will tell him what he needs to hear, not necessarily what he wants to hear."

Pilate nodded his head as though he was making some mental note of my comment, before his right hand came to his lips in reflection. "Yes, you're probably correct on that point."

If there was more he wished to discuss, the moment passed as a quiet knock at the door drew his attention: the same secretary who accompanied me to this office, stepping just inside the door announcing, "Sir, there is a representative from the high priest here to see you. Seems he has a matter of some urgency."

Rising to his feet indicating our time was finished, Pilate gave the man a quick wave of the hand. Ushering me to the door, he said, "I wish we had more time to talk about our soldiers and how you've made a difference in their training. You have information that needs to be shared with others and so I'll schedule another time to meet with you on that topic. You are fortunate you can concentrate on soldiers instead upon matters of political and religious dithering. Be assured, I'll keep your future desires in mind. I will also keep you in mind as special tasks come our way. A man in my position always needs to have trusted men available for extraordinary, unusual events that arise from time to time."

****

I walked slowly back to Antipas' palace stopping to look at some of the fine weavings and jewelry the merchants displayed along the narrow streets, their efforts to entice my interest unsuccessful as I saw nothing my wife would find pleasure in wearing. While I aimlessly strolled along, the busyness of the city all around me, I reflected again on my meeting with Pilate. If nothing else, this influential leader knew it was my heart's desire to someday return to Rome. I was also grateful to know that despite my many apprehensions about Antipas, it appeared his sensitivity to my longings had struck a chord with the man. Perhaps I had misjudged him.

Upon reaching the palace, there was a non-stop flurry of activity filling the courtyard. From all trunks of luggage being unloaded from the wagons and the hustling of the servants back and forth carrying various items of merchandise, it was apparent the tetrarch and his party had arrived from their time of relaxation. While neither Antipas nor Herodias was in sight, Kish's voice carried across the square as he supervised the movement of all the belongings, providing direction to the organized chaos all about him, giving evidence the time spent under his father's tutelage had not been wasted as the servants followed his instructions, moving with speed and a clarity of purpose, everyone in motion in an ordered fashion.

When he came out to inspect the wagons, Kish saw me standing off to the side. Smiling he said, "Centurion, as you can see, Antipas has joined us. Although he is a bit winded from his journey, he asked me to tell you to have dinner with him tonight so you can elaborate on the report you sent him a few weeks ago." Drawing closer to me, he lowered his voice. "Did Pilate have anything to say about Jesus? I thought he might want some type of report from the last few days."

Glancing about, I spoke in a whisper, "That subject never came up. Perhaps Jesus' movements the past few days are less important considering all the other activity of the Passover or maybe the high priests haven't seen fit to kept Pilate informed. Right now I'm in no position to know, so I won't hazard a guess. Concerning Antipas' invitation, please convey my delight to dine with him this evening. For now I'll be going. It appears you have enough to worry about right now."

Kish gave me a wry smile. "Yes, I do. While my father drove me hard as he trained me, as I look around, I'm grateful for his stringent counsel." With that said, he turned his attention back to insuring that the orderliness continued. I watched for a moment longer, impressed how this young man refused to let any sign of pandemonium or turmoil take over the ongoing process as he made his presence felt everywhere at once, issuing orders to some, encouraging others, never halting for a moment, any signs of sorrow of his father's death put aside for the time.

****

The tetrarch greeted me warmly when I arrived at his suite of rooms. Now used to the decorum the man enjoyed, the elaborate decorations of fine silk and materials no longer held me in awe. Surprised I was the sole guest, a meal of well prepared fish and fine fruits served by Kish appeared as soon as we sat down on the heavy cushioned reclining couches. With the pleasant smell of the meal as a backdrop, Antipas spent considerable time talking about the beauty of Tyre, its climate, its spectacular views of the sea. Once Kish cleared the main course, leaving a delicious red wine and fresh fruit, the tetrarch's voice took on a more thoughtful tone. With a large cup of wine in his hand, he asked, "Well, tell more about your search for this Jesus fellow. After reading your report, I suspect for brevity's sake, you omitted some details."

I moved forward in my seat, looking at the ruler for a moment judging which details I could provide which would satisfy the man's curiosity. "As you gleaned, he is a most interesting man. He travels around Galilee and the surrounding region with a very dedicated group of men whom he teaches his views of religion and their god. As I mentioned in my writings to you, from everything I can determine, he has a positive impact on the small towns and villages he visits, teaching and preaching, and most importantly to the people, he spends a great deal of his time healing their illnesses and disabilities."

I paused to sip some wine to slow my speech. "While I'm still not sure how he is able to accomplish these feats of healing, I'm convinced they occur because so many bear witness to these events. It's not clear where he and his men live, although the region around Capernaum is a possibility. With your knowledge of the Jewish religion, you can appreciate far better than I, how some people might consider him the Messiah written about by your prophets."

When I said the word "Messiah", Antipas' head jerked up as he almost spilled his wine. "Messiah you say? Some think of him as Messiah? That is most interesting as well as troubling to a degree. Please, go on. I've a few things to tell you when you're finished."

Not knowing where he was going or what information he already possessed, I proceeded with my rehearsed dialogue. "I've found no evidence suggesting Jesus or his men receive any compensation for these deeds he performs. Unlike the priests, who we both know extract monies from the people from time to time, Jesus and his men apparently do not. I'm not sure how they sustain themselves for there is no indication they profit from their service to the people. From a political point of view, I've heard nothing of Jesus or his men speaking against Rome or against you. One comment attributed to him when queried about money was 'Render on to Caesar what is Caesar's, render on to God what is God's', but I'm not sure if this statement is accurate. In sum, regarding a direct threat against you or Rome, I don't see one at this time."

"No threat, you say," he smirked. "Ah, Aquila, in some many ways, you are a most naïve man." He put down his cup. "There are many others who don't agree with you. We'll talk about that when you get finished," Antipas said with a smile.

Considering his comment and manner, I decided to open myself a little more. "Sir, to give you an idea of this man's popularity, I witnessed from afar his entry into Jerusalem several days ago. He was riding on a donkey as the people matted his way with palm leaves and their cloaks. With so many shouting his praises, it was clear he is a very popular man. Recent reports indicate he went to the temple and took the merchants there to task for selling their wares in this sacred area. While I'm sure this raised a ruckus, I don't know what the long term implications of this are, but from what occurred, I'm certain he has the attention of the religious rulers."

Antipas stood up and began pacing the floor. The torches and candles spread throughout the room portrayed him in a haughty moving series of pictures on the walls as he moved about, rubbing his chin repeatedly as he walked about. When he finally sat back down on the thick cushions, he filled his wine cup to capacity. Almost surely drunk, his words came out slurred. "Centurion, you're a good man, one given to facts and figures, one who sees the world as black or white, good or bad. You take men at their word, not anticipating their ulterior motives. You expect people to be as honest with you as you are of them, admirable traits to be sure."

After swallowing half his cup of the red nectar, he finished his comparison. "I, on the other hand, am much more suspicious, more leery of what a man says or does as opposed to what he really means. I'm more skeptical of human ambition, believing most men have an inherent lust for power." He chuckled at his last statement. "Yes, as I consider this more, you're like an arrow pressing toward a goal. I, on the other hand, am more like the bow, directing, and launching out many arrows in a flurry knowing that if I shoot enough arrows, I will accomplish what I want."

With nothing to add one way or the other, I drank more wine.

After taking a large gulp of his wine, he pressed on. "For your profession, your personality traits are appropriate. However, as a political figure, I deal with life differently, my experience teaching me to always look for what others are trying to take away from me, or to be mindful of how they might seek to take advantage of me. Life to me is a game: if someone takes something from me, I lose and the other person wins. To you Jesus is not a threat. He is simply a man who is helping others without asking for something in return, a most worthy goal from your point of view." His voice quaked as he thundered, "But to me, this man Jesus constitutes a major threat because he is taking away power and prestige that should be mine, and mine alone!"

Antipas stopped for a moment, his voice returning to a more calm tone before rising in vehemence once more, the longer he spoke. "In my view, as the people give Jesus more respect and honor, they give me and those like me, less and less. To our religious leaders, anyone who builds a following among the people reduces their power and their influence, to say nothing of the financial implications to them. His entry into the city two days ago and his actions at the temple will most likely be a defining moment for him. The chief priests, in particular, want a permanent solution found to rid themselves of this man once and for all because, as I said, he is a direct threat to their influence, something they've grown accustomed to through many generations.

I sat still trying to wrap my arms around all his words and their meanings. Antipas did not seek my counsel as he continued to vent, his thoughts becoming clearer to him the longer he spoke.

With narrowed eyes, his lips now pursed, he continued.

"Although I've only been in the city for a few hours, I've already heard there is a scheme afoot to eliminate this man. While I've heard no specifics, something is in the works. You need to know that because, while I hear your comments and try and balance them with others I'm privy to, there is something much larger going on here. You're fortunate in many ways, that while you've not been afflicted with the political disease some of us have, as a man of the sword, you may be once again called upon to be the instrument used to carry out others' decisions. While this may not seem fair, it's reality."

It was now my turn to fill my wine goblet, to pause and reflect upon the deeper meanings of his words. Why was it that men, if they could be called such, like Antipas and his religious counterparts, seldom wanted to dirty their own hands implementing their deadly decisions? My thoughts raced . . . What kind of plot was Antipas alluding to? If this was a Jewish matter, a religious issue, could this really involve me as a soldier of Rome? Unlike at Machaerus, here there were many capable of dealing out any punishment ordered by the religious rulers. I looked down at my sandals, the leather a constant reminder that as a soldier, my duty to Rome always came first. Duty first! But where was my duty to another innocent man?

I nodded my head slowly, "I understand what you're saying. If I have a part to play in this matter, I will do my duty as required. Is there anything else?"

"Yes . . . yes there is. I'm glad we had this discussion, if for no other reason to let you know the time spent on your search for this man was not in vain. With Jesus now here in the city, anything decided by the chief priests will be easier to conclude here rather than chasing the man down in the countryside. Some of my sources tell me the priests believe they may be able to get some help from one in Jesus' inner circle to help trap him. From your knowledge of his intimate group of followers, is that possible?"

A traitor in Jesus midst? Would any of those men who believed as earnestly as Philip betray their master? After a quick moment in thought, I shook my head. "I really can't say. I've only spoken with one of them. If the others close to Jesus believe him with the same intensity as this one man, I doubt any of them could be persuaded to violate the trust they have in him. However, since I've only met this one man out of perhaps a dozen or more, I can't speak with absolute certainty on this matter. From my perspective, I would say it is possible one of them may turn against him, but it's highly unlikely."

The tetrarch considered my words but did not respond. After another long period of silence, he declared, "I guess we'll just wait and see."

Then he began to chuckle. "It seems as though the priests are still considering alternatives, so I'll let them proceed without any interference or advice from me. After all, the people still link my name with John's demise. For now, I intend to stay on the periphery of all this. If they ask, I'll relay what you have told me. It is time they bore the brunt of this issue instead of me."

Then he glanced at me out of the corner of his eye. "Aquila, I would also appreciate if you would let me know what Pilate may be thinking about all this. I understand you saw him today. Did the subject of Jesus come up in your discussions?"

How subtle! First he confides in me and now he wants to act as a spy providing him Pilate's innermost thoughts! I would not, could not act on his behalf. Trying to keep the ire out of my voice, I returned his glance with a hard stare. "Pilate and I discussed matters of training and personal. Regarding any other concerns, I will not breech any confidences given to me by Pilate. Let me be very clear on this. I will not breech any confidences given to me by Pilate."

"Oh, of course, I understand," he said, stammering as he sought to backtrack from his comment, his face reddening a bit. "I only meant if there was something Pilate thought I should know please don't hesitate to pass it on to me. Of course, I meant no inference you should put loyalty to me ahead of your loyalty to Rome. That would be . . . ridiculous."

An icy silence filled the room. "You are correct, Antipas. I'm glad we understand each other. That would be ridiculous. Is there anything else you wish to discuss?"

Without any other meaningful conversation, I left Antipas' chambers. Obviously the concerns about Jesus were growing. Why else would Antipas feel the need to pressure me to act as a spy against my chain of command? Yes, the pressure concerning the affairs of Jesus must be mounting.

Chapter XVI

Jerusalem
Province of Judea
March 31, A.D. 34

With no training requirements or any specific instructions from Antipas, it seemed this morning could be invested in learning more about Jerusalem. After mentioning my desires to Kish, within an hour, he sent word for me to meet him at the entrance to the palace. When I arrived, standing next to him was an elderly short, stocky man with gray hair giving him an air of great intellect, his blue eyes bright and clear. He held an old worn stick in his right hand to provide him insurance as he walked. At first glance could have been Tobias' twin, the man I'd met at the Jordan.

"Centurion, this is Shamer, an old friend of my father's. He has a vast knowledge about Jerusalem and the surrounding area and is available to be your guide today."

After acknowledging my thanks to Kish, the old man said nothing until we took our first steps outside Antipas' holdings. "Kish told me much about you, Centurion. What would be your pleasure, places to enjoy revelry, places to shop for fine things to send to your family?" Yet before I replied, he rambled on, "Those are the usual haunts of the men who war Rome's uniform, but my friends tell me your interests are different. Do they speak the truth, Centurion?"

I gave the man an easy smile. "My interest should not be too challenging for a man like you, Shamer. I simply want to learn more about your city, how it came to be, and about the people. I've been traveling throughout your land for many months and now I've several hours to appreciate your capital city. So with that simple guidance, I place myself in your hands."

Shamar merely nodded as he led the way in an easterly direction walking haltingly because of his debilitation through the narrow streets now somewhat familiar to me. After making our way along the first block where markets teemed with the masses purchasing their breads, their fruits, and their meats. The smells of all these foods blended together into a rich pleasant aroma that periodically turned rancid as they mixed with the foul stench of the donkeys, sheep, and goats, all occupying the same crowded spaces. We stopped to sample some local baked bread, freshly made from a combination of wheat and rye. After greeting my companion with a friendly smile, the owner of this small business provided us a bench to watch the coming and goings in the constricted thoroughfare. As the last of the crumbs of the warm bread fell to the ground, Shamar began his first discourse.

"Jerusalem sits upon a plateau inhabited for over two thousand years and it has known many masters. King David and Solomon, his son, were our two men most influential in first building the walls, and in Solomon's case, bringing great wealth to the city and constructing the temple. Our city has been torn apart and then rebuilt more times than I care to count. I could bore you with many names involved in these changes of ownership but for now, let's head for temple. Forgive me, but at my age, it will take some time to get there.

Before we took our first steps, I asked, "Can we attribute all this activity to the ceremonies this week?"

"For the most part, yes, although the city is normally quite busy. Many of live here, however, enjoy the increased business activity, although the noise and the disorder is something my bones can do without." He looked around carefully before challenging the impatient throngs whirling around us. "Come."

****

The Temple with its massive walls dominated Jerusalem's landscape making up twenty percent of the entire space inside the city walls. While I had passed close to it several times the past few days, I had given little consideration to what lay inside. With Shamer's halting steps slowing our pace, we trudged up the slight incline to the outer ring of the temple area, an area called the *soreg*, a low wall surrounding the entire complex.

The old man glanced at the opening through the wall, "Entrance into the sacred areas of the temple is restricted to Jews, but you are permitted into the courtyard. Between your uniform and my standing in the community, no one will challenge us." With that said, we marched up the steps passing through what Shamer called *the Beautiful Gate* into a large open area, shaped in a large square, porticos running all along the interior walls, made of cedar, supported by stout marble pillars.

"As you see, Centurion, many people gather in this courtyard, many hoping to pass on their petitions to the priests who are the only ones allowed to enter the Temple sanctuary through the *Nicanor Gate* you see there," pointing toward another gate with his stubby finger. "Several days ago, Jesus caused quite a commotion here. If you look closely, you may see the results of his tirade, the feather or two from a dove or a small coin, maybe some straw still not swept away yet, all the result of him challenging the merchants and money changers who were conducting business in this place. Oh, that must have been quite a sight watching him throw their wares and profits up in the air, "the man smirked as he looked about.

Inspecting the ground closer, the old man was right; tell-tale signs of Jesus' rampage lay all around me.

The old man kept his eyes upon me. "I just thought you should see this place. I won't tire you with what happens inside the sanctuary, certainly nothing like what you experience with your Roman gods, other than to say it is inside there, sacrifices are made for our sins, the priests seeking atonement on our behalf for our transgressions before Almighty God."

"Are you saying only your priests have the ability to communicate with your god and they do it inside there?" I asked pointing toward the tallest walls of the sanctuary clearly visible from our location.

"Yes, simply put, you could say that."

My mind quickly transported me to Nain, to Nazareth, to Capernaum, and to the people I'd talked with, trying to assimilate my knowledge of Jesus with Shamer's teaching. If Jesus was some supreme being with a relationship his god, no wonder the priests would feel threatened, their sense of purpose and power came from these tall beautiful walls and their colorful dress. Is that what Jesus felt a few days ago -- abhorrence for how some men misused their power, through tall buildings, and pompous grandeur instead of touching and ministering to the masses? Here I was trying to avoid all the confusion of the past few months and now I was right in the middle of it again. It was time to escape.

"Shamer, I've seen enough. Take me to see what makes Jerusalem different from other capital cities I have seen."

The old man glanced up at me, his right eye turned up in puzzlement. "Alright, Centurion, of course, as you wish. Follow me."

****

"Since you've just seen the grandest place in Jerusalem, let's walk along the walls toward the south end of the city." After a few slow steps the old man stopped and asked, "Because you've spent considerable time with Antipas, I'm surprised you haven't asked me any questions about his father."

"What do you mean?"

"Because the temple suffered so much because of the wars experienced by our city before his reign, Herod decided to rebuild it. It was his pride and joy. While he spent his money lavishly throughout the territories he governed, nothing approached the funds he used to complete the construction of the temple in his seventy years upon this earth."

I leaned against the hard gray stones of the wall allowing the old man time to catch his breath. "I haven't spent much time delving into the history of Antipas' father. Do historians consider the rebuilding of the Temple to be the highlight of his life?"

The old man rubbed his cheek for a time looking sadly at the rough stony path at our feet. Pursing his lips together, he gave me a thoughtful stare. "From my perspective his highlight you've just seen. I'll have to give your question more time. For now, that is my most positive comment."

As he leaned heavily on his crutch, he spoke softly. "On the negative side, there are several points for your consideration. First, Herod was an extremely jealous man, afraid of anyone who he considered might be lurking about ready to impinge about his power and pride. This anxiety led him to execute one of his ten wives, a beautiful dignified woman, for some martial indiscretions, maybe on her part or maybe on his."

The old man paused before adding, "Then later, almost at the end of his life, this character flaw caused him to kill two of his sons, Antipater III, his oldest son whom he executed only five days before his death and then another son, Aristobulus. Herod murdered both men because they grew impatient for their chance to follow him as ruler. As you can take from this, the man employed fear and intimidation as his chief way of governing."

I nodded at the old man's words, saying nothing.

The old Jew took a few more steps before stopping again, this time with tears in his eyes as he maintained his balance through the heavy pressure he put on his heavy wooden rod. "And then there was another offense, this one more egregious than the others combined. It too occurred when Herod was an old man."

"Who did this involve?"

"Children . . . many, many children." Tears now streamed down the man's face.

****

We took seats on a large rock near a small garden near the wall, other passers-by questioning this strange scene, a Roman Centurion trying to comfort an old Jew whose head lay buried in his hands. Because of my uniform, no one interfered.

Once Shamer gathered himself, his story poured out. "It all started over thirty years ago when Augustus, the Emperor, decided to have a census made of the entire Roman world. This decree required every man return to the home of his birth to register and as you can imagine, this created great turmoil with many people on the roads, all seeking shelter at the same time as they traveled about. There was one such family traveling to Bethlehem, a small town a half days journey south of here, the man and his young wife, she great with child, ready to give birth almost any day. When they arrived at Bethlehem around dusk one night, they sought refuge in the town's inns but no rooms were available anywhere. The innkeepers there wanted to help but there was nothing available."

"So what did this man do to care for his family?"

"The only thing he could, the only option left to him."

"And that was . . . ?"

"To bed his wife and himself down in an area around some feeding troughs, or *mangers* as we call them, part of the stable for the animals, in this case an area that extended out from a large cave owned by the man who rented the couple this space. You've been around enough animals to know what this must have looked like, smelling of the daily activities of the animals, certainly one of the least convenient places to care for a woman ready to give birth, but again, this was the only shelter available."

I watched the old man, his head down. I blurted out, "So what does this have to do with Herod?"

The man raised his head. "Everything, Centurion, everything." After exhaling a great sigh, he continued, "Within a day or so, this young woman gave birth to a beautiful boy and this is where the story turns. Seems three Magi, men of considerable means from some lands far to the east, arrived in Jerusalem with their considerable party of servants seeking an audience with Herod, meeting him most likely in the same building you slept last night.

They told him they had been following a bright star in the western sky for many days believing this star foretold of a miraculous birth of a boy they called, 'The King of the Jews'. These men told Herod the star had stopped its movement somewhere over Herod's land and they had come to worship this newborn and assumed Herod knew something about this.'" Smiling, Shamer said, "Every time I think of this story, I can see Herod's face getting red, suspicion written all over it as he heard the Magi's proclamation."

I adjusted my seat on the hard rock. "Alright so these men are following this mysterious star, they meet with Herod, so . . ."

"Herod then seeks counsel from his most learned men who frantically search the writings of ancient prophets eventually finding some writings from Micah which stated the Messiah would be born in Bethlehem. Our great ruler then asked the Magi to search for the child and when they found him, let him know the location so he might go and also worship the babe."

"Based on Herod's jealous streak I can see where this is leading."

"And eventually the Magi did as well. After traveling to Bethlehem and finding the child in the care of his mother and father, these wise men showered the new born with precious treasures – gold, incense, and myrrh – and then as I understand it, each had a dream which warned them not return to Herod. These three followed their dreams and returned to their land by another route, never passing on any information to Herod."

"And when Herod learned of their deception, he sought to kill this child?"

The man's face now became filled with pain and anguish before answering my question. After a very long pause, his words came out in a whisper. "Exactly. He was so angry he dispatched a swarm of soldiers to Bethlehem but since he didn't know who to look for, he ordered his men to kill all the male children two years and younger living in the vicinity of the town." Shamer sat quietly, wiping the tears from his eyes. "Estimates of the children murdered ran into the hundreds but there is no real way of knowing."

The old man stopped. "Centurion, I see the question on your face so let me answer it now. The child's father, the object of Herod's search, also had a dream telling him of Herod's intentions. Upon being awakened by this dream, the father gathered up his family and fled that same night to Egypt where they stayed until learning of Herod's death."

"Did this family ever return here?"

Shamer gave me a wide toothless grin. "Yes. They returned to our land resuming their lives in their home town, the mother caring for the child who was soon joined by other siblings in the household as the father returned to his trade as a skilled carpenter."

With a queasy stomach I asked, "Where did they settle down?"

"Joseph and Mary went back to their hometown of Nazareth."

To break away from Shamer's words about Nazareth, I muttered something about having to return to Antipas' palace, but he stopped my hasty retreat. "Centurion, before we part company, may I speak freely?"

"By all means."

"You seem to have a genuine interest in my people and our way of life. I don't know how or why, but I sense the lives of my people are somehow interwoven with yours. I don't know why I sense this but I do. I pray it will all lead to God's glory. I will leave you now."

Before he took two steps, I called out to him. "Wait. Tell me how you know so much about the birth of this one little boy and Herod's involvement in the death of all those children?"

The old man fought to keep his balance, his body tilting slightly to one side. "I lived in Bethlehem for many years before I moved to Jerusalem. In my younger days I was in innkeeper there. Oh, I'm not the one who provided the young couple their meager lodging, that man was a friend of mine. Sadly for my part, I was one of those who turned Joseph away when he came seeking shelter the night he and Mary arrived in our town." The man's eyes looked down. "I was one of those who had no room for them. Then later when Herod's soldiers descended upon my village, despite my best efforts to hide my one year old son, the soldiers, many of them dressed like you, found him, butchering him before my eyes. The memories of those days will never leave me. Every time I see a small baby boy, I see my only son again."

Without another word the old man turned and slowly made his way toward the southern part of the city, leaving me behind with thoughts about Jesus, Joseph, Nazareth, and Messiah co-mingling. When would this end?

****

Despite my musings on the Jews and this man from Nazareth, I took time meditating anew on who I was and on my country and my army. My mind grappled with what I knew, what I had been taught. It kept coming back to one clear strident answer. Rome, Rome was my call, my destiny. It was my duty, my chosen duty, to obey her commands. With my thoughts harden once more, coursing through my veins, I straighten my back and returned to Antipas' palace with a new spring in my step. The mid afternoon gave off radiant warmth which encouraged me to seek relaxation in Antipas' pool before the sun went down. It was time to enjoy the pleasures afforded me since the gods deemed that I be a Roman Centurion.

****

Arriving back at the palace Kish greeted me, his voice tense. "Kish, what is it? Something troubling you?"

"No, everything seems to be going well. Although my father is not here for me to lean on, I believe the preparations are in place for the celebration of the Passover meal tonight. With so many details to attend to, and, being the perfectionist I am, I always want this celebration to be honoring to God. I believe I've done everything my father taught me. Without his counsel, I've no one to recheck the details."

227

"Ah, Kish, you're a smart man. From what I know about your father, I'm sure he taught you well, down to the smallest detail, no doubt." What else could I tell the young man? He faced a new challenge, a new responsibility. Now was not the time to introduce any misgivings into his thought process.

The man smiled his agreement. "Yes, of course, you're right." As I turned to walk away, he glanced around to make sure we were alone before he asked, "I'm curious, have you heard anything about Jesus or his disciples? I'm told he spent these last few days near Bethany, a small village a short day's walk to our east. Since today is the first day of the Passover, I anticipate he'll celebrate this most holy day somewhere in Jerusalem."

More Jewish muddle - Passover. "Kish, since you brought it up, what exactly is Passover, its significance?"

"I've only a few minutes . . ." Pointing to a nearby bench, Kish hurried his words. "First, do you know fifteen hundred years ago our people were enslaved in Egypt?"

"When I was stationed there I recall hearing something about that, but I never paid much attention to it."

"A long tale made short is the Jews were enslaved in Egypt for several generations before God remembered an unconditional covenant he made to us promising we would settle in this land where we now walk, and that we would live here for all time."

"Alright, I think I understand. Go on."

"To meet his pledge God raised up a man named Moses to free our people from Egyptian bondage. Moses, through God's providence, made numerous appeals to the Egyptian pharaoh to let the Jews leave Egypt, but the pharaoh would have none of it because their work as slaves was vital to the Egyptian economy and their way of life. Even after God then wrought nine devastating plagues upon Egypt, these had no effect upon this ruler. God then decided to bring down a tenth plague, the most destructive one imaginable."

Kish stopped to emphasize his next point. "God instructed

Moses to have all Jews on one specific night kill an unblemished lamb and place the blood of this animal on the door frames of their homes as a sign that God's people lived there. The Jews were also told to eat a meal consisting of roasted meat from the lamb, along with bitter herbs and unleavened bread as a sign of their trust and obedience to God. His final instruction was the Jews must remain in their homes on that one night until the next morning. The Jews followed Moses' instructions to the letter."

I held up my hands. "Kish, you've got to slow down. I'm trying to stay with you in all this detail – plagues, pharaohs, slaves, blood of lambs, door frames. What's the point to all this?"

Kish sighed, letting out a deep breath. "I apologize, this story is so familiar to me I forgot it's new to you. I'll speak slower. We're almost done." Then he took another breath before going on. "On the designated night, God swept over the land of Egypt, striking down the first born sons in every home which did not have the blood of the lamb on its door frame. Can you imagine the terror when every Egyptian household lost its first born son on the same night? But the Jews, all of whom, followed God's instructions, remaining safely in their homes as God's wrath passed over them. No harm came to them. Death did not visit their homes." The young man had been speaking faster and faster as his story reached its climax.

"There's the story. That is where the name, Passover, comes from. Because the blood of the lamb protected our people, God's vengeance, his wrath, his angel of death 'passed over' their homes."

I stared at the man, shaking my head in amazement. "It is difficult to fathom all that. What did the Egyptians do? How did this pharaoh react?"

"As you can imagine, the entire Egyptian nation devastated. All that death! Did I mention this death sentence also applied to their livestock as well? With his nation now suffering because of his decision, the pharaoh summoned Moses during the night imploring him to lead the Jews out of Egypt as quickly as possible. Without hesitation, Moses organized the Jews to leave the only homes they had ever known. Imagine six hundred thousand men and their families and their belongings preparing to leave. What a massive effort this must have been! Miraculously, Moses accomplished all this in a short time and the journey to the land promised them by God began. Within a day or so after their departure, the pharaoh changed his mind and decided to pursue the Jews. That is another amazing story about how God saved his people from this pharaoh which will have to wait until later."

With the sun now setting in the west and the warm air giving way to the cooler night air, Kish sat back, "I'm out of time, Centurion. Anyway that should give you some idea about why this holiday is so important to us. As the people celebrate the Passover tonight, you'll notice the city will be quieter, many people remembering what we've just talked about, celebrating God's protection of us as our nation returned to the land He promised us."

My mind raced as I compared my gods with Kish's. I could not recall a time when Mars or Jupiter had ever made their presence known to such a degree to my countrymen as the Jewish god did for his people. What did all this mean? "I'll say this for you, Kish, between you and Shamer, you keep my interest in your stories. I'm sure I'll have some questions after some reflection on all this."

"Of course, I understand."

If Kish was going to say more, one of Antipas' inner-circle approached us. With an evil smile on his face, he smirked, "Antipas has some news for you two. Follow me."

With no choice but to honor the summons, we got up, trying to keep up with this messenger as he walked with a purpose toward Antipas' living quarters. Surrounded by several others unknown to me, the tetrarch reclined on his favorite couch, sipping from one of his ever-present wine goblets conversing in hushed tones with those closest to him. With candle light flickering about him, Antipas wore a satisfied smile as he spoke amiably to his guests. When he saw us, he slurred his greeting. "Ah, Aquila and Kish, two of my favorites."

Pointing to the men at his side, he said, "These men are representatives from the chief high priest himself, Caiaphas, bearing some good news. As a courtesy to me, Caiaphas wanted me to know of a plan in place to arrest the man who has occupied a great deal of my time and yours. I'm talking, of course, about Jesus. Sometime this evening, Caiaphas expects to arrest this man. I don't know all the details about how or when this will occur but I want you two to change your plans for this evening."

Kish and I looked at Antipas and then at each other before I blurted out, "Antipas, are you sure about this? While I've never met the high priest, I've talked to another man recently who told me of a time when Jesus slipped away from a similar precarious situation. From the way the man told me his story, I've no reason to doubt if Jesus wished to do so, he could avoid capture again."

Antipas assessed my comments through his drunkenness. "I appreciate your comments, Aquila, I really do, but I don't think he'll get away this time. It seems Caiaphas has considered all possibilities. I'm sure you'll agree with me the word of the high priest is much more trustworthy than the story of some commoner you met along your travels." With a curt wave of his hand, he turned to Caiaphas' minions, "Wouldn't you agree with me, gentlemen?"

As the guests guffawed, I realized the futility of any more discussion so I held my tongue.

"Aquila, do you recall I mentioned earlier the priests may have found one of Jesus' men who would be willing to lead them to his master? Well, it happened! One of them has agreed to provide the priests some specific information in exchange for a sizable reward." He looked at me with great intensity in his eyes. "As we discussed, it seems every man has his price, even one of Jesus' most intimate followers. Antipas stopped for a moment to savor another swallow of his wine, smiling, "For being such a smart man, Jesus should never have come to Jerusalem. But he has, and this will be his undoing."

With Antipas and the men around him exchanging smiles and

laughter, it was Kish who interrupted their banter. "Sir, what will this mean for your Passover meal? Shouldn't that be where our concentration is tonight, on the reverence and its meaning?"

Antipas looked up, gazing at the young man. "Yes, Kish, of course . . . of course. Thank you for reminding me. I want you to have someone else serve me my Passover meal as I have an important task for you." He tugged at his royal clothes assuming a more strict posture. "Because you know your way around the city so well, I want you to go with these two men to Caiaphas' home and keep me informed about activities there. Since Jesus is a Galilean, I may be needed later tonight to render some sort of advice and I want to be ready if called upon."

Turning to me, he continued, "Centurion, since this matter now appears to be reaching its conclusion, there appears little for you to do at this point. Perhaps you and I can share some of my best stock of wine later this evening, celebrating the conclusion of your search."

Looking around at those who stood close to his shoulders, I had no desire to associate with men such as these. What was the point? I had my loyalties and they had theirs. "Antipas, while I appreciate your invitation, I'm not feeling well. After a night's sleep, I'm sure I'll feel better in the morning. Good night." With that said and not wanting to hear anymore about something I couldn't stop, I wanted to separate myself from such men as quickly as possible.

Once into the fresh night air near the main gate of the palace, I stared at the stars overhead as they quietly twinkled down upon the world. Based on Kish's narrative of the origin of the Passover celebration, I assumed most inhabitants of Jerusalem were in their homes celebrating the symbolism of this event, how the blood of a quiet, gentle animal could be packed with such power. Then the night sky grew brighter as moon made its presence known, the sight of the bright white ball marked with gray splotches shining down --- down on the stains on my sandals. Would more blood be spilled again before the moon rose again tomorrow night?

How strange. Blood was seen by many on this Passover night

as a sign of protection, while to others like Antipas and Caiaphas, they wished to see blood from a man they viewed as a threat to their way of life. How strange.

"Centurion . . . Centurion," the insistent call came from the darkness, the voice Kish's.

"Yes? What is it?"

The young man's troubled face came close to mine. "I'll be leaving with Caiaphas' men in a moment. I'm taking another man to act as a messenger. As the evening unfolds, I'll dispatch him to you if necessary to keep you informed of what is happening. I have a bad feeling about all this. For Caiaphas and the Sanhedrin to kill Jesus, they'll need Pilate's concurrence."

"What are you talking about?"

"I don't have time to explain now. Just by ready if a message reaches you tonight."

Chapter XVII

Antipas' Palace
Province of Judea
Early morning, Friday, April 1, A.D. 34

The ordered steps of the guards going by my room on their quiet vigil kept me alert, expecting at any moment a knock would interrupt the stillness. Then several hours before dawn different steps approached my room, softer, hesitating in front of my door, before a gentle knock preceded a muted voice, "Centurion? Centurion?" Opening the door to the flickering light of the torches stationed along the hallway, I saw the same servant who had given Kish, Joanna, and me news of Jesus' rampage in the temple. "Yes?" I asked.

The man, still fearful of my knowledge about Jesus, looked around to make sure the hallway was clear before whispering, "The high priest arrested Jesus last night. Kish wants you to meet him outside the entrance to Fortress Antonio just before dawn." The man bowed. "Those were his exact words." Was this a trap, some test of my allegiance to Rome or to something else? The man before me must have sensed my discomfort because he relayed the message again with more conviction. "Those were his words, Centurion, 'The entrance to the Fortress Antonio just before dawn.' "

"I understand. Go wake my soldier Maurus. Tell him to meet me at the palace gate in fifteen minutes. If he questions you, tell him, 'We both knew a Centurion named Theodosios.' That should convince him your message comes from me. Do you understand? Theodosios."

"Yes Centurion." Without another word, the man moved in the direction of Maurus' sleeping area.

****

Not surprising in the hours before dawn, the area around Pilate's headquarters was still, the steps of the guards marching back and forth at their posts the only noises heard, the guards giving us strange looks after discovering our presence in the shadows of the high walls near the fort's entrance. Maurus, as if by magic, found several moth-eaten blankets for us to wrap ourselves in to ward off the cool night air as we leaned against the broad, grayish white pillars of the government building. While I knew he wanted to ask many questions, something about my demeanor caused him to keep his thoughts in check. Kish's request was clear – outside the entrance. All we could do was wait, bundled up in these thin blankets, giving us little comfort against the cold, hard stones.

What had Antipas said? This wasn't about Jesus' good deeds; it was about power, prestige, and money. He was one man against the chief priests, one man standing against generations of the status quo. The more I thought about this, the less optimistic I became for this good man called Jesus.

****

Maurus was the first to hear the footsteps approaching. "Centurion, someone's coming this way."

I sat up quickly, shaking my head to get fully awake. Although the eastern sky showed its first signs of the coming dawn, it was still difficult to make out the man's features as he ran toward us, stumbling every few steps, exhausted. As he got closer, I recognized Kish and called out to him.

Recognizing my voice coming out of the shadows, he came to us, out of breath, totally spent as he bent over, putting his hands on his knees. After a few minutes, Kish was able to stand erect. "They're coming. I'm sure of it. They're only a few minutes behind me. They'll be bringing Jesus here." Gasping for more air, he went on. "They seek an immediate audience with Pilate . . . It was terrible. They beat him and beat him. They want him dead!"

His breath came in great gulps. "You must do something. You must tell Pilate about Jesus. Pilate knows you. He'll listen to you. You know Jesus is a man of God. My father said you did. Please, go talk to Pilate!"

Why was this up to me? While Jesus intrigued me, I had no allegiance to him. Yes, I knew a great deal about him but I owed him nothing, yet something drew me to consider Kish's fervent plea. If I spoke up, what risks would I be taking? Something deep in my soul caused me to reply, "All right, Kish, if the priests bring Jesus here, I'll try to be near Pilate and see what I can do. Maybe I'll have a chance to speak and maybe not. I'll do my best."

The young man nodded, "Today will be a defining day. I just know it." The three of us stood near one another yet our minds must have been worlds apart: Kish's focused on the fate of Jesus, mine on divided loyalties, and Maurus trying to piece our words together as he stated dumbfounded, "Centurion, what do you care about this Jew? What's he to you?"

I gaped at Maurus. Valerus would have understood, but not this man. "No time right now. Just stay close to me. Today I require your loyalty and trust. I'll explain all this to you when I can." Turning back to Kish, I ordered, "Tell me what you saw. Be quick about it."

"Everything started late last night. After celebrating their Passover meal, Jesus and his men left the city, going east to the Garden of Gethsemane near the Mount of Olives because Jesus wanted to pray there. Late in the evening, Judas, the traitor, guided Caiaphas' men and some priests to the garden to arrest him. There was a scuffle between one of Jesus' followers and the servant of the high priest, but Jesus calmed everyone down even as they bound him. As I understand it, they took him first to Annas' home."

"Who's he?"

"The former high priest, his son in law is Caiaphas. Although the old man still wields a great deal of influence, he's in no position to render any official judgment which is why the mob then took Jesus to Caiaphas's home. I was there watching as the guards brought Jesus, his hands secured, into the large room where the *Sanhedrin* had gathered."

"The Sanhedrin is . . . "

"The most powerful religious and political body in our culture. As chief priest, Caiaphas is its leader. This body rules over all civil and religious matters affecting the day to day lives of our people. While it is a powerful body, the Sanhedrin doesn't have power over life and death issues. They can only recommend such a sentence to Pilate. He is the final approval authority and that's why the priests are bringing Jesus here – to convince him to condemn Jesus to death."

"All right, I understand. So what happened at Caiaphas' house?"

"Although few outsiders are admitted to their official proceedings, because I work for Antipas, I was allowed entrance. The room was packed, the chief priests, the elders, the Sanhedrin, anyone in authority in attendance."

Kish stopped for a moment to collect his thoughts. "First, some of Caiaphas' men hurled insults at Jesus, but he remained silent, just looking at those around him. When Caiaphas asked for someone to testify against Jesus, no one stepped forward. After some prodding, several men got up and spoke against Jesus, but when questioned about the details of what they said, it was clear these men lied as their words conflicted with each other. Since Jesus remained quiet through all this, Caiaphas became quite frustrated. Things came to a head when Caiaphas asked Jesus if he was the Christ, the Son of God. There was not a sound in the room other than Jesus' voice when he answered, saying he was, and in the future, everyone would see the Son of Man sitting on the right hand of God."

"Jesus said that?"

Kish cried, tears rolling down his face. "Yes and when he did, the place erupted. Caiaphas immediately bored in attacking Jesus, tearing at his own clothes shouting, 'He has spoken blasphemy! He has spoken blasphemy!' exclaiming they didn't need any more witnesses. The crowd erupted, shouting and screaming. When they all finally quieted down, Caiaphas asked the Sanhedrin what they wanted done."

"Surely someone attempted to bring all this madness to halt."

Kish gazed at me with sadness, his voice filled with pain. "No, this great body of men with a few exceptions shouted, 'He is worthy of death! He is worthy of death!' Hearing this, the guards surrounding Jesus struck him and spat upon him. When order was restored, Caiaphas called for a vote which confirmed their judgment - Jesus should be put to death. After hearing those words, I snuck out of the room and raced here to find you."

As Kish was finishing his last words, the three of us looked up, the sky brightening, sharp yellow and purple streaks now painting the sky in glorious colors. We heard an unmistakable rumble like thunder in the distance, unmistakably a large crowd moving in our direction.

When we saw the van of the advancing hoard now several blocks away heading in our direction, I gave my orders. "Maurus, you come with me. Kish, you go to Antipas and tell him what is taking place otherwise he'll question your loyalty." Before either man could move, we spotted a bruised and battered Jesus, his hands bound in front of him being pushed and shoved simultaneously near the front of the thick crowd, the dawn's light bright enough to see dried blood around the man's face and on his clothing. Although he stumbled as they jostled him back and forth, the man's head remained erect, his posture as straight as his antagonists would allow.

Having dealt with mobs before, it always amazed me how rational individuals could be so easily swayed by the emotional speech of some charismatic leader. Why were we as humans so susceptible to stimulus such as this, acting as though we were drugged by some invisible potion bent on insuring our mutual destruction? Facing this threat, I knew we could not halt this crushing wave descending upon us. I repeated my orders to Kish while Maurus and I moved to be near the main doors of the fort where I anticipated Pilate would make his appearance.

****

Once near the fort's entrance, I watched the crowd halt as if by magic just outside the massive wooden doors staying away from the steps which lead inside. I learned later this was because Jewish law forbad its people from entering a Gentile building lest they become ceremonially unclean during the celebration of their Passover, one more example of another nonsensical religious ordinance which defied common sense, this strict adherence to their law paramount to these zealots.

With the sun's early morning rays now breaking through the eastern sky, the entire scene appeared like the first act in a long play as the unruly mob formed a semi-circle around Jesus, the main character in the play, the man bleeding from numerous blows. He stood silent, ramrod straight with the holy garbed priests surrounding him as they led the cacophony of insults hurled in his direction.

Suddenly the doors of the fort opened, a detail of Roman soldiers marched out, arranging themselves in a loose parameter around the crowd, the soldiers arrayed in full battle attire placed there by some clear thinking officer who was prepared for any contingency. Maurus and I stood on the steps next to the main doors which remained slightly ajar, the nearest Romans to the entrance. Over the deafening noise of the crowd, I heard movement behind the doors and then with great pomp, the doors swung wide open a second time.

Four Legionnaires led the way, two standing on each side of the door. Following them were two trumpeters who marched forward to the front of the steps and blew their instruments to announce the arrival of the governor of Palestine. As soon as their last notes ended, a confident Pilate stepped through the doors to face the mob. Behind him was Cato, the Centurion of the Legion, and several other officers in trail. Despite the early hour, Pilate's uniform was immaculate, the metal on his breastplate refulgent, not one hair on his head out of place. Surveying the scene before him, he glanced in all directions, acknowledging me with a nod before focusing his attention on the crowd. Once silence came over the assemblage, Pilate asked in his clear commanding voice, "Who is your spokesman?"

One of the high priests, the one adorned in the most elaborate purple and gold colored robe, a tall thin man with a peaked nose, a Promethean in my view, stepped forward and announced in his shrill voice he was Caiaphas' personal representative. Pilate then asked, "What brings you here at this early hour?"

The people now erupted in such a great clamor, it took their spokesman several moments to settle them down before pointing at Jesus, bellowing in a voice dripping with contempt, "This man is subverting the nation." Another priest, also adorned in spectacular holy garb, hollered from the fringes of the crowd. "Jesus opposes paying taxes to Caesar." A few others from the periphery, shouted out, "He claims to be the Christ, a king!" With these and other accusations being shouted out without any order to them, Pilate held up his hands for quiet, which the crowd reluctantly gave him only after noting the growing restlessness of the soldiers stationed around them. When quiet was restored, the chief spokesman attempted to sum up all the transgressions attributed to Jesus, "If he were not a criminal, we would not have him handed over to you."

Pilate paused to gaze at Jesus before his attention returned to the crowd's leader. "Take him yourselves and judge him by your own laws."

A low rumble spread throughout the mob and after some hesitation, their leader stared at Pilate answering with venom in his voice, "We have no right to execute anyone."

Pilate seemed taken aback by these words. He turned and looked at me and at several of his other officers who stood behind him before refocusing at the chief priest's representative and then at Jesus, who stared back at the governor. Pilate then turned to me. "Centurion, bring this man into my chambers. I wish to speak to him in private."

While all I intended to do was observe, and perhaps utter a few truths I knew about Jesus, now it seemed I was being drawn into the middle of this entire affair. Yet maybe, just maybe, if asked, and if I had the courage to do so, I could provide Pilate with some information he might find useful . . . If I had the courage.

After slamming my vitis into my chest in salute, I motioned for two of the nearest soldiers to go down the steps and bring Jesus with them as we followed Pilate and Cato back inside the fort. With the guards behind me shoving Jesus along, we proceeded down the hallway and into Pilate's office, the same place I had met with the governor a few days prior. When Pilate took a seat behind his desk and Cato stood at his right, the soldiers placed Jesus directly in front of the ruler. Jesus, the object of my search for many months, stood now just a few feet from me. He appeared tired but resolute, interested in the proceedings, but not frightened, no evidence of any fear or trembling on his part. Determination marked his face. He stood tall, his shoulders back, dried blood around his cheek bones and on the sleeves of his tunic.

Pilate looked at this man for a long time before beginning his inquisition. "Those people outside say you are a king. Are you the king of the Jews?"

Jesus returned Pilate's gaze with steady eyes before responding, "Is that your own idea, or did others talk to you about me?"

Pilate stopped for a moment before replying, looking closer at the man in front of him, a man who did not seem awed by the circumstances that led to this meeting. "Am I a Jew? It was your people and your chief priests who handed you over to me. What is it you've done?

Jesus' eyes remained steady. "My kingdom is not of this world. If it were, my servants would fight to prevent my arrest by the

Jews. My kingdom is from another place."

Hearing this, Pilate asked with some distain, "So you are a king?"

Jesus nodded his head and looked straight at Pilate when he answered, his voice clear and strong. "You are right in saying I am a king. In fact, for this reason I was born, and for this I came into this world to testify to the truth. Everyone on the side of truth listens to me."

Pilate got up from his seat and looked out the window behind his desk. "Truth - an interesting word. What is truth?" He paced the floor of his office staring out the window at the crowd below before telling Cato and the guards to take Jesus and wait in the hallway, leaving the two of us alone in his office. "Aquila, if you were me, what would you do? From what has been said here today, I certainly don't believe this man deserves a death sentence. Unfortunately I've placed myself in a vice."

Although struck by his comment, I remained silent.

Pilate shrugged his shoulders. "While its ancient history to some, these people seem to have a memory that never forgets. I've had two major disagreements with these Jewish leaders in the years I've been stationed here. Once I took some of their money from the temple treasury using these funds for their benefit, building a much needed aqueduct, but this project was not to their liking."

He paused for a moment, shaking his head as he continued, "Then a few years later, they accused me of insulting their religion by bringing some of our imperial Roman images into the city. For both of these indiscretions, Caiaphas and his priests lodged formal complaints against me to Rome. While I received only minor reprimands for these incidents from the Emperor, another occurrence which indicates I'm not cooperating with Caiaphas may lead to some serious repercussions regarding my posting here."

Since I took Pilate's comments to be rhetorical, I stood mute. Any courage I had to interject new information about Jesus dissolved in light of these revelations, his challenge now clear.

Would he risk his political future and oppose the Jewish leaders by standing up for his beliefs or would he cave in to their demands?

After wrestling with this issue for another moment, Pilate gave me a look of staunch determination. "Follow me," he said. Walking purposefully out of the room, he directed the guards to bring Jesus and follow him out to face the crowd. When we marched through the doors to reappear before the mass of people, cheers of anticipation grew louder, the noise unabated until Pilate held up his hands to quiet the tightly bunched assembly. Their silence, however, turned to cries of anger and fury when Pilate announced, "I find no basis for a charge against this man!"

The priests swiftly began to protest with greater vigor, inciting the crowd even more. As their level of displeasure increased, more Legionnaires came marching forward from the outskirts of the crowd, placing themselves at the bottom of the steps between Pilate and the enraged mob. After the efforts of the priests settled the people down, the leader addressed Pilate once more: "He stirs up the people all over Judea by his teachings. He started in Galilee and has come all the way here."

When Pilate heard the word "Galilee," he turned to me. "Is this true, Centurion? Is this man a Galilean?"

"Yes. This man comes from Nazareth, a small town west of Tiberias. He is known to many in Galilee as Jesus of Nazareth."

Pilate looked at Jesus and then back at the crowd before his gaze fell back on me. "Since Herod Antipas is here in Jerusalem, take this man to him. I want him to decide what to do. Go without delay."

****

After saluting Pilate once again, I ordered Maurus and the two soldiers with Jesus to follow me, leading the way back into the fort. Since I had no desire to confront the mob, we used one of the rear gates of the complex, intersecting with one of the quieter back streets leading directly to Antipas' palace. Once I felt our movement would not be interrupted, I dispatched one of the

243

soldiers ahead to alert Antipas of our coming.

As we walked through the gates of the palace, Kish was the first man to greet us. When he beheld Jesus, he made a slight bow before escorting us to the large room where Antipas held court when he was in Jerusalem.

Antipas sat on his royal chair at the far end of the room dressed in his most elaborate clothing featuring the grand colors of purple, red, and gold. Standing around him were four others, two of whom were the tetrarch's inept advisors, the other two dressed in priestly garb. These men sneered openly at Jesus fixing him with venomous stares, each ignoring the evidence of the earlier beatings on his face and on his clothing.

As my soldiers placed Jesus in front of him, Antipas smiled at Jesus in obvious delight of his predicament, the two men appraising each other in silence for a considerable length of time until the tetrarch rubbed his face with his hand before bursting out, "Jesus of Nazareth, I've looked forward to this day for some time. When I first heard about you and your adventures in Galilee, we thought you might be John returning from the grave. But once I confirmed you were not John, word reached me that many of my subjects in Galilee gave you credit for performing many great miracles. One rumor from some wayward wastrel even suggested you called someone back from the dead. Upon hearing this drivel, I asked myself if any of this could possibly be true."

With derision dripping from every pore of his being, Antipas went on. "And so now you're here in front of the Tetrarch of Galilee, the master of your homeland. I wonder if you would be kind enough to perform some miracles right here to help me understand the veracity of what others have said about you." Despite the early hour Antipas lifted his ever-present wine goblet, "Perhaps you could change this wine into water?"

When Jesus did not respond or even make a move to acknowledge these comments, Antipas' mirth quickly changed to anger; his sarcastic tone now abrasive and biting. "It is well you don't speak. I don't think you can perform any miracles anyway.

I think you're just a common man who is quite adept at fooling people with your quick wit and smooth tongue, masking realism with mystical foolishness."

When Jesus did not react to Antipas' words, those to the left and right of Antipas, began to lash out, asking Jesus questions about his teachings. Despite this interrogation, Jesus stared back at each of his accusers remaining still, unmoved by their insults. When it became apparent to Antipas, the man was not going to be baited into responding to any of these invectives, he whispered something to Kish, who hurried from the room. Returning moments later Kish held in his arms one of Antipas' elegant purple robes from the tetrarch's personal wardrobe. "Put it around him, Kish," Antipas commanded.

With the robe now around Jesus' shoulders, Antipas sneered, "It seems to me, if you're going to claim to be a king you should be dressed like one." While many in the room laughed at these remarks, Jesus held Antipas in a steady unflinching gaze, his composure remaining steadfast. Antipas sensing this called a halt to any further ridicule, announcing, "Centurion, take this man back to Pilate with my compliments. Tell him I have questioned this man and I find nothing to suggest he should be put to death." With a final disgusted look on his face, Antipas waved his hand at Jesus as if he were dismissing the lowliest servant in his realm.

****

We made the short walk back to the fort in haste, glancing behind me to make sure our detail was in good order. Satisfied with the soldiers deportment, their heads up alert, their eyes searching for any possible interference coming our way, my eyes met Jesus' for a moment, his gaze holding me in his grasp longer than I was comfortable. What was it about this man who seemed to look at me as though he knew everything about me? Could he really know my innermost thoughts?

I turned away from him to lead the way to the fort believing that with Antipas' declaration, Pilate would stand by his earlier decision to not condemn Jesus to death. The governor was a man of character. He understood the value of a life, even the life of a Jewish carpenter who invested his time in healing his fellow man. Surely Pilate would understand that.

Chapter XVIII

At the Antonio Fortress
Jerusalem
Friday Morning, April 1, A.D. 34

Once inside the fort, I maneuvered my detail to Pilate's office. Upon receiving permission to enter the governor's office, I found him standing by the window looking down at the crowd below, Cato not far from his side. "What did Antipas say?"

"Sir, Antipas agrees with you; this man doesn't deserve a death sentence."

Pilate's eyes narrowed as he listened to my report. He then began pacing around the room muttering, "This will not make them happy, neither this rabble nor their blood thirsty priests." Turning his attention on me, his words were simple and direct. "Follow me out onto the steps with your prisoner."

Trailing Pilate, all of us: Cato, Jesus, the soldiers, Maurus, and me assumed our previous positions as we faced the crowd, the uproar of those present increasing in anticipation of a favorable proclamation from Pilate. The Governor held up his hands asking once again for quiet.

"You brought me this man as one who was inciting the people to rebel. I have examined him and have found no basis for your charges against him." As those words filled the air, the crowd's displeasure with this judgment came out at once, fists pumping, cries of discontent intermingling with one another that only settled down when the soldiers on the periphery made some threatening moves. Before the noise was completely stilled, Pilate went on. "And neither has Herod Antipas, for after examining this man, he sent Jesus back to me, saying this man has done nothing to deserve death. Therefore, I will punish this man and release him."

When Pilate announced his decision, a crescendo of discontent spewed forth from the mob, loud enough to shake the stone pillars surrounding us, jeers coming from all quarters.

While the priests led the commotion, it seemed they anticipated this verdict for after quieting the crowd, they led the mob in a new direction. Their head spokesman cried out in a loud voice commanding a hush, "Pilate, what about the custom of the Feast?" this question appearing to catch Pilate off guard.

Looking at the man Pilate asked, "I'm not sure I understand your question."

The spokesman, a sneer of superiority on his face, broadcast his message in a louder, more insistent tone. "Have you forgotten that each year at the Feast, it is your custom to have one prisoner released from your prison who the people request?" With the words, the crowd stood silent, poised to hear the rest of the man's declaration. The priest, now knowing he held the momentum proclaimed, "Rather than release Jesus to us, we want you to release someone else. Release the man Barabbas."

Immediately the crowd led by other priests spread throughout the mob took up the chant, "We want Barabbas," this mantra growing more deafening with each shout. "WE WANT BARABBAS! WE WANT BARABBAS!"

Pilate turned to one of his secretaries who stood near the door behind us. "What do you know about this man their talking about?"

This thin officer immaculately attired in his uniform, but too much of a gentle soul to be a warrior, replied, "Barabbas has been in our prison for some time accused of taking part in a rebellion against us. We believe he committed at least one murder during the rebellion he helped incite." The secretary thought for a moment before concluding in his most bureaucratic intonation, "Sir, since both Barabbas and Jesus are charged with essentially the same crime, you could release Barabbas and let Jesus suffer his punishment instead."

With those words, Jesus' fate appeared sealed. There was

nothing I could do. Pilate now eyed Jesus, who heard this entire discussion, his gaze appearing to almost dare the governor to make a decision. Both men held each other's stare before Pilate broke eye contact looking down at the crowd before him. "Which of these two men do you want released?" he shouted, hoping perhaps after this short respite better judgment would prevail.

The crowd, however, now sensing a resolution of the matter, was not about to change its mind, shouting with even more vigor and resolve, "Release Barabbas! WE WANT BARABBAS! WE WANT BARABBAS!"

As the crowd's chant filled his ears, Pilate looked past me to catch the eyes of Maurus. "Maurus, take this man to the barracks and flog him. Bring him back shortly. Make sure he is not killed."

With a satisfied smile on his face, the man saluted Pilate and hastily signaled the soldiers next to Jesus and to follow him, heading in the direction of the soldiers' barracks. Watching them go down the hallway leading to the barracks, I followed along slowly knowing what was ahead.

****

At the soldiers' barracks, laughter and shouts of scorn greeted me along with the crack of a whip stinging the air in a steady beat. The scene was as I expected: in the open garden area exposed to the rising sun's ever increasing heat were almost two hundred soldiers, the majority of whom watched the beating taking place. At the center of the activity, with his arms tied to a rough, scarred wooden pole exposing his back, buttocks, and legs, was Jesus. Ten soldiers stood around him in a tight circle shouting in his ears, "You can't be a king," as they struck him with their fists, these men seemingly taking out all their frustrations for being stationed in the land of the Jews on this one man. To them, Jesus was just another Jew, one deserving of Roman justice.

A few feet away a man with the whip raised his arms signaling the soldiers nearest Jesus to back away to make room for the instrument of pain in his hands. The man snapped it again and again, each blow tearing into the exposed flesh, sending blood, tissue, and ripped skin flying in all directions, the result of the pieces of glass or bits of nails at the end of each strand of the whip. Maurus stood off in one corner of the garden letting the soldiers have their fun, waiting to call a halt to these proceedings knowing it was Pilate's intent that this man should live.

Unlike other beatings I had witnessed with impersonal detachment, this time I cringed with each blow of the whip, sensing every bite of the nails and the glass, the sting, the numbness, the flow of the crimson life sustaining liquid seeping from every wound. With each strike, Jesus' body sank lower on the pole as the man grew visibly weaker with each crack of this thrashing machine.

Sensing the end may be near, Maurus called a halt to the beating, directing the soldiers to untie Jesus, who amazingly, after considerable effort, stood up under his own power. The soldiers then put the purple robe given him by Antipas around his shoulders, the garment quickly soaking up the blood flowing from Jesus' battered frame. A soldier stepped forward and jammed a crown made from sharply pointed thistles down on Jesus' head, exposing his brow to a new assault, the blood flowing down Jesus' cheeks, ears, and neck. With the crown firmly in place, the soldiers mocked Jesus once more shouting, "Hail, King of the Jews," falling on their knees before him, bowing deeply in phony praise as they continued their chant. In a final gesture of disdain, one soldier spat in Jesus' face and struck him once again in the face.

Maurus came over to me grinning. "Centurion, I think we've accomplished Pilate's goal. Will you lead us back to him?"

I stared at Jesus and then at the soldier. "Yes . . . Yes, I will. Follow me."

****

Once more as we all stood in front of the mob, Pilate addressed them. "Look, I am bringing the man out to you to let you know I find no basis for a charge against him," saying all this as Jesus stoically gazed at the crowd wearing the crown of thorns and the purple robe around his shoulders. "And what shall I do with Jesus, who is called Christ?" Pilate shouted.

By now the crowd, of one mind because of the concentrated efforts of the priests, cried out in unison, "Crucify Him!" When the governor asked them again, their shouts became increasingly vicious and insistent, "Crucify Him! CRUCIFY HIM!" It made no sense. There was no reason for this lust of an innocent man's blood, yet it was happening right in front of me. All I could do was watch. Yet when I glanced at Jesus, he seemed unmoved by the shouts, the jeers, the unrelenting taunts. No evidence of fear or panic crossed his face, only a look of steadfast determination as he scrutinized each face in the crowd as they cheered for his death.

Facing this onslaught, Pilate looked at me, "Bring this man inside." an expression on his face which seemed to say, *"What else can I do?"*

Just inside the doors of the palace, Pilate perplexed asked the bleeding man, "Where do you come from?" When Jesus gave no answer, Pilate pressed him. "Don't you realize I have the power either to free you or to crucify you?"

Jesus then answered the governor, his voice firm and steady. "You would have no power over me if it were not given to you from above. Therefore the one who handed me over to you is guilty of a greater sin."

Pilate stared at Jesus again but said nothing. Resigned to a course of action, he led us back to face the crowd for the last time. With Jesus now in front of them again, some in the crowd shouted. "If you let this man go, you are no friend of Caesar. Anyone who claims to be a king opposes Caesar!"

Hearing this, Pilate sat down at the judge's seat, a small bench in front of him known as the Stone Pavement. Shouting out he said, "Here is your king," but the crowd cried out louder and louder, "Take him away! TAKE HIM AWAY! CRUCIFY HIM!"

Faced once again with this onslaught, Pilate motioned to

his secretary who stepped immediately to his side. After Pilate whispered something to him, this slender mousey man went back inside the building before reappearing a moment later carrying a small bowl of water and a towel, holding the bowl out to Pilate. Out of curiosity, an unsettling stillness took the place of the noise as the people watched Pilate put his hands into the water to wash them. He then took the towel, slowly and carefully drying his hands as he proclaimed, "I am innocent of this man's blood. It is your responsibility."

The people in the crowd now burst forth with a cheer as they followed the priests' lead. "Let his blood be on us and on our children," they shouted before taking up the chant once again to crucify Jesus. Had all these people abandoned their senses? Did they really have that much lust for innocent blood?

With a grimace on his face, Pilate turned to me. "Centurion, since this man is a Galilean, I want you to supervise his crucifixion. Before you do, see to it Barabbas is released. See that all this is accomplished as soon as possible." He was about to walk back into the inner confines of the fort, when he stopped to glance back at me. "Aquila, while neither of us agrees with this mob, we all must do our duty."

Easy words for him to say – He had washed his hands of this entire affair – leaving me to carry out his pronouncement. Do your duty. For a brief moment my mind was a blank. I stood still. I didn't hear the crowd. I didn't see Jesus or the soldiers around me.

"Centurion…CENTURION," Maurus' sharp voice brought me out of my stupor.

In the background throughout the entire exchange, he heard Pilate's order, and knew what was required. "Centurion, I'll prepare the detail. Meet us at the barracks."

I stared at my fellow soldier. "Yes, Maurus, you do that. I'll join you there after I go to the dungeon."

****

Somehow the guards at the dungeon knew of Pilate's decision, for upon seeing me, the head jailer led me straight to the man's cell without a word spoken between us, opening the massive wooden door for me to stare at an enormous heavy set man with dark complexion and dark eyes, a wicked sneer across his face. The cell, like John's at Machaerus, reeked of foul smells created by poor food, human waste, and the rats. The prisoner laughed wickedly when I spoke to him, doing little to hide his sinister nature, "It appears, Barabbas, your fellow citizens have selected another to die in your place."

The man chortled. "And why is that?"

I stared at the man, wishing for I could end his miserable life right now. "Others will tell you about this later. For now, just be glad you're being set free. Let me assure you, if you cross us again, you'll meet the fate you're dodging today." I didn't wait for a reply, nor did I want one. "Jailer, escort this man to the front gate and release him."

Watching the jailer unlock all the chains securing Barabbas to his cell, I thought about what lay ahead for Jesus. Over time crucifixions had became our standard Roman punishment as we dealt with slaves and foreigners, and those found guilty of sedition and robbery, our methods adopted from the experiences of the Egyptians, the Carthaginians, the Persians, and the Assyrians. It began with a vicious beating which Jesus had already received. The highpoint of the crucifixion was the hanging of the guilty on a wooden cross. Once affixed to the cross using nails pounded through the wrists and feet, the condemned remained in this position until death occurred ultimately from a combination of the scourging, exhaustion, malnutrition, and the sheer pain of the body trying to draw breath in this unnatural position, the conclusion normally coming in a day or two. My thoughts kept returning to Pilate's words – *Do your duty.*

****

"Is the detail ready?" I asked.

A smirk came to Maurus' sweaty face. "Yes. In anticipation of a heavy crowd wanting to watch our procession, I've given us enough men to escort this man to the hill. We've also been given two other criminals to be crucified today along with this fellow. From what I can see," pointing to Jesus, "I don't think their beatings were as severe as this one."

I nodded my understanding but said nothing as I tightened the strap on my helmet.

"Are you ready, Centurion? Is anything wrong?"

I replied angrily. "No, there's nothing wrong." After checking on the organization of our party, I ordered, "Open the gates." There was no reason to wait.

As the gates opened unto the main thoroughfare which led to our destination, a hilltop not far from the northwestern edge of the city called Golgotha, or by its nickname, 'Place of the Skull', onlookers crowded the streets.

To help bull our way through the crowd, I placed four soldiers in front to pave the way through the narrow streets, while I followed with two more guards. Behind me was Jesus, four guards around him. Following Jesus' group were the other two criminals, two guards with each of them. Maurus brought up the rear. The three condemned men carried their heavy wooden cross beams, which from the look of the scarred timber, it appeared these beams had experienced this walk before. One soldier in each group carried a sign indicating the charge each prisoner had been found guilty of committing. The sign in front of the two criminals stated they had been found guilty of robbery, while Jesus' sign, as decreed by Pilate, said, "This is Jesus, King of the Jews." Pilate's thoroughness in the making of this sign interested me for the words about Jesus appeared in all three languages common to the people of Jerusalem. As a last measure of mercy for those condemned to crucifixion, the procession to Golgotha normally followed a circuitous route through the city, allowing for the possibility of someone testifying on behalf of the guilty individual. If new evidence was revealed, a new trial would immediately be held. Just before leaving the fortress, Maurus told me we had been directed to take the most direct route to Golgotha, but when I asked who issued that order, he could not say.

Although the march to Golgotha would be short, each step would be a struggle for Jesus because of the multiple beatings he received since late last night. As our journey began, the crowd pushed in closer and closer, many craving for one more opportunity to watch this man suffer as they hurled insults at him, calling him a blasphemer, a hoax, and a scoundrel. With considerable effort our soldiers forged a path through the mass which pressed us on both sides. I wondered how many of these same people waved palm branches and laid their clothing at Jesus' feet as they sang his praises less than a week ago? Where were their praises of adoration now?

When I looked back to check on our progress, Jesus' strained mightily to hoist the heavy cross beam on his back, its weight causing him to fall down again and again, and with each fall, the soldiers nearest him beat him about the legs and back until he rose once more, a little slower each time. Unless I took some action, it appeared the man would die from exhaustion before we reached the hill.

Searching through the crowd, I saw a large, solid man, clearly capable of helping Jesus with his burden and who, unlike so many others, was not jeering or enjoying Jesus' plight. Pointing to the man, I shouted above the noise, "You there, come here." When this man did not heed my charge quickly enough, I ordered my soldiers into the crowd to haul the man before me.

Once in front of me, I shouted at the man. "Your name?"

Trembling with fear, the man pleaded, "Please, sir, I've done nothing wrong. My name is Simon of Cyrene. I brought my two sons, Alexander and Rufus, a great distance to be here to celebrate the Passover with me. I came to this street this morning because I wanted to see what all the commotion was about. Please, sir, I've done nothing wrong," Looking around at the unruly crowd, he pleaded, "Please let me go back to my sons."

I heard the man's entreaty but I ignored them. I needed a strong man now and he met that criteria. Pointing to Jesus, I ordered, "Carry this man's burden. He's not strong enough to do it himself. If you do as I say, no harm will come to you." Without another word, Simon looked first at me and then at Jesus before slowly reaching down, hoisting the blood stained beam upon his shoulders. As the two men stared at each other, Simon's eyes began to well up with tears as he saw more blood streaking down Jesus' face. With no words exchanged between the two, Simon followed a few paces behind Jesus who with his burden now lightened, continued to stumble with almost every step, although he now maintained a more acceptable pace.

As we passed through the gate which led to Golgotha, the crowd along our path became mixed, many still applauding for Jesus' crucifixion, but some new voices, mostly women distraught at the carpenter's circumstances, pleaded for mercy. At one point I saw Jesus say a few words to several of the women, but I wasn't close enough to hear this exchange before the soldiers nearest Jesus broke up this short conversation, encouraging Jesus to move along with a few well placed strikes to his back. Because the soldiers knew crucifixions could take a considerable length of time, they knew they could not return to the comfort of their barracks and begin a round of heavy drinking until the crucifixion reached its inevitable conclusion.

With Golgotha now in sight, we saw the barren wind- swept crest ahead, its peak marked with a number of sturdy vertical poles standing like sentries announcing to the three condemned men, they would not be the first to die on this rocky, dusty rise.

We stayed on the well worn trail in our slow climb up to the top and with the sun's rays now beaming down upon us, the bald top of Golgotha growing hotter by the minute. A large crowd of onlookers trailed us, those calling for Jesus' death in the majority while the smaller group, consisting mostly of women showed their sympathy to Jesus' plight, standing silent away from the noisier crowd, tears streaming down their faces.

I also saw some onlookers watching us from the Damascus Road, many of them approaching Jerusalem from the north, stopping along their journey for a moment to observe the scene before them. While some appeared interested enough to sit and watch for a spell, the curiosity of most of the travelers' lasted for only a moment before they continued on their way into the city.

When we reached the crest of the hill, Simon put down the beam next to Jesus as this brave quiet man nodded his thanks to the father of two. Simon held his gaze for a long time before he slowly descended down the hill. I too silently thanked the man for helping Jesus, although I wondered if it would have been more merciful to have let this carpenter die of exhaustion along the road rather than face death on a cross.

Chapter XIX

At Golgotha
Jerusalem
Mid morning, April 1, A.D. 34

It was now time to do my duty, my solemn duty as a soldier. To do anything less would dishonor me, my family, and my fellow soldiers. Although wanting to exhibit some degree of mercy and compassion to these three, it was incumbent upon me to adhere to the crucifixion protocols. At the top of the hill buried permanently in the ground the vertical wooden poles stood ready. With three men to crucify, I selected three poles nearest one another on the peak of the hill as the crucifixion site. Pointing to Jesus, I told the soldiers with him, "He'll go on the tallest one, the one in the center." Then after surveying the ground I told Maurus to move the other two men toward the poles on either side of Jesus. Little thought went into this decision; it just seemed like the right thing to do.

After dragging the condemned men to the places I designated, the soldiers offered each man a solution of wine mixed with gall to help deaden the pain which was sure to follow. After slurping this mixture down as quickly as possible, the two criminals started to cry and plead for mercy. When their pleas drew no reaction from the soldiers, they began to curse, their screams increasing in volume as the soldiers stripped their clothing from them. Before the sedatives could take much effect, we proceeded to the next step, nailing the men to the crossbeams which they carried on their backs from the fort. "Let's begin with the men on the sides," I said.

Knowing what was to come, it took all the strength my soldiers could muster to hold the two thieves down on the ground as they flayed about with every fiber in their bodies. It was not until the two were beaten almost into unconsciousness could we hammer the long, rusty nails into their flesh where the hands met the wrist, the instrument used for this destruction a large heavy metal mallet welded by the strongest soldier in our detail.

With each blow, blood shot up in all directions, sparing no one. As the mallet fell over and over, each man suffered in his own way, screams of pain coming from the depths of their souls. During this process, each man quickly lost the ability to retain his bodily fluids, the stench filling the air around us. After nailing the left wrist into the wood, each body was stretched to near its full length before we nailed down the right wrist. With the two hands now firmly attached to the wood, neither man had much energy left as they panted for air, a combination of terror and panic on their faces as the reality of their situation took over.

And then it was Jesus' turn. I stood near the soldiers who were to nail Jesus to his beam. Unlike the other two, he sampled the drink offered but he spat it out, shaking his head declining any further drink. Why was he trying to be so brave? Did he really wish to feel the bite of each blow of the mallet?

Regardless, after the soldiers stripped him of his clothes, unlike the men on his left and right, he laid submissively on the ground. While it was clear by the way his hands and arms tensed up as the soldiers held him steady on the beam, he felt each blow of the mallet just like those before him, but unlike the two thieves, the only reaction he made came from his teeth grinding against one another as the nails bit into his body. The pain he suffered was real, his body twitching each time the mallet drove the nails deeper and deeper into his flesh; unlike the other two, no cries of mercy came from his lips, only his eyes opened wide with each strike of the mallet, communicating the indescribable pain he felt.

When his gaze fell on me, I couldn't hold his stare, moving my eyes away to concentrate on the movement of the mallet up and down, trying my best to stay away from the spurts of blood coming from the violation of his body. I had seen this bravery, this resolve before, but where . . . Then I remembered . . . At the beheading of John, his look of dogged determination, the same as I saw on Jesus' face. What caused the faith of these men to be so deep? What did they know about their god that men like me could not fathom?

****

With the three now secured to the crossbeams, the soldiers used a ladder to haul each man in turn up the vertical poles, tying each in place using a set of ropes starting with the thieves first and then Jesus. As each of the three bore the brunt of their body weight on their arms and shoulders, the strain on them was visible as the long rusty nails pinned them, the wounds in their wrists now gushing with fresh blood. I went from pole to pole, inspecting each to insure it could hold the weight of each man. With this quick check complete, the soldiers bent the knees of each man before hammering nails through the center of their feet and into the vertical poles, this act as painful as the cruelty rendered upon the wrists moments before.

I inspected our work once more, the last fifteen minutes a blur, few words passing among the soldiers as they went about this grisly task. While most of these soldiers had previous experience in this macabre duty, this was the first time for three of the men with me. While they performed their duties as expected, their reactions varied from stoic compliance to gruesome determination. Satisfied with our efforts, I directed one of my soldiers to nail the signs declaring the crimes of each of these men to the top of each pole.

Looking around, blood was everywhere. Maurus, because of his prior experience, produced a bucket of water and some old rags to help me and my men wash away the stains of the day, the pail of water soon turning a dark crimson. After cleaning the majority of the day off my hands and wrists, I looked down. New stains appeared on my sandals. Jesus' blood was now next to John's.

****

The sun inched its way higher in the sky. For me and my men, it now became a matter of waiting. To amuse themselves, the soldiers decided to divide the clothes of the dying men, the clothes from the two criminals consisted of a short tunic, a girdle, and sandals which the men shared without a squabble. Jesus' clothes, however, become a matter of some discussion, as upon examination, the soldiers realized the value of the purple robe given to him by Antipas, the garment seamlessly woven in one piece from top to bottom. Rather than damage this beautiful piece, the soldiers decided to draw lots for it instead, with the winner having the garment for himself.

While this division of clothing was taking place, the condemned men on either side of Jesus continued to plead and beg for mercy, knowing all the while, the time to commute their sentences passed long ago. Jesus, however, spent little time watching us, focusing his attention instead upward as he peered into the skies above. As the time dragged into the second hour, he closed his eyes and put additional weight on to his legs, taking some of the pressure off his arms. After searching the sky, he cried out in a surprisingly strong voice, "Father, forgive them, for they do not know what they are doing."

When I heard his words, I stood transfixed. "Father, forgive them." It reminded me of John's final words: "Forgive them." Could we really be forgiven for killing such men? Was this god so merciful, he would forgive us, forgive me, for my part in these killings, these murders?

****

Before my thoughts could linger on that subject, Maurus pointed down the hill as a large gathering of priests came up the path toward the crest of the hill. Nodding to my soldiers, who understood my concern, they formed a loose line in front of the crosses, a signal to our visitors to keep their distance. Seeing my men arrayed before them, the priests stopped before reaching the soldiers, talking and gesturing among themselves.

Then, as if by silent command, they all begin to laugh and jeer at Jesus, paying no heed to the criminals on either side of him, their focus on this one man, pointing at him and hurling insults at him shouting, "Come down from the cross . . . If you really are the Son of God, get down . . . Show us a miracle, Jesus, and come down . . . Free yourself if you really are a God . . .Where are your angels now?" Despite the harshness of their words and the bitterness in their voices, this man from Nazareth paid them no heed, keeping his eyes closed.

When it became apparent Jesus was not going to react to them, one of the chief priests attired in his most holy garments, his voice dripping with scorn and ridicule, triumphantly proclaimed, "I told you. They say he saved others, but he can't save himself. I told you he was a fraud." The priest kept up his assault, but Jesus did not stir.

The soldiers had been watching all this, not saying a word. Now being spurred on by the priests, several of the younger soldiers joined in shouting at Jesus, "If you are the king of the Jews, save yourself . . . save yourself." Even as these chants filled the air, nothing happened except Jesus' strength began to visibly wane, his head sinking lower and lower on his chest. Nothing anyone shouted at him caused him to acknowledge them in any way despite the constant, abusive rhetoric pelting him.

After a time the priests grew bored and quieted down before retreating partway down the hill, their insults still directed at Jesus but not with the vehemence as before. With the sun nearing its zenith, some of the crowd began to filter back toward the city to seek shelter from the sun's burning rays. A few soldiers gathered up some of the clothes from the condemned men to form modest shelters to give us some relief from the oppressive heat. Jesus and the other two men had now been exposed to the elements for almost three hours.

****

One of the criminals, the stocky short man, the one who had screamed and cursed the loudest as he was being nailed to his cross, now began to challenge Jesus. "Some say you are the Christ. If you are, save yourself and us as well," a phrase he kept repeating over and over. When Jesus did not respond, the man's pleas turned into rage, as he started to curse Jesus in a similar manner of the priests, but despite these cries, Jesus remained still.

To my surprise, the second criminal, a tall, skinny fellow, who had been the quieter of the two, now spoke up in Jesus' defense, rebuking his fellow criminal. "Don't you fear God," he cried, his body racked with pain, his breath labored, long stretches between his words, "We're being punished justly . . . . We're getting what . . . we deserve." He then turned his head slowly in Jesus' direction, his voice raw with emotion. "This man . . . has done nothing wrong . . . nothing to . . . to share this fate with us."

Still keeping his eyes on Jesus, the man's next words came out in a hushed, reverent manner. "Jesus . . . remember me . . . when you come into your kingdom."

Through his pain, Jesus slowly raised his head, turning to look at this man. He seemed to gather in all the air he could before replying, "I tell you the truth . . . today you will be with me in paradise."

What an amazing statement for a man who would meet death in just a few hours. What was it about this man who appeared to suffer like other men, yet whose mind and emotions seemed to be above those around him? How was it he said nothing when insults came his way, but when a man stood up for him under these most dire circumstances, Jesus responded with understanding and encouragement? Why would Jesus, if he was this long predicted Messiah, promise paradise to a lifelong thief in his last moments on earth? What right did this criminal have to live in paradise anyway?

****

As I considered this strange dialogue between the two men, several of the women from the group who stood near the base of the hill well away from the insulting priests and their lackeys, approached Jesus' cross. Dressed in their traditional garb with long flowing clothing covering most of their features, their heads covered with scarves, only their faces visible. A younger man accompanied them, slim and medium in stature, a determined look on his face. When this group got close to Jesus' cross, they stood looking up at him, tears pouring unashamedly from their faces as they knelt before him.

I asked one of the women who was near the back of the group who these women and the man were. She hesitated for a moment as she stared at me and at the power my uniform represented, distrust and suspicion in her eyes. She ignored me at first, but when I asked again, she responded in a cold and biting manner. "Why should I trust you, a Roman? It is you and your kind who are responsible for this cruel act."

When I made no reply, she paused after a long moment of silence before responding in a softer, kinder tone. "Centurion, forgive me. Your honest question deserves an honest answer." After looking back at those near the cross, she said, "The woman nearest the cross is Mary, Jesus' mother."

I nodded, of course, Mary. I took new interest in the woman who now kneeled at the cross, her face beautiful, her bright blue eyes filled with compassion. She was of medium height, slender in build, and she moved with a mature grace. As could be expected, her attention was totally on her son, whose face now showed the strain of abuse heaped upon him. When I asked the woman about the man, she told me his name was John, one of Jesus' followers. I wondered if this was the man Philip told me about, one of the twelve devoted men who first told the others Jesus was the Messiah.

Despite the pain racking his body, Jesus seemed to sense the nearness of those gathered close to him. With considerable effort, as evidenced by sweat pouring from his face, he raised his head from his chest, his face twitching in agony as his eyes rested first on his mother and then on the man next to her. He said nothing for a long time before acknowledging Mary. "Dear woman, here is your son."

Then shifting his glance slowly to John, he whispered, "Here . . . here is your mother."

The two nodded their heads in understanding. No other words were spoken, although the women remained close to the cross for a few more minutes before Mary led them down the hill to resume their vigil away from the other small crowds gathered about. As I considered Jesus' instructions to John, it seemed he was charging this man with the responsibility for his mother's care rather than have his siblings, like James, assume this duty. Was this because John was the only man of his closest followers with enough courage to be near Jesus in his hour of need?

****

Suddenly, a large thunderous bolt of lightning shook the ground so close to all of us on the crest of the hill, we all ducked, cowering down on the ground. Like the others, because my attention had been on Jesus and his words and watching those nearest the cross, I had not seen the dark line of clouds now billowing around us, so black the sun seemed to stop shinning. Looking about for a place to hide, I watched our makeshift sun shelters disappear in an instant, the flimsy clothes flying in all directions, the clouds swirling above us, boiling with anger, heavy rain now pelted us in quick, sharp bursts, soaking us to the skin in a matter of moments, the claps of thunder and lightning intermixed, so severe the hair on my head stood at attention waiting for the next streak of bright light to strike.

With such fury above us, most of the crowd near the bottom of the hill dispersed in a matter of moments, running for the protection of the city. Despite the ominous skies and the crackling of the lightening, a few of the priests braved the elements to witness what we all expected to be the death of Jesus. The women, who had just been near Jesus, huddled close to each other at the bottom of the hill pulling their garments over their heads to shield themselves from the terror above.

Frightened by the severity of the storm and the darkness, my soldiers and I shielded ourselves among some nearby boulders, as the wind and rain howled around us, hurling its fury upon us, the stinging rain unremitting. Despite these conditions, our duty required us to stay and so we did. The men on the crosses seemed to barely notice the swirling maelstrom above them, their bodies not moving, their lives continuing to slowly wane, each breathe they took more labored than the last. The rains and winds and flashes of lightening went on and on, buffeting us. Despite my fears, I tried to maintain a confident, knowing look as my soldiers gathered around me in the shelter of our rocks, staring out from our observation post.

One of the soldiers, a younger one, looked at me with fear in his eyes. "Centurion, why are the gods doing this to us? Are they punishing us for killing these men?"

I guffawed, lying to the man, "Of course not. This storm was predicted. It'll pass. They always do," smiling at this man and the others as I wiped the rain away from my eyes, yet in my heart, I too wondered the same thing. Like my men I was frightened to the core, my heart churning. Was Jesus' god reacting to our torture of this man?

The rain, the lightening, the wind lasted over almost three hours until at last the rains began to slacken, even though the horrific winds still whipped the dark clouds above us, swirling them about like angry waves on a ocean. In the midst of this, Jesus cried out in a voice louder than the torrent raging about us, "My God, my God, why have you forsaken me?!" A few moments later, Jesus spoke again saying, "I am thirsty."

The priests, who had stayed close to the hilltop, began gesturing to one another. I heard one of them shout, "Listen, he's calling Elijah." Upon hearing Jesus' words, this priest dispatched one of his men to the city to retrieve a sponge filled with wine vinegar. When this man returned a short time later and with my permission, they lifted the sponge attached to a stick offering it to Jesus. The leader of the priests laughed, "Now let's leave him alone. Let's see if Elijah comes to take him down now." Despite the winds buffeting the black, gray clouds above us, these men continued to target their fury at Jesus, berating him with cries of, "Save yourself if you can," as they shook their fists at him. This continued for a short time until several large bolts of lightning ripped across the sky, striking close to where these men stood, sending them in a hasty retreat nearer the base of the hill, the object of their scorn once again now left alone.

****

Finally the gray-dark masses that weaved back and forth across the sky grew quieter. The two criminals on each side of Jesus gave no sign of life, their bodies still. When I looked at Jesus, I saw his chest move slowly in and out, grasping for every bit of air he could bring into his crippled body. Then, with almost super human effort, he lifted his head and opened his eyes wide as though studying the clouds as they passed by. He declared in a soft low voice, "It is finished." No one moved. We all waited to see if this was the end, the priests, the women with Mary, my soldiers and I all watching, no one uttering a sound.

As all of us held our collective breath, Jesus gathered his strength, pulling as much air into his lungs as he could. Then with a pronounced strain on his face, he cried out in a loud voice, "Father, into your hands, I commit my spirit." With upturned eyes, he gazed wide-eyed into the heavens above. Then all the air seemed to leave his body. He closed his eyes and his head dropped, thumping his chest, no indication of life remained.

Before any of us could make a move in his direction, the ground under and around our feet shook violently, the rocks rolling as if we were in a tidal wave causing all of us to lose our balance. At the same time the large rocks on the nearby hills seemed to split apart. I went to my knees and saw in the distance the burial grounds, where many of Jerusalem's dead laid in tombs, tremble as though a great force was pushing the ground upward. Without warning, some of these tombs appeared to split open and what looked like bodies came out of them. In an instant these bodies, if that's what they were, flew across the sky toward the city. The soldiers looked at me in terror. "Centurion, did you see that? Did bodies come out of those tombs? Are we dreaming? Are we under a spell?" each of us stood wide eyed, several of the men crying in terror.

No words came from my mouth as the events of recent months flashed like a blur before my eyes. The death of John . . . the trust he had in his god . . . Valerus' recognition of John's belief . . . Tobias' willingness to tell me about John . . . the young man's tale at Nain telling me of Jesus bringing him back to life . . . James' narrative of Jesus turning water turned into wine . . . Jesus' healing Jorim in Capernaum . . . the healing of the blind man at Bethsaida . . . Philip's firsthand knowledge of Jesus . . . Cuza's story of the Samaritan woman at the well . . . seeing Jesus face to face as he rode into Jerusalem on a donkey . . . the birth of the boy in Bethlehem . . . and everything I had witnessed since last night. Through it all, Jesus stood like a rock, unshakeable, resolute. Compassionate of others through it all. Like a god in his emotions but human in every respect as he suffered from the beatings, the sting of the whip, and pain of the nails. Was there any doubt? Could there be any other explanation, any other possibility?

I looked around me as the clouds parted, giving way to the deep blue sky as rays of the afternoon sun shined their warmth upon us, a zephyr giving us relief on our rain drenched faces.

We slowly arose to our feet, moving away from the rocks which had provided us protection from the elements, the men too shaken to say anything. The groups of priests and the women who had shared the tumultuous winds and rain of the past few hours, stared up at us, everyone staring at Jesus' cross.

In halting steps, I drew close to Jesus' cross. Staring up at him, I concentrated on his broken body. There was no movement of his chest, his blood, which had flowed so freely from all his wounds shortly before, had almost stopped, his head and hands and all of his features hung like a limp wet rag. No doubt Jesus of Nazareth was dead. I reflected on everything I knew about this man, his final words to his God. To no one in particular, I proclaimed, "Surely this man was the Son of God!"

Chapter XX

Golgotha
Jerusalem
Late afternoon, April 1, A.D. 34

With Jesus dead the women downhill gathered around Mary comforting her, too far away to be heard, their gestures and wailings indicated their great remorse. In sharp contrast to them, the priests and their minions smiled, nodding their heads in satisfaction as they pointed to Jesus' cross, their laughter carrying across the hilltop, one of them running excitedly toward the city carrying the announcement of Jesus' death. In spite of the sadness of the moment, the sun's rays heralded life and hope, while the crosses standing on the crest of the hill symbolized death, a slow, painful death.

Within a short time after the priests' messenger went into the city, another small crowd of men made their way out the city gates heading in our direction. When this second group, their self-importance apparent by their elaborate clothing, reached the priests near the bottom of the hill, they celebrated for several moments before continuing in my direction. I recognized some of them who had been major spokesmen in front of Pilate. Had it really only been a few hours ago when all this started?

They gazed at Jesus, talking among each other, pointing at the man as though he was a prized slaughtered animal, their focus solely on the one who had caused them such concern, no attention paid to the ones on either side of Jesus.

After studying the limp figure for a few moments, the spokesman of the group addressed me, his voice sharp and irritating, "Centurion, we've just come from meeting with Pilate. He told us to instruct you to break the legs of Jesus to make sure he is dead. The governor understands the urgency as our religious laws dictate this man must be removed from here before nightfall," the spokesman's demeanor grated me. He was one who expected others to jump at his every word and not be questioned. Under the circumstances, I found his words most offensive.

I stared at this pompous man standing straight and tall, his beard brushed and tended with care, his confident, self assured style in stark contrast to the men who hung on their crosses behind me, their bodies torn by nails, dried blood caking around their many wounds, their broken, bent shapes naked for all to see. After pausing to consider the situation and the man's loathsome manner, fire burned within me.

"I hear what you say about Pilate, but why would he give you such permission? Why are you in such a hurry?" Finding great irony in this, I went on, "I thought you wanted the whole world to see the punishment this man suffered to discourage others from committing similar offenses. We Romans allow the birds of the air to feed on such men for a day or two to insure their indignity continues. How is it you've convinced Pilate to order something different? This man is dead now. You can't harm him anymore." Looking at the priest, I asked, "Or, is it perhaps, you're in a hurry because you are still afraid of him?"

The man tilted backward as though I had struck him with my fist, glaring at me before he and the others clustered together, conferencing among themselves. After several moments of heated debate, their spokesman studied me closely as he replied, "It's obvious you don't know our religious beliefs and customs. There are two laws which we, as men of God, must obey. While your Roman methods are to leave these men here for several days, one of our laws states we cannot leave a dead man exposed to the elements overnight. Therefore, these men must be taken off their crosses before sundown," the men behind the spokesmen bobbing their heads in agreement.

"And we have a second law, which applies to our holy day of Sabbath, which begins at sundown tonight. This law does not allow us to do any work once the Sabbath commences, and since any effort to conduct a burial constitutes work, these men must be taken from these crosses now so we can bury them or we will be in violation of that law." With a smirk on his face, the man concluded, "As I'm sure you can understand, because we're men of God, we certainly don't wish to be in contravention with any of his ordinances."

I scowled at this man. How I wished for an excuse to draw my sword on this vile, despicable creature. He and his comrades had just killed three men, one of whom was not guilty of any crime, and yet now their concerns centered on violating some laws? What kind of God did they worship? What hypocrisy! From what I knew about Jesus, he could very well be the son of the same God these men were now trying to please, yet Jesus' relationship to their God didn't seem to matter to them. What concerned them now were laws, some edict, some proclamation. Were these commands man's or God's?

I turned my back to these pontificating theologians, glancing at my soldiers who heard our exchange. They had no real feelings one way or the other, no loyalty to these priests and certainly no loyalty to the men who hung naked behind them. They didn't know what I knew about Jesus nor did they care. This discussion made little difference to them. They knew by breaking the legs of those behind us, if any life remained in them, once their bodies would be supported solely by the nails through the hands, death by suffocation would come quickly. The breaking of the legs would only lead to the inevitable, thus allowing them to return to the pleasures of Jerusalem sooner rather than later.

After thinking the situation through, I ordered Maurus to have the soldiers carry out Pilate's instructions, the instrument of choice was the mallet, the same one used earlier to hammer the nails through the flesh. "Break the legs to the right of the man in the center and then the one to the left." When the crack of the mallet yielded no reaction from either man, I called for a halt. These two had been dead for some time. Studying Jesus' body once more I declared, "Maurus, don't bother, this man is dead. Leave him alone." Jesus had suffered enough. The priests thought about challenging me until they saw something in my gaze which caused them to reconsider protesting.

As I turned back to look at the priests, I heard a disturbance behind me. One of my soldiers, a man who had shown considerable hatred for Jesus, took it upon himself to thrust his javelin into the man's side, blood and a clear liquid, almost like water, flowing from body. The soldier sneered up at Jesus as he inspected the mutilation.

Stepping quickly in front of the soldier, I grabbed the man's weapon and broke it across my knee, screaming at him, "Don't ever do anything like that again!! Do you hear me?"

Pointing at Maurus, I shouted for all to hear, "When we return to garrison, assign this man a duty which he'll not soon forget. Make sure it humbles him to whatever degree you feel necessary." The man moved away, joining the other soldiers, any trace of a smile on his face gone. With my anger seething, no one came near me.

****

Withdrawing away from the others for a moment to regain my composure, my senses focused on the clearing sky telling me dusk was only a few short hours away. As I gazed once more around the hill, I saw another group of men coming in our direction led by two men who appeared quite aged by their gait, their garments identifying them as men of wealth. Servants followed these two carrying on their backs large earthen jars, bundles of cloths, and some wooden poles. Although their movement was slow, there was purpose in each step.

As this second group reached the crest of the hill, the religious leaders glared at them as they mumbled among themselves. One of the younger priests in the mob near me, caustically said, "Joseph, why are you and Nicodemus here? We've everything under control. The pretender is dead! There was no need for you to make the climb up here. We've accomplished the will of the Sanhedrin."

Neither of the two older men wavered as they completed their last few steps of their painful march. The leaders of the two groups now stood only a few paces apart, the older men glared first at the men decked out their religious garb before staring at me and my soldiers. Then, without a word, they turned their attention upon Jesus, their eyes fixed on the man, the nails, and the blood. As they focused on Jesus, the religious flock hurled comments and questions in their direction, words which became less respectful with time. Despite these verbal arrows shot in their direction, the two elderly men remained still, their eyes taking in every detail of the cross of Jesus, deep sorrow on their faces, tears welling up in their eyes.

The man who the priests addressed as Joseph turned to speak to me, his voice strong and clear. "Centurion, I have spoken to Pilate and have his permission to come and take this man's body for a proper burial. However, before we do this, he directed me to tell you to report to him at his headquarters. We will remain here awaiting your return."

Before I could respond, the religious rulers drew back as their leader addressed Joseph once again. With his voice dripping with malice he said with his chin thrust out, "What are you doing Joseph, you and Nicodemus? You're both prominent members of the Sanhedrin, highly regarded members, I might add. You were there when we voted to have Pilate to kill this man." The man pointed a bony finger in their direction. "Why are you now having second thoughts? Can't you see what a scandal this will cause? Think about your reputations. What will others say? You and your families will be disgraced."

The man called Joseph did not respond, but turned again to focus upon the nails which held Jesus fast to the wood. "We will wait here for you, Centurion." Staring back at the priests, he addressed them, directing his words at each man in turn who stood facing him. "During our council meeting last night when we decided this man's fate, I remained silent. While I did not vote for this action, neither did I have the courage to oppose it. It is only now, after seeing this innocent man die, I have found the boldness to do what is right. While you and the others will no doubt taint my record and that of Nicodemus, we know our loyalty must be to God first, not to men."

He smiled at his companion. "As you will recall, some time ago, Nicodemus attempted to calm us down, telling us of how this man, Jesus, spoke about God's love, but we didn't listen. We ignored his counsel. After the events of last night, the two of us realized our biggest regret is we did not confront your evil intentions when we had the opportunity."

Here was courage in action, courage, albeit too late to affect the outcome of the day, but courage and boldness nevertheless. I thought back to another man of courage, my trusted friend Valerus who dared to express his desire to know John's God.

With Joseph's words ringing in their ears, the priests drew themselves into a cluster, their arms waving about, confusion in their midst. To circumvent any thoughts they might have, I announced for all to hear, "Maurus, I'm going to see Pilate. I don't expect to be gone long. See to it that no one and I mean no one, touches any of these men who died here today. Is that clear?" When the man acknowledged my order, I turned to Joseph. "Sir, I will go to see Pilate according to his instructions. To avoid any confusion may I ask your full name, sir?"

The man looked at me and then at his former colleagues. He brought himself to the position of attention, standing as straight as his tired frame would allow. "My name is Joseph of Arimathaea." He looked at his companion. "And my friend with me is Nicodemus. Pilate knows both of us. We will wait here for you to return. Thank you, Centurion, for your prompt and courteous attention to this matter."

In a gesture of profound respect, my vitis smacked against my breastplate. These two men deserved this salute. They were men of honor.

****

"Sir, I understand you wish to see me?"

"Yes, I do."

Pilate got up from his chair behind his desk and leaned against it, getting straight to his point. "I understand the man Jesus is dead. His death came sooner than I anticipated. The man looked strong enough to last well into the night, maybe even until tomorrow. Anyway, is my information correct? Is he dead? What about the other two?"

"All three died within the last hour. From my observation of Jesus, I'm sure all the beatings he received since last night contributed to his succumbing so quickly. It's always difficult to predict how long anyone will react to such punishment."

"Yes, that's true." Pilate said nothing for a few moments before he began to pace around the room. "It's been a very strange day, Aquila. I'm glad it is almost over. Even my wife told me of a dream she had about this man, counseling me to have nothing to do with, as she called him, 'that innocent man'." He stared out his window at the now empty courtyard. Having resolved something in his mind, he dismissed me. "Give Joseph my blessing to bury this man he is so concerned about. I trust this affair will now be behind us so we can return to normal activity. It's hard enough to govern the politics, the economy, and the security concerns of these people under normal circumstances without complicating everything by adding the religious fervor of their Passover and all this Jesus talk into the mix."

He gave me his final comment before I saluted him. "You've done your duty well today. I knew I could trust you."

****

Nothing had changed during my absence from Golgotha, the uneasy standoff between the two older men and their former associates added to the stillness of the place. Jesus and other two men remained undisturbed on their crosses, while Mary and the

275

women with her, continued their hushed vigil further down the hill.

Since there was no need to delay the burial process any longer, I ignored the priests and spoke directly to Joseph. "In accordance with Pilate's instructions, take charge of Jesus' body according to your customs. My men and I will dispose of the other two men after you're finished."

With these words now the law of the land, several of the priests made ready to protest, however they held back on their objections upon the command of their leader who split his contempt between Joseph and me.

With a nod, Joseph said, "Thank you, Centurion. We'll be expeditious and reverent in our task." Then he signaled his servants to come forward to approach the cross. Led by their masters, the servants closed in around Jesus' cross and began to pry the nails from Jesus' feet. After considerable effort, they managed to loosen the nails without further damage to the body. With the feet now free, one of the servants used our ladder, setting it against the back of the cross to loosen the ropes which held the horizontal beam in place, allowing the servants to lower the body, still attached to the beam, to the ground. Then with great care they removed the nails from the wrists, careful to limit any more damage to the tortured frame.

The priests watched all this without interfering, although there was a great deal of muted talk taking place. With the body now on the ground, the priests began to drift away in small groups toward Jerusalem, their goal accomplished. The group of women, with the way clear to approach the top of the hill, stood nearby, watching Joseph and those with him as they continued with their self–appointed task.

With the body now free from the nails, the two older men, assisted by their servants, laid Jesus on a clean, white linen cloth. A white napkin was placed over Jesus' face as these men carefully cleaned the body using a mixture of myrrh, a perfume made from a plum-like fruit, and aloes, an embalming fluid extracted from a lily plant, contained in the jars the servants carried up the hill. The wounds on Jesus' hands and feet received extra care before the body was wrapped in white linen cloth. After inspecting the work, Joseph directed four of his servants to place the body on the wooden frame of the funeral bier, inserting poles through each end of the bier so the men could transport the body. While I had witnessed some of this cleansing when Cuza died, I found the care and thoroughness of Joseph and his men superb, their attention to detail beyond reproach, the veneration given to Jesus' body demonstrating their love and respect for this man.

As Joseph's men gathered up all the material they had brought with them, I asked, "Where are you taking him?"

Joseph pointed to a beautiful garden area, down the hill toward the west, a short distance away. "As a man of some wealth, I long ago purchased a new tomb cut into the rock in the garden over there. I intended to use it for my burial, but based on the events of these past few days, it is more fitting to have Jesus buried there. It is a serene place, away from onlookers."

Joseph paused for a moment sighing, before shaking his head. "If you have no other questions, we will be on our way."

"How will you keep onlookers away from the tomb?"

"When the tomb was cut from the rock, a very heavy stone was placed nearby. Once we place the body in the tomb, the stone will be rolled into place, sealing the entrance. In anticipation of this being my final resting place, I can assure you, the stone is substantial, so heavy, it will take all these men to roll it into place once we are done." After I nodded my understanding, Joseph walked to the front of the procession to complete his mission in sorrow.

I sensed the man's heartache and shame. He and I were kindred spirits. Both of us, in our own ways, felt we let opportunities to testify on Jesus' behalf slip through our fingers. Neither of us had the courage while Jesus lived to stand up against the authorities over us. Both of us kept our mouths closed as we did our duty. What else could we have done? Had we rebelled and stood up for Jesus, someone else would have taken our place and the end result would have been the same. While it seemed wrong, it appeared his death was inevitable.

As Joseph and his small caravan began their slow walk down the hill, I noticed the women began to trail Joseph and his men, the women walking past me, staying a respectful distance behind the funeral procession. As they passed by, I recognized one of the women. It was Joanna.

Dressed in simple garb, her clothes grayish in color, her body protected from peering eyes, only the front of her face exposed, Joanna answered my question before I could ask. Through the tears running down her cheeks, she said, "We want to see where they take our Lord. Perhaps in a few days, we may be permitted to anoint his body with spices. Right now, we wish to be close to Jesus and draw comfort from one another."

I nodded as she hurried to catch up with the other women. Suddenly she turned back and said, "Aquila, we've watched as you did your duty today. While you could have been harsh and cruel to those three, you discharged your duty with compassion. Thank you." Before turning to catch up with the others she added one more comment, a smile accompanying her words, "My husband was right . . . You are a good man."

Compassion! Had I really been compassionate, been a good man? I had my doubts about that. I didn't feel compassionate or good when Jesus' blood spurted from his wrists as those rusty nails tore into his flesh, or as his body jerked in pain as the mallet struck the heads of the nails over and over again. No, I didn't feel humane or tender. The only feeling running through me now was sorrow. Looking up, I watched the women as they continued on their sad journey.

There was still work to be done before we could leave this place of death. With just me and my soldiers about, I ordered Maurus to organize the men to take the two criminals down from their crosses and dispose of them in accordance with the crucifixion mandates.

In sharp contrast to the tenderness and love shown by Joseph and his men for the body of Jesus, the two remaining bodies received a far rougher treatment from the soldiers under Maurus' direction. There was no linen cloth, no myrrh, no aloes, no attempt to be gentle while pulling the nails from the dead flesh, the soldiers' motivation was to complete the task before dusk so they could drown the memories of this day away with the strong drink. I watched the scene, detaching myself as best I could from its cruel conclusion. While one body would be placed lovingly into a burial tomb purchased by a rich man, protected from prying eyes and the small animals, the bodies of these two criminals who shared death on the cross with Jesus would be thrown in to a garbage cart before being dumped into the city's refuse pit to be food for wild dogs and carnivorous birds of prey led by the ossifrage, the largest vulture in the land.

When our task was complete, we left Golgotha behind, darkness rapidly closing around us. As the last rays of the sun dipped below the horizon, I thought about the priests. They had accomplished what they had set out to do: to kill a good man, a man who had miraculous powers, a humble man who had a unique relationship with his God, such a rich relationship that seemed to say he was the Son of God.

Chapter XXI

Fortress Antonio
Jerusalem
Evening, April 1, A. D. 34

By the time we reached the fort, I wanted nothing to do with any Jews or their religion. What kind of people could so callously desire the death of a man who claimed to be their own God's son and do all this in the name of the religion they claimed to revere? It made no sense. Rather than go back to Antipas' palace, I desired a place of familiarity, a place where my roots felt grounded, where others knew my values and beliefs and appreciated them. This night would be spent with my fellow Roman officers at the Fortress Antonio.

Besides being Pilate's headquarters, one side of the large complex provided the billeting for the Legionnaires, the place where Jesus had been scourged. On the opposite side of the complex were billets for the officers, my brothers in arms. Each area had its own dining space and places of relaxation, good order and discipline calling for this separation, the same concept I introduced to Shallium months before. Fellowship and kinship would be in abundance, opportunities to renew old acquaintances and tell soldier stories about those with whom we had served would be the order of the day. This would be my place of refuge.

While the dining area designated for the officers was not elaborate, it was functional, room enough to accommodate fifty men at wooden tables where they could enjoy reasonable food and copious amounts of wine. If a Centurion wanted to be alone, his decision would be respected. If another wished to fill his gullet with all fruit of the vine he could hold and be undisturbed, that too would be respected.

Seating alone in a corner table with my second voluminous cup of wine held firmly in my grasp, the Centurion of the Legion, the *primus pilus*, Cato, the one who had stood next to Pilate earlier in the day, surprised me when he slapped me on the back, occupying the seat on the bench opposite me. He was an impressive man, tall in stature, with powerful arms and legs, his bald head shining bright, the soldiers joked he shaved his dome several times a week. The men of the Legion loved him. He was fair yet tough, strong yet compassionate, his warrior exploits legendary. He was our role model, the consummate, professional soldier.

Since each level of any legion, centuries – maniples - cohorts - legion, had one Centurion in charge, Cato had risen through the ranks to reach the pinnacle of our career path. Pilate depended upon him for wise and steady counsel regarding the units under his control. Without question, Cato's sage advice kept many a commander from great embarrassment over the years, his presence at all the proceedings earlier today his *modes operandi*.

"Aquila, from everything I saw and heard today, you had a very interesting time: standing up to a mob, releasing a criminal back into society, and then crucifying three men. How were you so fortunate to have all these opportunities come your way?" Cato laughed softly as he helped himself to a cup of wine. "Or maybe I should ask, which of the gods did you anger to for all to be heaped upon your shoulders?"

"I'm not sure about angering the gods, but you're right, it was a most interesting day." I took another gulp from my cup, trying to forget the events he mentioned. I liked this man but what could I share with him? "Today was a culmination of events that evolved over many days," I said slurring my words.

"Well my young Centurion, I've got all night and we've plenty of wine." His smile was friendly enough, his words invited a response. "But before you begin, I should tell you while you were at Golgotha we also had some excitement here in the city today. Did you hear about the curtain in the Jewish temple being torn from top to bottom?"

My eyes left my cup to look at the older man. "I have no idea what you're talking about."

"In their great temple . . . after the rain and the wind and lightning finally stopped . . . the Jews came running to us in sheer panic. Seems that when earthquake hit, the large curtain in their temple tore apart." Cato paused for another drink, wiping the excess off with the sleeve of his tunic. "I've never been in the Jewish temple, but from what I understand, it has three parts. The first is the largest, called the courts where all Jews can enter. The second part is called the Holy Place, where only the priests are allowed while the third area, called the Most Holy Place is even more restrictive. Only the high priest can enter once each year to atone for the sins of all Jews. I'm sure there is much more to all this, but this is my simple understanding. Anyway separating the Holy Place from the Most Holy Place was this huge curtain."

"I was in the courtyard a few days ago so I have a general idea of where you're talking about."

"Good. Apparently, when the earthquake hit, this curtain between the two holy places tore from top to bottom and fell to the ground. I'm told it was an extremely heavy piece of woven cloth which took many men to lift into place. When it crashed, it almost killed one of their priests."

"During the earthquake, you say?"

"That's my understanding. Why do you ask?"

Was now the right time to trust someone: the curtain, the earthquake, tombs flying open, Jesus' death, all this happening at one time? Could it be that the God of the Jews was telling his people Jesus was his son or were all these incidents a series of coincidences? Doubtful, but . . . ?

Looking around the large room watching the unabashed revelry occurring all around us, men like me involved in drinking contests, arm wrestling, good natured joking, all meant nothing to me. Leaning closer to Cato to make sure my words would be for his ears only, I whispered, "Cato, this might just be a coincidence, but from what you said, it seems this curtain came down near the time Jesus died."

Pausing to form my thoughts with care, my next words shot out. "Over the last few months I've learned a great deal about this man Jesus which I dismissed. Although the stories were unbelievable, defying logic at every turn, with the events of these past few days, and from what I saw today, I'm beginning to believe Jesus might be some kind of Jewish God, maybe even the one they call Messiah." I put my wine cup down, gazing into space before turning back to capture Cato's eyes. "And now he's dead, killed by the same people he may have come to help."

Cato stared at the scarred wooden table in front of us. Then he took another large swallow from his cup. Was he going to berate me, or laugh at me? Had I opened my mouth to the wrong man?

Like me, he looked about, insuring our privacy, the tone of his voice much like that of a father teaching a son. "Aquila, I've been a soldier for a long, long time and I'm not easily swayed by rumors or gossip, innuendoes or unfounded suppositions. Not much surprises me anymore. From the stories I've heard these past few months, and from my own observations, your thoughts about Jesus have merit."

He leaned in closer to me. "Some things in life can be attributed to chance, or, as you say, to coincidences, but with Jesus, there are too many stories, too many incidents, too many witnesses, to ignore. When all these accounts attributed to Jesus are taken together, my conclusion is similar to yours."

I stared at this warrior. What was he saying?

Cato's mouth turned up into a wry smile. "I see by the look on your face, my words come to you without any warning." He chuckled a bit. "I suppose it's time to let you in on a closely held secret. Believe me when I say no deception was intended by what I'm about to tell you. In fact, when I'm finished, my words may put your mind at ease. As a matter of some concern to both of us, keep what I'm about to tell you in strict confidence. Is that clear?"

With my head now spinning with this new revelation and my curiosity piqued, I stammered, "Yes, of course." Then it struck me. His joining me at this table was no casual happenstance. He chose to sit here to learn or to share something of value to each of us.

The man took another drink of his wine goblet stopping to savor its rich juices, smacking his lips together. "As perhaps you're aware, we senior Centurions have a unique communications system. Rather than use the message system of letters used by men like Pilate and Antipas, we employ trusted runners and short notes to share information with one another. This helps us keep in touch with various aspects of the command without getting the senior leadership more involved than they need to be in some of the more sensitive issues in the land."

After seeing my head bob acknowledgement this, he went on. "Before your friend, Valerus, sailed for Rome, I spent several nights with him reminiscing about old times when he and I soldiered together on the fringes of the Empire. During our talks, I sensed he was struggling with something very important. It was during one of our times together he told me about John, his beheading, and the faith this man demonstrated in his God."

Before continuing, Cato looked around the room once again to insure others would respect our space in the corner of the dark, dingy room which was now almost filled to capacity. "At first I dismissed all this as Jewish nonsense and the result of the strong medicines given to Valerus, but then I took it upon myself to learn about the faithfulness of John. Then several months ago, Lucius informed me of your visit to Capernaum and Antipas' interest in Jesus of Nazareth. So while you've been doing your investigation about Jesus on the tetrarch's behalf, I conducted a similar investigation to satisfy my own curiosity."

Wanting to ask a hundred questions, my mouth remained closed as Cato continued. "To answer the first question I suspect you have, the answer is no - Pilate is not aware of anything I've been doing in this regard. While I didn't have you followed, I pursued through my own sources, a somewhat parallel path to the course you chose. While I heard second hand many of the same stories others told you, I too had doubts. And perhaps like you, I questioned my allegiance to our Roman gods as the more I learned, the more I became convinced Jesus might very well be the man he claimed to be."

Pausing to search my face for my reaction, he went on. "I hoped for a different ending for Jesus today, even though my sources predicted his death days ago. While you couldn't see this coming, I had the perspective of distance and having a broader knowledge of the politics of the chief priest and his associates which influenced the final outcome." Cato gazed off to the side, a far-away look in his eye before he looked down at his hands. "I'm sorry Jesus is dead."

I sat still too stunned to reply. Leaning back against the wall, a great sigh came from the depths of my soul not knowing whether to be angry or relieved. Angry others were seeking the same information about Jesus without telling me, and yet relieved their conclusions mirrored mine. "As you've considered everything you learned about Jesus, after today, do you believe he was the Jewish Messiah?"

Dwelling on my question, the older man gazed looked thoughtfully at me. "Yes . . . yes, I do. What helps me reach this conclusion is my respect for Lucius and what he told me about his servant. If I had heard his story from someone I didn't know, I'd be more skeptical, but Lucius' personal testimony means a great deal to me, his report along with what the people at Nain had to say."

Cato rubbed his chin. "Aquila, just because I believe Jesus was who he said he was, doesn't mean you have to. Each man must decide for himself and besides, unless there's another miracle waiting around the corner neither of us knows about, the man is dead. All our conjecture about him means very little, for without his leadership, those who have followed him and believed in him have nothing."

Excited by his words yet drained from the day's turmoil, I needed time to absorb Cato's words. As I stood up to leave, he stopped me. "Just one more in case you haven't heard, the traitor, the one who gave Jesus up to the priests, is dead."

"Humph," I grunted. "What happened? Some of Jesus' followers come across him in a dark alley?"

"No. Seems after pocketing the priests' money, thirty silver coins to be precise, Judas had second thoughts and tried to return his reward to the priests. When they refused his request, he apparently threw the money in the temple and then went out and hung himself. Some of our soldiers found him."

I nodded my understanding, neither of us had much else to say. We held a common belief few others could comprehend, our mutual respect and kinship forming a bond much like a brotherhood. After we parted company for the evening, I relived the day's events as I cleaned my uniform. The dirt and blood came off my clothing and the metal parts of my uniform easily; the blood on my sandals was another matter. I could only hope the dark memories of the deaths of John and Jesus would someday disappear. Fortunately for me, the plentiful amount of wine I consumed allowed me to sleep that night.

****

As I prepared to return to Antipas' palace the next morning, Cato sent word for me to meet him near Pilate's headquarters. The man waited for me there, his words brisk and to the point. "Aquila, there has been a new development regarding the events of yesterday. Early this morning Caiaphas and some of other chief priests came to see Pilate. Seems the priests are concerned about statements Jesus made last week when he predicted that not only would he be killed, but that he would rise again in three days. They're afraid Jesus' followers may steal the body from the tomb, thereby claiming Jesus has risen from the dead as he said he would. Caiaphas told Pilate this second deception would be even worse than the first."

"So what did they want Pilate to do?"

"Their request, which Pilate honored, was for us to put guards around the tomb to secure Jesus' burial site. He gave this order to me and I've already taken action. To insure there will be no question of tampering, the first shift placed a seal around the stone. Guards will remain at the tomb for the next three days to cover the time Jesus gave his disciples. Once this period of concern passes, we'll stand down the guards."

"Interesting." Then my words came out slowly as the thought hit me. "Isn't it amazing how that even in death, Jesus still causes the priests to tremble at his words."

"I agree . . . nevertheless, I wanted you to know."

After thanking Cato, my mind kept rolling back to this new development as I made the short walk to Antipas'. Even after his death, the priests are still afraid of Jesus. Were they being cautious, or did they too believe his words? What would happen if Jesus' prediction came true?

This thought stayed with me as I passed through the gates of the palace where all was quiet. There was no energy, everyone appeared listless, downcast. When I asked about Kish's whereabouts, the servants informed me he was not feeling well and would not be available today. Perhaps like me, he just needed time to absorb all that had happened.

****

The next morning I rose early to go back to Pilate's headquarters, hoping to see Cato so we could discuss some old friends we both knew. With the sun beginning its dance skyward, I found him. After taking a seat on one of the benches overlooking the patio near the soldiers' quarters, we began a lively conversation about common acquaintances from the legions we had served. In the middle of talking about our time in Gaul, Cato stopped in mid sentence as he watched two men walking some distance from us. "Something is wrong. Follow me!"

I could barely keep up with him as he rushed down the steps into the patio, making long strides to catch up with two soldiers heading away from us. When we were almost upon them, Cato commanded them to halt, the two coming to the position of attention as they realized the Centurion of the Legion hailed them. "Aren't you two part of the guard detail at the tomb of Jesus?"

"Yes, Centurion," they responded.

"If you are on guard duty then why are you here? Make this a good answer. " It was clear Cato wanted the truth and would tolerate nothing less. No excuses, just the truth.

"Well, Centurion . . . "

"WELL is not an acceptable answer! I will ask once again. Why are you away from your post?"

The men looked at each other before the taller of two replied, a frightened look on his face. "Jesus is gone, Centurion! His body disappeared!"

Cato looked at each man, his eyes narrowing. "What do you mean 'disappeared'?! How? Don't give me any far-fetched tales. Give me the truth. Do you understand me? Omit nothing! Start from when you went on duty last night."

The two men trembled as the one who had been doing all the talking began while the other soldier nodded his concurrence. Both knew their only hope of survival was to tell Cato exactly what happened; anything less would put them in great peril. "Centurion, our shift began at midnight. It was a clear, calm night. It remained that way until just before dawn . . . then suddenly the ground around us shook!"

The soldier who was doing all the talking looked at his compatriot, beads of sweat coming down his face. "Then an angel appeared. . . He was bright as lightning, his clothes white as snow. He went over to the stone barring the entrance to the tomb and rolled it away as if it was a small rock, and then he sat on it. He saw us, but he didn't speak to us. We were so scared, we couldn't move. We were frozen in place, paralyzed."

"What happened then?"

"A few minutes later, two women carrying some spices came

down the path toward the tomb. When they saw the angel, like us, they became terrified. The angel spoke to them in a soothing calm voice, telling them Jesus was no longer in the tomb. He said Jesus had risen like he told them he would. Then this angel told them to go tell Jesus' followers what they had seen. Before they left, they were to look inside the tomb to verify that Jesus was no longer there. He then told them Jesus was going ahead of them to Galilee." The second soldier kept nodding his head confirming what the first man said.

"The women stood still for a long time before one of them got up the courage to look inside the tomb. When she came out, she cried out saying Jesus was not there. Both women looked at the angel who just nodded his head. Then the two of them ran back up the path toward the city."

"And you two? What did you do?"

"Centurion, we sat still, petrified of the angel who then just disappeared, afraid of being accused of not doing our duty, afraid of Jesus who somehow got out of the tomb."

This time the second soldier spoke. "We decided to go tell Caiaphas, since he convinced Pilate to set up this detail in the first place. We saw him just before we came here. When we told him everything we just told you, he held a short counsel with the priests. They told us to tell anyone who asked, 'His followers came during the night and stole him while we slept.' "

The soldier then reached under his belt, dangling a large bag of treasure. "They gave us this money and said if this report gets to Pilate, they would satisfy his concerns and keep us out of trouble." The man's head dropped. "We were on our way to hide the money for later."

The other man chimed in. "Centurion, that's the truth . . . The angel, the stone, the women, the bribe. Everything -- it's all true. We didn't fall asleep at our post. When the angel appeared we were just too afraid to do anything."

Cato stared at the men. "For now, I choose to believe you. But you've made one critical error. You went to see Caiaphas instead of coming to see me. Therefore, the money you received from him will be given to the general fund of the Legion. You will say nothing of our discussion to anyone unless I personally give you permission. Is that clear? Is there anything else you have to tell me? Anything you've left out?"

When both men shook their heads, Cato sent them back to their quarters, but not before sternly counseling them once again about not saying anything to anyone as he relieved them of their bag of coins.

Neither of us spoke for what seemed a long time. We looked at each other, both of us trying to get our minds around what we'd just been told. "Can it be, Aquila? Is it possible Jesus arose from the dead as he said he would, that an angel rolled the stone back freeing the man from his tomb? Could he really have done that?"

I shook my head as I too found myself at the juncture of belief and disbelief. "I helped nail him to the cross! I saw him take his last breath! I saw his body wrapped in burial cloths. And yet . . ." My mind raced back to the boy at Nain. If Jesus could raise that boy from the dead, why couldn't he do the same for himself? While it seemed impossible, many other stories I had heard about Jesus also sounded at first too implausible as well. Yet . . .

How I wished Cuza was here. Perhaps Kish could help me understand all this. He seemed to share much of his father's faith. Could others help me understand any of this, Philip perhaps? Could Kish get me in contact with him? Considering my part in Jesus' death, why would any of Jesus' disciples agree to see me? Excusing myself, I hurried back to Antipas' palace.

Chapter XXII

Antipas' Palace
Jerusalem
Early afternoon, April 5, A.D. 34

Halting just inside the gates, I sensed excitement in the air. Something was different, or was something different in me? While others saw Jesus die from a distance, I was right there watching him suffer, seeing his blood flow from his body, concentrating on the anguish, the pain on his face, my eyes searching his as he took his last breath. His death was no hoax, no fabrication and yet these new tales brought hope.

Taking solace in the garden, I sat on one of the benches wondering again and again, could the statements of two frightened soldiers possibly be true? Like many stories told by soldiers, the truth could be stretched so thin, it could become almost unrecognizable, yet the two guards did not waver from their testimony under the intense scrutiny of Cato. While part of me wanted to deny their words, it was difficult to imagine the soldiers embellishing too much from what they experienced when facing the barrage of questions asked them. I still had to wonder, could they really have seen an angel? Did such creatures really exist? The old man at the Jordan told me about John's father seeing an angel but . . . .

Everything I had seen and been exposed to these past months led in a circle with Jesus always at the center. Did he have the power, like a God, to overcome death? And what about all the miracles, could they all be true? The thought occurred to me, if one of Jesus' miracles was true, then why wouldn't all the others be true as well? Conversely, if one miracle could be proven false, wouldn't that mean the rest could be false as well?

Yes, that's it. Review the miracles. Judge them for their veracity.

First, did Shallium's father and the young man in Nain lie about Jesus raising the young man from his coffin? No, it seemed both told the truth and many townspeople would verify their account. Then there was James' story about Jesus turning water into wine. By his account, I believed every word he said. Certainly Lucius and his servant held me captive as they told me how Jesus healed Jorim, each verifying the account. Then there was the testimony of the man on the beach at Bethsaida who described how Jesus restored his sight, his enthusiasm certain and undeniable.

What about all comments others made to me about Jesus – the innkeeper, Philip, Cuza, Kish, Joanna? Everyone who spoke about Jesus was always positive and clear in what they described. Even the second hand stories told me by Cuza led me to think of Jesus acting in a manner unlike any other man I'd ever known. My own observations of his entry into the city, his response to his accusers at his trial, and then the way he faced death gave clear evidence of his uniqueness.

No evidence had come forth from anyone contradicting any miracles attributed to Jesus. Nothing! While I hadn't interviewed anyone with the purpose of disproving his miracles, surely if any part of these stories were false, someone, somewhere, would have given me some inkling of any inconsistency. At Jesus' trial, the priests presented no evidence to counter any of Jesus' miracles. If there were any blemishes, certainly the priests would have been quick to bring such damning evidence to Pilate. Since they had not done so, this must mean there was no such evidence to refute, nothing to disprove any of the truth of Jesus' claims. There was nothing from any source I could recall suggesting Jesus was not who he claimed to be.

My mind kept repeating my words on Golgotha: "Surely he was the Son of God . . . Surely he was the Son of God!" So if my words were true, where should I go from here? What could I do? My mind kept going around in circles searching for some logical answer. In my heart I felt I already knew the answer.

****

"Centurion… CENTURION. Are you all right? I've been watching you for a few minutes. I couldn't tell if you were sick or having some spell. Are you all right?"

I shook my head slightly, gazing up at Kish. "Yes, I'm . . . I'm fine. I've news for you."

He smiled down at me, excitement in his voice. "Perhaps I've already heard your news. If you're coming to tell me Jesus' tomb is empty, that information reached me earlier. Even though I've not heard the whole story yet, I've been told enough to know that the tomb is empty! Jesus has risen from the dead just as he said he would!

The young man could hardly contain himself, his words gushing out. "When we first heard this, some thought you Romans stole the body, but that made no sense because Pilate had nothing to gain by creating religious unrest. Nor was it logical for the priests to seize the body either, for this would have given credence to Jesus saying he would rise from the grave. Besides, who could get into the tomb with your soldiers guarding it? The only explanation any of us could reach was that the women's story was true - Jesus rose from the dead just as he said he would. As you can imagine, everyone is waiting for more information or perhaps a sighting of Jesus, some kind of evidence we can touch and see. I expect to hear more from my mother when she returns."

When he got his breath, Kish went on. "For now, we all have many questions. Will he return to us and save us from oppression? I just don't know. And in the meantime, we don't know what Caiaphas and the priests will do or what actions they'll take."

I placed my hand on Kish's shoulder, the emotions of the past week finally catching up with him; the loss of his father, the crucifixion of Jesus, and now this new revelation. "Kish, I'm much like you. I don't know what to believe. It seems to me all any of us can do is wait. Wait and see if Jesus chooses to reveal himself to someone."

Did I really believe the words coming from my lips? Would Jesus really be able to show himself at some point? Wasn't it enough for him to rise from the dead? "What are Jesus' men saying about all this? What is their advice?"

"I don't know. I imagine their thoughts are much like ours – hopeful yet confused, desiring to show faith, yet frightened of what Caiaphas will do. As much as they want to believe Jesus has risen, I'm sure they're confounded like all of us. For now, I agree with you. We should try and remain calm and see where this all leads. I am my father's son; it is in my nature to act although I don't know what I can really do."

Kish looked at the ground, his shoulders down. After a great sigh, he glanced up. "You're right. We'll wait for Jesus. If and when he decides to appear somewhere, we'll all rejoice."

Upon hearing those words, I turned away. Yes, some would rejoice and some of us would tremble in fear; fear because of the great distress we caused him when he lived among us, me in particular! First I killed his friend, John. Then I killed him. If Jesus returned from the tomb, could he ever forgive me? Their blood was on me. I could never be forgiven! If Jesus did return from the dead, I would run as far from him as I could.

****

More than a week passed as Antipas decided to remain in Jerusalem for a longer stay than originally planned. Despite a long standing dispute involving power, Antipas confided in me that he and Pilate had become friendlier as a result of Antipas' support of Pilate's disposition of Jesus, the two dining together several times in the past few days. This was good for me personally, as at some point they might discuss my desire to transfer to Rome. At least this thought crossed my mind when Antipas told me of their new relationship.

Meanwhile, each time I saw Kish, he related third or fourth hand accounts of sightings of Jesus, stories originating first with a woman who maintained Jesus spoke to her near the tomb that first morning. Another tale came from two men who claimed as they were walking from Jerusalem toward the village of Emmaus, several hours west of the city they had a conversation with Jesus. And finally Jesus' closest followers declared he had appeared to them the night he arose as they met in a locked room.

I listened to these tales with great interest. Despite the enthusiasm expressed in these stories, they seemed contrived, almost like dreams made up by wishful thinkers. While part of me wanted to believe what I heard, the guilt I felt for my part of breaking Jesus' body was too great, my memories of watching him strain for his last breathe too real to be captivated by these supposed sightings.

The thought occurred to me how the power and prestige of Jesus' intimate followers would increase if they spread these stories and others believed them. Weren't these men like the rest of us, seeking fame and glory for themselves, or did they have a different motivation, a different perspective? Judas' treasonous acts had shown, despite his intimate knowledge of Jesus, these men could be like the rest of us, each having human frailties, desires for lust, and power, and prestige. Could their sightings really be true, not motivated by personal gain or personal glory?

During the middle of the second week after Jesus' death, as I passed through the garden of the palace, Joanna approached me. "An opportunity has come up I believe would be of interest to you. Can you meet Kish at dusk this evening? I think you'll find what he has to show you most interesting."

Such a mysterious request could not be turned aside. Joanna and Kish had always been trustworthy, just as Cuza. They would not lead me astray. "Of course, how can I refuse? Is there some reason why this meeting can't take place now?"

Joanna smiled. "No, that's just not possible. Please meet Kish at the front gate at dusk." Although her words were not a command, I took them almost as such. During the remainder of the day I wondered what lay ahead, a secret meeting no doubt, new information about Jesus perhaps.

****

When I arrived at the gate at the appointed hour, Kish was waiting for me. Without a word he led the way east through the city streets, past the temple, and out the *Valley Gate,* toward the Mount of Olives. We stayed on the road toward Bethany before turning on to a less traveled path which led into a garden filled with shapely olive trees and large boulders, the beauty and solitude of the place breathtaking, the stars making their presence known in the eastern sky, their lights sparkling through the limbs of the overhanging trees. Only the subtle noises of our footsteps and those of the night creatures on their nocturnal wanderings interrupted the quietness of the ground around us. We stopped in a small clearing, "Kish, what is this place called? It seems like paradise on earth."

He studied the clearing around us. "This is the Garden of Gethsemane. It was here Judas led Caiaphas' men to arrest Jesus before they took him to stand in front of the Sanhedrin. Jesus and his disciples prayed here many times. I brought you here because this seemed a good place for you to meet some friends of mine."

As soon the words came from his lips, four men stepped from the shadows of one of the large trees. My first reaction was to draw my sword, but something held my hand down as I gripped the handle, waiting and watching as these men came closer. In the dim light of the stars, I immediately recognized two of the men; one was Philip, who gave me a knowing nod, and the second was Reuel, my faithful soldier, who, while he did not render a salute, gave me a respectful look. The other two were not familiar to me; one an imposing muscular fellow with dark, curly hair, a serious, intense look on his face while the fourth individual reminded me of Cuza, smaller, older with gray hair, his frame and manner unremarkable.

With these men now standing in front of Kish and me, Kish spoke first. "You know Reuel, of course. He has been a follower of Jesus for a short time and asked to be with us tonight. And you know Philip." He turned to the third man. "This is Thomas, another of Jesus' followers. This fourth man is Cleopas. These men come in peace and bear you no ill will."

While I acknowledged Kish's words, I remained on guard, glancing from one man to the next wondering if others lay hidden in the darkness ready to pounce on me to take revenge for my part in Jesus' death.

Philip was the first to speak. "Aquila, it is good to see you again. Until we can discern Caiaphas' intentions, this is the best place for us to meet. We understand he is hunting for us and so we must be   on guard."

Still not knowing what to say, I looked about remaining silent yet vigilant. Why was I here? Philip must have noted my concern because he waited for me to look back at him before he spoke again. "Jesus loved coming to this place and so we feel close to him when we're here." Then he smiled, "And who knows, maybe he'll come here to be with us one night. What a blessing that would be. . . Kish has told us about your conversations with Cuza. Given what you discussed with our friend, it occurred to us you should hear what Cleopas and Thomas have to say. Perhaps their accounts of their recent experiences will help you in your search for the truth."

As I listened to Philip, I glanced back at Kish, and then at Reuel before shifting my eyes toward the other two men wondering what they could add about Jesus. Without any prompting, Reuel broke in. "Sir, before the others speak, I must tell you about how I've come to be here tonight. As I mentioned to you on that day on the road to Tiberias, because I've been privileged to accompany you in your search for Jesus, I was moved to ask myself similar questions to those you asked yourself. Then when Jesus and his men came to Jerusalem, I saw Philip quite by accident and because I had seen him at Bethsaida, I felt I could ask him questions and after we talked, he introduced me to Jesus."

The young man, now with tears in his eyes, shook his head slowly from side to side. "It was an incredible meeting. He was everything the others told you about him. While I serve Rome, my heart now follows Jesus, and while I watched from afar the events leading to his death, I believe he has risen from the tomb just as he said he would." The soldier looked up, staring at me. "Centurion, there are many others like me in our ranks. While we will continue to serve Rome faithfully, our eternal trust is in Jesus as our Lord and Master. I'm here because of my respect for you. I just wanted you to know that."

Nodding my understanding, the words and stature of the man who spoke told me something was different about this meeting, his words communicating the establishment of a bond, much like the one I felt with Cato, a brotherhood of men equal in the sight of our creator.

Then Cleopas stepped forward. "When the others asked me to come here, I was afraid; afraid to face a Roman Centurion with my story." The man paused, glancing at the others, all of whom gave him reassuring nods. "Then I realized I have no need to ever fear those who wear your uniform – I've seen the risen Jesus. I've spoken to the one who has conquered death!"

I gazed at this man assessing him once again. "Forgive me, I don't understand."

Cleopas smiled at me. "On the third day after Jesus' death, a friend and I were walking toward Emmaus, a village west of Jerusalem, talking about Jesus' death and how earlier that morning several women claimed to have gone to the tomb, and finding it empty, they passed on a fantastic story saying Jesus was alive."

The man halted to gaze at the city in the distance before continuing. "As my friend and I continued along on our journey, a stranger joined us, asking what we were talking about. When we relayed this story to him, this man launched into a lengthy dialogue telling us how foolish we were and how slow our hearts must be to remember what the prophets had spoken about. This man reminded us, 'Did not the Christ have to suffer these things and then enter his glory?' As we studied this man closer, we remembered what Moses and other prophets had written."

I stopped the man. "Are you suggesting that Jesus' death was foretold? That your God allowed this to happen? Why would he do such a thing?"

Cleopas ignored me. "As we approached Emmaus, this stranger acted as though he was going on, but at our urging, he stopped to eat with us. It was then this man took the bread, gave thanks, broke it, and gave it to us. When he did this, Centurion, it was like scales fell off our eyes; we could see this man in front of us was Jesus." He gave a great sigh, "Before we could ask him any questions, he disappeared, vanished before our eyes."

"So what did you do?"

Cleopas chuckled, "We ran back to Jerusalem and found Philip and the others and told them this good news – that we had seen Jesus alive! The women were right! Jesus is alive!" Now out of breath, the old man stood silent, a wide smile on his face.

Before I asked Cleopas any questions, Thomas addressed me in a strong, deep voice. He was equal to my height, a sword at his side. "Centurion, while my story is brief, it may help as you wrestle with all you've seen and heard about our Lord and Master.

"I've been a loyal follower of Jesus for several years. Some consider me a bit of a hot head and from time to time, I've proven them right." He chuckled, "Maybe that's one of Jesus' greatest gifts, blending so many different personalities into a common belief." Then he stopped for a moment as he stared at me. "And like you, I have strong beliefs about my duty, in my case, duty and loyalty to Jesus."

The man's eyes bored into me, "Despite everything I saw Jesus do and everything I heard him say, when he died on that cross, my courage left me as I doubted . . . doubted everything the man taught us. When Joseph and his men wrapped Jesus in the white linens of death, I felt abandoned, alone, forsaken. Later, however, I experienced something that I will hold on to for the rest of my life. Because Kish related to us some of your struggles, I wanted to meet you to tell you what happened to me." The man stopped, putting his hand on my shoulder much like a brother would do, "Perhaps after listening to what I have to say, like other Romans you know, like Lucius and Cato to name a few, you too will become a follower of Jesus."

Me, a follower of Jesus! Why would he have me? "Thomas," I said, attempting to deflect some of the man's words, playing for time, "you said you saw Joseph wrapping him in the linens. I didn't see you there with the women and John."

"I wasn't on Golgotha. I was one of those who spent the day sitting along the Damascus road watching the events of the day. I didn't have the courage to come closer. I saw you nail Jesus and the other two to their crosses. Even when John and the women drew near to Jesus, I didn't have the nerve to join them for fear of ridicule." The man gave a great sigh. "I was there through the dark period and the earthquake and when the skies finally gave way to sunshine. All I could do was watch from a distance, concerned about me and what would become of me instead of focusing on my Lord."

Here was another man like me, like Joseph of Arimathaea, who felt he let Jesus down. How many more were there like us who had the chance to stand up and speak on Jesus' behalf, but we sat still, unmoved by the circumstances around us?

Thomas' eyes stared into the night sky fixing on some distant star. "Despite those many months watching Jesus heal people, raising some from the dead, hearing him speak, watching him perform miracle after miracle, some of which you've learned about and many others which you've not, I abandoned Jesus in his greatest hour of need. When he died, I was so depressed, not understanding the events of his last day: the arrest, the beatings, the trial, and then the crucifixion, I went off to sulk, away from my friends. I just couldn't understand why Jesus didn't defend himself or lash out at his accusers; why he didn't use his miraculous powers to save himself."

Tears come down his cheeks. "On on the first night after he rose from the tomb, my friends told me Jesus appeared in our room where we hid, but since I was out wallowing in self pity, I wasn't there. When I joined them later and the others told me what happened, I was angry. I said that until I could put my fingers into those nail holes and put my hand into his side pierced by the soldier's spear, I would not believe he was alive. I just couldn't. Looking back at my arrogance, I realize what I fool I was."

The big man rubbed his mouth collecting his thoughts. "Then a few days later, we assembled once again in that same room, the doors and windows locked. Suddenly without any warning or fanfare, Jesus stood among us. Right there in our midst! After greeting each of my friends, he focused his attention on me, just me! He held out his hands to me saying, 'Put your finger here; see my hands.' Then he pointed to his side and said, 'Reach out your hand and put it in my side. Thomas, stop doubting and believe!' "

The man stopped, too overcome with emotion to speak. After gathering himself, he fixed his eyes on me. "Aquila, Jesus should have dismissed me for my disbelief, for my doubts, for my uncertainty, for my fears. Who could blame him? Yet, in spite of my shortcomings, he loved me and gathered me into his arms." With the shake of the head, he went on, "He loves me more than I deserve. When he spoke to us later that night, he taught all of us a valuable lesson, one I'll never forget. He said, 'Because you have seen me, you believe; blessed are those who have not seen and yet have belief.' "

He pointed a finger at me. "Aquila, I tell you this because you have been blessed. You have seen the Son of God. You have looked into his eyes, into his face. You have seen him suffer and die. While you have not seen him since that day, I have. And I tell you He is alive! It is time for you to believe what you know is true. It is time to put away your doubts and fears. It is time for both your heart and your mind to come together to embrace the truth you already know."

Oh, how I wanted to believe Thomas. Because Jesus and his disciples had forged a deep bond, it was understandable Jesus could forgive them for their indiscretions. Thomas and the others had been a part of Jesus' ministering to the multitudes; they witnessed his miracles; he counted them as his friends. There was a bond there. But as for me, what had I done? I had killed him. His blood was on my hands, on my sandals. I had killed his friend, John. Even if Jesus was alive, how could there be enough love in him to accept me and to forgive me?

I shouted out, "But I killed him! How can he forgive me? How can his father, your God, forgive me? I killed his son!

Chapter XXIII

Kish's was the first to attempt to put my mind at ease. "Aquila, almost everyone ran away from Jesus when you took him to Golgotha except you. You were there standing next to him in the last hours of his earthly life. While you feel unworthy of Jesus' love and forgiveness, none of us deserve his love. Think about the criminal who died on the cross next to Jesus who stood up for him. Did that man deserve Jesus' love?"

"I . . . I can't really say."

"Aquila, the others and I have had long conversations about that criminal," Philip said, his feet shuffling around. "It seemed he didn't believe in Jesus until almost his last breathe yet Jesus forgave him of his sins, telling him there would be a place in paradise for him."

Philip went on, looking around at the others gathered around me in a loose semi-circle, pointing to each one in turn. "Your sins may be different than ours, but we have all wronged God. We are all like that criminal, in need of Jesus' love and his forgiveness. In some respects, it is really quite simple. If we believe Jesus is who he said he is – The Son of God – he promises, like he did with the one criminal, to prepare a place for us in paradise. We must be willing to make a public proclamation. You know what is amazing, Aquila? You were the first to utter that phrase for the world to hear."

Silence surrounded us until Philip continued. "We are just now beginning to understand some of Jesus' teachings as we reflect upon what we witnessed these past few years. We've come to realize nothing he ever did or said was by accident; everything had a purpose. Think about it: his coming here at Passover and dying on the cross is similar to the celebration of Passover which our people experienced in Egypt many years ago. Although we're still grappling with everything that happened these past few weeks, there are just too many similarities to ignore."

An owl's cry not too far off in the woods interrupted the man's train of thought as we all turned to listen. When nothing followed the cry, his next thoughts came out in slow, halting phrases. "Now we're trying to remember every phrase . . . every miracle . . . every teaching . . . trying to put everything together we've learned from this man." Philip put his hand on my shoulder, nodding his head much like father would do as he taught his son a great lesson. "It will take us much study, but we do know that, like the criminal on the cross, we must believe in him to enjoy paradise with him. Just as Thomas and Kish have said, he only asks us to believe He is the Son of God! Can you do that, Aquila? Can you believe the words you spoke? 'Surely He was the Son of God'?"

Oh how I wanted to accept what Philip was saying. "But," I gasped, "can I forgive myself? The deaths of two innocent men are on my hands!" the memory of watching Jesus drawing his last breathes still clear in my mind.

"While you were a vessel for those who caused the deaths of John and Jesus, you were doing your duty. We believe Jesus understands and is ready to forgive you." Philip stopped for a moment as he looked me squarely into my eyes. "Forgive yourself, Aquila. We believe God has. He is ready to receive you into his family of believers."

He paused giving me an opportunity to absorb all that had been said. "Jesus came here many times to pray and we have followed his example. As we pray now, I want you to join us. Will you do that?"

"But how do you pray? What will I say?"

"Just talk to God, Aquila. Tell Him what is in your heart. Ask

Him to forgive you. Ask Him to receive you as a believer, that
Jesus is His son. If you seek God, He will find you."

I still wasn't sure what I would say or how I should proceed.
I watched the others kneel down in the moist grass, their eyes
closed. I knelt down next to them closing my eyes ready to listen,
to what I did not know.

We were a strange collection of men: one was a fisherman
with rough hands dressed in common clothes, another an intensely
zealous man with a dark beard, and then there was an older man,
whose soft spoken words came from his lips with such conviction
and promise. Knelling beside them were the chief servant of one
of the most influential rulers of our time and two members of the
most powerful army in the world, one young soldier filled with
the youthful enthusiasm and fervor, and me, a man who vacillated
back and forth between wanting to believe what I had seen and
heard, yet still wrestling with the deeply held notions of the past.
Could I put all my history behind me and plot a different course for
my life?

The others prayed in turn, first praising God and thanking
Him for his many blessings. Then they prayed for those like me
to find peace in our hearts to believe Jesus was the Christ, the Son
of the Living God, their yearnings impassioned, filled with great
intensity. It was though they expected Jesus to be side by side with
us, so close he could hear every word spoken, so different from my
prayers uttered to my Roman gods, unsure if any of my deities ever
listened or cared about my requests.

This time was different. There was a presence nearby I sensed.
Could it really be that Jesus, the man I crucified, was now close to
us? Was that possible?

When the others finished praying, there was a quiet stillness. I
knew it was my turn to speak to God. My heart said "Yes", but my
mind and my tongue moved at a snail's pace. Finally, after much
hesitation, my thoughts tumbled out.

Slow at first, in halting words and phrases, my pace quickened the more I asked Jesus over and over to forgive me of killing him, of nailing him to the cross, of not standing up for him in front of Pilate and Antipas. I asked him to forgive me for killing John. I asked him to help me believe He was truly the Son of God, not even sure what that phrase meant. I voiced every thought that had been stored in my heart these past months, telling him of my meetings with so many who talked about him and his miracles. This was my chance, my first real chance to tell this unseen God and His Son of all the thoughts and feelings that had gripped my soul for so long. Then I asked Jesus over and over to forgive me for my part in his death.

I don't know how long I prayed, the others did not interrupt me. When my heart and my mind ran out of thoughts I lay spent on the ground. Philip prayed once again after me, thanking Jesus for me and for what I had expressed. When he said "Amen," we rose to our feet.

Looking up I saw the first rays of the sun breaking through the eastern sky, the pinkish, purple sky in the east, the darker tones to the west like so many others dawns before them, yet this one somehow seemed different. Or was it because I felt different? It was then I looked down. Was it possible; after all this time, after all the heartache? I touched them to be sure, but it was true. The stains on my sandals were gone! John's blood gone! Jesus' blood gone! No sign the stains had ever been there! Tears flooded down my cheeks. The others looked at me in silence.

It was Philip who filled this void. "Aquila, Jesus washed your sandals clean. He cleansed them in a miraculous way that nothing else could because you believe He is the Son of God . . . And if we could see your heart now, we would see an even greater miracle. You see, like us, he washed the stain of guilt away. He cleansed you. He has forgiven you."

And with that I fell on my knees once again, praising God!

****

It has been a number of years since I penned the words you've just read. Many things have happened since. My faith and belief in Jesus has magnified as he has blessed me in many ways. The same cannot be said for some who appeared in the previous pages.

Four years after Jesus' resurrection, Caius Caligula, the man who replaced Tiberius as Emperor, discovered that Herod Antipas, perhaps at the urging of Herodias, conspired with a Roman officer, Sejanus, and the king of Parthia against the Roman Empire. Called to Rome for questioning and facing overwhelming evidence against him, Antipas admitted his aspirations of wanting a kingship, partly due to his jealousy of his nephew, Agrippa I. Caligula's judgment gave all the lands which Antipas governed for forty three years over to Agrippa I, banishing him first to Gaul and then later to Spain where he later died. To her credit, Herodias accompanied Antipas into exile.

After rendering his report to Tiberius on the circumstances of Jesus' death, Pilate remained governor of Judea for several more years until an incident in Samaria between his soldiers and a group near Mt Gerizin got out of control. This incident led to the execution of some notable men of Samaria, prompting another round of complaints against Pilate which resulted in his termination as governor of Judea after ten years. Upon reaching Rome and being judged harshly by Caligula, Pilate, apparently wearied with the misfortunes surrounding him, committed suicide. While rumors suggest Pilate's wife became a follower of Jesus that has never been confirmed.

Caiaphas' eighteen year tenure as the Jewish high priest in Jerusalem ended about the same time as Pilate's dismissal, his responsibilities passing first to Jonathan and then to Theophilus, both sons of the former high priest Annas. I never heard another word about the man.

Of Jesus' most intimate followers, there have been many stories of how they have fared over the years but with few exceptions, the details are known only to God.

After Jesus' resurrection, Mary, along with Jesus' most ardent followers, met together constantly in prayer undergirding an ever expanding group who believed in Jesus. Through their actions, the numbers who believed their testimony about Jesus swelled dramatically, giving rise to a movement no government could stop. While I know nothing of Mary's specific role in this growth, many whom I've met attest to her faith.

Because I left the Jewish lands soon after Jesus' resurrection, Joanna passed into history. I picture her growing old gracefully, always remaining a stalwart follower of Jesus.

James, Jesus' brother, was touched by the events of Jesus' life in a most profound manner, eventually occupying a prominent position of leadership in Jerusalem and throughout the larger area of those who later became known as "Christians." Later James wrote a significant epistle to comfort and encourage the Jews scattered throughout the lands. Called "The Just" by many, his life ended when some Scribes and Pharisees in Jerusalem beat and stabbed him to death during the time Porcius Festus was Governor of Judea.

After Jesus' resurrection, word reached me that Philip continued to be used by God traveling first to Phrygia with another follower, perhaps Nathanael, before eventually reaching Hierapolis, a pagan city devoted to the idolatry of a gigantic serpent. While telling the people there about Jesus, it is said these two men were martyred; Philip suspended by his neck from a tall pillar and Nathanael flayed to death by knives.

Thomas, like so many of Jesus' followers, went into a pagan world on behalf of Jesus. Unconfirmed reports suggest he ventured to the far off land of India where while building a church there, a pagan priest pierced his body with a sharp spear killing him.

John, the man who appeared with Mary on Golgotha, remains under Roman rule in exile at Patmos, a rocky, barren island in the Aegean Sea, a place used by my government to banish criminals, using them to work in the mines there. Despite the desolation of Patmos, I understand John communicates with Jesus' believers through letters carried by those who visit him from time to time.

No words have reached me concerning the lives of Joseph of Arimathea or Nicodemus. From my brief encounter with them as they stared down the priests on Golgotha, I picture both of them living out their days talking to anyone who would listen about Jesus.

As for me, I continued in the profession of arms for many years, telling of my experiences concerning Jesus to other Centurions. In some cases they listen, in other cases not so. Cornelius of the Italian Regiment is one who after a time turned to believe in Jesus. I understand he has had some dealings with Peter, one of Jesus' most strident followers. One who did not appreciate my words so much was Julius, a Centurion in the Imperial Regiment. While not negative to my comments, neither was he taken by them. I've been told recently however, his heart may have been touched by Paul, a devout Christian who journeyed with him during a tumultuous voyage from Caesarea to Rome, a venture where his ship wrecked on the island of Malta. Perhaps sometime later we will learn more about their adventures. What a story that would be.

Sadly, I never saw my friend Valerus again. He died before I reached Rome.

As a final word for your consideration, I've enclosed a portion of a letter I wrote to my son, Felix some years ago which summarizes much of what I've learned over the years.

. . . Once I made the decision to believe that Jesus is the True God, one unlike any other and that he has power over life itself, my priorities and my purpose for life changed. I know he has forgiven me of sins and I am a new man with a new outlook and a new perspective. Things that once seemed so important to me have become less so. I try to stay away from those who want to drag my spirit down into the pit of despair and triviality, spending more time now with those who believe as I do; that God has put us here to

glorify him and to praise him.

For the most part my personality has not changed. I'm still disciplined in my approach to life, still driven to succeed and to achieve goals, still passionate about my country and those who serve with me, but I'm more caring about the plight of those around me. While not as compassionate as Jesus demonstrated, he teaches me day by day to be more like him. I will continue to be a work in progress until I take my last breath.

I would like to tell you because of my belief in Jesus everything in my life is better and I have no challenges, no issues or problems of great importance confronting me, but that would not be true. Things don't always go my way. I still make poor decisions. I still do not treat everyone in a manner fitting of my belief in God but I'm learning. Nevertheless, regardless of how many days I have left on this earth, I know I have the love of Jesus in my heart with each and every step I take.

In my notes I wrote about the day Antipas and I went fishing on the Sea of Galilee. The owner of the boat talked some about the importance of having an anchor holding his boat on solid ground to avoid dangerous waters. As I reevaluated my life, I realized I too needed an anchor and that anchor for me is Jesus. Because I rest in the palm of his hands, I know he will keep me from troubled waters. I now depend upon him to keep me rock steady as I travel through the storms of life.

My question to you, my beloved son, is, do you have such an anchor, one that holds you steady as you face the storms of life? If you don't, I implore you to seek Jesus. Enjoy the peace I have in knowing him. As Cato *told me, this is a decision I cannot make for you. Each man must make his own decision, his own choice. But the choice you make has eternal consequences . . .*

Your loving father, Aquila

CPSIA information can be obtained at www.ICGtesting.com
Printed in the USA
BVOW010232080413

317559BV00002B/10/P